SLATEWIPER

FORGE BOOKS BY LEWIS PERDUE

DAUGHTER OF GOD

SLATEWIPER

SLATEWIPER
LEWIS PERDUE

To Mark Burnett
Looks like we've walked
some of the same dark
corridors. Great bouncing
ideas off you.
Best
Lew
8-19-03

FORGE®

A TOM DOHERTY ASSOCIATES BOOK
NEW YORK

SLATEWIPER

Copyright © 2003 by Lewis Perdue

This book is printed on acid-free paper.

A Forge Book
Published by Tom Doherty Associates, LLC
175 Fifth Avenue
New York, NY 10010

www.tor.com

Forge® is a registered trademark of Tom Doherty Associates, LLC.

Library of Congress Cataloging-in-Publication Data

Perdue, Lewis
    Slatewiper / Lewis Perdue.—1st ed.
      p.   cm.
    "A Tom Doherty Associates Book."
    ISBN 0-765-30111-3 (alk. paper)
    1. Genetic engineering—Fiction.   2. Women scientists—Fiction.
 3. Bioterrorism—Fiction.   4. Japan—Fiction.   I. Title.

PS3566.E69122S53 2003
813'.54—dc21

                                                              2002045496

First Edition: July 2003

Printed in the United States of America

0   9   8   7   6   5   4   3   2   1

To Raymond Verdes (January 12, 1930–June 24, 2002),
Lieutenant-Colonel, French Foreign Legion, a gentle,
kind, talented man, whose spirit war could not defeat.
You have earned your ultimate peace.

And to his partner and companion, Dr. Wolfgang
Schröder, who holds a special place in our hearts.
We pray God will bring you comfort.

ACKNOWLEDGMENTS

I AM A VERY FORTUNATE WRITER.

I'm fortunate that my agent, Natasha Kern, believed in this book from the beginning, all the way back to 1995, when no one believed that terrorists could get their hands on gene-engineered bioweapons.

I'm doubly fortunate to have an incredible editor, Natalia Aponte, who saw past the thriller McGuffin and realized this was a book about people and the way we allow ourselves to be divided by race, rather than united by our shared humanity. Natalia kept me writing about the people and what the whole thing meant and refused to let me write just a lot of cool action scenes.

Natalia is my rabbi to the incredible team at Tor/Forge, especially Tom Doherty, whom I have known for decades; and Paul Stevens, who seems to keep everything rolling along; and the marketing and sales team who have done the bang-up-est of jobs at making sure you, the reader, could get your hands on this and my other books.

I'm incredibly fortunate to have loyal readers, who continue to e-mail me about books of mine they read back in the early 1980s.

I'm fortunate to know Mary Evelyn Arnold, who, in addition to being a good family friend, is also a take-no-prisoners proofreader, fact checker, and continuity tester without whom I would constantly embarrass myself.

And finally, I realize that Megan, my wife of twenty-two years, is good fortune who transcends anything I could write. And, indeed, I never wrote a damned thing that was any good before I met her.

1

Typhoon clouds churned across Tokyo's September skies. Beneath the clouds, down in the unfashionable northern prefecture of Toshima, workers at Otsuka General Hospital struggled through the gathering noontime dusk to clear the sidewalks of the dead and dying before the torrential rains began to fall.

Hundreds of the sickest lay scattered about like cordwood, blanketed by a miasmic stench that rose from suppurating skin abscesses and bloody diarrhea. Some were silent, others moaned in high-pitched whines as loudly as their weakened bodies would allow. The rotting stumps of arms, legs, and fingers attracted flies and showed bare bones. Flesh seemed melted off the skeletons of the dead.

Those in earlier stages of what the newspapers were calling "the Korean Leprosy" sat in stained trousers and skirts, hung their heads between their knees, moaning and coughing. Here and there, entire families gathered, creating microcosms of the crowd with their dead, dying, and walking wounded. Mothers and fathers cradled their children in futile attempts to protect them from a horror that attacked from within.

They matted the sidewalks, the lawns, the ambulance loading ramps; they filled the empty parts of the parking lot, even the spaces between vehicles. The truly fortunate lay thick in the hallways of the emergency room, where medics from the Self-Defense Forces went through the existentially futile motions of pumping the victims full of antibiotics and intravenous drips.

At the perimeter of the hospital grounds, SDF soldiers garbed in disposable overalls, masks, and rubber gloves worked away at the crowd, loading the live ones onto litters and into olive-drab transports. The gelatinous remains of the dead were scooped up with shovels and placed in a hodgepodge of commandeered makeshift containers: barrels, metal tubs, ice chests, soft drink coolers, even children's plastic wading pools.

Among the carnage walked three men: a white-haired Japanese man, about seventy, wearing a white physician's coat, and two blond Caucasians in jeans and sweatshirts who towered over him. The tall Caucasians each carried a large duffel. All three wore rubber gloves and surgical masks that left only their eyes showing.

The two Caucasians wiped steadily at their eyes that watered against the sharp caustic mist hanging over the hospital grounds. Around them, scores of SDF soldiers walked about spraying a disinfectant solution from large backpack pump applicators normally used for applying lawn chemicals.

The trio moved in lurches, a few steps in one direction and then a stop as the white-coated figure stepped ahead of the two others, turned to them, and blocked their way. They exchanged words, then one of the Caucasians would start off in another direction, leaving the Japanese man scurrying to catch up and repeat the process.

"We really have things well in hand," said the white-coated Japanese man as he stepped into the path of the other two once again. Dr. Yoshichika Iwamoto was chief administrator of Otsuka Hospital, professor at Tokyo University, and former member of the Diet. "You really didn't need to come," he insisted. "It is very kind of you, but so very unnecessary." Like most Japanese doctors, Iwamoto spoke English. Like many of them, he considered it a barbaric tongue.

Iwamoto's face showed none of the internal turmoil stirred up half an hour before when the two U.S. Army doctors had arrived unexpectedly. He wore his *shiran kao*—his nonchalant face—and tried to explain to them that this was an epidemic, a matter for specialists, that they would only be in the way. To his dismay, they had demonstrated that they were, indeed, experts in this sort of medical emergency, even pulling out published papers the two had coauthored, brought along for just this anticipated problem.

What Iwamoto really wanted to explain to these ill-mannered intruders was that this was a Japanese situation, something like a family emergency to be dealt with as discreetly as possible. That NHK, then other television stations, had broadcast stories since the outbreak of Korean Leprosy a week ago was intolerable. To air one's own dirty linen was disgraceful, unacceptable. He shook his head now as he thought about the broadcasts and the newspaper articles that followed. Soon, there had been attention from foreign journalists—more *gaijin*. Whatever happened to Japan for the Japanese? Kurata-*san* would fix that.

The news reports had brought these *gaijin* doctors. That alone was an insult, evidence of their lack of faith in his ability, in the ability of the entire Japanese race. Big, white, racist bullies who automatically assumed that little wheat-colored people couldn't handle things by themselves and so forced their filthy "help" on them. Iwamoto seethed inside. And their bad manners! They had arrived unannounced; it embarrassed him that they had given him no opportunity to welcome them properly.

They were so arrogant these *ketojin*, these Americans.

He said a small prayer of thanksgiving that at least they weren't Japanese forcing their help on him. That would create an *on*, an obligation, a debt that he and the hospital would be duty-bound to repay. Fortunately, *gaijin* were without virtue, without value. Those without virtue could not create *on*, nor were they to be afforded the courtesy or protection due true sons of Yamato. Iwamoto knew his only obligation was to rid himself of these two pests as quickly as possible, to keep them from hindering the removal process that was proceeding so efficiently.

They walked along in silence for several steps, making a wide detour around a man who retched convulsively at the edge of the street.

"I'm afraid you will not be comfortable," Iwamoto said hopefully as he stepped ahead of them and stopped their progress once again. "Our sanitary facilities are quite overstressed."

"No problem," said one of the *gaijin*. "We're Army. We're used to being uncomfortable."

"It's part of regulations," joked the second as he headed off in another direction.

Iwamoto cringed inside as he scurried to catch up with him. *How could they be so insensitive as to ignore his distress? How could they miss such obvious communication?*

Blocking their path, Iwamoto marshaled his resolve and tried again. "Ah, you see, we have limited supplies and equipment. I am afraid that—"

"Brought our own," the *gaijin* said almost simultaneously. One slapped the big duffel bag for emphasis, then turned and continued walking in yet another direction.

Desperation welled up hot and sour in Iwamoto's throat as he set out after them again.

In the distance, thunder rolled; stiff winds tore at the trees and rolled off the massive hospital building in chaotic gusts. Looking hopefully at the sky, Iwamoto maneuvered himself in front of them again and stopped. Instead of speaking immediately, he made a point of studying the weather carefully. The two Caucasians looked upward for a moment, then back at him as he spoke.

"These very early typhoons can be serious," he said. "It could be dangerous for you here." He looked expectantly from one white face to the other. "Perhaps you will be needed by your *own people* at Camp Zama."

The *gaijin* shook their heads synchronously, as if their necks were linked by gears. Almost as precisely, they turned and resumed their stroll.

Iwamoto made an audible hissing sound as he sucked in wind through pursed lips; he pursued them yet again. The older physician was winded by the time he stopped them again, this time just yards from the entrance to the hospital.

"It's a disgusting disease," Iwamoto said. "The soiling, the rotting, the bloody discharges—the odors."

Pungent antiseptic now masked most of the nauseating stench that earlier had hit the Caucasians like a squirming fist in their bellies as soon as they had stepped off the train at the Shin-Otsuka rail station.

"Look, Doctor, we've been through it before," said Lieutenant Colonel Denis Yaro, M.D., infectious disease specialist with the U.S. Army 9th Corps, stationed at nearby Camp Zama in Kanagawa Prefecture. "We're big boys. This won't be the first time we've gotten shit on our nice white coats. We happen to think this is a pretty important situation, and we'd like very much to help you to get to the bottom of this weird strain of glanders—if that's really what it is—but if you don't want us here, then why don't you just come out and tell us that?"

I have been, Iwamoto thought to himself. *But you are too thick to hear me.*

"Cool it, Denis," cautioned Jim Condon, M.D. Condon was another army light colonel, an epidemiologist and internal medicine specialist whose offices adjoined Yaro's at Zama's Medical Corps facility.

They had come—in violation of specific orders for all of Zama's physicians to stay clear of the area—as volunteers, partly because they wanted to help and partly because Yaro hoped to snag a sample of a totally new, undiagnosed disease that could be turned into a publishable paper.

Iwamoto fought to control his anger. When he spoke, it was formally, stiffly. "The pathogen has not yet been identified," the doctor continued. "It does not seem to be any known bacteria, virus, or even a prion or single-celled amoeba or other organism. Because of this there seems to be no natural immunity and as a result, none of the patients has, so far, survived."

Condon and Yaro thought they saw a faint look of satisfaction.

"The genetic fragments we have been able to identify at this very preliminary stage of the investigation indicate that it could be identical to the unknown variant a-087 that killed all the inhabitants of that small settlement on the northeast coast of Cheju-do."

Yaro nodded his head. Condon saw the lightning in his colleague's eyes. Just two weeks previously, more than nine hundred people on Cheju-do—a small island in the South Sea some fifty miles south of the tip of the Korean Peninsula—had been wiped out before help could arrive from the mainland. Nobody knew where the disease had come from, but it ravaged the settlement and then, ten days later, seemed to self-destruct.

"You should also know," Iwamoto said, "that it is clear that this is a biotype that is more likely to exist in a carrier state specifically restricted to the Korean race. I believe—"

"Carriers! Race!" Yaro's tone was contemptuous. "You know as well as I do there is no such thing as a Korean race!"

Iwamoto stumbled back away from the tall white man and quickly caught his balance.

"This is all about power and politics and nothing about science," Yaro continued, his voice deep and angry. "But your use of those words— your use, Doctor—on television has been a disaster for Japan's Korean community. Your implications in all those interviews are impossible to miss. You're telling everybody what they want to hear: that Koreans are carriers of this dirty disease because they're racially inferior."

"I resent your implications that I—"

"Look, asshole, I was watching the television when you told one interviewer that it was as if the gods had invented the perfect disease to personify a race of people despised almost universally by the entire Japanese nation."

"Calm down, Denis." Jim placed a hand on his colleague's forearm. "Back off." But Yaro took another step toward Iwamoto.

"You're fucking Nazi hypocrites, Doctor. You and your countrymen. You occupied Korea, forced the people into slavery, kidnapped Korean women, and locked them into army-run brothels as "comfort girls" that soldiers raped day after day. A lot of people calling themselves 'doctor' used Koreans as convenient laboratory animals for Japanese medical experiments."

As Yaro advanced, Iwamoto stumbled over his own feet and sat down hard on the well-tended turf.

"That's enough, Doctor," Condon said firmly as he grabbed Yaro by the shoulders and wrestled him back. Iwamoto got slowly to his feet and dusted himself off. Jim Condon stepped between the two men.

"If this truly is only a Korean disease, then it poses no threat to my colleague or me, does it, Doctor?" he asked. "Why should we be concerned?"

With Yaro no longer an immediate threat, Iwamoto felt the searing anger rising from deep in his gut. He closed his eyes for a moment, trying to center his emotions. He looked deep inside to avoid being provoked by the *keto*, but it was to no avail; he would later offer prayers to remove the shame of losing control.

"Of course it is a Korean disease, you round-eyed fools! We have the genotype. That is why this should mean nothing to you, nothing at all. These are *Koreans*! The dogs that these animals eat have more value, don't you understand? Treating them is beneath the dignity of the medical profession."

Iwamoto's outburst stunned them like a slap in the face. For a long moment silence grew large and awkward. Condon finally filled the void. Softly, his voice cold with barely restrained anger, he said, "Doctor, in our country, even dogs get medical care."

"Yes, and in your country, you also sleep with the *kurombo*—niggers— so what more is it necessary to say?" Iwamoto spat as if the words themselves had contaminated his mouth.

"Thank you so *very* much for your enlightened worldview. But we, Doctor, came here to figure out how to cure the dogs."

Yaro was quivering with anger. Condon turned him around, handed him the duffel he had dropped, and led him toward a family of six sprawled on an old tarp some ten yards away.

"There is no cure; there is only death!" They heard Iwamoto screaming after them. "Suit yourself! You are wasting your time! Only death! Only death!"

Fifty yards away a tall, young Japanese man dressed from head to toe in hospital white held a clipboard and walked from one devastated family group to another, taking notes and an occasional photo. Tears soaked the upper edge of his surgical mask. As Iwamoto's words ricocheted across the hospital's immaculately landscaped grounds and found the ears of Akira Sugawara, the tall, young man turned from the body of a four-year-old Korean girl and her grieving parents and watched Dr. Iwamoto walk away from the tall *gaijin*.

What is this hell? Sugawara wondered again. An irresistible alien gravity clutched at his heart, creating a weight so profound he was sure it would rip out the whole organ and carry it to the center of the earth.

What is this hell? And why had his uncle sent him to document it?

2

THE BARRAGE OF GENETICALLY ENGINEERED FLAVR SAVR TOMATOES BEGAN
SLOWLY—AS IT ALWAYS DID—MAKING RED, WET THUMPS AGAINST THE BIG,
HEAVY SUBURBAN. The Flavr Savrs arced out of teeming mobs that lined
both sides of the brick-paved road, a new street cut at great expense
through the Maryland countryside west of Bethesda. The road had its
own exit off the Beltway and led straight to the gates of the GenIntron
Corporation.

The mobs lining the street surged against the striped crowd barriers
as the deep metallic burgundy Suburban approached; riot-clad policemen stationed along the crowd barriers looked nervously about, at the
crowd, at the approaching Suburban, at themselves. As the police urged
the crowds back behind the barriers, their hands lingered near service
revolvers, batons, tear gas grenades, radios. The *whack-whack* of a helicopter's blades echoed in the street.

Those not throwing tomatoes waved signs demanding "No More
FrankenFoods," along with scores of other placards calling for an end to
genetic engineering, genetic testing, genetically altered foods, genetically
engineered pharmaceuticals and vaccines. Most prominent among the
signs were the slick and expensive ones from Hands Off Our Genes, a
well-funded operation run by Elliot Sporkin, a biotech demagogue who
knew nothing about science and everything about making a profitable

career off the fears of a scientifically illiterate populace.

Inside the big Chevy truck, the postcard view of the countryside and the soft early morning light painting the mountain all rosy and warm under a clear blue sky quickly faded to an impressionistic red as the tomato barrage crescendoed.

Without consciously thinking about it, Lara Blackwood switched on the windshield wipers as she scanned the crowd, recognizing many of the same anger- and hate-distorted faces who cursed her day after day. Just ahead of her, a police escort—two motorcycle outriders and a van full of riot police added for today's annual meeting—accelerated toward the heavily guarded entrance to GenIntron. Lara pressed on the accelerator to keep up with them. The morning sunlight painted brilliant rainbows in her short black hair and made the star sapphires in her earrings glow like deep blue embers. They had been a gift from her father who brought them back from a mission in Kashmir more than twenty years before.

Founder and CEO of GenIntron, Blackwood was a rare woman among the old boys' club of biotech entrepreneurs, bursting to prominence by developing profitable disease treatments from "introns": parts of the human genome that others had dismissed as "junk DNA." The media loved to lavish print space and airtime on this tall, attractive woman who bootstrapped her Cornell Ph.D. in molecular genetics with an athletic scholarship that took her to dual Olympic bronze medals in rowing and sailing.

As the wipers cleared wave after wave of red pulp and juice, Lara glanced at her passenger, a tanned, silver-haired man in his late forties, dressed in the conservative pinstripes, white shirt, and boring rep tie that were the uniform for the top people at First Mercantile American Bank & Trust. Jason Woodruff, president of First Merc and GenIntron's newest board member, smiled at her.

"You put up with this every morning?" he asked.

"Almost every," she replied. "Not usually this extreme. They save that for special occasions like today." She gave him a thin smile.

His head was in constant motion as he took in the crowd surrounding them. "They're all here, every nutcase. I never imagined there were so many."

Lara glanced over and smiled at the naked astonishment on the banker's face. Welcome to the real world, she thought as he read the signs aloud.

Woodruff saw the smile on her face and frowned. "You actually enjoy this, don't you?"

"Enjoy what?"

"All"—he waved his arm to take in a street's worth of roiling movement, noise, and anger—"this."

"What makes you think that?" Lara asked.

"You're smiling."

She gave him an even broader smile now, full of even white teeth, followed by a low chuckle that might have been confirmation or denial.

Woodruff frowned. Like most bankers, he found ambiguity subversive and spontaneity unsettling. He was more comfortable with hard numbers, conservative businesspeople, clients who deferred to him by virtue of his position as head of America's largest bank. He frowned. Lara was neither, did neither.

Woodruff admitted he had never understood her, not as an entrepreneur, not as a woman, and certainly not as the brilliant scientist the rest of the world seemed to think she was. She was too tall, strong, too full of appetites and ambitions for a woman. Women shouldn't be like that.

"There's one with a big yellow star of David," he said mostly to himself, "it says 'No More Holocausts,' and then . . ." He squinted. With amazement in his voice, he continued, ". . . and then 'Death to the Nazi She-wolf.'"

Woodruff turned to her. "What . . . ?"

"Our genetic screening tests," Lara said. "A lot of people think they'll be used for some kind of new eugenics program. You know, define a 'normal' test for the gene sequence, eliminate the rest." She paused to hit the windshield washers. "Dumb shits," she muttered. "That's not what we do. Reality's just too inconvenient for the delusional worlds these people live in."

Still scanning the crowd, Woodruff shook his head. "I guess that's what the placards are about from the Down's syndrome group there that seems to want you dead as well." He paused. "Yes, I see the sign clearly now: 'I'm not . . . not a mistake; I don't . . . don't need fixing.' That's from the Down's syndrome group," he said, turning toward her.

She nodded. "We might actually have had a treatment for Down's by now if the animal liberation lunatics hadn't broken into the labs in our old buildings and liberated the monkeys," Lara said evenly. "Four years of work gone in one fit of animal rights rage."

"Well, your animal rights friends are over there." He pointed to the left side of the street. "Then there's the Operation Rescue contingent," he said, pointing to the right. "Let me guess. They're against screening because it might mean an abortion?"

"You're a quick study, Jason," Lara said as she deftly steered the Suburban around a burning plastic trash can that came rolling out of the crowd. "You'll make a fine addition to the board." Her sarcasm was so subtle he decided to imagine that he hadn't heard it at all.

The crowd's screams grew louder, though they were still tolerable inside the custom O'Gara-modified Suburban.

"What are they screaming?" Woodruff asked anxiously as he watched the distance increase between the Suburban and the police escort.

"Oh, the usual." She smiled faintly.

"And the usual is?" He was annoyed by her flip reply and that smile. That damned enigmatic smile.

"Well, here. Listen for yourself." She reached for the window switch and started to lower his window. An angry roar shot through the crack.

"Don't!" Woodruff snapped in alarm as he ducked away from the barely opened window.

Discrete words were still hard to distinguish above the rumble, but "Killer bitch!" seemed to come through loudest.

Lara laughed, then she closed his window against the sound.

"I don't understand," he said. "They *hate* you . . . and you actually *like* that."

"Jason," she said evenly, "these are the most marginal of the marginal—extremists who understand nothing but fictional nightmares. Considering all that, I'd check myself in for some heavy-duty electroshock therapy if *they* liked me."

They drove in silence as the GenIntron gates grew closer. Flavr Savrs continued to pelt the Suburban.

After a long while Lara broke the silence. "So? You want to tell me what it is you came to say?"

"Pardon?"

"Don't be coy, Jason. You didn't ask me for a ride this morning to be a good energy-conserving citizen."

"I told you, the Beemer—"

"Is in the shop." She shook her head. "Right. Uh-huh."

"But—"

"Jason, the last time you rode with me was the day you wanted to make sure no one else was listening when you told me that your gutless bank was cutting off my credit line and if I knew what was good for me I'd reconsider the buy-out offer that Daiwa Ichiban had made."

"You know as well as I do that when we yanked that credit line, it was the best thing that ever happened to you."

"I'm not fond of being forced to do things, Jason."

"Yeah, well the acquisition instantly made you rich."

"Unlike you, I don't see money as the most important thing in life."

"That's easy to say when you've got millions."

Lara heard the whine, the jealousy in his voice.

"But that's not the message that Daiwa Ichiban told you to deliver to me today, now is it?" The banker failed to reply. She shook her head. "They've sent you to do the dirty work again, but you can't work up the *cojones* to tell me."

He hesitated. Then: "You're a has-been; you're history. Today's your last day as chairman and CEO."

"That would be chair*woman*," she corrected. "And don't be absurd. There's six months left in the transition. I have some important lab work to finish before that happens."

Woodruff smiled for the first time.

Suddenly a piercing cry shot through the crowds lining the right side of the street. Lara looked over just in time to see a bloodred, jellylike blob fly out from the midst of the Operation Rescue members, shedding drips as it flew. It slammed against the windshield, leaving a broad slimy smear before the powerful wipers batted it off the windshield and into the animal liberation protesters on the other side of the street.

"What the hell was that? It looked like a fucking fetus."

"It was," Lara said as she hit the washers again to clear the smear from the windshield.

"It was?" Woodruff's voice had edged higher, heading toward hysteria.

"Fetal pig," Lara said matter-of-factly. "Like those from high school. The Operation Rescue people buy them by the barrel . . . for effect."

"It looked so . . . human."

"That's the point," Lara said. "It's—"

Like an overstressed levee giving way, the crowd barriers on the left side of the street collapsed. Infuriated animal rights protesters, agitated by the fetal pig, stormed toward the Operation Rescue contingent. Instants later a guttural cry erupted from both sides of the street as protesters of every stripe overwhelmed the underguarded barricades and poured into the streets.

"Uh-oh," Lara said as the crowd closed in on them. She pressed the accelerator to get closer to the police van. The Suburban quickly closed the gap, seconds later only feet behind it.

On the right, the animal rights crowd drew first blood with the Operation Rescue members. The police van came to a complete stop as the crowd pressed closer. They were close enough now to be blinded by the television camera lights safely behind the GenIntron fence.

Then a pavement brick tracked a lazy ballistic curve out of the crowd and glanced off the windshield's expensive armored glass.

"Oh, God!" Woodruff cried out instants later as the Suburban shuddered beneath a hailstorm of pavement bricks. He flinched away from his window as bricks smashed into it. Outside a cry of jubilation swept through the mob as they saw him jerk his head away.

"Don't let them see you react," Lara said evenly. "It just encourages them."

"Don't . . . what?" He gaped at her slack-jawed. "You . . . you're a fucking lunatic!"

At the gate, GenIntron security and riot-clad reinforcements hired for the annual meeting moved forward, battering the edges of the mob with batons but making little progress. Tear gas canisters arced into the mob. Up ahead, television news crews, hungry for good bang-bang for the six-o'clock news, rolled their tape.

Protesters began rocking the Suburban and the police van.

"Jesus, Lara, *do* something; they'll turn us over and kill us! Don't just sit here, floor it and get us through the fucking gate!"

"Bad move," she replied calmly.

"But they're trying to *kill* us!" His voice quivered, partly from the violent rocking, mostly from fear. "It's self-defense," he insisted hysterically.

Lara shook her head. "See those TV cameras? When they roll the edited footage, you won't see bricks and bleeding cops. You'll see a big fucking Suburban mowing down innocent community activists."

"But—"

"Just hold your fucking water, Jason. Try not to mess in your pants, okay?"

Pale now and perspiring heavily, the fight seemed to drain from him; the banker slumped in his seat.

Ahead of them, it was clear that the police van had stalled.

As the crowd rocked both vehicles more and more violently, the solution came to Lara; she slipped the Suburban into gear and released the brake. The huge car, with the overpowered engine, lurched forward. The sudden movement destroyed the mob's rocking rhythm. She tapped the accelerator and collided softly with the police van. It moved forward slowly. The move surprised the rioters who were trying to overturn it. They fell away as the Suburban pushed the van forward steadily, slowly.

That night the TV video showed protesters making a show of lying down in front of the van, then scrambling away at the last second. The toothy blond anchorwoman seemed upset that both the Suburban and the police van reached the safety of the GenIntron compound, robbing her of a bigger story that might have gotten her national exposure and a ticket to a larger market.

3

LARA BLACKWOOD STORMED DOWN THE TUBELIKE CORRIDORS OF GENINTRON'S MAIN RESEARCH WING LIKE FATE IN SEARCH OF DESTINY.

The hundred-yard-long, gleaming tile hallway was one of three in the complex. Each was lined with laboratories and segmented every one hundred feet by pneumatic airlock doors. The first impression was that of the inside of a subway train whose far end had been stretched to the vanishing point. The design had won numerous awards and been enshrined in two famous New York museums.

"Stop!" Woodruff called from behind her as her broad, determined strides steadily distanced him. He jogged for a moment to catch up. "Don't do anything you'll regret."

Lara stopped and whirled so quickly the banker stumbled into her.

"What you really mean is you don't want me to do anything that *you* will regret." Her voice was low and full of loosely restrained violence. She stood nearly nose-to-nose with the six-foot Woodruff. "Well, you can bank on *that* happening, mister." He quickly backpedaled away from her.

Just as quickly as she had stopped, Lara turned and resumed her double-time march down the futuristic corridor.

Woodruff watched her grow smaller in the distance and then walked to a hall telephone to call security.

Thirty yards away Lara stopped to swipe her magnetic ID card over the security reader. Moments later she was prompted to enter her password on a compact keyboard. Instants later a set of pneumatic doors sighed open. In this section the corridor was lined with thick, greenish, blast-proof glass windows that led on to laboratories beyond. Most labs in this corridor had solid stainless-steel doors, airlocks, and "gray area" decontamination zones flanked by additional security keypads and retinal identification systems. These were biosafety level (BSL) 4 labs, reserved for the most lethal of the lethal and for creating forms of life that had never existed in nature and which might be catastrophic if released from the lab.

With the right enzymes and a snip of DNA from here and there, life could be created that a decade before could not have been imagined. Scientists clipped genes from yeast, fungus, dogs, frogs, algae, and people's next-door neighbors and reassembled them at will, the Legos of molecular genetics. All DNA was equal on the molecular level. This was democracy at the nano-level: one nucleic acid base, one vote.

It was here that Lara had doggedly pried open the genome's secrets of ethnicity that had opened the door to GenIntron's first commercially successful drug: a treatment for Tay-Sachs disease. Her personal research had located the right sequences that allowed other drugs to deliver targeted treatments for diseases that disproportionately afflicted other ethnic groups—well-known ones such as sickle-cell anemia for people of African descent, cystic fibrosis for northern European Caucasians—and scores of lesser known syndromes.

She had been able to find the treatments by focusing on introns—so-called junk DNA—that had been ignored by other researchers. For it was here in these vast stretches of DNA that others saw as a wasteland that she spotted opportunities and made them come to fruition by manipulating the introns to fold or unfold in ways that altered the mechanisms by which vital proteins were produced. By creating new molecules never seen in nature, molecules that were active only in the presence of DNA found in specific ethnic groups of people, she could relieve pain, suffering, and death.

Just ahead, a tall, lean man with café au lait skin, graying hair, a sharp prominent nose, and ice blue eyes stepped from an adjoining corridor. He waved at her, began to smile, and then saw the look on Lara's face.

"What's the matter?" he asked as he fell into step with her.

Ismail Brahimi, who had won a Nobel Prize while teaching molecular biology at Cornell, had cofounded GenIntron and as president had run most aspects of the company for the past two years. Brahimi had been Lara's choice to become the company's second CEO, but the new Japanese owners had passed him over in favor of Edward Rycroft, head of research. Rycroft was a brilliant but moody researcher whose greatest strength, aside from his ability to alienate people, was his lust for the Nobel Prize and envy of the wealth that Lara and Brahimi had accumulated from their founding of the company. Being the honest, ethical man he was, Brahimi had refused to engage in the shadowy, backstabbing intrigue and politics that would have been necessary to dethrone Rycroft.

According to Brahimi, Rycroft's appointment was, like everything else in the world, "God's will." Lara was not as sanguine.

"Woodruff. Kurata. That's what's the matter," she tersely answered his question.

"What else is new," he said grimly.

"They're kicking me out."

"What else is new?"

"Today." She stopped at the laboratory door with her name on it and punched in her password. "Woodruff hitched another ride with me."

"What brought that on?" he asked.

She shook her head. Shrugged. "Some kind of tantrum in Tokyo, I guess."

The LCD above the keypad flashed ACCESS DENIED.

"Shit," Lara muttered. She reentered the numbers. Again, ACCESS DENIED.

"What's wrong with the system?"

Instants later the airlock door down the corridor *whooshed* open, disgorging Edward Rycroft followed by a uniformed GenIntron security guard armed with a nightstick and pepper spray. Jason Woodruff trailed at a safe distance.

"You probably want to miss this," Lara suggested. "It's not going to do your career here any good."

"Uh-uh. Nope. I'll stand by you on this one."

Lara looked fondly for a moment at this kind, gentle man whose deep religious faith made him brave and tough when circumstances required.

"No. Really." She insisted, "Go."

"All right, but—"

"Ismail, there is nothing you can do here but make your own life more difficult. So go!"

"As you wish," Brahimi said reluctantly, then walked away.

Lara turned toward Rycroft and his approaching retinue. "Let me into my lab," she shouted as they approached.

"It's not your lab anymore," Rycroft replied, his words veneered with a House of Lords accent that almost camouflaged his working-class Midlands roots. He stopped an arm's length in front of her. The gray-uniformed security officer stood just behind him.

Lara looked at the face of the guard and realized that she recognized him vaguely only by face and couldn't remember his name. In the months following the purchase of GenIntron, all her loyal corporate security staff whose names and life histories she knew intimately had been replaced with personnel from another Daiwa Ichiban subsidiary. There was professionalism here, she knew, but no sympathy.

Beyond the guard, Woodruff shifted uncomfortably from foot to foot.

"What do you mean it's not my—"

"You sold the lab when you sold the company."

"But we had a *deal*," Lara insisted. "Kurata himself agreed that I got to use the lab until I finished the work I started. There's a major paper from it."

"The policy has changed." Rycroft said evenly, tilting his chin up ever so slightly. "As you know, economic conditions have forced Daiwa Ichiban to make sure that all of its companies are operating with as little waste as possible."

"Waste!" Lara took a step toward him. "You're calling me waste?"

The security guard moved to protect Rycroft. "That's all right." He raised his arm to stop him. "She's not going to hurt me."

"You wish," Lara said harshly.

Rycroft wavered uncertainly. A charged pause hung between them for a long moment.

"My work is in there and I'll drag your butt to court if I have to."

"It is no longer your work," Rycroft said wearily. "Indeed, you know as well as I do that it has never really been your work. You did the work using corporate time, facilities, and equipment."

Exasperated, Lara loosed an audible sigh. "Yes, Edward. I am aware of that. I'm nearly finished, so why don't you let me take things to the end so the company can have the benefit of the knowledge." Unconsciously her right hand massaged the earring's sapphire.

"Decisions have been made at the highest levels," Rycroft said. "I am not authorized to countermand them."

"At least let me get my notes—"

"They are GenIntron's notes. I believe we have the necessary staff and resources to take the work to fruition."

Lara frowned, opened her mouth to argue, when the realization hit her.

"You're going to steal my work for yourself, aren't you?" Her voice rose loud and harsh. "Your ambition and ego have so far outpaced your intelligence and scientific ability that you're willing to plagiarize me to get ahead."

"That's an unbecoming accusation to make," Rycroft replied. "It is simply a matter of resource allocation. Your lab is urgently needed for more vital work," Rycroft began. "Daiwa Ichiban has decreed that maximum resources must be devoted to monetizing research and capitalizing on profitable opportunities."

Lara stared at him with slack-jawed amazement.

When Rycroft spoke again, his voice was filled with arrogance and condescension. "So, dear, this is the reality: your access has been terminated. Your remote system log-in accounts have been eliminated. Security has been informed that you are no longer to be allowed through the gate. I am in charge now and that is the final word. Run along now. Go to Washington and take the advisor's post the White House offered you. You are no longer welcome here."

Lara stepped back, her shoulders sagging with defeat. For just an instant Rycroft smiled broadly; the security agent relaxed; even Jason Woodruff stopped his nervous fidgeting.

Before any of them could react, Lara moved swiftly forward, her right arm folded like a wing. Using her right elbow and forearm like a bludgeon, she hammered Rycroft full in the face, then stepped quickly forward, knocking his feet cleanly off the floor.

"Monetize *that*, dear," she said.

The security guard grabbed for his pepper spray.

"Don't!" Lara barked and grabbed his wrist; the guard froze. Rycroft moaned on the floor and bled from his nostrils.

The guard was taller than Lara by a head, but she was in better shape and he knew it. In fact, he had listened carefully in his first days on the job, during the transition when Lara's departing security guards had each passed along stories about her: some true, some apocryphal, but all dealing with her strength and physical ability. Especially true were the stories about her excellence while attending the same martial arts and firearms classes required of all the GenIntron security guards.

"Help him," Lara told the guard without taking her eyes off his face or the iron grip off his wrist. "I'm leaving now."

He let her take the pepper spray from his hand. They stepped apart. When the guard bent down to assist Rycroft, she turned and strode away.

The dead and dying stretched to the sunset like neatly planted rows in a garden that vanished somewhere over the distant horizon. In the pale ocher hues of the setting sun, Akira Sugawara strolled among the rows of death flanked on his left by Tokutaro Kurata and on his right by Edward Rycroft. They smiled and walked, farmers amid a bumper harvest.

The plants in this crop looked up at them, faces tight and flat with pain, mouths wide with cries that made no sound in the warm, waning light. Rycroft smiled. It seemed all so natural; this was the way things should be. The sores and lesions, the melting flesh, the exposed bones— well, that was what this crop was supposed to look like.

Sugawara walked along, unconcerned that he couldn't hear the words spoken by Rycroft and his uncle, yet understanding every thought and nuance as they estimated the harvest, talked of the extraordinary yield compared with what they had sown, second-guessed the weather, and anticipated the rewards of bringing it to market.

Yes, they agreed, this would be an exceptional harvest, extraordinarily profitable, eminently worth the risk they had taken.

In an instant the air turned icy as the sun slipped toward twilight. The wind howled now with the deafening cries of pain and screams of agony of people clawing at their feet, clutching at their pants and legs. Sugawara felt the horror of their bony fingers clutching at his flesh, then felt his bowels loosen as the flesh began to melt away from the faces of Rycroft and Kurata like wax loosened by fire. The two men loosed great, unending ululating screams like the sirens of hell.

All around the two men, the faces of the plants grew whole, the lesions healed; babies and rows upon rows of families smiled.

Sugawara wondered about this for only a moment before a bright crushing pain like death itself slashed at his very soul; he felt his own face dripping on his chest. He looked at his hands in horror as the skin and flesh flowed, exposing first the suppurating flesh and then tendons, then bones. Hands clutched at his entrails and tore at his guts.

Then, as he had every night since walking the grounds of Otsuka General Hospital, Akira Sugawara forcibly awakened himself, tangled in his knotted, sweat-drenched bedsheets.

4

AN EARLY SNOW SIFTED INTO THE GENEVA EVENING AND FILLED THE GATHERING DARKNESS WITH LARGE WET FLAKES. Just inside the glass doors to Banque Securité Internationale du Geneve, Sheila Gaillard stood with a dark-suited man and gazed out at the traffic jamming the rue du Rhône, tied up by drivers unable to cope with the first snowfall of the approaching winter.

"You are positive you would not like for me to summon one of our drivers for you?" He tried to keep his eyes on her face, but—as they had for the past hour—they strayed to her breasts for just a moment. The plunging neckline of the short cashmere dress gave him a generous view.

Sheila looked over at the obsequious banker and dismissed him as just another walking sack of semen in a suit.

"No, thank you," Sheila replied demurely as she handed him her coat. "It's a beautiful evening for a walk."

"Of course," he replied as he obediently took her coat from her and held it out. "As always I will personally notify you when the deposit arrives."

"Thank you." She turned and extended her arms backward toward her coat. As she slipped her arms into it, she took a half step backward as if stumbling. His erection prodded against her butt; she rubbed herself sideways against him for just an instant.

"Oh, goodness," she cried out as he caught her. One of his hands caught her full in the breast and then quickly moved down to her waist.

"I ... are you ... I mean ... , " he stammered.

She looked up and gave him her most grateful rescued damsel look. "My heel must have caught on something," she said. Her heel had last caught on something for real a number of years before puberty. She stood up and shrugged her way into her coat as they both looked down at the seamless marble floor.

She put on her hat, buttoned the coat, and stepped into the night. Sheila turned to look at him and saw that he was still looking at the floor, face flushed, erection shoving against his fly; she smiled at him and walked away.

Men ... warm dildoes with legs ... fun, disposable. If only she had time.

With long, confident steps unhindered by the snow on the sidewalks, Sheila made her way along the Rhône toward the pont de la Machine, the pedestrian-only bridge over the river.

Pausing at the midpoint of the bridge, Sheila leaned against the railing as if to check her watch; she scanned the crowd for signs of surveillance. Not that she expected to find any; it was simply an unconscious part of her life. She did notice the snow was getting finer as the evening wore into night and the temperature dropped. She acknowledged an admiring glance from a middle-aged man and checked her watch again; she was right on schedule. The scientist from Daiwa Ichiban's Belgian subsidiary had arrived from Brussels the night before, lured by the prospect of making a killing by selling the manufacturing process information for an antidepression drug that had netted his employer almost a billion U.S. dollars the previous fiscal year. The scientist thought he was meeting a representative of Daiwa Ichiban's main corporate rival without realizing that his E-mails had been intercepted by the company's tightly woven security filter and passed along to Gaillard.

Rejoining the stream of pedestrians, Sheila cautioned herself not to expect too much from the meeting with the man. He was probably acting alone; there was probably no corporate conspiracy. But it was her job to make sure that leaks were closed and all those responsible were held accountable. She reached the end of the bridge and crossed with the light over to the place des Bergues. The street began to ascend, and Sheila picked up the pace, enjoying the muscle burn in her calves and thighs as she outpaced the flow on the sidewalk.

Making her way over to the rue du Mont-Blanc, Sheila continued up-hill toward the place de Cornavin.

Fine flakes of snow the texture of powdered sugar reflected the diffuse glow of the streetlights and seemed to fill the night with a swirling, peach-colored fog.

Down on the place di Reculet where the streetlights were farther apart than in nicer sections of Geneva, a lone man stepped up on the sidewalk and hesitated for a moment. He looked back up at the elevated tracks of the Gare Cornavin. With the quick nervous movements of a sparrow, Martin Allard looked around: up the rue des Gares, down toward the place de Montbrillant, behind him at the narrow, dark passage des Alpes that ran beneath the train tracks. He plunged his right hand into the pocket of his raincoat and wrapped his fingers around the surprisingly thin envelope that would soon become the retirement fund that had always eluded him.

He smiled to himself, trying to dismiss the black fear that squirmed in his belly. Just a few more minutes and life would be a lot brighter. The plain biochemist with the forgettable face took a deep breath and plunged into the labyrinth of narrow, twisting lanes that surrounded the place des Grottes. He passed an old man, slipping along the sidewalk, poking at the snow with a cane. But other than the old man, the night was silent, save for the faint shuffling sounds his steps made in the snow.

He'd already decided that the warm Moroccan coast was where he'd go. He thought of the white buildings, the beaches. A man didn't need a lot of money to live grandly there. Not much money at all.

His head was filled with the vision of a grand hotel and palm trees when a low, sensual voice came out of the darkened doorway on his right and cut through his reverie.

"Hello, Martin."

He flinched at the sound of her husky voice, and cowered away from her as he struggled to keep from urinating in his pants.

Sheila launched herself fluidly from the doorway. Before the terrified scientist could take another step, she embraced him with both arms as a lover might, pressing her body against his, pressing her firm breasts against his chest. She smiled as she watched the predictable transfiguration of his fear and amazement into a fog of negligent lust that left no room for caution or flight.

Her own heart quickened in anticipation. She felt her nipples grow hard as she ground her pelvis into his and felt him stir and harden against her. His breath smelled of alcohol and licorice and she noted the faint memory of cheap aftershave and the lingering fecal smells of tobacco smoke. The odors failed to diminish her own desire; her breathing quickened; the hot, silky wetness between her legs mounted as she slipped her left hand to the small curve at the back of his neck. She caressed the fine hairs that grew there, moving her fingers up and down the back of his neck, counting to herself, up again and then back down, lingering now at the base of his neck.

Eyes wide open, Sheila fixed his gaze and moved as if to kiss him. She felt her heart pounding against his. His erection was like stone now and he was beginning to thrust at her, pleasuring himself through all the layers of warm winter cloth. But it wasn't the man's pitiful tumescent tool that propelled Sheila toward her own climax. Her gathering heat came with her foretaste of the future.

With their lips hovering a ragged breath apart and preoccupied by his pre-ejaculatory obsessions, the small scientist from Belgium failed to notice as Sheila used her right hand to grab something from her left sleeve.

Sheila felt the heat rise like a great irresistible tide and race upward from her belly. Allard never saw the stainless-steel glint of the scalpel Sheila held in her right hand nor did he notice the surgically honed blade as it flashed silently through the darkness and plunged deep between the vertebrae she had so precisely marked with the index and middle fingers of her left hand.

Her stint as a surgical resident served her well as she shoved confidently on the scalpel, working it first through the capsular ligament, then through the synovial membrane. The razor-sharp blade slid upward deftly between the lamina, then she felt resistance decrease as the cutting surface plunged through the dura mater and into the nerves of the spinal cord itself.

Sheila shuddered for just an instant as the man fell instantly limp. She reveled in the flash that swept through her and left her skin electrified.

The scientist felt his bowels and bladder go first, filling the darkness with an offal stench.

Sheila let him go and stepped back and watched as his legs collapsed beneath him. Luxuriating in her own post-orgasmic afterglow, she watched as Allard spun to the ground.

For Allard, the night spun; he tried to hold out a hand to break his fall, but his insensate arms hung limply at his side like dead meat.

He felt the pain as he hit the pavement heavily. Moments later, he felt her hands, grabbing him by the cloth of his coat, dragging him back into the darkened doorway. She moved her purse to one side and then propped him up against the shuttered door. Windblown trash collected in the corners of the doorway—cigarette butts, scraps of paper, coarse grit.

Allard's heart beat wildly as he lay there looking up at her, the smell of his own offal clogging his nose. He tried to move his legs, his arms, tried to turn his head. But the rebellious muscles refused to obey.

"What have you done?" he cried, unable to will his lifeless legs and arms to do his will.

"You've been pithed," she said.

He looked blankly up at her waist. She leaned down and tilted his head back so he could see her face. For the first time, he noticed the scalpel in her gloved hand. Recognition dawned slowly.

"We used to do it with live frogs in the lab," she explained. "Surely you did the same at some point in your education? Hmmm?" Sheila knelt by his side and used the index and middle finger of her right hand to gently caress his cheek. She smiled at him. "Surely you remember? Sever the spinal cord in just the right place, and the frog is completely immobilized, yet stays alive almost indefinitely so you can dissect it and watch its insides work. People are like frogs in a lot of ways."

The scientist looked down at his arms and legs as he tried to move them. His mouth opened to form words, but the sounds never came. Tears formed in his eyes as he realized what she had done.

"That's right, sweetheart," she said calmly. "You're a quadriplegic. With proper care, you'll live for years and years. They'll put a catheter up your putz and they'll probably have to do a colostomy and put a bag there to catch all your shit."

She smiled; tears glistened in his eyes.

"I need some information," Sheila said.

"Why not just ask?" he replied. "I'd have given it to you without"—his eyes danced wildly—"this."

"You have a reputation, a reputation for never talking, for misleading. I needed to give you an incentive."

The scientist gazed silently up at her. Then: "I'll give it to you. Just make me okay again. You're a doctor. Please . . ." His voice broke into sobs. Tears streamed down his face. "I'll do anything, anything, just don't leave me like this; I'd rather be dead."

"Most would," Sheila said. "But a severed spinal cord is forever. No doctor in the world can make it grow back."

The deep expression of shock that played across his face as the realization set in made her smile. She went through his pockets and quickly found the envelope.

"Now," she said, tapping his forehead with a corner of the envelope, "Tell me who else is working with you."

"No one."

"You're sure?"

"No one. No one," he cried.

Satisfied, she bent low over his groin, her fingers fumbling with the zipper of his pants. In moments, she had pulled his penis out. To the scientist's wide-eyed horror, it grew hard in her hand and stood erect.

Suddenly Sheila let his erection drop and stood up. She rummaged in her purse for a premoistened paper hand towel. As she stood there, carefully wiping her hand, she looked down at him and said, "It'll get hard like that almost without warning." She wadded up the hand wipe and tossed it in the corner of the doorway.

"There's a different set of nerves that works your erection, the same ones that control your breathing, your digestion. Only there's no way you can get rid of the tension—not unless you ask one of the nurses, or orderlies, to jerk it for you.

"It'll be like that for years, Martin. I want you to think about that. I want you around as a living example of what happens to those who steal from Daiwa Ichiban." She paused. "And if you're nice about it all, maybe I'll come back, and if you beg hard enough . . ." She paused as she leaned over to pick up her purse. "Maybe one night I'll kill you.

"And if you decide not to be nice about things, just remember: the police are going to find it hard to believe your story about me. After all, you're a thief. We have the records from your computer. You talk about this and the company will file the papers and have you arrested. The police will simply think you were double-crossed by your contact. They'll nail you and throw you in a prison hospital where the inmates and attendants will sodomize you until your rectum rots out."

The man whimpered.

Sheila Gaillard rummaged about in her purse for a second, placed a plastic safety cap on the scalpel. Finally, she withdrew a pint of cheap brandy and unscrewed the top. Then, slinging her purse strap over her shoulder, she knelt beside the scientist, and before he could resist, she jammed the open rim of the bottle in his mouth.

Reflexively, he drank from the bottle, then tried to stop. Sheila frowned, then pinched his nostrils. "Drink up, asshole," she demanded.

"Or I'll leave your prick out 'til it freezes hard with frostbite."

He drank until the bottle was nearly empty. She poured the remainder of the contents over his chest and neck.

Sheila smashed the bottle on the stone doorway next to his head. Then carefully sorting through the shards, she selected a flat, daggerlike piece and deftly held it in the gloved fingers of her right hand. In a single swift motion, she lifted his head with her left hand and plunged the shard deep into the pith incision she had made in his neck.

He shrieked with pain as she lowered his head, the shard still protruding from his neck. Then she stood up, took a final look at his crumpled body, his stiff penis, turgid and red against his trousers. Then she turned and walked away. His screams filled the night.

Inside the train station, Gaillard confirmed the time and track for the express to Paris, then seated herself in the coffee shop. As she sipped at the bitterness of a double espresso liberally corrected with a rough local eau-de-vie, she turned on her wireless phone and paged through her voice mail.

Most were routine inquiries from customers of the small biological materials business she maintained as a front for the frequent travel her real work for Daiwa Ichiban demanded. She forwarded all of the routine voice mails to her staff in Osaka who would handle the orders. With those out of the way, she concentrated on the important one from the chairman of Daiwa Ichiban.

"I assume your current assignment for me has been successfully completed. Please arrange to meet me at my estate near Kyoto," said Kokutaro Kurata's digitally recorded voice. "I wish to consult with you about a possible new assignment which has just presented itself. Bring your German associate. I must go now for a very important ceremony."

5

TOKUTARO KURATA STOOD FOR A MOMENT UNDER THE GRACEFULLY CURVED EAVES OF THE YASUKUNI *JINJA*, AN ARCHITECTURALLY UNREMARKABLE BUT PO-LITICALLY FORMIDABLE SHINTO SHRINE IN CENTRAL TOKYO. Like the eighty-one-year-old Kurata, the *jinja* played a prodigious role in the rediscovery of the soul of the Japanese people.

Lean, tall, and unbent, Kurata looked up at the dark scudding sky; his eyes followed the first marble-sized raindrops fall downward, watched them leave dark circles on the sand-colored pavement leading to the *jinja*. A respectful crowd erected umbrellas and stood patiently behind a rope cordon. Ten paces away, dressed in the officer's formal ceremonial uniform of the Japanese Ground Self-Defense Forces, stood Kurata's nephew, Akira Sugawara, who prayed that he was successfully hiding his discomfort from his uncle and the massive crowd.

Akira found discomfort in his own discomfort. Had he not graduated at the top of his class from the National Defense Academy and served his tour with the GSDF with honor and a file filled with the highest commendations? Should he not be comfortable at a ceremony honoring fallen soldiers? He knew the answer but would not admit to himself that it was the character of those being honored that created the tension in his heart. He was not supposed to feel this way.

He marveled, instead, that despite the weather, a prodigious crowd with no such concern or discomfort had come to worship at the Yasukuni shrine that immortalizes Japan's war dead as *kami* or gods. Those here this day were but a fraction of the eight million Japanese who visited the shrine to pay their respects every year. More than two and a half million war dead had been deified as gods since the *jinja* creation in 1869 by the Meiji emperor. As Japan's most important *gokoku*—"defending the nation shrine"—Yasukuni focused national attention on what kind of nation Japan would become. Since the founding of Yasukuni, warriors setting out on dangerous missions had traditionally parted with the saying, "See you at Yasukuni." They would meet again, inevitably, as spirits or in the flesh.

Most Japanese revered Yasukuni and its beloved *kami* without thinking about wider social or political implications.

Beyond the shores of Japan, however, the shrine was a source of international controversy and suspicion because many of the most beloved of Yasukuni's gods included those who planned the occupation of Korea, the rape of Manchuria and China, the Bataan Death March, the surprise attack on Pearl Harbor, and those who conducted hideous and inhuman medical experiments on innocent civilians that equaled and often exceeded the atrocities of the Third Reich. At the godhead of this pantheon was General Tojo, executed as a war criminal after World War II.

While the world beyond thinks that Japan has moved past the war crimes of the Pacific War, those who perpetrated them are still venerated by the public and by those at the highest levels of government.

Kurata smiled, gratified to see that the crowd worshiping at the public areas of Yasukuni was so large on such an inclement day. He breathed deeply of the brisk typhoon air, delighted in the way the swirling gusts plucked at his dark business suit and combed through the generous shock of white hair that appeared so frequently in editorial cartoons both in Japan and in the international press.

As head of the Daiwa Ichiban Corporation, the largest industrial *zaibatsu* in Japan, Kurata commanded international influence and power. As a descendant of an ancient family whose members were carefully documented for more than eighteen hundred years, he loomed large in debate over the nature of the "Japan-ness" of the nation. It had been his destiny, he told his closest associates, that he had been chosen to help lead Japan's rebirth, its rediscovery of its sacred roots.

Kurata had been a youngster in the final days before Hiroshima and Nagasaki and attended a navy training school where he trained for a suicide mission along with hundreds of thousands of others who had volunteered for a fight-to-the-death defense of Yamato, the spirit and essence of Japan.

He was inspired, as were his compatriots, by the valiant defenders of Saipan, who had fought the barbarian invaders to the last, then killed all of the civilians and children and, finally, themselves rather than suffer the ultimate indignity of being taken prisoner. So it was for every one of the thousands of islands in Japan.

Kurata had been trained to ride astride a special steerable torpedo adapted for long-range distances. His mission was to set out at night with hundreds of others, stealthily advancing on the Allied invasion fleet, head just above water. In a last rush to destruction, they were to steer the torpedo at top speed into the nearest ship.

Hiroshima and Nagasaki and the emperor's recorded plea for cooperation with the Allied forces ended his hopes of being enshrined at Yasukuni as a *kami*, but the prestige wrought by his willingness to die for his country had advanced his career and shaped his deepest beliefs.

There was movement in the crowd now, and Kurata saw a small elderly woman dressed in traditional silk kimono recognize him. An instant later a murmur rolled through the waiting crowd. Some pointed discreetly, others bowed deeply. Sugawara's discomfort deepened.

With this recognition, Kurata's well-dressed bodyguards moved to his side; "the defender of Yamato," as the newspapers called Kurata, had many enemies among the leftists.

Kurata returned the recognition with a slight bow of his own. An instant later he heard behind him the muted voice of the prime minister, Ryoichi Kishi, as he spoke with the Yasukuni shrine's *kan-nushi*—the head priest. Kurata turned and stepped back into the doorway. He waited for the two men to approach.

Like Kurata, the prime minister wore a modest dark blue suit. Beside him walked the *kan-nushi*, dressed in his formal robes. The *kan-nushi's* flowing headdress bounced with each step. The two men stopped short of the doorway and bowed. As befitted his station and prestige, Kurata returned a shallower bow to each man. He faced the priest. "Your stewardship is most excellent. I am most confident the *kami* must be pleased with the ceremonies today and with the new exhibition in the Yushu-kan."

Just minutes before in the shrine's very restricted inner room, the head priest had finished conducting a private ceremony for Kurata, Kishi, Sugawara, and more than two hundred *jiminto* who stared at Kurata's nephew with a mixture of envy and curiosity. The *jiminto*, Diet members of the Liberal Democratic Party, included most of the prime minister's cabinet. Preceding the ceremonies, the group had toured the Yushukan, one of the buildings—some said the most significant—in the shrine complex. With the generous financial support of the Daiwa Ichiban Corporation and the enthusiastic political backing of the Diet, the Yushukan had become a museum that worshiped Japan's role in World War II.

"You are most kind." The priest bowed deeply. "We are not worthy of your generosity."

"Please forgive my forwardness, but I must insist on recognizing your excellence."

"Of course. There is no forgiveness warranted, Kurata-*sama*," the priest replied, using the most honorific form of address.

Conversation rattled from the opposite side of the shrine.

"I am so very sorry," the priest said as he looked toward the source of conversation, "but if it is agreeable with you, I will supervise the exits of the *jiminto*."

Kurata and the prime minister nodded their agreement. With a deep bow, the priest left.

Kurata gestured for Sugawara to join them.

"You know my nephew, I believe?" Kurata said to the prime minister.

"Of course," the prime minister said with a faint bow. Sugawara returned it with a deep bow of respect. The prime minister nodded approvingly as he studied the ribbons and medals that paved Sugawara's uniform.

"Akira has just recently returned from post-doctorate study in America and has joined Daiwa Ichiban as my personal assistant. Perhaps one day he will lead the company."

"Just so," said the prime minister, looking at Sugawara. "I am familiar with your service. The Nibetsu was stricken when you decided to leave active duty at the end of your commitment."

Akira looked uncertainly at his uncle, then back to the prime minister. The Nibetsu Investigation Division was the secretive intelligence section of the Japanese Ground Self-Defense Forces. Akira had risen quickly through Nibetsu's ranks, propelled by his quick intellect and a doctorate in computer science from Stanford. Along with his academic excellence, Akira had excelled in the service's martial arts and weaponry instruction, a combination that had assured his selection for the GSDF's first units of antiterror, special operations forces and had been promoted in record time to the rank of *Itto Rikui*, the equivalent of captain in the American army.

"It's all right," the prime minister said reassuringly. "In my position I know many things which are often best left unspoken." He smiled.

"I am please that you have remained on reserve status. Your considerable talents are an asset to the whole country."

"Thank you, Prime Minister." Sugawara bowed deeply.

"But now," the prime minister continued, "you have with your uncle a worthy responsibility to which you must devote your considerable talent."

"Thank you, Prime Minister." Sugawara bowed again. He caught a signal from his uncle, then politely stepped back out of earshot as Kurata turned to the prime minister.

"You seem to be wavering in the face of the foreigners," Kurata said. "One of your cabinet members came dangerously close to apologizing for the accomplishments of our glorious fight."

Under political pressure from the Koreas, China, and other Asian nations, Japanese officials had issued mild "regrets" over school textbooks and other state-supported activities that denied that the rape of Manchuria had ever happened and that characterized the Japanese role in World War II as one of "liberation." Lawsuits had multiplied against Japanese corporations that had used POWs as slave labor and against the government itself for its sanction of enslaving Korean women to be used as prostitutes for the armed forces.

"*Hai*, Kurata-*sama*," the younger man acknowledged. Kurata looked over this handpicked prime minister, wondering if the new generation had the right steel. Millions of younger Japanese had begun to pick up the nationalist fervor in the 1990s and continued to fill the ranks of those who recognized just how special, different, superior were members of the Japanese race.

"Begging your pardon, wise one," the prime minister said. "Those expressions are for foreign consumption only since governments are so easily sated with words. You may rest assured that we will not change our textbooks and we will continue to conduct ourselves as best advances us as a nation."

Kurata nodded faintly. "Just so." He paused for a moment. "Appeasement is filled with danger. For you and for our special people."

Sheets of wind-whipped rain hammered at the pavement as one of Kurata's security guards spoke into a lapel microphone, listened for a moment to his wireless earpiece, then turned toward the two men. He bowed, stood at a respectful distance, and waited to be recognized. Kurata nodded, and the man stepped forward.

"Begging your forgiveness, Kurata-*sama*, but I believe it is safer for you to board your car at the rear entrance. There are no crowds there."

Without hesitation Kurata shook his head. "Your concern is appreciated a thousand times, but a true son of Yamato does not flee from danger. He welcomes it."

"As you wish, my lord," the security guard said as he bowed deeply. It was a ritualized conversation that had repeated itself countless times in thousands of places. It was more than a challenge to keep alive a man who insisted on embracing death itself.

"Also, please alert Kishi-*san*'s driver that he wishes to ride with me," Kurata added. "We will have a conversation on the way to his office and then you will take me to Narita airport."

"*Hai*, Kurata-*sama*," the security guard acknowledged with a deep bow. From long experience, he knew that when the most sensitive matters were to be discussed, words were most secure when spoken inside Kurata's limo.

Knowing all this, the security guard murmured into his lapel and scanned the crowd to make sure his men had unobtrusively worked their way to the front of the crowd.

Seeing his men in place, the guard again spoke into the lapel microphone; seconds later, Kurata's armored Mitsubishi limousine pulled up to the entrance followed by the prime minister's car and security retinue. The very large security guard who rode next to Kurata's chauffeur leaped out before the limo had come to a halt and fought open a very large umbrella, fought to keep the wind from wresting the umbrella away.

A cry rose from the crowd as Kurata waved the umbrella away and, with Kishi at his side and Sugawara following behind, walked proudly into the slashing rain, past the opened door to his limo, and directly into the crowd, whose cries of adoration rose above the howls of the wind and rain. As the rain hammered down on his head, Kurata bowed, he shook hands, he said his thanks to those who wished him well and told them he intended to keep their faith and justify their trust in him. Most paid no attention to the prime minister.

"They adore you," the prime minister said when they had climbed into the Daiwa Ichiban Corporation limo. Sugawara sat on the jump seat opposite his uncle. The men wiped their heads and faces with warm towels handed to them by the driver.

Kurata looked at the prime minister. "Ah, but I am merely a symbol.

They adore not me, but the restoration of the *Yamato damashii*, the spirit of Japan, *neh?*"

Buttoned down in its armor, airtight and sandwiched by security cars front and back, the limo moved gracefully away from the Yasukuni shrine. The prime minister watched the shrine's crowd recede in the limo's tinted glass. He shook his head slowly, then turned back to Kurata.

"Please overlook my contentiousness, but it is you they love," said Kishi, distracted and, to Kurata's ears . . . envious? Kurata also noticed the prime minister had slipped back into his native Osaka-*ben* accent, a sure sign he was fatigued, perhaps worried. Osaka-*ben* was considered a coarse variation of the Kansai-*ben* spoken by the people of the Osaka-Kyoto-Kobe region. Some found the dialect offensive. Indeed, Kishi's national influence had floundered until he engaged a speech pathologist who taught him to speak flawless "standard" Japanese, actually a modified Tokyo dialect. By contrast, Kurata spoke Kyoto-*ben*, considered the most elegant form of the language, the only "true" Japanese, by language purists and the new neonational movement.

Kurata found the envy in the prime minister's voice an unbecoming, disappointing loss of personal control, but Kurata showed no recognition, no emotion.

"You inspire," Kishi said. "I merely administrate."

Kurata was silent for a moment as the limo merged into the jammed traffic of Uchibori Avenue, inching its way toward the Diet building.

"One must believe to inspire," Kurata said, then fell silent for a moment. "You and I are different parts of the way to the same goal. There is the wind, the kite, and the hand on the string. *Yamato damashii* is the wind; I am the kite; you are the hand. Without all three, there is no flight." *And the Daiwa Ichiban Corporation steers your hand so that I fly where I wish.*

"Friend, you and I have spoken often of the need to renew the national spirit, to cleanse us of the cultural erosion from outside," Kurata continued. "Without a shared myth of who we are and where we came from, we cannot remain great. A culture defines itself through its shared illusions. Without the myth, there is no culture. And without purity, there is only pollution.

"Just look at the Americans: even though they allowed the genetic pollution of their bloodlines by intermarriages, for many years they were a great nation because their different peoples made personal origins secondary to a shared national illusion of who they were. Now, they are spinning apart like the Balkans because no one wants to be an American first; every group insists on the primacy of its own origins, rituals, culture, ethnicity."

Prime Minister Kishi nodded solemnly. He looked out the window at the torrential rain that slammed into them sheet after sheet, drumming a tattoo on the limo's roof.

"Of course," Kishi said finally, "the mixing of so many disparate peoples laid the seeds of this destruction. We cannot allow that to happen here."

The telephone rang. Kurata nodded his agreement with Kishi's statement and picked up the handset. The LED indicated that this call—like most of his—was encrypted to bar prying ears.

"Moshi-moshi," Kurata said into the mouthpiece. *"Hai,"* he responded. *"Hai, hai, ichiban!"* He hung up the telephone.

Kishi gave no notice that Kurata had engaged in a telephone call, no matter how short. To acknowledge this would be impolite, an invasion of privacy.

"The cleansing proceeds as scheduled," Kurata said. Kishi raised his eyebrows. "This is the tenth day; there are no more new cases of the Korean Leprosy. It is according to what my scientists assured me. And not any new cases—not a single one—among Japanese."

"What of that—"

"Not Japanese at all," Kurata said quickly. "That entire family was Korean; they tried to pass by using counterfeit documents. They fooled the government. They fooled their neighbors. They could not fool the Slatewiper."

"Congratulations." Kishi nodded. "It has underscored to the general population the dangers of allowing *gaijin* to live permanently in our midst and the . . . wrongness of accepting them. This is a great thing for Japan that you have done. History will mark this very June day as the moment the *kiyome* began."

Kurata shook his head. "The purification is not yet done," Kurata said. "Only ready to begin." He fixed Sugawara with a serious expression as if to say: *Make sure you have recorded this conversation faithfully.*

Sugawara nodded, hoping his expression did not betray the leaden sadness in his chest.

The C&O Canal through Georgetown teemed with its usual Sunday crowds of joggers, hikers, walkers, toddlers, elders with walkers and

canes. Bicyclists threaded their ways among babies in carriages and grop-
ing teenagers. All of them crunched their disparate paths along the rut-
ted ochre gravel towpath. Trees verged both sides of the path; their
arching limbs created a tunnel of such brilliant fall foliage it seemed to
burst into flames every time the brilliant noontime sun emerged from
the partly cloudy sky.

Edward Rycroft and Jason Woodruff walked shoulder to shoulder,
puffing eagerly at the Players cigarettes that the Englishman chain-
smoked.

"Beautiful day," Woodruff said.

"I would assume that all this is about more than a nice day." Rycroft
glared at him. He loathed small talk.

"Of course it is," Woodruff replied defensively. They walked half a
dozen more paces. "One of my Saudi private banking customers asked
me for a favor yesterday."

"And?"

"Somehow he has a hint of what happened in Tokyo."

Rycroft shrugged. "There's more speculation about that than JFK's
assassination. What's that have to do with me?"

They dodged a jogging stroller propelled by a young woman with
auburn hair and well-formed legs in shiny purple spandex tights. Silently, the two men passed half a dozen more people before the crowd
thinned and they could continue the conversation.

"He wants us to make something that will do the same thing to Jews,"
Woodruff said eventually.

"That's entirely understandable," Rycroft said.

"He's willing to pay an enormous amount for enough material to wipe
out every Jew in Israel."

A thin smile softened Rycroft's face. "There are a lot of Jews in Israel."

"There's a lot of money in this client's bank account."

"Is this a Saudi government thing?"

Woodruff shook his head. "Not officially, but—"

"But government funds have found their way into your client's account."

"You have the picture."

They continued in silence for perhaps half a minute. Then Woodruff
spoke again. "Your part of the deal is worth twice as much as your
GenIntron stock options are worth. Cash. Anonymous. Numbered account. No taxes. Finally we can get the money we deserve."

Rycroft nodded as they reached the end of the towpath and turned right down the hill toward the river.

"I can do this," Rycroft said as they reached the bottom of the hill and turned left under the elevated Whitehurst Freeway. "Especially now that we've got that evil bitch off the premises."

"There's still that sanctimonious asshole, Brahimi," Woodruff reminded him. They walked in silence for several minutes and reached the riverside bike path paralleling the southern end of Rock Creek Parkway and headed south toward the Kennedy Center.

"Not a problem," Rycroft said. "The actual production is done in Tokyo. He doesn't have access to data from there."

"But isn't the formulation done here?" Woodruff asked. "I thought the Rockville lab was the one that actually prepared the specific sequences that target ethnic groups."

"True, but that was done in Blackwood's lab. I'm the only one with access to that now. I can prepare the sequences personally."

When they reached the Watergate complex, they stopped at a pedestrian light and waited to cross over toward Foggy Bottom.

"How much are we talking about?" Rycroft asked.

"Fifty million."

"Each?"

Woodruff nodded.

"That's awfully cheap for delivering an entire sanitized country over to them."

Woodruff frowned. "Don't get greedy."

Rycroft shrugged, lit a cigarette from the remains of the previous one, then tossed the smoldering butt on the sidewalk. "You know, if your Arab buddy is willing to pay that much, it seems to me that there is no end to the amount of money we could make if we're careful."

The light changed and the men walked across.

"I'm not sure I like where this is going."

"That's not my problem," Rycroft said tersely. "I think that we should open this up to a discreet number of others. The Arabs aren't the only ones who would like to rid themselves of pesky people who inconveniently inhabit land they could put to better use."

"And how would you do this?" Woodruff asked warily.

"A small meeting. Very small. Very private."

"I don't know," Woodruff said slowly. "If Kurata gets wind of it, we'll find ourselves on the business end of Sheila Gaillard and her Nazi sidekick."

"My point exactly," Rycroft countered. "That's true regardless of whether we get a hundred million or three hundred. So why not maximize the return for the risk we take? Sell it to the highest bidders."

"I suppose," Woodruff said reluctantly.

"Excellent! I'll send you my short list for invites. You can handle the details. Singapore for the meeting I imagine."

"But—"

"You handle the details, I'll supply the bugs." He extended his hand. "Do we have a deal?"

Woodruff hesitated.

"Wouldn't you rather have a hundred million or more instead of fifty?"

After a long moment, Woodruff smiled, gripped Rycroft's hand, and shook. "Deal."

6

NESTLED IN THE BOW PULPIT OF THE *TAGCAT TOO*, HER SIXTY-FIVE-FOOT STEEL KETCH, LARA BLACKWOOD RECLINED AGAINST THE SLICK NYLON SOFTNESS OF THE SPINNAKER BAG, LOOKED BACK TOWARD THE STERN, AND SIPPED AT A GLASS OF DRY ROSÉ. The remains of her lunch rested in a paper plate at her feet: the ragged heel of a baguette, an almost-finished rind of Reggiano Parmesan, and a ragged pyramid of oil-cured Kalamata olive pits. The sounds of a Mark Knopfler guitar solo drifted up from below.

She closed her eyes and rubbed at them. Deep leaden fatigue from the night-long solo sail down the Chesapeake Bay pressed her ever deeper into the spinnaker fabric. The night had been long but successful; the new night-vision starlight and thermal imaging system she had installed functioned perfectly both from the cockpit and on the remote display belowdecks. It was far better than the old one that had failed just off Cape Hatteras in a driving rainstorm.

In the faint breeze, Lara could hear the rustling sounds of the Sunday *Washington Post* she had picked up at the marina's convenience store. Eyes closed red against the rising sun, she listened as water lapped at the pilings; mooring lines groaned; halyards slapped gently at masts.

What in hell was she doing? she wondered. Next to the rage that burned inside over her clumsy ouster from GenIntron was the growing amazement that for the first time in her adult life she had enough time and money to do anything that she wanted—even revive her lifelong dream of successfully completing one of the great solo around-the-world races.

Lara opened her eyes halfway and took in the fog banks tearing themselves into smaller and smaller pieces under the heat of the lazy September sun.

Then she closed her eyes and remembered her boating hero, Isabelle Autissier, who had sailed solo around the world twice in one year, once in the BOC Challenge in 1990–91 and again in the Vendee Global.

Lara had met Autissier in Capetown during the 1996–97 Vendee Global when a rogue wave, measured at more than ninety feet on the radar of a U.S. aircraft carrier, pitchpoled both their boats. Autissier limped into port with a broken rudder. Lara's boat, a fifty-foot carbon fiber sloop, the *Tagcat*, sank. Of the sixteen boats that started that Vendee Global, only six made it home.

Shortly after she returned from Capetown, GenIntron's board told Lara they would resign en masse and scuttle any prospect of an IPO if Lara continued to enter life-threatening races. She honored their wishes.

After the IPO, she had used part of her newfound wealth to build *Tagcat Too*, incorporating all of the lessons she had brought home from her near-death experience off the Cape of Good Hope along with a number of innovative comfort features that allowed her to sell her house and live comfortably aboard the boat full time.

The phone rang then from belowdecks. Lara's hand went to her waist before she realized that it was the *Tagcat Too*'s landline phone ringing. It rang again. Reluctantly, she got up and climbed down the forward hatch. It rang again. She hurried now. Only the White House had the number.

Dressed in a ratty gray A³ America's Cup challenge sweatshirt and paint-stained cargo shorts, she made her way aft toward the navigation station packed with computers, satellite guidance systems, sophisticated communications, and a special telephone the White House had installed just two days previously.

Lara made her way swiftly along the narrow mahogany-paneled passage covered with framed photos and certificates screwed securely to the walls. There were the bronze medals, the photo of her on the foredeck of *Heineken* during the Whitbread race, the one hundred-ton coast guard captain's license, and the faded, yellowing certificates from her earliest sailing days when she placed first in the 420-class High School Nationals and first in the J/24 class of the Rolex Regatta.

Living aboard a sailboat had given her a connection to her first love even if she lacked the time to sail it. And now the compact space also seemed to embrace her, hold her womb-tight, and bind tight all the painful burning rage and dense, dark sorrow that had gnawed at her every waking moment since the final scene with Rycroft. Having her work ripped away so suddenly and finally was what she imagined it was like to lose a child.

Passing through the dining saloon, she glanced briefly at the "New E-mail" icon on her laptop and the piles of papers, books, and magazines that filled the space.

As she reached for the phone, Lara gazed at the snapshots of her father taped on the bulkhead between the sonar and the night-vision displays. He had been a very large man, over six feet seven, and a former SEAL. Next to that was a fading photo of her mother, Else, who had died giving birth to her. She was Dutch, had the same brilliant eyes as Lara, and like most from the Netherlands, she was a very tall woman. The Nazis had killed Else's parents and the rest of her family in a massacre of resistance fighters outside Amsterdam.

Else, who had been a constable with the Amsterdam police force, met Lara's father at a U.N. conference on refugees in Brussels.

Lara had long been fascinated with Holland and the sturdy nation's ingrained tolerance of others and their ability to wrestle success and affluence from a raw climate and a soggy, near worthless patch of earth. Their high educational level and dependability made GenIntron's Dutch subsidiaries the most efficient and financially productive in the world. Not to mention that with all the tall people—statistically the Dutch are the tallest nation in the world—she didn't stand out in a crowd as she did everywhere else.

After her mother's death, Lara's father retired from the navy to raise his daughter alone. He was a brilliant, resourceful man who quickly built a successful consulting business in Alameda testing marine gear and vessels for both the military and civilian manufacturers.

The phone rang again; Lara checked the LCD display that told her it was the White House calling but that it was not a secure call and she need not activate the encryption features. Lara picked up the handset.

"Blackwood," she answered.

"Ms. Blackwood, this is Irene Whitehead with the White House switchboard calling."

"Good morning."

"Yes. Well, thank you. I'm sorry to bother you on a Sunday, but I've got a very persistent caller from Tokyo holding, an army doctor, Colonel James J. Condon, who says he knows you and must talk with you. I didn't want to give out your home number, but he says he has to talk with you about something that's a life-and-death matter."

Jim's face came quickly to her and made her smile. They'd met in an advanced molecular genetics seminar during her final year of graduate school at Cornell. He'd been a second-year student at the medical school and had been paired with Lara for the hands-on parts of the seminar. He'd been an able lab partner, meticulous, often brilliant. They'd stayed in touch for several years and continued to exchange holiday cards and amusing jokes via E-mail. She had even had her GenIntron staff consult for him when he had been stationed at the Armed Forces Institute of Pathology.

"Of course," Lara said quickly. "Go ahead and connect us, please."

As soon as the operator put Lara on hold, the earpiece filled with a characterless New Age instrumental musical score of the kind the new president favored.

"Yuppie elevator music," Lara muttered as she opened the main companionway hatch with the stormproof Lexan bubble that allowed her a clear view of the deck, winches, sails, and lines without going topside in foul weather. It was more than the inconvenience of the wet and cold. Topside in a storm was a quick way to die. Cool moist morning air rolled in through the open hatch, bringing with it the scents of flowers from somewhere beyond.

The bland music from the earpiece continued; Lara grabbed the wireless phone headset from its hook next to the phone, placed it over her head, and switched it on. Freed from the cord, she moved about the navigation station, straightening up its contents, absently running diagnostics on the electronics, the computers, remote cams, and the satellite Internet connection as she waited for the White House to connect her.

She had worked with a talented Dutch marine architect to design the *Tagcat Too* in a way that incorporated all of the lessons she had learned from her ill-fated circumnavigation. She had designed the electronics and computer system and even done much of the programming. The hull had been crafted in the shipyards of Rotterdam and outfitted by the best shipbuilders this maritime nation had to offer.

She had added night-vision Web cams to the bow and stern. Together, the cameras not only allowed fans a real-time peek, but they also gave Lara extra eyes on deck when bad storms forced her to remain below and guide the *Tagcat Too* using the electronic helm. From here, she could trim sails, jibe, and even raise and lower the main, mizzen, and jib using the electric roller furling systems.

The diagnostics ran flawlessly as the hold music continued to assault her ears. It sounded like someone had tried to take one of the sexist, racist, homophobic songs of some rap performer and set it to orchestral strains. As bad as it was, it was still an improvement over the original since she didn't have to listen to the song's crude, crypto-criminal lyrics.

Running the Web cams in local network mode, Lara pulled up the images on the laptop screen. The mast-top camera could be moved up and down and in an arc of more than 270 degrees. Lara powered up the twin diesels one by one for their weekly check and tested the powerful electric bow thruster that ran off the diesel's generators.

She was working the manual throttle and bow thruster controls when the telephone scratched and clicked. "Hello?" a tentative voice at the other end said. "Hello? Lara?"

"Jim?"

"You bet."

"It's been a while."

"Too many years."

"More than I'd like to count," she said.

They chatted for several minutes, then Condon interrupted, voice turned strained and anxious. "Lara, I don't want to seem abrupt, especially after all these years, but I'm up to my ass in a real bear of a problem—"

"Not a problem," Lara said as she cleared a pile of *New Scientist* and *Economist* magazines off the nav station seat and located a pen and pad of paper for notes.

"Please don't misunderstand," he said quickly. "If it's not . . . appropriate or something, just let me know, okay?"

"Give me a break, Jim," Lara said. She made space to write by moving aside a pile of Saturday's mail all covered with pale yellow change of address stickers. "Just lay it all out."

The phone line fell silent for a moment.

"Well? So tell me."

Condon told her about the "Korean Leprosy" outbreak in Tokyo.

"I read about that," Lara said. "But I'm surprised it hasn't been played up more over here."

"It was just a bunch of dead Koreans," Condon said with a deep irony. "Nothing important to the Japanese media." He paused. "But it sure hit like a bomb," he said. "From what I can tell, it looked like whatever hit these folks started a general cellular lysis process—it's amazing: cell walls just disintegrated, dissolved. It started with the skin and voluntary muscles. First, these awful sores and then it was like the people began to melt as the disintegrating tissues actually sloughed off their bones. Most of the victims die spectacularly when the blood vessels give way and they just seem to explode blood. It just goes all over the place. And it seems to be contagious."

"Oh, my God," Lara whispered.

"Yeah. My comment exactly. This sucker is a real slatewiper," Condon said. "Especially if you happen to be Korean. It cut through them like a wet towel over a smudged blackboard. Then less than ten days later, poof! It was gone."

Lara shivered. "You say it hits Koreans only?"

"So far," Condon said.

"What does it look like?"

"Good question."

"How so?"

"Well, I have samples but there's no cellular structure under the microscope and nothing else I can identify."

"What do you mean?"

"The samples don't react to any antigen tests, they won't grow on either agar or live cells. The samples seem to be chemically inert."

"Jim, why aren't you talking to CDC or maybe Fort Detrick?"

"Mainly because my commanding officer is pissed as hell that we bent regs and went to the hospital to get samples at all. We're not supposed to stick our nose into their business, something about diplomacy and the precarious political nature of U.S. installations there at all."

"Well, that's pretty easy to understand, especially given that new Japan-first government that wants all U.S. bases and military presence eliminated. It's been front-page news here for more than a year."

There was a long silence. Finally, Condon sighed. "I suppose. On the other hand, I have these terrific samples, but my commanding officer mutters court-martial every time I bring them up. I want to send them to Fort Detrick or the CDC to look at, but I'll get my ass in a sling if I try that without my CO's approval. And getting that's a bureaucratic hassle in the best of times . . . ninety-seven levels of bureaucracy, paper requests signed off on by a hundred people. Taking weeks and weeks." He paused. "We didn't have the time."

"Like the time you picked the lock on the lab supply room?"

Condon laughed after a long pause. "Exactly! No way we could have aced that sequencing exam without the correct markers, right?"

Lara laughed with him, then sighed. "What can I do for you?"

"I thought maybe your company might be able to help out."

"My *old* company," Lara corrected him and then explained her current position. "But you're right, GenIntron would be the place to start."

"Then you'll do it?" Condon asked hopefully.

The line echoed with the ensuing pause. Lara stood up and leaned against the teak paneling. For the first time she was aware of her heart thumping in her chest. She smiled briefly at the excitement, the challenge of a new mystery. But the smile quickly faded as she realized that unless Condon was badly wrong about the new syndrome hitting only Koreans, then one of her worst nightmares had come true: someone had tested a bioweapon that was activated by specific gene sequences likely to be found only in a particular ethnic group. And they had done it with some sort of unknown disease. She had to help him because she had to know what was going on.

She looked at the snapshot and remembered the words her father said over and over and over like a mantra: "Do the right thing. No matter how hard, no matter how dangerous, no matter how difficult. We all die sooner than later and if doing the right thing makes it sooner, then you will have died a hero."

Dead hero had never been a life goal of hers, but she knew she not only had to do the right thing here, but she had to do it the right way. There was the issue of actually helping Condon. Anyone at GenIntron who collaborated with her would certainly get fired if Rycroft found out. He was a wickedly vindictive little bastard and she wouldn't put it past him to file some kind of lawsuit.

"Well," Lara said tentatively. "Let me think about it for a bit. I'll E-mail you."

The disappointment in Condon's voice was palpable as he spelled it out for her, then repeated the address to make sure she got it.

"Okay," she said. "I'll get back to you very quickly."

"Okay," he sighed. "You're the boss."

"Not anymore." The deep void of loss and separation burned again in her chest.

When they rang off, the digital phone switch in the White House basement—through which the connection had been routed—noted the end of the call and entered the details in its log, indexing the retrieval location for the digitized file containing the entire conversation.

Lara went immediately to her laptop in the dining saloon and logged on to a free Yahoo! E-mail account that she had opened years before when she wanted to surf Web chat rooms with another persona.

She entered the E-mail address that Jim Condon had given her.

"Send me a Hotmail or Yahoo E-mail address. If you don't have one, get one. Use extreme caution. Tell no one else. I may not control the company anymore," she wrote, "but I've still got resources. Summarize our phone conversation and what you found in Tokyo. E-mail that to Ismail Brahimi at the Hotmail address in the cc: box above. Then send half your samples packed in dry ice and copies of all your notes and the photos you took to him at his home address."

She entered the address of an old Victorian in Harper's Ferry that Brahimi had been restoring for more than five years.

"Find a commercial cold storage facility and store the other half of the samples and your notes and photos. Keep this secret."

Lara hesitated for a moment, then at the very end wrote, in capital letters: "WATCH YOUR BACK." Then she clicked SEND.

7

North of Kyoto, a narrow lane snakes its way from village to village, through the rugged wooded cliffs and hills of the Rakukoku, following an ancient serpentine route through countryside bathed in history.

A white Land Rover crept along the road with Sheila Gaillard at the wheel. She searched the woods that came right down to the road shoulder.

"Keep an eye out for the wall," Gaillard said in fluent German. "I miss it half the time."

Her passenger, Horst Von Neuman, nodded as he scanned the passing scenery, looking for the unsigned break in the trees, a grown-over, ostensibly unpaved track that did little more than part the trees. He was a lean, severe man with close-cropped sandy hair and deep, hungry blue eyes.

"There." Von Neuman pointed to a spot marked by a massive old tree highlighted in the directions.

Gaillard slowed and pulled over to the shoulder. She waited until there was no traffic from either direction before pulling into the space between the trees. They drove into a green tunnel lined with the arching branches of a dozen varieties of trees. The pavement, camouflaged to resemble a dirt track, hummed under the Land Rover's tires.

Suddenly the road doglegged acutely to the right; Gaillard slowed and prepared to stop. Just around the dogleg, a large log blocked the road. Gaillard pulled up to it and stopped. They rolled down their windows. Gaillard turned off the ignition.

"It's amazing," Von Neuman said, scanning the thickly wooded terrain. "I can't see them, but I know they must be there, watching."

Gaillard nodded. "And listening." She looked at her watch: 3:58, two minutes early.

Tokutaro Kurata was a worshiper of nature and of the deities of the forest and of the streams, as befitted a devout follower of Shinto. Accordingly, he wished this path up to his ancestral estate to resemble a simple country road. What Kurata wished, Kurata got. The concealment of all the necessary conveniences and security had cost far more than those of conventional design, but cost was not a concern. Kurata was prepared to pay whatever it cost for the grounds of all his residences around the world to look as if not one cent had been spent at all.

At precisely 4:00 P.M., two uniformed security guards emerged from their cleverly camouflaged bunker, one of a series that ringed the fifty-acre estate, all linked by underground passageways and packed with electronic gear that monitored sound, infrared, vibration, even the telltale scents of human beings.

One of the guards, a tall, fortyish man built like a pro football defensive lineman, approached the Land Rover. The second, who looked like a much younger brother to his partner, stood warily next to a thick hickory tree cradling the Shin Chuo Kogyo 9mm parabellum submachine gun issued to all of Kurata's security personnel. Heavier armament, both men knew, was concealed in the forest, trained on the visitors at this moment. It would instantly tear them to pieces if their intent seemed hostile.

The older guard stopped by the open driver's window of the Land Rover and silently waited for Gaillard to speak.

"Gaillard and Von Neuman," Sheila said tersely. The guard nodded and pressed a key on his walkie-talkie. Instants later the woods made a faint hydraulic sound as rows of steel barrier posts rose from the ground in a broad "U" shape around the Land Rover and an area large enough to contain a semitrailer. The "log" in the road closed the top of the "U," assuring that anyone trying to fake their way into Kurata's compound would remain for questioning if their identifications failed to pass muster.

The posts extended some four feet out of the ground and then audibly locked into place. This done, the guard plucked a device off his belt that looked like a pair of binoculars with a small keyboard fixed to the top. The device beeped twice as the guard pushed the buttons, then he handed the device to Gaillard.

"Look inside until it beeps again," said the guard. Gaillard took the portable retina identification scanner and held it up to her eyes. He knew that for scheduled visitors like her and Von Neuman, their unique retinal blood vessel patterns had been downloaded from the mainframe and stored digitally in the scanner's memory to allow a quick match. For authorized but unexpected visitors, the retina scanner was hooked via an encrypted, secure wireless network to allow real-time access via satellite to Daiwa Ichiban Corporation's supercomputers in Tokyo and Kyoto.

The scanner beeped, and Gaillard handed it back. The guard looked at a small LCD display next to the keyboard and nodded. He walked to the other side of the car. The scanner beeped as he reset it. He handed it to Von Neuman with the same instructions he had given Gaillard.

Seconds after Von Neuman passed his retinal scan, the "log" arced its way clear of the road allowing the Land Rover past the first line of security. They drove fifty yards before another set of guards—this time Japanese—stopped them and made Gaillard and Von Neuman speak for the voice analyzer.

Cleared again, Gaillard and Von Neuman stepped out of the Land Rover and turned it over to a guard for parking. Only Kurata's limo or the cars of those with him got to continue up the drive to the top. The guards then escorted them to a Mitsubishi sedan and opened the rear doors for them. The reinforced, armor-plated doors with their thick greenish ballistic glass latched securely when the doors were closed. Identical glass separated the passenger compartment from the driver.

"No handles inside." Von Neuman pointed to the doors as the car accelerated.

"Herr Kurata is a very cautious man," Sheila replied.

Von Neuman nodded approvingly.

They came suddenly out of the trees and there, looming in the distance, was Kurata's estate, a three-story wooden palace that resembled the Kinkaju-ji, the Golden Temple with its gently curving rooflines and railed porches that encircled every level. Like the Golden Temple, most of Kurata's mansion was surrounded on three sides by a mountain lake set amid dense trees and rugged hills. The 750-year-old structure had been built by Kurata's ancestors only to fall into disrepair until Kurata's business empire enabled him to restore it to its original beauty.

"Kurata's estate is laid out in Shinden style, along three sides of a big 'U' with his huge main hall at the bottom of the 'U,' down by the lake," Gaillard explained. "The other two sides are long, narrow buildings and walls that stretch from the lake almost to the entrance up at the public road. The interior space is filled with streams, ponds, statuary, and gardens. And while it outwardly resembles the Golden Temple, it is easily six or eight times larger.

"It's also a national monument open to the public on holidays," Sheila continued as the Mitsubishi made its way along the winding road. "It's part of the 'I belong to you, you belong to me' myth that Kurata cultivates."

"Great God!" Von Neuman was pointing out the windows. "What are these huge lizardlike creatures? They're the size of an alligator."

Sheila smiled.

"Komodo dragons," she said. "Native to islands near Okinawa and nearly extinct. As it happens, the microclimate of Kurata's estate is ideal for them so Kurata's won the hearts of the green movement by setting up a colony on his grounds, complete with scientists to monitor the colony, zookeepers to keep the dragons happy, and a steady stream of live animals—sheep, goats, calves—to keep the dragons fed."

"And I suppose it is a security enhancement as well?" Von Neuman said.

Sheila smiled and nodded.

Finally, the Mitsubishi pulled to a subtle stop in a small parking area at the sheer cliff at the base of Kurata's mansion. After freeing them from the car, the chauffeur took them around an artfully arranged boulder, which blocked the line of sight to an elevator set into the rock. He unlocked the doors with a key and then locked it behind them after they stepped in.

The elevator emerged at the top into a small gazebo in a copse of chestnut trees. Two Japanese men, both wearing business suits, faced them when the doors had opened. One was older, medium height, and by the faint bulge of a shoulder holster, obviously a guard. The other was much younger, athletically muscular, and tall, even by Western standards.

The young man extended his hand first to Sheila, "Welcome," and then to Von Neuman, *"Wilkommen."*

When Sheila shook his firm, warm hand, it seemed almost electric in her grip. She met his gaze and surprised herself when she grew suddenly moist and warm.

"I am Akira Sugawara."

"Gaillard. Sheila Gaillard," she said abruptly, then quickly broke eye contact and retreated from the handshake. Her racing heartbeat startled, then angered her. Annoyed by the loss of control, she struggled to restore the comfortable interior icy coolness that governed her life and made her successful. *Heat is bad,* she cautioned herself. *Emotions loosen control; they deflect focus. They can get you killed.* Even as she wrestled for composure, Sheila admitted that this handsomely tall Japanese man was undoubtedly very desirable genetic material.

From reading her dossier, Sugawara knew Gaillard was a strange but effective part of his uncle's security apparatus, her role continually pivotal in ways that remained vague and unspecified. But even knowing this did not prepare him for her strange reaction to a simple handshake. He kept this from showing in his face and voice as he shook hands with Von Neuman.

"I will take you to meet my uncle who is looking forward to your visit," he said finally. Sugawara escorted them from the gazebo followed by the older guard.

Instants later they entered a landscape that looked like a bit of Kurata's native Kyoto transplanted to the new world. He frequently referred to it as an island of civilization surrounded by savages.

Sugawara guided them along a long stone path running slightly uphill underneath a graceful tunnel of maple trees. A thick wall of cane, restrained by a bamboo lattice fence, ran along both sides. Along either side of the stone walk was a handrail made of bamboo.

A simple one-story structure lay at the upper end of the path.

"That's a replica of a famous teahouse in Kyoto," Gaillard told Von Neuman in German.

"Begging your pardon," Sugawara said in slightly accented German. "To be precise, this is a faithful replica of the Koto-in, a subtemple of Daitoku-ji. The original was built in 1601 by Hosokawa Sansai, a lord in feudal times who was devoted to tea and accordingly constructed a tearoom in this subtemple."

Von Neuman and Gaillard exchanged silent glances. Gaillard said, "Thank you." Sugawara bowed. Sheila tried to hide the annoyance she felt at the unwanted heat the young man's words generated low in her belly.

They walked around the replica of the subtemple and down a narrowing zigzag path that led through an otherwise impenetrable wall of bamboo. Minutes later they emerged into what could only be called a green world, rolling landscape shaded by trees and carpeted almost completely in moss down to a small pond overhung around its perimeter with trees and lush vegetation. A small stream ran down to the pond, making soothing noises against the stones. Sunlight filtered through the dense leaf canopy and cast a green light into the already green world.

In the middle of the stream some thirty or forty yards away stood Tokutaro Kurata, a white flowing robe in the traditional style rolled up to his knees and tied in a knot to keep it from dragging in the water. Splashes of water covered the robe. He held a misshapen basketball-sized stone and looked around the streambed, head cocked as if listening to music.

"Shhh." Sugawara stopped and raised his arms. They all stood silently as Kurata placed the stone in the stream, stood back, listened, then picked it up again and tried another position. Occasional Komodo grunts filtered faintly into the silence.

This went on for more than half an hour until Kurata finally nodded to himself, turned, and acknowledged the presence of his visitors. Kurata indicated with a nod of his head that he would meet his guests at a simple wooden bench just above his current position.

Kurata made his way up the hill, pausing frequently to listen to the stream. Finally, he greeted Gaillard and Von Neuman, dismissed the older guard, and sat on the bench. "Please sit," he directed them.

As they walked, the older guard tilted his head for a moment and held his hand up to a discreet earpiece. After a moment he put his hand on Sugawara's shoulder and said quietly, "Sugawara-*sama*?"

"*Hai.*"

"Security reports that Mr. Rycroft has arrived."

"*Domo.*"

After they joined Kurata, the elder statesman remained quiet for several minutes listening to the sounds of the water gurgling over the rocks.

"There are forty-one varieties of moss here." He paused. "Back in Kyoto, there is the *Koke-dera*—moss garden—at Saiho-ji, which has forty-two varieties. More varieties will grow here, but growing them all would be presumptuous of me." He smiled, then paused again. In the silence, the sounds of the stream seemed to make words that could almost be comprehended.

"You see the Saiho-ji was designed in 1339 by a Zen priest who felt that moss symbolized the timeless aspect of nature and the transitory essence of man." He looked away from them and gazed as his garden. "Eventually moss covers hewn stones and all man-made objects, bringing to naught all of man's creations."

Kurata looked back at the two sitting with him; he looked for comprehension but found none to his satisfaction. Western minds were incapable of appreciating the beauty in the ultimate deaths of us all. He did not let his contempt show. He had a use for these lower creatures, even the *kurambo*.

They were tools for his hands, logs to be milled and shaped for his creations.

Finally, he looked at Sugawara and asked, "Where is Mr. Rycroft?"

"I was informed that he had reached the first security checkpoint just before Ms. Gaillard and Mr. Von Neuman arrived in the elevator."

Kurata nodded noncommittally. Then to Gaillard and Von Neuman he said, "This is my new assistant, Akira Sugawara, my eldest daughter's eldest son. He received an education at the Stanford University in California, and now, fortunately for me, he knows everything."

Kurata laughed; his grandson bowed deeply. This was, apparently, a running source of amusement for them both.

Turning serious again, Kurata said, "Please deal with Akira as if he were me. He acts with my authority; his young eyes, ears, bright mind, and spry body will accomplish what my failing body and senses cannot. I have no sons of my own and wish that one day he will develop the right spirit to step into my shoes."

"Of course," Gaillard said.

"Good," Kurata said. "I will be occupied with many things in the coming days, so I will delegate your liaison to Akira."

Kurata sat in silence for a moment listening to the music of the stream.

"So," Kurata said finally, focusing on Gaillard, "you must wonder why I was so insistent on this very quick meeting."

"You always have wisdom behind your actions, Kurata-*sama*," Gaillard replied.

He nodded in agreement. Just then, voices drifted from the direction of the Koto-in replica. Rycroft's overbearing tone could be heard clearly. Moments later the new CEO of GenIntron strode angrily toward them, clearly familiar with the path. Two of Kurata's suited guards flanked him.

"I'm very sorry to be late," he said as he approached. He still wore a bandage on his face. "I had to interrupt some very critical research. Then the idiots at the airport had to search every bloody thread in my suit-case." His cultivated British accent was distinctly nasal.

Kurata raised his eyebrows faintly. Sugawara struggled to suppress a smile as he looked at the bandages on Rycroft's face.

"We are happy you could join us," Kurata said evenly. "Please be seated. I was about to begin."

Rycroft looked awkwardly about and chose an empty stone bench as near to Kurata as he could.

"It's the matter of Miss Blackwood," Kurata began.

"I don't understand," Rycroft interrupted. "I took care of that very decisively. She is a non-entity."

"Silence, Edward!" Kurata said harshly. "Do not interrupt me again."

Rycroft opened his mouth and then thought better of it, letting his face settle into a mask that was equal parts frown and pout.

Kurata looked at Sheila Gaillard. "Originally I called you because Ms. Blackwood exhibited some . . . extreme behavior"—he looked at Ry-croft's bandaged face—"when she was informed by Dr. Rycroft that she no longer had access to her laboratory or research accounts." Gaillard looked at Rycroft and raised her eyebrows questioningly; Rycroft glared silently at her.

"Ms. Blackwood is a brilliant and resourceful woman whose behavior that day clearly demonstrates that she can also be unpredictable. While I would like to continue to avail ourselves of her abilities, my original call was to make sure you were fully briefed on her in case some sort of . . . intervention became necessary."

Kurata nodded toward Sugawara, who produced a file and handed it to Gaillard. "This is a file I have prepared for you on Lara Black-wood," Sugawara said. "She has been successful because of the attrib-utes mentioned by Kurata-*sama*, and although I have not actually met her, all available data confirms that she has a commanding physical presence because she is tall, athletic, and fit." And beautiful, he thought to himself, remembering the hundreds of captivating photos of her—many attached to newspaper and magazine articles—that he had read in assembling her profile. But the videotapes were the most compelling. They showed not just a beautiful, intriguing woman, but one with strength and character. She was as tall as most men and stronger and yet had a commanding sexual femininity that attracted and intrigued him.

Gaillard accepted the folder. "Thank you. I'm sure this will be useful."

"Since my call to you, another incident has just recently occurred that makes your intervention necessary," Kurata said and again gestured for his nephew to continue the thread.

Sugawara pulled a slim notebook from one inside coat pocket and opened it.

"Among the duties I have the honor to perform for Kurata-*sama* is to produce an historical record of Operation Tsushima. As part of these duties, I was present on the grounds of Otsuka General Hospital following the test deployment of the Korean Leprosy vector." Sugawara swallowed against the sour memories as the smell came back to him suddenly. And with them his head was filled with the images of grieving families and, worst of all, the looks of innocent wonder on the faces of the youngest victims, too young to interpret the horror around them and in their bodies, too young to understand their own imminent deaths.

"I observed there two foreigners. After further inquiry, I learned that they were American doctors from Camp Zama who had come to the hospital to investigate the outbreak. I gave this information to Daiwa Ichiban security who subsequently identified the men and have monitored their activities. I received a communication today that one of the doctors made contact with Ms. Blackwood and requested help in identifying the pathogen in the samples they obtained."

"That's clearly impossible," Rycroft interrupted. "We have most definitely terminated her access to corporate resources."

Sugawara nodded. "True as far as we can tell."

"What do you mean by that?" Rycroft snapped.

"Simply that her well-known resourcefulness is cause for continued vigilance."

"Resourcefulness," Rycroft huffed, then reluctantly fell silent.

Kurata stood up and walked over to a table-sized boulder covered with a coarse moss that had sprouted spore pods. He stared at the stream with his back to his guests. A late afternoon breeze stirred the crowns of the trees, plucking from them the first leaves of fall. "For now, I would like for us to continue to monitor Ms. Blackwood to determine if direct intervention is necessary." He turned to face them again. "I am flying to Washington with the prime minister tonight for a previously arranged meeting with the American president. Because of recent events, I have arranged for an opportunity to meet with her and see if there may be a way to gain even a small amount of her co-operation."

Then, singling out Gaillard with his gaze, he said, "I believe you must intervene quickly and decisively with these American army doctors. You and your colleague."

The wind gusted sharp and cold, stirring the leaves into whirl-dances. "*Hai*, Kurata-*sama*," she replied.

8

As darkness sifted in among the trees of Tokutaro Kurata's estate, Akira Sugawara sat by himself on his uncle's favorite stone bench and struggled to hear the notes of the stone placed there earlier in the day. What he heard in their places were the screams of anguish and the wet, ragged noises of death that blanketed the hospital slopes as the grotesque experiment finished its rampage of an entire block of Tokyo's Korean ghetto. Sugawara pressed his hands against his ears, but the noise only grew louder.

"Damn!" he cursed softly. The sounds of the Korean Leprosy had not left him alone for a second, not sleeping or awake, eating or relieving himself. It was always there, a hissing, screaming, weeping chord of black clashing notes that accreted in his heart day by day and grew heavier and sharper as the seconds passed by.

Sugawara gazed at the elegant woodlands and struggled to find the beauty in the mosses planted there. Instead he found the whole scene trivial and pornographic next to the suffering caused by the Slatewiper.

"Your uncle is proud of you." Sugawara turned to see the bent figure of Toru Matsue walking slowly through the sculpture gardens by the koi pond. Sugawara got up and went to him.

Sugawara bowed. "Good evening, *Sensei-san*."

The two men stood silently for a long minute, silently watching the lazy undulations of the koi. They made an incongruous pair: Sugawara, just over six feet tall, lean, muscular, young, limber, straight in stature; Matsue, grizzled, stiff, bent by age and arthritis so that he appeared even shorter than his five feet six.

"Your uncle is proud of you," Matsue said again.

"I am grateful for that, but unworthy of his praise," Sugawara replied.

The two men spoke in Japanese in deference to the older man's preferences and his lack of proficiency in what he called "the devil's tongue."

"He wished for me to convey his encouragement."

"Just so," Sugawara commented. He looked over at the oldest of the family retainers. Matsue had served the clan for more than sixty years, first as a retainer to Sugawara's father and after his death employed by Kurata to teach him the essentials of the Japanese spirit.

"You are progressing satisfactorily; Kurata-*sama* places more trust in you each day."

"I thank you for your kind words," Sugawara said. "I will try my best not to dishonor you."

Following Sugawara's doctoral studies at Stanford, he had returned to Japan and was viewed as a *kikoku-shijo*, a "child returning to its own country." With increasing frequency, such children returned carrying Western influences—pollution as many called it—and were thus viewed with suspicion. It became an increasing problem in the 1950s and had only grown worse as Western ways and speech infiltrated the culture, creating an entire *kikoku-shijo* culture. Traditionalists feared that it would eventually eclipse the true ways.

Kurata had long been troubled by his nephew's disturbing *kikoku-shijo* tendencies. To set the young man on the proper path and assure that Sugawara was fit to eventually assume the mantle as head of one of Japan's oldest clans, Kurata appointed Matsue as Sugawara's retainer, guide, and teacher in *Nihonjinron*—the art of being Japanese.

Nihonjinron was an ancient code, a set of manners and mannerisms strictly prescribed and underpinned by an equally rigid set of cultural beliefs and moral imperatives that had evolved over the years into something that outsiders mistakenly thought was the same as Bushido—the code of the samurai warrior. But *Nihonjinron* subsumed Bushido and went further and deeper. To the old-line generation like Kurata, it was *the* way, the only way of being truly Japanese. It started with the genes and it concluded with the unswerving dedication to *Nihonjinron*.

Finally, Sugawara spoke.

"I am troubled, *Sensei-san*."

Matsue turned his head toward the younger man and raised his eyebrows.

"Please excuse my presumptuousness by daring to voice this troubling thought," Sugawara began. "As you know, I have the ultimate respect for Kurata-*sama*, but is it not a duty to speak up when one feels his lord's actions may not be wise?"

"It is rarely appropriate," Matsue began, "and then only after much reflection."

"*Hai*," Sugawara agreed. "I had no sleep last night, reflecting upon Operation Tsushima."

"What troubles you?"

So many things, Sugawara thought. The concept of killing people for one. He closed his eyes for a brief moment of reflection and saw in the personal darkness the young round faces, eyes wide with innocence, filled with tears and, finally, closed by death. He wanted to unload his doubts and his fears, but he knew Matsue would not understand. He opened his eyes and said, "I wonder if this is the most"—he paused, searching for the word that would accurately reflect his thought without giving away his true feelings—"most *efficient* way to solve the Korean problem."

"Do you have an alternative to offer?" Matsue asked.

"I thought, perhaps, they could be resettled," Sugawara said. "Relocated back to Korea."

"And if they do not wish to go?"

Sugawara glanced away, at the fish. "I am so sorry, Matsue-*san*, but I do not have that answer."

"You must have no doubts about your duty," Matsue said, reminding Sugawara of one of the central obligations hammered into every Japanese child and faithfully carried into adulthood. "You may offer—respectfully of course—your advice on the best way to complete a task, but it is not your place to question the wisdom or the correctness of accomplishing that task, the correctness of which was determined by consensus, by the collective wisdom of many very respected men."

"*Hai, Sensei-san*," Sugawara said as he bowed deeply to indicate a sincerity he did not entirely feel.

"That is good," Matsue said. "Otherwise you will seem like a *narikin*."

Often applied derogatorily to post World War II nouveau riche Japanese, a *narikin* refers to a pawn that has been made into a queen. In a culture where all power was derived from conformance and acceptance by society, a *narikin*, rich or otherwise, was despised as a lone-cowboy big shot lacking any legitimate authority to exercise its newly acquired power. Such people were shunned, whole families isolated in stunning loneliness that brought all but the most dedicated loners back into the pack.

Matsue turned from the pond and shuffled toward a large Rodin bronze. Sugawara followed.

As he walked, Matsue asked the younger man, "May I assume that I need not remind you of your *on* to Kurata-*sama*?"

"Of course not, *Sensei-san*. Kurata-*sama* is my uncle, my family. This binds me with *gimu*, repayments that can never meet even one ten-thousandth of my obligation in this lifetime," Sugawara said, an acolyte reciting his catechism. "He is also my liege lord which binds me through *giri*, which must be repaid equally to the obligation assumed. I will be fortunate to have repaid even half this obligation by the time of my death. Only my duty to the emperor surpasses that to Kurata-*sama*."

"Very good," Matsue said as he approached the bronze. He stopped and looked at the expressions on the faces of the figures in the bronze.

When Sugawara had joined him, Matsue said, still looking at the bronze, "Observe the expressions on the faces. See the crude, primitive expressions of emotion."

"Yes, *Sensei-san*," Sugawara said.

"The expressions are like those of monkeys and other hairy apes," Matsue said. "Their facial muscles and the brains inside their skulls are not as highly evolved as ours; they are not capable of the subtleties and expressions we are, *neh*?"

"That is taught as correct, *Sensei-san*," Sugawara hedged. His less-than-absolute answer earned him a frown from the older man.

"Never forget, young Sugawara, you have the blood of Yamato flow-ing in your veins," Matsue said sternly. "We are the *shido minzoku*; the other races are but apes. We are a pure race, the purest in the world—the DNA research by Kurata-*sama*'s laboratories has proven that beyond doubt. The Yamato Sequence is in every gene, held by our race and no other. Even other areas of science support the power of purity. Just look at the laser beam. It is powerful because it is pure, one single frequency of light. It can burn and cut because it is not polluted by many different colors. And so it is with the *Yamato minzoku*, the race of Yamato.

"As for the Koreans—and the Bangladeshis and the filthy Filipinos and the debris from the mainland—they are vermin; they threaten the purity of our race. We must remain pure to remain powerful. There is no choice but to eliminate the threat. Do not forget this!"

The old man repeated the slogans that had finally made their way out of the meeting halls of the neonationalist faithful and had begun to seep into the policies of the Diet, the prime minister's office, and into every branch of government.

Sugawara's mind swirled with conflict. At the very deepest level, he was bound by *giri* and *gimu* to do his uncle's bidding. The rule was clear: one's obligations always took precedence over one's sense of right and wrong. This made his decision easier.

At an immediate level, Sugawara feared Kurata's ruthlessness, his quickness to punish or eliminate those who opposed him. And perhaps more than anything else, he needed the protection that Kurata's power offered him. He was, after all, guilty of many things that he had already done in his uncle's service.

His heart sank as he thought of what he had already seen, what he already knew, and the certain knowledge that he would learn and see worse. From his years at Stanford, he knew that at least by Western standards he was already guilty of knowing about a crime and not reporting it. His only chance of survival was Kurata's protection. But that protection would come only at the price of loyalty and compliance. He was trapped—had trapped himself by his own actions. If only he had rebelled earlier! When he returned to Japan from college, he had many friends who were trying to shed the old ways. He should have clung to them, but the old ways and the rigid imperative to comply with them forced good people into bad behavior. He swallowed against the wad of guilt in his throat.

"Yes, *Sensei-san*." Sugawara bowed. "Please forgive my confusion. It is not my place to question these decisions."

The toddlers' screams that filled his head grew louder.

9

THUNDEROUS APPLAUSE ROCKED THE WASHINGTON HILTON'S GRAND BALLROOM AS LARA BLACKWOOD MADE HER WAY DOWN FROM THE DAIS LUGGING A BRIEFCASE FULL OF THE NOTES AND DOCUMENTS THAT HAD MADE THAT MORNING'S PRESENTATION THE HOTTEST MEDIA EVENT IN A MEDIA-CRAZED TOWN. Her speech, delivered to a packed audience of scientists, government officials, and media from forty-three countries, had enraged some in the audience but encouraged most of the others.

The event—the White House genetic treatment symposium—had been scheduled long before Lara's White House appointment, but since her arrival, she had energized the proceedings and elevated them from the realm of dry and mostly obtuse papers to an event CNN had termed "the United Nations of human genetics." Never before had the general media paid so much attention to the real issues—the science beneath— a subject that was so poorly understood, misinterpreted, and demonized. It was what she had intended.

At the base of the dais, Lara plunged into a swirl of people that crowded around her all wanting her attention. Like a successful politician, she shook the nearest hands, patted the nearest shoulders, looked into every pair of eyes that met hers. Lara's stature and energy made her stand out and it took only moments for the television camera crews to surround her. One network sports anchor called her "a supersized

Anna Kournikova" while the political press felt superior comparing her looks with Julia Roberts and her stature with Janet Reno.

"Lisette Hartley, CNN," said the first reporter to emerge from the jostling scrum that mobbed Lara. The CNN reporter followed the blocking of her cameraman and shoved a mike in Lara's face. The brilliant camera lights caught the full striking luminosity of the rare, deep red Sicilian amber earrings she had acquired in Malta the day after winning the Tour de Mediterannée single-handed race with *Tagcat Too*. Each earring was carved into a heart and contained a tiny insect.

"Were you really serious when you warned that genetic research could produce some sort of 'ethnic bomb'—a biological weapon capable of wiping out one race or ethnic group and leaving others untouched?"

She squinted for a moment at the intense light.

"Facts speak for themselves," Lara said as she set her briefcase down and withdrew from it two sheets of paper.

"This," Lara said as she straightened up and shoved one of the sheets at the reporter, "is the current list of diseases mostly confined to one ethnic group or another. Cystic fibrosis affects mostly Caucasians, Tay-Sachs mostly Ashkenazi Jews, sickle-cell anemia mostly African-Americans, and so on down a list that numbers more than two hundred at the present time."

Lara paused as she again bent over her briefcase and pulled from it another photocopy and held it up so the CNN cameraman could get a close-up for later broadcast.

"This is the—much shorter—list of ethnically linked diseases for which cures and treatments exist, cures and treatments that key off the sick individual's specific DNA sequences that cause the disease."

Looking directly at the camera, Lara said, "I know a little about this because more than half of these treatments were developed by my former company, GenIntron. If we can develop a pharmaceutical that targets a specific DNA sequence identified with a particular ethnic group, then it's *theoretically* possible to develop a killing agent that operates the same way."

"But research on offensive biological warfare is outlawed by international treaty," another television on-camera personality countered aggressively. Lara turned toward the source of the challenge and found a young, immaculately coiffed blond woman with expensively even white teeth, too much makeup, and a two-thousand-dollar designer suit.

Lara shook her head slowly and gave the woman a look that wordlessly asked how she could possibly be so naive.

"We've seen clearly that treaties cannot be enforced among terrorists. And if that is the case, can you keep Serbs from wanting to kill Muslims or Muslims from killing Jews or Hutus from killing Tutsis or . . ." She hesitated for a moment. "Or today's neonationalist Japanese groups from using the technology to rid the country of Koreans and other 'undesirables'?"

A buzz swept through the assembly. Her company had been bought by a Japanese-owned corporation and they were all wondering where she stood.

The blond woman's mouth opened and shut several times. Lara imagined the woman's brain like her mouth, futilely gasping in pursuit of an intelligent thought, much like a fish out of water. Not for the first time, Lara felt terrified that most people got their news from watching television.

Before the blond TV personality found either thoughts or words, the CNN reporter broke through the excited buzz.

"I thought you said the concept of race was an outmoded one," the reporter asked, obviously having done her homework. "That there isn't a gene for being black or Japanese?"

"Technically that's right," Lara replied. "There is no one gene; in fact there is no coherent DNA profile for any given race. In fact, there is as much or greater genetic variation among people of a given race"—she used her fingers to place visual quotation marks around the word—"more variation there than there is between people of different races."

"So how do you explain the theoretical ability to produce an ethnic bomb," Hartley persisted.

"Because people who live in a certain area for long periods of time, those who, by custom, intermarry among their own group develop certain genetic sequences that are the same. It's less a racial thing than a process of genetic familiarity. We see it among the Amish and among most of the world's rural populations who don't migrate and who marry among those they know best. All that's required to create an ethnic bomb, as you call it, is the ability to search through the DNA to find the right sequences."

Another shouted question came from the mob of reporters, but before Lara could answer, a very tall, painfully lean, young man in a pin-striped suit pushed his way through the crowd. The television reporters recognized him an instant after Lara did. Peter Durant, White House health care policy wonk and, not incidentally at this occasion, the man charged by the president's chief of staff with "riding herd" on her.

"I'm sorry to interrupt you," Durant said, facing the cameras, "but Dr. Blackwood is urgently needed at a meeting at the White House." Lara looked questioningly at him; Durant angled his head toward the ballroom's exit. Following his glance, Lara saw Durant's two Secret Service agents standing—outnumbered and nervous—just beyond the clot of television reporters.

Durant was one of the few non-Cabinet-level people to warrant Secret Service protection. His proposed changes to the health care system struck raw nerves in tens of millions of people and, not surprisingly, provoked all manner of death threats. ("Just one more argument for government-funded psychiatric care," he was fond of saying. Those who didn't realize that Durant lacked a sense of humor thought he was making a joke.)

Genetic testing combined with mandatory abortions for fetuses that tested positive for expensive birth defects was a cornerstone of Durant's cost-containment program. Lara had clashed with him frequently on this, arguing that mandatory abortion deprived women of personal choices in the same way that banning abortions altogether did. It was a hot debate that had spilled over into the newspapers more than once. Each story brought more death threats, aimed primarily at Durant.

Because of this and the protests that had plagued Lara as president of GenIntron, she had been offered a security detail, but so far it had been unneeded. The crazies seemed attached to GenIntron, not to her personally. She enjoyed the ability to take a walk alone again.

Making her apologies Lara followed Durant from the ballroom into a service corridor. The two Secret Service agents Lara had spotted were joined by three more who melted out of the crowd and formed a sort of rear guard as they walked among trays stacked with dirty dishes from the luncheon.

When the security detail had discreetly distanced themselves, front and rear, Durant turned to Lara. "I've never seen someone piss off so many people as fast as you've done." He exhaled audibly and rubbed his face in frustration.

She studied his face and, as always, found more to like than dislike. She had gone out with Durant socially a handful of times and came home each time amazed that a man this intelligent could be so monomaniacally focused on one topic and only one topic and could not or would not talk about anything else. He was the stuffiest person she had ever met in her life. She finally stopped accepting his invitations because deep policy discussions about co-payments and employer-mandated co-payments did not go well at all with French First Growth clarets.

They walked in silence for several paces before Lara replied. Stepping gingerly over a mound of what had pretended to be rubber chicken a few hours earlier, she said evenly, "Who am I meeting at the White House?"

He shook his head slowly, leaned over, and said, "You didn't say what we expected today."

"Then you didn't read my speech."

"This whole matter was *discussed* with you," Durant hissed angrily. "The president feels—"

"Cut the crap, Durant," Lara snapped. "The president doesn't *feel* anything half the time; he listens more to his Prozac talking than to you, me, or anyone else."

Durant opened his mouth to reply, then thought better of it as they neared the freight elevator and caught up with the Secret Service agents on point. Lara and Durant said nothing as the elevator arrived. One Secret Service agent boarded the car even as the scarred doors rattled open. An instant later, he emerged, satisfied it was empty, and held the doors.

"We'll meet you at the bottom as instructed, sir," said the point agent.

Lara watched him lean in and push the button for the lower garage level.

"Jesus Christ! You don't *know* what you're doing!" Durant said in a shouted whisper as the elevator doors closed. He closed his eyes and swiped at his face with his left hand.

"I'm sorry?" Lara raised her eyebrows coolly.

"You're not just dealing with the White House now," he warned as the elevator descended. "There are other *interests* involved."

"My interest is in good science," Lara said. "You can take your political bullshit and—"

Durant turned to face her and it was then that she saw the concern in his eyes.

"Lara, like it or not, political bullshit is what our lives are all about for as long as we are associated with government. It's not pretty, but it doesn't matter whether you govern or are part of the governed, political bullshit is part of life, so you better learn to live with it." He paused as the elevator rattled downward. "Call it what you like, but this is all about your recent extracurricular activities."

"My what?"

"You're playing with fire here ..." He inhaled a loud and strained lungful of air as he stared at the elevator's ceiling, its bare fluorescent lights.

"Fire?" Lara asked, her voice softened now by the fear she saw. "How? I'll bet this is all about campaign contributions. I know the president and his party get huge piles of cash from Kurata and a legion of his executives. They even tried to twist my arm once."

Durant chuckled unexpectedly.

"What's that for?"

"Just trying to visualize what someone would look like after attempting to twist your arm."

He smiled. "Look, I know what you and others think about me." His voice softened. "But I really do care about the issues and the people that the whole health care morass affects." He paused, struggling for words. He turned away from her and spoke vaguely toward the elevator ceiling. "Clearly politics is not your cup of tea. You're a brilliant woman who has added immeasurably to medicine and I am concerned that your position in the White House might be in serious danger because of your assistance to those doctors in Tokyo. You are seen as something of a loose cannon."

"Fine," she snapped. "If the president wants to cut me loose, it's his call. I don't need this crap." She stood face-to-face with him, her nose almost touching his. She waited.

Finally, Durant shrugged, then turned away. "As you know, I have unprecedented access to the president and I hear things. Often those things are not intended for my ears. And I have been concerned over the past day or so that you may have unwittingly involved yourself in something which is far bigger than it seems."

"But all I did was offer a little pro bono assistance to an old classmate—"

"I hear what you're saying, but the buzz I am picking up says you're nosing around something big, something that involves alliances, national security interests."

"Hold on!" Lara protested. "Don't you think we've got a duty—a public health duty—to scope out that bug. It's just a plane ride away from the U.S."

Shaking his head vigorously, Durant said, "I don't know details, but from what I can tell, it's bigger, much bigger than you can possibly believe." The elevator rumbled to a stop. "We may not like it, but protecting ourselves from global terrorism, the ability to reach out and stop them, means that we have had to get into bed with a lot of people we don't like; we have to bend overseas and make compromises that were unacceptable before 9/11. I believe that's what you've stumbled over and that's why the president personally wants you to make sure you forget ever getting that phone call. It's the best thing for the nation, for the world . . . and it's the best thing for Lara Blackwood."

He stepped out as the elevator doors opened, then turned to her. By the way he stood, blocking the opening, he didn't intend for her to follow him.

"Please use your best judgment," he said as the doors began to close again.

10

STEAM GHOSTS DANCED FROM THE IRON STREET GRATES IN THE DARKNESS OF THE TOKYO NIGHT. Dim lights from a distant street reached into the depths of the narrow alleyway and backlit the steam, giving life to the ghosts.

Lieutenant Colonel Denis Yaro heard a snicking chunk behind him, turned just in time to see glints off a sword reach out of the impenetrable predawn shadows and cleanly slice Jim Condon's head from his shoulders.

"Oh, man!" Yaro said, syllables slurred into a single word. He wobbled in place on sake-stunned knees and squinted into the gloom. The dark little alleyway in the Kabukicho district left little to see and much to the imagination.

"I shou'nev'drunk th'las'un," Yaro slurred as he swayed unsteadily. The fly of his pants was still half-zipped from their visit to the *nopan kissa*, the no-panties coffee shop they had stumbled into looking for directions. "You can'b'lef whad'I'm hal . . . halut . . . halucin . . . seein'."

The hollow-melon thunks of Condon's head hitting the cobbles and the geyser of blood from his severed carotid arteries sobered the army doctor. The swift decapitation was not an alcohol hallucination. Condon's body slumped; reflexively, Yaro stepped forward to catch him and was rewarded by a face full of blood still forcefully being expelled from the active but lifeless body.

"Dear God," Yaro said clearly as he unsteadily wrestled the body of his friend gently down to the wet cobbles and laid it next to the head. Still fighting the alcohol for clear thought, Yaro's mind fought to bring order to the nightmare. For a ridiculous instant, Yaro worried about the concussion the head must have suffered. "Oh, God. Oh, God."

"Your god can't help you now," said a woman's voice from the blanket of darkness.

"Wha'?" Yaro wiped at the blood in his eyes and scanned the night. He saw the glint of metal first, reflecting the faint light from the distant thoroughfare. Then a very tall, lean man carrying a sword stepped from the darkest shadows. Behind him, he saw blond hair dimly backlit like the steam and below it an athletically lean woman with large breasts.

"Do not call for help," said the man. "Or you will swiftly join your friend here."

Looking up at the man, Yaro thought he looked vaguely familiar. A nearby drinker at one of the restaurants? In the back of his mind, a small disquieting voice said that it was not a good sign that he had allowed him to see his face.

While the man stood directly in front of Yaro, the woman circled around the physician. Instants later Yaro felt a cold point of metal at the back of his neck; it burned as if frozen.

"Do not move," she said. Yaro started to nod, thought better of it. "Now tell me who is your source."

Yaro's thoughts raced. "I don't know what you're talking about," he said finally. An instant later Yaro felt the back of his neck burn, a tickle of blood dripping down his neck.

"You do not play games with us, Doctor," said the man in front as he waved his blade just millimeters from Yaro's face. "You were seen at the hospital prying into matters that do not concern you. You have learned of Tsushima from some source and we will know who it is."

"I don't know about any Tsushima," Yaro insisted. "We were just trying to help, to treat the sick. Ouch!" The blade penetrated more deeply.

"Please don't think we are such fools," the man said. "We know it is no accident that every other military doctor in the U.S. forces was restricted to base. We cannot accept that you just volunteered to help." The man now placed the tip of his sword at the base of Yaro's right eye.

"Unless you tell us exactly what we want to know, you will lose first one eye, then the other."

Yaro closed his eyes. "I don't know. I don't know what you're talking about." The smell of blood was hot, metallic, in the narrow alley.

"You had better know," the first man said. "And know quickly."

"Tsushima," Yaro managed to croak after a long moment. "Tsushima Straits . . . 1905 . . . Japanese defeated Russian fleet . . . made Japan a world power—"

Yaro screamed when the sword cleaned out his right eye socket.

11

FLICKERING LIGHT FROM THE ROARING FIREPLACE PLAYED AGAINST THE DEEP-
ENING AFTERNOON SHADOWS AS THEY SETTLED IN THE CORNERS AND RECESSES
OF THE WHITE HOUSE BLUE ROOM. The air-conditioning blew constantly.
Lara Blackwood sat next to the fire in an 1817 Bellangé armchair and
fidgeted with the altimeter and barometer settings on her watch.

She looked at the flames and—not for the first time on this deepening
late afternoon—remembered a staff cocktail party only a month or so
ago where the same psychiatrist who wrote the president's Prozac pre-
scriptions had told her privately that the president had charged him with
creating "the proper emotionally supportive atmospheres to empower
success" in all of the rooms of the White House.

"Fire and ice, yin and yang, opposites in the right proportions" were,
according to him, the keys to all success. Emboldened by too many
vodka martinis, and jammed against Lara in a packed, noisy room, this
half-drunk headshrinker had expounded on his theories at length, all the
while trying to look down the relatively scant cleavage revealed by
Lara's modest silk cocktail dress. The packed room had been jammed
like a rush-hour Metro train and he took full advantage, pressing his
shoulder against her breasts at every chance.

It was, to her thinking, a relatively minor annoyance in exchange for
his frightening insight into a frequently unhinged White House occupied

by a man despised by the electorate, voted in nonetheless because they disliked the other candidate even more.

Now, as she had done over and over again since the president had unexpectedly summoned her that afternoon, Lara stared at the fire, felt the cold air, shook her head at the memory of the drunk shrink behind it.

Shifting to keep her foot from falling asleep, Lara looked at her watch. She had now wasted an hour and a half. She looked expectantly at the door, frowned when it did not open, then looked up at the ceiling, willing the man in the Oval Office just above to get his butt in gear.

With an audible sigh she hoped would be recorded on the listening devices she assumed studded each room, Lara stood up and, for what seemed like the thousandth time that afternoon, examined the pair of Sevres vases on the mantelpiece. A brochure, undoubtedly dropped by a tourist earlier that morning when the room had been open to the public, informed Lara the vases were made around 1800 and had been purchased by President Monroe for his card room, "known as the Green Room," the brochure explained. Lara gazed at the delicate vases, decorated with scenes of Passy, "a suburb of Paris," the brochure explained, "where Benjamin Franklin lived while he was minister to France." She wondered where all the giants had gone.

Turning away from the mantelpiece, she turned in a slow circle, taking in the portraits hung on the walls: Andrew Jackson, John Adams, Thomas Jefferson, George Washington. Even the portrait of James Monroe had been painted by another famous American, Samuel F. B. Morse, the telegraphy pioneer. These were giants who built a nation; why did it seem only dwarfs had ruled these rooms for the last half century? Had the people themselves shrunk? Were the mediocre dreams of the electorate simply fulfilled in the leaders they deserved?

Before she could ask herself another unanswerable question, Lara heard voices from the hallway. She turned as the doors opened; she gasped faintly as the first person through the door was not, as she had expected, the president, but Tokutaro Kurata, chairman of the Daiwa Ichiban Corporation, the man who had forced her from her own company. Kurata was followed by a man she recognized from his news photos: Japanese Prime Minister Ryoichi Kishi; the two men took half a dozen paces and stopped. Only after the two Japanese men had entered the room did the president follow, closing the door behind him.

"Lara, I believe you know Mr. Kurata?" the president said without preamble. Lara looked at the president closely, and even from the distance saw the softness around his eyes that told her he had taken his Prozac that morning. While it had moderated his rages and wild mood swings, it deprived him of a certain intellectual edge—defanged his killer instinct—that she felt a leader in his position needed.

Lara nodded. "It's been some months," she said as politely as possible.

"This is Prime Minister Kishi," the president announced. The prime minister gave a very shallow formal bow.

"How do you do?" Lara asked, trying to keep a look of distaste from her face. Kishi had slugged his way up in Japanese politics, serving as the chairman of the ultranationalist Kokuhansha Party. He and his cohorts were true believers, nationalist ideologues who had stirred up and then ridden a wave of right-wing sentiment to the top of the government. They fervently believed in racial purity, the restoration of the Japanese spirit, had even called for death to those more moderate politicians who, even timidly, suggested Japan had been the aggressor in World War II and therefore owed an apology to anyone.

A short awkward silence followed the introductions. Lara looked from face to face—up at the president, down at the prime minister in the middle, and directly at the head of Japan's most powerful *zaibatsu*.

Kurata broke the silence. "The president was kindly giving us a tour of this most historical of government mansions when he mentioned you happened to be here. I insisted that I stop in and pay my respects."

"Just happened—?" Lara shot the president a sharp glance that quickly faded when she saw the look of concern on his face.

Alright, Twinkie. I'll play your bullshit game now, but you'll pay later for keeping me in the dark on this one.

Without skipping more than half a beat, she smiled at Kurata and said politely, "How kind of you to think of me."

Wordlessly, he gave a faint acknowledging bow and turned to the other two men.

"I don't wish to delay your important business," Kurata said to the president and prime minister. "I am an unimportant bystander to your matters of state, so perhaps you would permit me to remain here with Miss Blackwood while you continue?"

Lara thought it sounded more like an order than a request. Regardless, the president and prime minister agreed so quickly it left no doubt in her mind this had been prearranged. The president opened the door for the prime minister, allowing him to leave the room first. Then, before closing the door, the president turned toward Lara, resting his hand on the well-polished brass doorknob.

"Please give Kurata-*san* your close and patient attention," said the president. Without waiting for a reply, he turned quickly and closed the door behind him, thus granting himself deniability while leaving no doubt that whatever Kurata said carried the sanction of the White House.

Kurata stepped closer to Lara. He wore the same dark blue suit (or one like it since rumor had it he had only two suits and they were identical) he had worn during the final negotiations for the takeover of GenIntron. Lara had actually seen him only twice, once at the end of negotiations and again at a signing ceremony. The rest had been handled by Kurata's underlings. She had never been alone with him.

As he drew nearer, she noted the hand stitches in his suit, the enameled Daiwa Ichiban Corporation pin in his lapel.

"Would you like to sit down?" he suggested.

Lara shook her head and replied politely, "No, thank you."

She saw the flicker of a frown and understood it. Kurata was an average-height Japanese man of his generation—about five feet seven. While post-war nutrition and medical care was producing a new generation of taller Japanese men, Kurata was still four inches shorter than Lara and she realized it galled him to look up to her, even slightly.

"Very well," he agreed flatly, then looked at the fire.

The silence stretched into a minute, then two, punctuated only by the hissing and popping of the fire and the low background hum of the air-conditioning. Such silences hold much less tension and embarrassment among the Japanese than in Western cultures. Lara held her tongue, watched the fire.

Finally, Kurata looked toward her. Lara turned her head and gave him a direct stare, something women did not do in the Japanese culture. It was interpreted as aggressive, sometimes sexual. She allowed herself the faintest of smiles as he hesitated for a moment.

"We are most grateful for the fine and productive organization we have inherited from you," Kurata said. "The fine foundation you built has allowed us to make dramatic strides in the few short months since the transaction."

Lara nodded her thanks and fought against the anger that urged her to demand he get to the point.

"GenIntron's contributions have set significant events into motion," Kurata said. "Events that will have enormous impact upon the world."

Come on! Say what you want to say.

"However, it has come to my direct attention," Kurata continued, "that you've had some unauthorized communication with a party who has gained improper knowledge of our activities."

Lara furrowed her brow.

"There is very much for you to gain by cooperating with us," Kurata continued. "You are a significant stockholder, and although you have been made comparatively wealthy by our transaction, you have much, much more to gain by simply remaining uninvolved in company affairs, thus allowing plans to proceed uninhibited."

"Are you speaking about those cultures from the Tokyo epidemic?" Lara asked.

"That is the matter at hand," Kurata said. "If you do not wish to forget the matter for your personal economic reasons, I must appeal to you to think of your personal safety."

Lara was stunned and had to remind herself to keep her mouth from falling agape.

"Are you threatening me?"

She opened her mouth, then quickly shut it against the angry words that struggled for release. Instead of speaking, she turned and walked to the windows, now darkening with the gloom of early evening. Breathing quickly against her anger, Lara looked out across the ellipse at the Washington Monument. In the foreground, she saw four red lights marking the landing zone for the president's helicopter.

Kurata's image was reflected in the darkened pane, superimposed on the monument.

"Historical events you cannot stop are in motion," Kurata said so softly Lara strained to catch the words. "You can profit by these events, or you can be crushed by them. The choice is entirely yours."

He stood there expectantly, waiting for an answer.

You killed all those Koreans, didn't you? she wanted to say. But she said nothing; instead, she watched his impassionate face reflected in the glass. "Regardless of how you feel, you must decide whether you wish to share in the historical events that are unfolding."

Lara's mind raced. Her first impulse was to slap his smug face and tell him to fuck off and read all about his new, improved ethnic cleanser in the *Washington Post*. But what proof did she have that Kurata and his neonationalist goons were somehow using genetic engineering, maybe even her own work at GenIntron, to selectively kill Koreans? For anyone to believe her, she needed proof and that could come in just hours. Ismail Brahimi's last E-mail said he was almost finished analyzing the samples that Jim Condon had sent.

Ismail Brahimi would help her find the way to attack the problem. But finding that way would be impossible if her every step was dogged by Kurata and his goons. She decided that surrender, at least for a short while, was her best path to victory.

She bowed her head slightly. "You are, as always, a persuasive man, Kurata-*san*."

He raised his eyebrows, surprised this had been so easy. But, Kurata thought, for a man like himself surprising things could be done. Especially when dealing with women; especially when dealing with half-breeds, even famous ones like this one.

"Please excuse me," Kurata said. "It is not I who am persuasive but the concept, *neh?* A Frenchman—Victor Hugo, I believe—said that 'an invasion of armies can be resisted, but not an idea whose time has come.'" He smiled. "You are a very smart woman to see that this is such an idea."

Lara swallowed against the bile that welled up in her throat. "Of course, Kurata-*san*."

He bowed. "Please forgive me for taking up so much of your valuable time. I will leave now so as not to inconvenience you further."

Lara bowed, making sure it was sufficiently deeper than his in order to show her subservience. *You slimy hypocritical bastard.*

"There is no inconvenience," Lara filtered the anger from her words. "You have enlightened me."

Kurata turned, walked to the doors, and was gone.

Sheila Gaillard adjusted the disposable surgical mask on her face as the United Airlines flight leveled out over the Pacific Ocean east of Japan. To save a few cents, United and other American airlines recycled the cabin air so many times and allowed so little fresh air in that they created a perfect environment for disease to breed. All it took was a single sick person coughing or sneezing and the hazardously recycled air made sure that every person in the cabin would be exposed to their microbes and viruses within an hour. The mask caused her some odd stares at times, but it was far better than getting sick.

In the aisles, flight attendants shoved their stainless-steel meal carts down the aisles, assaulting the shoulders, elbows, and knees of hapless passengers jammed into seats unsuitable for human beings over eighty pounds. The carts oozed with the school cafeteria odors of yet another attempt at what this airline thought passengers would be stupid enough or hungry enough to consider as food.

"I'd rather eat bugs and pond slime from survival school." Gaillard managed a faint smile of agreement despite her pounding headache. She turned her head slightly and from the corner of her eye spotted the in-flight food critic across the aisle, a young woman in air force blues with pilot's wings, as she refused the offer of a disposable plastic dish filled with vague lumps of something masquerading as meat. Her seatmate, another female air force pilot, nodded enthusiastically as the two women shared a heat-twisted Payday candy bar and a stale bag of toasted almonds one of them had found at the bottom of her carry-on.

Sheila coveted the candy bar and cursed herself for being so rushed that she broke her cardinal rule of international flight and was forced to fly on a U.S. airline. The haste had been necessary because Kurata thought the Blackwood woman was going to be trouble and wanted her to personally keep an eye on her. Twelve rows up, Von Neuman was jammed miserably into a bulkhead seat by the smelly rest rooms.

This flight was certainly confirming her worst opinions of American airlines. Other than that little Southwest Airlines that she didn't have much occasion to fly, American airplanes were just airborne urinals with surly flight attendants and arrogant check-in staff whose competence level rivaled, but could not quite rise to the level of the black mold that grows at the bottom of a shower curtain. She continually heard that Northwest was even worse and that anyone with an IQ bigger than their shoe size would hitchhike rather than get on one of their aircraft.

She shut her eyes and rubbed at them until a night sky full of colored stars filled her head. But no amount of pressure could alleviate the nagging throb that started just beyond the hairline over her right eye and seared deep into her brain. Involuntarily, her fingers combed through the hair there and gently explored a thin ragged scar. When she had a headache like this one, the scar always seemed to be hot, on fire. The surgeons had done a fine job of minimizing its size and visibility, but it was always there to remind her of a life she no longer lived and could only faintly remember.

She was twenty-seven when her old life died. She'd left Bellevue Hospital in New York City for the night having put in a thirty-two-hour stint sewing up the Darwinally challenged of the island: drunks, street toughs, yuppie slime who drove their Beemers too fast, and the occasional victim who really didn't deserve what they got. The hospital's medical staff saw her as a talented physician and gifted surgeon until the last time she boarded a subway.

After being forced off the train by a group of parolees who gang-raped her for hours, beat her with a length of steel rebar, and left her for dead with a sharpened screwdriver jammed in her head, it was all her former colleagues could do to save her life.

While surgery and physical therapy reassembled her in better physical condition than before, her personality—the sense of who she was—changed completely from serious, studious, and courteous to aggressive, moody, abusive, and frequently out of control.

The rapists' screwdriver had ripped through her frontal lobes like a bomb obliterating the solid, stable, reliable citizen and likable person she had been.

Every bit of her education and knowledge remained intact along with her rock-steady hands and phenomenal ability to absorb new information and make sense out of it.

Three months after returning to work, she was fired for assaulting an operating-room nurse with a scalpel after the woman handed her the wrong hemostat. The assault had been the culmination of an escalating series of absences, missed appointments, and insults hurled at staff members.

Two rows behind her, someone sneezed. Sheila ran her fingers around the edges of the disposable surgical mask and pinched the soft metal clip at the bridge of her nose to make sure it was still as well sealed as it could be.

A generous severance payment along with disability insurance kept her going for months as she tried to sort out what had happened to her. In the intellectually lucid periods between crippling headaches and memory blackouts, Sheila made herself the star patient of her new medical practice. She found ample documentation in both popular and medical publications that frontal lobe injuries were well known for altering the victims' personalities, most frequently turning model citizens into miscreants and criminals.

The most famous of all was railroad foreman Phineas Gage who survived an accidental explosion in 1848 that drove a sharp, three-foot seven-inch steel bar clean through his head, entering just under his left cheek and exiting the top of his head. The shrewd, considerate, conscientious worker quickly deteriorated into a grossly profane, capricious, irreverent, and self-centered man who, according to his friends, was "no longer Gage."

She knew how that felt as she went through her Web pages and writing, not recognizing the person who had created them as herself. And while she learned there was no cure for the poorly understood condition, she found out she had been lucky, probably because the screwdriver had drilled a relatively small path through her gray matter. Unlike many other frontal lobe-damaged victims, she showed no lack of planning ability and experienced no problems with her memory, speech, or ability to learn or to move. She did find it much harder to motivate herself and get moving on tasks and occasionally failed to get the punchline of a joke. She also found other people tedious, boring, beneath contempt, and completely uninteresting if they didn't serve her sexual or occupational needs.

When she went through old receipts to prepare her income taxes, she couldn't fathom why she had bothered to donate money to the Red Cross and other charities. It now seemed like a foolish waste of money.

The problem that had concerned her most had been the blackouts. She'd be doing something normal and then the world would go blank. Hours later she would usually find herself in bed or on the sofa. Infrequently, she would find herself in a familiar place like the medical school library, the corner bodega, or in a cab.

One night during this time, just before midnight, she found herself naked on the deck of a Long Island beach house engaged in sex with three men and a woman. Sheila never penetrated the memory blackout that brought her to the house. As hard as she tried in the years that followed, the last thing she could remember was the headache that buckled her knees and the brilliant neon lights that filled her vision. Nothing about what must have been a deliberate and ordered decision to locate and take herself to what she learned was an expensive and exclusive "alternate lifestyles" facility.

The crippling headaches stayed away as long as she paid frequent visits to the Long Island beach house where she quickly became a sought-after sex partner. She also found that the fits of uncontrollable rage, the tardiness, and the verbal abuse that had gotten her fired also remained at bay. What neurons had been rewired to produce this strange relationship with the deep buried pleasure structures in the brain? she wondered. What neurotransmitters and hormones were in play that interacted with the rearranged structures of her brain?

Quickly she learned that research had no answers and that neuroscience had not evolved sufficiently to address the questions her new behavior had raised. She threw herself into absorbing every word of research on the topic and when she was done was appalled at how little humans really knew about their own minds and how the neurons in their heads governed—or failed to govern—their behavior.

Freed of the headaches and able to bring her emotional outbursts under control, Sheila attempted to get her old job back, but on the morning she was supposed to appear for her final job interview she found herself, instead, recovering from a blackout on the Staten Island ferry.

Depressed by the failure, she grew increasingly obsessed with the men who had raped and beat her. One had been caught, but skipped bail set by a judge who didn't seem to care what had happened to her. The police were overworked and had moved on to other, fresher crimes where failure to act carried greater political consequences than cold cases, especially those involving ill-tempered, pushy, foul-mouthed victims.

A flight attendant tapped Sheila on the shoulder.

"Dinner?" the flight attendant asked.

"Yeah, but it's pretty clear from the stink that somebody forgot to load it onboard."

The flight attendant shrugged apathetically and moved on to the next seat.

Sheila visualized her naked, spread-eagled, handcuffed to a bed, and skinned of every last square inch of epidermis.

Just like the men who had raped her. One by one, she had tracked each of them down and handcuffed them at gunpoint. She had lost none of her surgical skill and after finishing with them, wore their skins like a pelt coat, just as she had read about Mayan priests doing. Then, she made sure they were alive before soaking them with gasoline and setting them ablaze. Their screams had given her a rush that touched the deepest spots in her soul and lifted the darkness of her memory lapses. For months, she tried to work out what sorts of neuronal rewiring might have been triggered by the extreme emotions, the transcendent feelings, and the dreams that allowed her to relive the pleasure night after night.

The literature was clear that the brain could rewire itself to overcome injury and that even intense thinking and learning changed brain topography and nerve cell configurations. So it was, she concluded, reasonable to believe that the chemicals produced from her experiences with the rapists had certainly allowed her damaged tissue to reconnect, to establish whole new pathways that bridged her incapacities and allowed her to develop new, better ones.

After she killed the last rapist, the memory blackouts never returned. She was confident they never would as long as Kurata gave her enough work.

12

THE SCUDDING CLOUDS HAD BEGUN TO SURRENDER TO VAGRANT PATCHES OF BLUE SKY WHEN LARA FINALLY STEERED HER SLEEK CARBON-FIBER ROWING SHELL BACK INTO THE YACHT HARBOR. Sweat dripped from her face as she pulled with a passion against the oars until her thighs and back and shoulders burned hot and tight against her damp skin. Her breath came deep and rhythmically, unstrained and eager for more.

She rowed for all she was worth as she turned down the main channel. Even though the wind had diminished and the chop was minimal, the water sang quick, sharp *shup-shup-shup* notes against the racing hull.

Stress and anger were never things Lara could deal with emotionally. Never calm and rarely sanguine, she had learned as a child that emotional stress demanded physical release.

Her father had been clear about that. "Call it a runner's high or whatever else you want," he told her time after time. "But extreme exercise creates extreme relaxation by producing endorphins and a whole host of other brain chemicals that aren't even close to being identified."

Extreme physical exercise was his meditation and "Feel the burn," his mantra. Even after retiring from the SEALs, he kept up a physical training regime more suitable for his former unit than an aging business consultant. Up until the day he died in the crash of an experimental high-speed watercraft at age seventy-six, he was still running the beaches of San Diego and climbing the mountains east of there.

"I'm running away from old age," he liked to joke. "If I slow down, it will catch me." She knew now that even if you could outrun old age, death was always faster.

There was truth there, she knew, as she pulled the paddles free of the water and glided toward the end-tie where the *Tagcat Too* weighed gently against her mooring lines bow toward the harbor entrance.

A wolf whistle shot across the main channel. "Hey, baby!"

Lara traced the whistle's echo to a fleshy man lounging in the stern of a large, expensive white powerboat. She thought he was a lobbyist or something and he seemed to be on his boat at all hours, usually entertaining small groups of people.

"We ought to get together." He took a drag on a cigarette and waved a brown mixed drink at her as she glided past. His intense gaze was all too obviously fixed on her breasts. Sweat had made her Lycra bodysuit cling; her nipples pressed expansively against the stretch fabric.

"Lose the beer gut and cigarette and we might have something to talk about."

The man leered at her and made an obscene gesture with his middle finger. It was their usual routine and had grown almost amicable. Men like him were a lot like dogs chasing cars. They thought she looked sexy from a distance and then had second thoughts close up: most men did not like women tall enough to look them straight in the eye. Not to mention those who stood eye to breast with her ample bosom. Women just weren't supposed to have both muscles and boobs.

Lara placed her oars on the dock and then climbed easily out of the shell and pulled it out of the water. She stretched for a moment, then walked quickly to the main hatch of the *Tagcat Too*, dialed in the combination, and went below to check for voice mail or E-mail from Ismail. Nothing.

Back on the dock, she hosed down the shell and paddles with fresh water, dried them, and put them back in their locked dockside storage. Loud laughter and the strains of forced bonhomie drifted across the water from the large powerboat as a man she recognized from television news as the white-haired chairman of some Senate committee or other shook hands with the boat's owner. A blond with a Barbie figure and stiletto heels decorated the senator.

Lara coiled the water hose and hung it on the dock box hook next to the faucet, climbed aboard the *Tagcat Too*, and after looking over the deck to make sure all was in order, descended belowdecks with the image of the blonde in her head and how easily the woman fit into a time-worn role: woman as ornament. A moment of envy surprised Lara as she checked to make sure the boat's hatches were secured. Not that she really *wanted* to fit into the trophy woman role, but her size and stature meant that she couldn't try it on, even for a night, just to see what it might feel like.

She checked her E-mail again and then moved aft of the cockpit and opened the teak door to her stateroom. There she stripped off the Lycra and tossed it into the dirty clothes bin. The blond ornament easily attracted men who were comfortable with her. Lara envied that comfort. She had made people nervous for as long as she could remember. In school, those who were uncomfortable with her size retaliated with taunts and jeers that drove her deeper into her studies and her sports where she could excel and escape the insults that dogged her through school hours.

Carefully removing her earrings, Lara massaged the piercing between her thumb and forefinger and went to the custom-built, velvet-lined jewelry drawers that held her collection of earrings.

There were scores of earrings in the drawer and a total of sixteen drawers, each about a foot wide and long and an inch deep. A friend once joked that she had earrings like Imelda Marcos had shoes. She carefully placed the earrings in the drawer and let her eyes lovingly move over row after row, some priceless, others completely worthless without the memories attached. It was true. She loved earrings because they were one of the few things she could walk into a store and buy right there, on the spot: no alterations, no waiting. Other than clothing from a sporting goods store, almost everything else she wore had to be tailored or custom-made. Even necklaces and bracelets had to be altered before they would fit her frame. Being tall and strong had taken her places that few other women could go, but the older she got, the more she wished she could just be a normal-sized woman with a normal life with a normal man. And children.

Normal, she thought as she turned on the hot water in the shower, was highly underrated. The on-demand propane water heater came to life. Lara walked naked into the dining saloon to check the E-mail one last time and then stepped into the shower.

Ismail was the most normal man she knew, but then someone with a Nobel Prize was hardly your average guy. She loved him as a brother and a colleague, someone she had struggled with to build a company and create ways to heal. There was a time, probably back in college, she supposed, when they might have been lovers. But then, as now, he was a devout Muslim who believed sex outside of marriage was wrong. At first, she'd thought his unwed celibacy was quaint and old-fashioned, but eventually she found it comfortable because it allowed them to work long hours together without sex becoming an issue. Then, not long out of college, they were collaborators and then cofounders of a new company. Both felt that romance with coworkers was a greased slide to disaster.

They had behaved logically, rationally, she thought as she massaged the shampoo into her hair. Being levelheaded had certainly paid off for both of them, but she wondered now whether or not they had both paid too high a price.

Not that she hadn't tried to make up for lost times, but a depressing string of one-night stands had left her burned out. Just about the only people confident enough to ask her out were other athletes, but most were totally self-absorbed and unable to keep up intellectually; the only exception had wound up as gray dust at the World Trade Center. She could never look at those awesome clouds of dust storming down the canyons of lower Manhattan without thinking of him, as part of this great roiling ghost that had carried away so many hopes and dreams.

The phone rang.

Cursing under her breath, Lara shut off the water and walked swiftly to the extension in her cabin. The caller ID readout displayed Ismail's wireless phone number.

"Ismail!" she said, picking up the receiver. "I was worried."

"Not as much as you're going to be." His voice was grim. Static reigned on the fuzzy connection.

"Where are you?" Lara asked.

"Heading to La Jolla," he said faintly beneath a crescendo of static. "As soon as I got the initial results I knew we'd need more work, but I think they're watching me pretty closely at the lab. I knew I couldn't do it there so I arranged for a little help from Scripps."

"What do you mean?"

"The organisms that your friend sent contain artificial DNA bases."

"Dear God!"

A long crackling pause filled the earpiece.

"Yes," Ismail said finally.

The entire genetic code of life is written by four DNA bases, adenine, guanine, cytosine, and thymine all strung together billions of times like beads in the DNA double helix. Each series of three bases along the DNA strand forms a *codon* that is specific for one of only twenty amino acids that, with few very rare exceptions, are used by all living things from yeast to human beings.

A gene is nothing more than a string of three-base codons that tell the cell how to assemble the corresponding amino acids into a useful protein. A cell assembling a protein from DNA, for example, would know that when it found the codon, CAT, it was supposed to stick in a histidine amino acid, TGG coded for tryptophan and TAG was like the period on the end of a sentence, marking the termination point of the protein.

The two helixes of DNA are held together by bonds between specific bases: adenine always pairing from one helix strand to another to thymine and cytosine to guanine.

But because there are only four bases in DNA, it restricts the number of amino acids that a cell can use to make proteins. Synthetic DNA, as pioneered by scientists at the Scripps Research Institute and Cal Tech, incorporate two new DNA bases that can be incorporated into DNA and expand the range of amino acids that can be formed. This allows the production of proteins never before produced in the organism.

"So what have we got here?" Lara asked. "I'd bet on Xanthosine phosphoramidite for one of the bases."

"Yeah, but the other one is a true mystery," Ismail continued. "I looked for every possible nonpolar isotere of thymine and came up with nothing."

"Oh, my God, Ismail! That means it might be one of mine! You know as well as I do that molecular shape is more important than hydrogen bonding for sticking the two DNA strands together with the C-G and A-T pairs. That's why I created that series of synthetic DNA bases for gene therapies."

"It *could* be one of yours," Ismail said slowly. "But remember that others are working on synthetic DNA as well, so it might be—"

"I don't believe in coincidence," Lara said. "We've got an unknown synthetic DNA in a sample of a pathogen from Tokyo right about the time I get booted out of my lab . . . and this comes after the company gets bought by a Japanese billionaire whose headquarters is in Tokyo."

"I tend to agree," Ismail said. "But there's something even more disturbing."

"That's hard to believe."

"All of the cytosine molecules in C-G pair bonds in the pathogen are methylated."

"Oh, no." Lara leaned against the bulkhead. "Ismail, remember: when cytosine and guanine pair up in human beings, the cytosine almost always has a methyl group attached."

"I know," Brahimi said. "I know."

But Lara continued, thinking aloud. "This methyl group is missing in the same C-G bonds in bacteria and other human pathogens. This C-G sequence allows the human immune system to key in on the unmethylated sequences and launch a generalized immune response that is the body's first line of defense."

She paused to think about what she had said. The impact forced her to sit before she spoke again, this time in an uncharacteristically quiet whisper. "My God, Ismail: a pathogen with methylated cytosine in its C-G sequences would be a stealth bomb able to launch an attack without setting off the front-line troops."

"Which is why I called in sick and took the first flight I could get to San Diego. There's half a dozen people here who've studied on GenIntron grants and used our labs."

"Dear Lord, Ismail. What if they've linked our process for ethnic sequence activation and instead of coupling it with therapy, they've attached a synthetic, fatal disease."

"I pray that is not the case."

"We may need more than prayers," she said. "Synthetic pathogens mean that the human body can't fight it, can't produce antibodies."

"If God wills it, we can do something about it."

The call suddenly disconnected in a hailstorm of static.

"Ismail? Ismail?" Nothing but static. "Damn!" She slammed the phone into the receiver and went to the built-drawers to search for clothes.

Fighting the black, heavy dread that grew like a stone deep in her belly, Lara dressed quickly in cargo shorts and a Washington Marathon

T-shirt. Ismail called back to say that he had arrived at Scripps and would contact her when he had more.

Lara then quickly made her way to the nav station and retrieved Jim Condon's phone number from the notepad there. She dialed the number, but got no answer.

13

EVEN AT 2:00 A.M., THE STREETS OF TOKYO'S KABUKICHO DISTRICT WERE STILL THRONGING WITH REVELERS BASKING IN THE NEON GLOW, LOOKING FOR FUN, LUCK, MUSIC, INTOXICATION, CINEMA, SEX. Just northeast of the Shinjuku train station and less than one thousand meters from the Royal Gardens, the Kabukicho district pulsed every night until the rising sun cleared the streets and sent *sararimen* dragging into their offices bloodshot, bleary, flushed, flustered, and smelling of breath spray.

A discreet dark limousine pulled to a halt and double-parked at the curb next to a Mitsubishi bearing a decal proclaiming, "Honor the warriors of the Great Pacific War." Cars behind and in front bore the same decals.

At the sight of the double-parked vehicle, a policeman wearing white cotton gloves stepped from his *koban* and headed toward the limo, intending to wave it on before it blocked traffic.

As he approached, he watched two large, tall, dark-suited men—obviously bodyguards—step from the front of the limo. One opened the rear door. A young man stepped out who looked vaguely familiar to the policeman. When Tokutaro Kurata stepped out, the policeman stopped in his tracks. He stood there, half gawking, as the entourage approached. Kurata and the young man walked abreast, one bodyguard in front, another in back.

The policeman bowed deeply as Kurata passed.

"You make me proud," Kurata said to Akira Sugawara as they made their way past a doorway that burst with the manic jangling and flashing of pachinko machines. Kurata's nose wrinkled as if he had smelled something unpleasant. Pachinko parlors were run by Koreans.

"Thank you, Uncle," Sugawara replied. "I have had a good teacher."

Kurata smiled. "It will take them months to disentangle the agreement they have entered into."

"No doubt," Sugawara agreed, thinking of the five Americans they had just dropped off at their hotel after an evening of dining and drinking. The men were owners of a large software company that had asked Kurata to help them crack the Japanese market with a joint venture that could circumvent the "quality assurance inspections" the Japanese government had used for more than twenty-one months to prevent the sale of the product.

"They have a good company," Kurata said as they made their way through the fragrant *hibachi* smoke of a curbside *yakitori* stand. "I want it."

"*Hai*, Kurata-*sama*."

"Acquire it in the usual manner. Make them desperate and they will sell at an advantageous price."

"*Hai*." Sugawara pulled a small memo pad from the breast pocket of his plain navy blue suit and scribbled a note.

"Europe is a boutique; America is a farm. We take what we wish and leave them what we wish them to have."

"*Hai*."

They walked on silently for several moments, through a throng of young men ogling the window of a *noppan kissa* ("orgasm but no intercourse" read the sign) for the no-panty coffee shop. They passed other examples of the district's thriving ejaculation industry: the peep rooms, pink salons, Turkish baths, date clubs, massage parlors, mistress banks, enema-on-stage shows, live sex acts, and even the *sekuhara*, where women dressed up like office workers, took money from men who paid to harass and, for more yen, bed them.

Interwoven with the pink industry operations were legitimate restaurants and bars, theaters, cinemas, shops, music clubs, video arcades rumbling with digital thunder, and an all-night food shop. Sugawara noted that many doorsteps had a small pile of salt, a purification ritual to cleanse the inhabitants within.

As they passed another *noppan kissa*, Kurata looked in and made a derisive snorting sound. "That is a good place for a woman. Women are holes to be borrowed for producing children," he said, quoting the ancient Japanese proverb.

"*Hai.*" Sugawara felt dirty for not disagreeing.

Kurata nodded sagely. "But remember—" He stopped abruptly and turned to face his nephew.

Sugawara took half a step, stopped, and gave his uncle a bow. Front and back, the bodyguards stopped instantly in midstride.

"Remember," Kurata resumed in a conspiratorial tone, "that no matter how much pleasure they give you, never trust them; never trust a woman even though she has borne you seven sons," quoting another old Japanese saying.

"*Hai.*" Sugawara bowed deeply to keep Kurata from seeing the disgust on his face. He was thankful for the darkness.

They resumed their walk in silence, turned a corner into a narrow alley. It was darker than the main street, but a bright light shone halfway down, illuminating the *kanji* characters that identified the restaurant to which Kurata was leading them, keeping his commitments even if it took until two in the morning.

When Sugawara was sure his uncle had finished speaking for a moment, he said, "You asked me to follow the issue of the woman, Blackwood."

"*Hai,*" Kurata replied. "Now there's a woman who would have been better off putting her pussy to work and not her brain."

Sugawara felt his cheeks flush. He swallowed and remained silent until Kurata spoke again.

"Tell me."

"The monitors on her telephone indicate that her friend, Ismail Brahimi, is resourceful and has taken the samples from Tokyo to be analyzed at the Scripps Institute," Sugawara said.

Kurata frowned. "That's most unfortunate." They walked a dozen steps in silence. "Do we have assets at Scripps?"

"I am sorry, Kurata-*sama*, but we do not at this time."

Kurata raised an eyebrow and made a sucking sound with his lips. "Then we have few alternatives," he said finally. "You must direct Ms. Gaillard to deal immediately and conclusively with Blackwood, Brahimi, and his contact at Scripps. Both Blackwood and Brahimi have intellects that are bright and powerful, but they cannot continue to shine if she remains our enemy, *neh?*"

"As you wish," Sugawara said. He turned his face away to keep Kurata from seeing the expression of anger and disgust on his face that would not hide behind any attempts at disguise. It was an unspeakable loss to humankind to murder a brilliant Nobel Prize winner and a woman on track to win one herself. Sugawara took a silent deep breath and held it a moment to calm himself.

"Excellent," Kurata said, leaving the end of the word hanging in a manner that let Sugawara know the man was not finished, only thinking. "Make a note."

Sugawara nodded.

"As you and I have discussed previously, accidents attract less attention to us than something that appears to be a crime. There are many people who can kill. That actually takes very little talent. But Ms. Gaillard has served me for so very long because her genius lies in the arranging of accidents that are invariably fatal. Tell her to make sure this is no exception."

"*Hai*, Kurata-*sama*," Akira acknowledged as he swallowed against the bitterness that rose in his throat.

As they drew nearer to the restaurant, singing could be heard from within, songs with a martial cadence belted out by men whose fervor for the lyrics far exceeded their talent for melody. It was a military song bar, where Japanese businessmen dressed in old military uniforms strapped swords to their belts and posed for photographs in front of painted World War II scenes. These were bedrock supporters of Kurata's plans for *hakko ichiu*. The phrase had defined Japan's goal in its aggression in WWII and, now, its predatory designs using money and trade as weapons.

Snatches of the words echoed in the alleyway.

"*Sonno*"—literally, "revere the emperor"—"*joi*"—"expel the foreigners." Sugawara remembered the words to the song, words his father and uncle had taught him. He listened to the snippets of sound and filled in the missing words; he knew the part about *junshi*—the samurai's honor of following his lord unto death, and the glory of *junshi* in service of *Sanshu no shinki*—the mirror, sword, and jewel of the imperial insignia.

Sugawara had been in hundreds of these bars from Kyushu to Hokkaido, always with Kurata, always standing aside as the audiences lionized the "defender of Yamato" as a contemporary messiah. He was always amazed at how young most of the participants were; most, like Sugawara, were too young to have played any role in the Pacific War, many had not even been born then.

Every so often, Sugawara would even recognize an officer or enlisted man he had served with in the Self-Defense Forces and occasionally a professor from his days at the National Defense Academy. He was perplexed at how these younger men sang the loudest as the words scrolled across the television monitors and cheered the hardest when the old newsreels played scenes of Japanese victory.

"In sacrifice is our joy," came words from the song bar, "there is no reward better than glorious death."

These, Sugawara thought, were the Japanese equivalent of the young German neo-Nazi skinheads, but instead of suppressing the movement, the Japanese government encouraged the song bars, promoted memberships as ways for young businessmen and bureaucrats to make alliances that would advance their careers. Their uniform was not the skin head but the business suit, their weapons not clubs and firebrands but the yen, the *zaibatsu*, the bureaucracy. They did share, however, the same enemies: Jews, foreigners, and any others who did not act, look, and think just like they did.

For these *sarariman* samurais, the war was not only not over, but it was being won this time.

"All glory to *Yamato zoku*"—the Japanese race. Words spilled into the alley and filled it with an increasingly emotional volume. "All strength to *Yamato damashii*"—the Japanese soul. "One hundred million hearts beating as one." Sugawara cringed, tried not to listen to the final lines that had already played in his head. "For we are destiny, the unique, the *shido minzoku*"—the leading race.

As hard as Sugawara found it to understand, the *Jiminto*—Japan's ruling Liberal Democratic Party—had been successful in its attempts so far to resurrect the cult of the emperor's divinity.

While the American occupiers and the Constitution they had written for Japan forbade the worship of the emperor, they did not take action once the Imperial Institute revived, nor had they protested when, in 1960, Prime Minister Hayato Ikeda and his cabinet confirmed the divinity of the emperor and the role that the sacred mirror—the *yata*—played in the Japanese identity.

As Sugawara walked toward the restaurant, he heard the lyrics more clearly now, but more importantly, heard the unquestioning faith behind the words. How could so many people believe so literally in the divine nature of a man, just a man?

By 1973 the nation was celebrating another ritual banned by the Americans, the *kenjinogodoza*—the worship of the other two imperial insignia, the sword and jewels. Four years later Emperor Hirohito recanted the words he had spoken in 1946, words demanded by the American victors, renouncing any claim to divinity.

Then there was the Yasukuni shrine, where all of Japan's war dead—including war criminals surely as evil as the worst of Nazi Germany—were worshiped as gods. The shrine was legitimized by the visits of every prime minister, cabinet minister, and eight million people every year.

It infuriated Sugawara. Why were the Japanese people so willing to be led by liars and frauds?

Kurata stopped suddenly and put his hand on Sugawara's shoulder.

"*Hai?* Kurata-*sama*." Sugawara stopped.

"I have been thinking, just now. It seems as if we are in the process of eradicating many of the thorns that have pricked us over the past weeks and months." Kurata paused and looked thoughtfully at his nephew. Sugawara knew from experience to be silent and patient. His uncle nodded slightly to himself and continued. "We—by this I mean patriotic Japanese and not just Daiwa Ichiban—for years we have been plagued by the efforts of an organization known as *Shinrai* which has sought to embarrass us for our heroism in the Great Patriotic War."

"*Shinrai*, the truth?"

"Yes. They are a loose gang of malcontents and emotionally disturbed people, fanatics really, who have supported lawsuits against the great companies that made our war effort possible. They have stirred up emotions and even prompted the Chinese to take certain actions regarding us and our great country."

He paused again and cocked his head toward the singing from just inside the door. The wind rifled at their coats like a pickpocket.

"I believe now is the time for us to begin eliminating these worthless pigs," he said. "To stop their lies and to block their efforts. A file exists in my desk which I wish for you to read, and to discuss with Ms. Gaillard a program for their neutralization."

"*Hai*, Kurata-*sama*."

Kurata nodded, then walked briskly through the open door into the restaurant. Sugawara followed him. The bodyguards followed Sugawara. They stood at the entrance, in a small dimly lit reception area illuminated mainly from the bright light spilling in through the open door to the main bar where a song was ripping toward its final notes. Two men stood next to each other, looking into the main room.

"I tell you, something must be done," said a very slight, short man holding a clutch of printed menus in his hand. "They will take over unless some new divine wind comes to sweep them away."

Sugawara looked at his uncle and made a hand gesture that asked if Kurata wanted him to interrupt the men, to announce their presence. Kurata shook his head, wagged his index finger.

"That communist bastard should be killed! Imagine the prime minister apologizing for the Great Patriotic War," said the second man, a large round man Sugawara recognized from the newspaper photos as the owner of a sumo stable and a member of the Diet from Kurata's ultra-patriotic party. "At least we held firm in the Diet."

The thin man snorted. "What are you going to do about the lawsuits? The Koreans, the Americans, Dutch—all the stinking *gaijin* are filing reparations suits."

"We will change any laws that would give them grounds," the fat man said. "Besides, no Japanese judge will find in favor of these lice. And those that do?" He drew a finger across his throat.

"That's all very well," the thin man persisted. "But I hear they're also filing suits against companies, corporations. They think the *zaibatsu* may pay them off as a public relations gesture, something to keep from tarnishing their reputations and sales, especially in Korea and China."

The fat man shrugged. "They must do what they must do. We can only ease the path they choose."

The thin man glanced behind him, saw Kurata standing there.

"Kurata-*sama*!" the thin man said and dropped the menus on the floor. He bowed deeply. The fat man followed suit; Kurata, Sugawara, and the bodyguards returned the bows, each with the degree merited by their relative status. "We are honored; your followers are anxious to see you."

A murmur of conversation had broken out in the main room after the conclusion of the last song. The thin man kicked the spilled menus out of the way and conducted Kurata into the room where more than two hundred men sat, drank, smoked.

The owner did not have to say a word; the people nearest the door recognized Kurata and immediately grew silent as they bowed deeply. Within seconds, the entire room filled with a shrinelike silence. Kurata bowed; Sugawara and the bodyguards bowed as well.

Sugawara looked around the room and, again, was struck by how young the audience seemed. New progeny bred on an ideology of the past, giving birth to what had been aborted before the previous generation could succeed. Here and there, Sugawara spotted dashes of familiar color: the gray-blue of the Ground Self-Defense Forces, khaki work uniforms of the Marine SDF, and the light blue of the Air SDF. Among the Ground SDF, he spotted a rainbow of uniform pipings identifying the men as infantry (red piping), armor (yellow), ordnance (light green), and airborne (white). He said a quiet prayer of thanks that he recognized none of the faces. As Akira scanned the tables, his eye fell on the remains of the previous generation; a table of six grizzled and shrunken old men sitting at the head of the room in their place of honor—the remains of the *Seikonkai*—the Refined Spirit Association. They were the most active of the veterans' groups from the 1960s, when all American oversight vanished, up through the 1980s, when death came more and more frequently.

The *Seikonkai* were honored by the Tokyo government, awarded the highest honors, and afforded the highest respect by civic organizations. The *Seikonkai* was founded by Dr. Shiro Ishii and was composed exclusively of veterans of the infamous Unit 731. It was, Sugawara thought, as if Josef Mengele and his subordinates had been recognized as heroes by modern Germans, honored with declarations from Bonn, Berlin, and every other municipality.

"...to be here tonight," Kurata had begun speaking. Sugawara focused on his uncle's words, even though he had heard them a thousand times.

"You are the cutting surface of Yamato's sword," Kurata was saying, "the first and most valuable line of defense against the *gaijin* and those of our own people who would pander to the *gaijin* and destroy our unique culture. For we are not just a nation but a single tribe united by our common ancestor, the great Jimmu. We are the purest race on the earth, the purest the world has ever known—or ever will know— because the other races have polluted their bloodlines with inferior genes. We are strong because we are pure; just as a laser cuts because its light is all pure, we are strong and will prevail because of the purity of our blood. We feel as one, believe as one, act as one." His voice rose. "We *are* one! We are Yamato!"

The audience roared.

Kurata stood there, a grim satisfied smile on his face. He nodded as the assembly applauded.

"We must remember we are at war with the world that would stain our hands and blood," Kurata resumed as the room grew silent again. "We are divine people; why else would the kamikaze"—the divine wind—"have saved us so many times, have kept the filth from our shores? We are blessed! I *believe* the kamikaze will come again to sweep us clean of filth and banish our enemies."

Again he paused to let the audience cheer.

"We must all do our parts to earn the divine intervention. We must fight; we must not relent; we must not compromise. We should all remember the words our beloved *Showa Tenno*"—Emperor Hirohito—"delivered on the occasion of his eighty-fifth birthday. On that day, after communing with the spirits at the Yasukuni shrine, he told the nation that when the day came for Japan to rise again in war against the evil arrayed against us, the spirits of Yasukuni would rise with his divine army."

A sepulchral silence filled the hall as Kurata lowered his voice. "You are the emperor's army. *Banzai!*"—ten thousand years.

"*Banzai!*" echoed the crowd, again and again like mortar rounds exploding.

Akira Sugawara was astounded that simple sounds could be so painful.

14

Late morning traffic made its way easily along Pennsylvania Avenue and through the intersection with Sixteenth Street just west of the White House. Five stories above the intersection, Lara Blackwood stood by the windows of her corner office in the New Executive Office Building and watched the tops of cars and taxis and buses moving to the silent metronome of the traffic light. Like a nervous tic, her right wrist seemed to rise and turn of its own accord, bringing her watch up to eye level.

"Damn," she muttered again. Time was moving like drifting continents; the forever night had turned into the forever morning. She yawned, covered her mouth, squeezed her eyes shut for a moment, then opened them, half hoping she'd wake up from a very bad dream.

Right before dawn, she had fallen into a troubled sleep after completing an outline of her alternatives that charted the resources she could use against Kurata, listed the people and agencies not controlled by Kurata or the White House, and singled out those on whom she could rely for protection. It was a depressingly short list.

Turning now from the window overlooking Pennsylvania Avenue, Lara walked to her desk and took another sip of coffee. It was cold; she grimaced and drained the cup, hoping the caffeine would help her shake the persistent sense of surreality that had descended on her from the moment Kurata had walked out of the Blue Room. She felt detached, as if she were floating in some preternaturally bright spot, outside herself, watching herself, observer and observed.

She didn't know what to do, how to feel. Her father had been an enormously intelligent man, physically imposing and emotionally self-contained. He was a solitary man with few buddies and the conviction that he was better off relying on himself. He had brought up his only child in the same mold.

She realized that she had no close friends to run to other than Ismail. As she sat down now at her desk across the street from the White House, she wished desperately there was someone on whom she could call for help, to protect her. She had never picked a fight with the White House before, nor with a *zaibatsu*. A mammoth global conglomerate like Daiwa Ichiban had almost unimaginable resources and was unconstrained by either laws or ethics.

A knock at her door startled her.

"Yes?" Lara answered. "Come in," she said, turning the legal pad to a blank page. The door opened.

"This just arrived." Lara's secretary, Sandra Robinson, held up a plain manila envelope as she walked over to Lara's desk. She was a neat, plain woman who could be thirty-five or fifty-five and wore a sweater, blouse, and skirt, regardless of the temperature. Sandra Robinson had efficiently served a steady stream of White House appointees and thought her lack of political opinions her greatest virtue.

"By courier," she said as she laid it on Lara's desk. "It's been x-rayed; it's okay."

"Thank you," Lara said as she picked up the envelope.

Sandra looked at Lara's coffee cup. "I've got a fresh pot brewing; want more?"

Lara shook her head. "No, thanks."

The secretary closed the door behind her.

Lara looked at the envelope with her name and office address typed neatly on a plain white label with no return address. She slid her index finger under the flap and tore it open.

The envelope contained the front page neatly torn from a Japanese tabloid newspaper and a single sheet of plain bond paper with no letterhead or other distinguishing marks. With growing anxiety, Lara unfolded the newspaper. It took her a moment to recognize that the large photo on the cover was that of a large rat, feasting on a decapitated head.

"Dear God!" She pushed away from the desk and stood up, backing away from the grotesque image. Nausea squirmed in her belly, only to be replaced by cold knots of fear as she slowly deciphered the Kanji characters in the blazing headline: "American Army Doctors Killed; Police Blame Gambling Debts To Yakuza."

She forced her eyes from the headline back to the photo and to the photo caption. "The severed head of U.S. Army medical doctor Jim Condon was discovered by trash collectors in an alley running through the notorious water trade sector. His body was discovered nearby, alongside the horribly mutilated body of another American medical doctor, Denis Yaro."

Lara snatched the newspaper and turned it over.

"Oh, God." Her lips moved silently. "Dear God." Lara felt like a truck had hit her; she sat down jerkily, gripping the armrests of her chair, fighting the nausea that rose in her throat.

Frantically, she looked through the envelope and quickly examined the papers again to see if there was any indication of who had sent it.

After several long moments, she noticed that the bond paper that had come in the envelope contained an English translation of the article, thoughtfully enclosed so she wouldn't miss translating even one word. She willed her hands not to shake, urged her heart out of her throat and back into her chest as she pulled out her cell phone and dialed Ismail Brahimi's cell. It rang four times, then rolled to voice mail.

"Ismail, be careful. Be very, very careful. Jim Condon and Denis Yaro are dead. A Japanese newspaper said they were killed over gambling debts, but I don't believe it."

Lara sat very still and closed her eyes, concentrating on her breathing and damping the electricity that crackled all over every square inch of skin on her body. In moments, each breath came to her deep and regular; her heartbeat and her thoughts followed suit and she felt the deep, centered calm that sustained her when storms and heavy winds hammered her on deck. Someone was trying to scare her. Who? She just knew it had to be Kurata. And if he couldn't scare her, would he go further? Had he been responsible for Jim's and Denis's deaths? Would he come after her? What did the president have to do with this? Had he simply lent the White House to Kurata for the man's own secret purposes like he had to so many wealthy campaign contributors or was the Oval Office in the loop?

The questions fed on each other in a tangled snakepit of doubt and uncertainty.

Lara reached for her phone and punched in Peter Durant's direct number. His voice mail answered.

"Damn!"

She dialed his cell and got the same result.

"Peter, this is Lara. Call me as soon as possible. It is an emergency."

For a long moment, she considered taking the tunnel under Pennsylvania Avenue to the White House and tracking him down. The conversation with Kurata came back to her and she thought better of it.

Flipping the legal pad to its last page, Lara looked at her action plan. She had to cash in some GenIntron stock and add it to the rainy-day cache onboard. Then she needed to buy fresh ammunition. That much was clear. She had cruised extensively in the Caribbean and Indonesia where piracy was too common and thus carried a solid selection of firepower that she routinely fired at a range across the Potomac in Arlington.

But no matter how good the firearm, old ammunition could go south, cause a jam in automatics or simply not fire. Of course, she'd have to go to Virginia to obtain the ammunition since all of the guns she had locked up securely on her boat were illegal in the District. Despite well-meaning gun control laws, criminals obtained the weapons they wanted while honest citizens went naked and unprotected.

15

LARA STEERED HER SUBURBAN OUT OF THE NEW EXECUTIVE OFFICE BUILDING'S UNDERGROUND LOT. Dodging a homeless man with three overflowing shopping carts tied together like a train, she edged the big armored vehicle into a lurching stream of reluctant traffic and headed for Arlington via the Memorial Bridge. Deftly navigating the confusing maze of blocked and one-way streets that had been closed or redirected to prevent terrorist attacks on the White House she dodged a battered white cab that ran a stoplight at G Street and avoided a skateboarder who barreled across the street without looking.

"Darwin welcomes you with open arms, you brainless twit," she muttered as she watched the skateboarder in his knit cap and baggy clothes careening the wrong way down a one-way cross street.

As she drove on, Lara's mind continued to race, asking more questions without answers. More and more, however, her thoughts began to settle into chaotic orbits around a deeply disturbing thought: her life's work, the ideas and processes she had created to save lives, had been turned into a deadly weapon.

Guilt sat heavy and dark in her heart as she wondered how long it would be before the black market arms trade would include vials of gene bombs along with Stinger missiles, AK-47s, and napalm pods. There was no doubt that once gene bombs were perfected and tested effective, they'd be sold on the open market.

The emptiness within her grew colder, hollower as she realized that if used discreetly, gene bombs would allow an aggressor to wage war without the victims being aware that they had been attacked—until it was too late, if ever. In an era when new, emerging diseases like Ebola fever, or the "flesh-eating" staph bacteria, made for big headlines, a major gene bomb attack could stealthily annihilate whole populations overnight without an attacker showing his hand.

Lara shivered for a moment. Dear God! How could it come to this? Thinking back on it now, each of the steps—the founding of GenIntron, the choice of research, the financial dance with First Merc that had led to the financial crisis that had led to the sale to Daiwa Ichiban Corporation—that once seemed so innocent and logical to her now resonated with sinister vibrations. She had felt those vibrations, chosen to ignore them, actually had no choice if her company was to survive.

She finally reached Constitution Avenue and lifted her blinker handle to turn right when her cell phone rang.

Hoping against hope it was Ismail, her hopes soared as she snatched the phone from her purse and pressed the talk button.

"Lara?" It was Peter Durant's voice, filled with concern. Her heart fell.

"I need to see you, Peter. I need to talk with you." She filled him in on the deaths of the two army doctors.

"I don't know," Durant said doubtfully. "It seems like you're getting upset over something that sounds like an accident."

"Then why would someone send me the clips and try to scare me?"

Static filled his thoughtful pause. "Did you report it to security?"

The Secret Service and Executive Protection Service guarded the White House and its office buildings.

"No." Lara replied.

"Why?"

She hesitated. "Because . . . because I'm not sure who to trust."

"Surely you can't be thinking the president has anything to do with this?"

"I don't know what to think," Lara replied, then described her meeting with Kurata at the White House.

"I don't know," Durant replied. "I just think you're taking all this too far, reading things into this that aren't warranted."

"That's because you *choose* not to see it, Peter," she said angrily as the light changed and she made her turn. "You're just like every fucking body in this stinking town who has this moral tunnel vision that conveniently blocks out whatever isn't tied to their own selfish goals!"

The State Department buildings loomed on her right as Lara pulled into the left-hand turn lane that would take her around the north side of the Lincoln Memorial. Again, she wondered where the giants and heroes had gone.

"That's a cheap shot, Lara." Durant was angry.

"Will, don't you see that Daiwa Ichiban bought GenIntron so they could get the last vital pieces they needed to perfect a gene-targeted weapon? This is what that so-called Korean Leprosy is all about."

"Geez, Lara, I think your imagination is running away from you. I can't see how you can justify the wild conclusion you've just leaped to."

"Look, let's talk."

"Things are awfully tight today," he said reluctantly. "The president—"

"Fuck the president!" she snapped. "This is important, Peter."

"Oooh-kay." He hesitated. "I'll meet you in my office at nine tomorrow morning."

"Can't we meet outside the White House."

"Lara, my office at nine tomorrow," Durant said sternly, then hung up.

"Asshole." Lara steered her Suburban right onto the Memorial Bridge. When she was finally heading south along the parkway toward the Pentagon she tried Ismail's cell phone again.

"I think we should have some results this afternoon for sure," said Craig Bartlett as he skillfully drove his battered Volvo skillfully through the narrow, winding two-lane shortcut that twisted through the hills between LaJolla and Rancho Bernardo just north of San Diego. He was a senior researcher in molecular genetics at the Scripps Institute. Ismail Brahimi sat in the passenger seat next to him when his cell phone began to ring.

"Hello?" he said. "Hello?" The earpiece crackled with static. He shook his head and pressed the end button.

"Not much signal here in the hills," said Bartlett.

Brahimi nodded. "Thanks for the hospitality. I could have stayed in a hotel."

"You know I couldn't let that happen."

"Thanks," Brahimi said with a cheerfulness he did not feel. Something was hideously wrong in the samples from Tokyo.

Bartlett squinted into the dazzling sun as he turned the wheel right, left, right again, steering the Volvo through the narrow asphalt road's tight blind turns.

Behind him, a man with a hard hat and dressed in Cal Trans orange work clothes made his way out of the sagebrush and dry chaparral and placed a line of orange cones across the road. After making his way back into the brush, he keyed his walkie-talkie and said one word.

"Now."

The road grew narrower, even more torturous, as the Volvo neared the summit of the hills that separated the coast from the inland area. He downshifted for the hairpin curve he knew would take them over the crest.

"Holy Jesus! What is that?" Bartlett yelled as they rounded the hairpin turn. Brahimi looked up just in time to see a jackknifed propane tanker truck dead ahead, its long bomblike trailer completely blocking the road. His mind filled with television news images of propane tankers burning, pillars of fire that soared into the sky.

Bartlett stood on the brake, felt the tires break loose and start to skid. The propane tank raced ever closer. Eyes wide with fear, he steered into the turn; the Volvo slid toward the tank sideways now, slowing almost imperceptibly. For an instant it felt as if the car was going to roll, then it regained its equilibrium.

An eternity later, amid the sulfurous stench of skidding rubber and the screams of tortured tires, the car came to a rest just feet from the disabled tanker.

"Fucking hell," Bartlett said as he leaned his head against the steering wheel and took a deep swallow. After a long moment, he sat up, took a deep breath, and loosed a long shuddering sigh. Beside him, Brahimi fought to control the shaking in his hands as he looked at the truck.

"What in the world is this?" Brahimi said as he opened his door. Then he spotted the driver lying facedown in the road. "Look!" He pointed to the driver. Both men hurried out of the Volvo, and made their way toward the truck. Both men tried 911 on their cell phones. But there was no signal.

Movement on the hill above caught Brahimi's eye. He stopped and looked up at the top of the hill above the road. When he did, he saw a lone figure, a tall, lean person, legs spread, silhouetted against the bright sun. The person stood too far away to tell whether it was a man or woman, or to make out the small metal box held in one hand, or to see an index finger as it pressed the small red button on the box's front panel.

16

"UNBELIEVABLE. Unfuckingreal," Lara Blackwood muttered as she leaned over a growing pile of paper spewing from a small HP LaserJet in the dining saloon. Next to the printer, the hard drive indicator light on her laptop blinked continuously. It would take hours before the printer would catch up with all the data she had downloaded from the Internet, some of it free and easily available, some that came from proprietary databases at exorbitant costs.

Lara grabbed another stack of paper from the printer and yawned as she looked at the top sheet. It could take days to read it all, but read it all she would. Somewhere in the torrent of information, she believed, was the information on Kurata that would help her understand how he was involved with the Korean Leprosy and why. More important, perhaps there would be just the right bit of data that would tell her what she might do.

She read through pages that contained the second or third variant of Kurata's biography. They had all seemed the same, yet Lara tried again and again, hoping that one of the accounts or perhaps the newspaper articles might contain that unique piece of information she was looking for. She scanned the pages quickly, skipping over the now-familiar story: Kurata, Kyoto native, heroic youngster, son of an old samurai family, trained and ready for suicide torpedo missions against the American fleet, brought into the family's herbal medicine business, which he quickly built into an international business acquired in 1955 by the Daiwa Ichiban Corporation, a small, new company with great aspirations.

Over the next twenty years, Kurata rocketed up the corporate ladder as he built Daiwa Ichiban into a *zaibatsu* with international interests and ownership in banks, steel, electronics, shipping, pharmaceuticals, chemicals, heavy manufacturing, shipbuilding, and automobiles.

Along the way, he grew into an icon of the neonationalist movement. The old mythologies of Japanese racial superiority, emperor worship, the divine origins of the Japanese people, and the notions that a Caucasian world had unfairly ganged up on Japan accreted about him one layer at a time until he had become the black pearl of Japan.

In 1976 Kurata threw his considerable influence and Daiwa Ichiban's inestimable wealth into the battle to sanitize the nation's textbooks and cast a good light on the Japanese role in World War II. Thanks to his efforts and the concurrence of the national government, Japanese schoolchildren learned that the war had been caused by Caucasian aggressors. Japanese invasions of its neighbors were "advances" and the subjugation of slave laborers was "mobilization of labor."

By 1977 the Japanese Education Ministry's new history guidelines for the basic history of Japan had reduced World War II to six pages out of several hundred. Most of those six pages were occupied by photos of the atomic bombing of Hiroshima, tallies of Japanese war dead, photos of the fire-bombing of Tokyo, and other "Caucasian atrocities."

The next year Kurata led the charge to rehabilitate Tojo and thirteen other convicted Japanese war criminals and successfully had them enshrined as deities in the Yasukuni shrine. Every prime minister since that time, except for Morihiro Hosokawa, has visited Yasukuni to pray to Tojo and the other war dead.

Lara shook her head slowly as she got up and took her empty coffee cup into the galley for a refill. She took a sip, then returned to the damning evidence spewing from her printer.

It was Kurata, the pages told her, who had led the outrage against Prime Minister Hosokawa back in the late 1990s when he suggested that Japan owed the world an apology for its aggression in the Pacific. Kurata made sure that Hosokawa's political career died a quick death.

One member of the Diet who had agreed with Kurata's viewpoint was Shintaro Ishihara, who said that Hosokawa deserved death for his suggestions an apology was needed. Ishihara, who coauthored a neonationalist, racist, Caucasian-bashing book with Sony Corporation Chairman Akio Morita called *The Japan That Can Say No*, became a rabid apologist for the right wing, implying among other things that the Japanese invasion of its neighbors had actually been good for them.

"The Asian countries that are booming economically—South Korea, Taiwan, Singapore etc.—were all controlled by Japan at one time before or during World War II. Thanks to intensive effort, including Japan's contribution, the countries are making rapid and social economic progress. You cannot say that about any place where Caucasians were preeminent."

"Oh, man," Lara mumbled as she took another sip of the coffee. "Tojo redux."

The database slipped into the full text of articles from various newspaper and magazine articles. One indicated that Kurata had personally funded a steady succession of fanatics, including the one who shot and wounded Hitoshi Motoshima, the mayor of Nagasaki, after Motoshima's suggestion Emperor Hirohito bore responsibility for war crimes.

No definite link was ever proven, but article after article implied that Kurata's hand, his charisma, and his money had guided and sustained Japan's militarist movement back to its pre-World War II attitudes. Further, the articles implied, the Japanese people—conditioned to conforming to social norms that demanded that "the nail that sticks up *must* be hammered down"—seemed happy to go along with its leadership.

Analysis articles from the database concluded that Japan's economic difficulties of the mid-1990s and again in the first years of the new century had fueled support for the right wing, which blamed the problems on Caucasian-inspired conspiracies and on the country's small, but visible communities of Indians, Koreans, Bangladeshis, Filipinos, and other inferior races.

Reading the last page in the stack she had picked up in the printer, Lara sighed. Why didn't she know this before? The articles on the database were all individually available, but no one had ever pulled them all together before. Were editors afraid to offend? Had the purchase of media companies by Sony and other Japanese corporations chilled the discussions? The thought made her shiver. She put her coffee cup down and took another pile of paper from the printer.

Now, as Lara read the most recent hard copy, the deep empty blackness that boiled in her heart turned tight, twisted, and cold. The database search for Kurata and Daiwa Ichiban had churned out information on secret Japanese medical experimentation units, which had performed horrific medical experimentation on hapless Chinese civilians in Manchuria and on captured Allied prisoners of war. There was a Unit 731 and a doctor named Shiro Ishii; the name seemed vaguely familiar to Lara. She grabbed a pen and marked the name. The text indicated that Ishii was a "Japanese Mengele" who, among many other atrocities, had frozen thousands of innocent people to death in order to study frostbite and hypothermia. Occupation authorities had not prosecuted him for his war crimes because the American army considered him a genius in bacteriological warfare. Instead of punishment, they rewarded him and hundreds of his colleagues with immunity and comfortable government-subsidized lives in exchange for their cooperation in the development of weapons to fight world communism.

The historical text described multiple "experimentation" centers in Manchuria, in China, in the Philippines, in Indonesia, and in Japan itself. Nausea and loathing filled her as she read the details of the torture, perversion, and crimes against nature that had been officially sanctioned by the Japanese government, with the knowledge of Emperor Hirohito himself.

The text veered suddenly away from medical atrocities to the Japanese government's official policy of rape as an instrument of war. "I witnessed the rape of a Chinese woman by seventeen Japanese soldiers in rapid succession," testified a young professor at the University of Nanking, his words captured in a National Archives database containing documents of the Tokyo War Crimes Trials. "I do not care to repeat the occasional cases of sadistic and abnormal behavior in connection with the rapes, but on the grounds of the university alone, a little girl of nine and a grandmother seventy-six years old were raped." Trial witnesses estimated that within six weeks of the Japanese occupation of Nanking, twenty thousand women were raped. Many of them were also mutilated and murdered.

"Young girls and women between thirteen and forty were rounded up and gang-raped," Hsu Chuan-ying, a sixty-two-year-old official of the Chinese Ministry of Railways, told the War Crimes Trial. "I visited one home where three of the women had been raped, including two girls. One girl was raped on a table, and while I was there blood spilled on the table was not all dry yet."

"Fucking monsters!" Lara slammed the papers on the table and stood up so abruptly the chair tumbled over backward and thudded dully into a half-full shipping box. "You fucking animals make the Serbs and the Taliban look like Mother fucking Teresa."

Breathing quickly against the bands of anger that strapped her chest, Lara set down her coffee cup and climbed up on deck for some fresh air. The midnight night wind was unsettled, the faint distant whispers of a hurricane making its erratic way offshore of the Carolinas. Lara reveled in the wind and turned to face it.

How is it that we haven't known these things about the Japanese? she wondered. We knew about the Nazis, but never knew the Japanese massacred more than six million innocent civilians—mostly "inferior" or "polluted" races like the Chinese and Koreans and Filipinos and Caucasians?

Up in the parking lot, beyond the chain-link fence, a shiny Beemer swam through the crime lights' sodium orange sea, cruising for a parking space. Beyond the ostentatious German sedan, a group of young teens in baggy pants huddled and talked on the sidewalk. She watched them for a moment. It was hard to tell whether they were just kids killing time, or a street gang who thought it was time to kill. The gangs frequently vandalized the marina buildings and occasionally broke in to burglarize boats. Funny, she thought, how the gun control laws never stopped them.

The Japanese had equaled or exceeded the atrocities for which the Nazis were known and had done so with a bloodlust that rivaled Idi Amin or Pol Pot. Yet, no one knew . . . or seemed to care.

Did the United States still feel the need to maintain their end of the Faustian bargain with Japan's Mengele now that communism had imploded? Were such immoral bargains inevitable? If we had to do evil in order to protect our ability to do good, then what did that say about the good we tried to do.

Lara's white-hot anger suddenly turned against her as she realized that by selling GenIntron, she had sold out her convictions just as surely as the government who protected the imperial monsters of Japan who had equaled the Nazis for sheer evil.

In the distance the teens drifted way. Lara went back below, carefully locking the hatch behind her. She walked carefully toward the bow, checking to make sure hatches were properly secured.

Lara returned to the dining saloon and the mounting printout. The computer search had turned up the proceedings of the 1989 Conference on the Meaning of the Holocaust for Bioethics at the University of Michigan. Shocked, Lara read the page and learned that Shiro Ishii, the Japanese Mengele, had been honored by the Japanese government in 1984, awarded the Outstanding Award for medical research for his work on "temperature regulation in humans." That work, she knew from her earlier reading, had been based on torturing innocent Chinese civilians and Allied POWs in vats of freezing water to see how long they stayed alive, and how hypothermia progressed to death. How could they? How could the modern-day government of what purported to be an enlightened nation give such honors to a hideous monster?

Then, as she read, it got worse. Not only had Ishii been honored, but those who had worked with him at Unit 731 had risen to positions of great power, influence, and prestige in Japan, including various heads of Japan's National Institutes of Health, its surgeon general, prominent faculty positions at the Universities of Tokyo, Kyoto, Osaka. Many were employed in responsible positions by such well-known companies as Takeda Pharmaceutical Company, the Hayakawa Medical Company, and—she caught her breath—the board of directors of the Daiwa Ichiban Corporation and its subsidiary, NorAm Pharmco.

"Oh, my God," Lara said faintly; the nightmare her life had become grew terrible in a way she could never have imagined. Her hands shook as she read the page over and over again, hoping perhaps the names would disappear. Tears came. Kurata had appointed two of Ishii's cohorts, Japanese war criminals in their own rights, to fill the slots on the GenIntron board vacated by her and Ismail Brahimi.

17

THE TWO-STORY, ECRU BRICK BUILDING OF LABORATORY 73 STOOD AWAY FROM THE REST OF THE FACELESS, NONDESCRIPT BUILDINGS IN THE VAST TACHI-KAWA COMPLEX AT THE WESTERN FRINGES OF TOKYO WHERE THE PACKED URBAN JUNGLE GAVE OVER TO RICE PADDIES AND GROVES OF BAMBOO.

Tachikawa was an ancient city in the plains just east of the Chichibu Mountains, visible only on those infrequent days when the Tokyo smog relented. Despite its ancient roots, Tachikawa was a gritty suburb for those who worked in the vast factories of the modern *zaibatsu*: Honda, Mitsubishi, Toshiba, and a thousand more.

In more recent history, Tachikawa had served as the Japanese war machine's center for research and development. The research facilities were among the first occupied by Allied troops after Japan's surrender. Because of the long delay between the surrender and actual occupation by U.S. troops, most of the very sensitive materials from the research and development center had been parceled out among the scientists and researchers who hid the materials as bargaining chips against prison or execution.

By 1977 when the U.S. turned the base back over to the Japanese Self-Defense Forces, caches of documents, papers, lab books, and even prototypes were still being unearthed in personal gardens and the ancestral village homes of those related to the workers. None of the scientists who worked at Tachikawa had been prosecuted by the Tokyo War Crimes Court.

Most of the buildings had returned to housing Japan's most sensitive defense-related research and development, including that of the FSX fighter aircraft, with which Japan intended to leapfrog U.S. dominance just as it had done with semiconductors, televisions, autos.

From the top windows of the three-story, brick building that housed Laboratory Three, the designers of the FSX could just barely make out Laboratory 73, hidden behind bamboo thickets and secured—even from the rest of this high-security compound—by two electrified, twenty-foot fences topped by concertina wire. Dogs and armed men patrolled the no-man's-land between the wires. Laboratory 73 even had its own separate entrance so its workers did not have to mingle with those from other labs. While only an elite few Japanese and Americans knew of Laboratory Three and its work on the FSX, none of the workers at Laboratory Three had even the slightest notion about what might be happening behind the walls of Laboratory 73.

Laboratory 73 was conducting precisely the same kinds of research and development it had before and during World War II under the command of Army Lieutenant General Shiro Ishii. It had then been known as Unit 731.

Laboratory 73's roof bristled with satellite dishes that connected its supercomputers via fiber-optic-quality links and secure encrypted communications to other supercomputers located around the world and operated by its research partners. Laboratory 73 was the central ganglion in a global web that encompassed the many labs of the Daiwa Ichiban Corporation and its subsidiaries, including NorAm Pharmco and now GenIntron.

To maintain strict security and to prevent the people actually doing the research from knowing what the overall picture looked like, pieces of the research were carefully parceled out among peripheral labs and brought together in only one place: Tachikawa. Even at Tachikawa, only a handful at the very top had the complete picture. One of those was Kenji Yamamoto.

A scientist by training, Yamamoto's job was no longer research. After thirty-five years as a Lab 73 scientist, he served as the manager of Laboratory 73's mass production facility, which was charged with manufacturing large quantities of the substances developed at the center.

He stood at the window that looked out toward the mountains and struggled to control the anger that seethed within him. He took a deep breath, then turned to face his tormentor again.

"I cannot stress any more strongly than I have how dangerous is your demand the production be increased so quickly," Yamamoto said. He pulled at a cigarette and exhaled, adding to the smoke that already hung like geological sediments in neat horizontal layers.

"Bloody hell, Kenji!" The sheer tidal wave of anger nearly overwhelmed the usually precise BBC English. "All you've fucking done for the last frigging three months is tell me what you *can't* do. I'm telling you now what you *must* do. Kurata's set the date, and unless you're bloody well ready to fall on your sword, I suggest you get your lazy arse in motion."

"Rycroft-*san*, please to listen to prudence," Yamamoto pleaded.

Edward Rycroft clenched and unclenched his fists as he glared at his production manager.

"Kurata doesn't want prudence," Rycroft snapped. "He wants results—and a lot of dead Koreans."

"But your newest production method is unproven," Yamamoto persisted. "It is fast, but it needs to be better tested."

"Look, Kenji. Who designed the production method for the test in Tokyo?"

"You did, Rycroft-*san*."

"Did that work *just* like I said it would?"

"Of course, Rycroft-*san*, but—"

"Did the earlier test in Korea work just like I said it would?"

"Yes, but—"

"Do not fucking interrupt me one more time, do you hear me?"

"*Hai.*" Yamamoto bowed.

"That's more like it." Rycroft lowered his voice. "Now listen to me, Kenji, and listen good, because I will sack your arse if I have to say this again. *I* created the processes, and they worked *precisely* as I predicted every time. *I* created this new process, and *it* will work as precisely as the others because *I* say it will. Don't forget you're dealing with a scientist who is half a step away from the Nobel Prize. How *dare* you question my judgment?"

Yamamoto swallowed hard against the humiliation and bowed deeply. "*Hai,* Rycroft-*san*."

"Then get to it." Rycroft marched to the door and opened it. "Kenji, if the materials are not ready when needed, your family will regret your failure for generations."

Rycroft stepped into the hallway. When he slammed the door, it sounded like a grenade exploding.

18

RAIN PEPPERED THE WINDSHIELD OF THE PRESIDENT'S LIMOUSINE AS IT MADE ITS WAY UP CONNECTICUT AVENUE TOWARD CHEVY CHASE.

"They say it's barely hurricane strength but nothing to be trifled with. Somewhere over North Carolina, I believe. Spawned some tornadoes behind it and wiped out a whole county full of trailer parks," the president said to Lara. He sat next to Peter Durant on the plush seat facing forward. Lara sat alone across from them.

He shook his head. His voice was graver when he said, "This surely won't help the turnout today." The president wore golf shoes and a floral Hawaiian shirt. He shook his head. "Won't help it at all." He paused as he fidget-fondled a gold-headed putter presented to him by the sultan of Brunei.

"I cannot possibly believe that you could say that at a time like this!" Lara Blackwood waved a copy of the morning's *Washington Post* at him. It was folded back to the article on the fiery deaths of Ismail Brahimi and Craig Bartlett. Her tears of earlier in the morning had crystallized into anger and resolve. "It is positively criminal for you to worry about the rain spoiling a political fund-raiser when talented people are dead and one of your loyal corporate contributors is about to loose a terrible contagion that is going to kill hundreds of thousands of Japanese Koreans."

The president looked at Peter Durant.

"I know how much this loss must have upset you," Durant began. "But this all seems like a remarkable string of coincidences." The president nodded. "The article quotes the California Highway Patrol as saying that this was clearly an accident."

The limo slowed as, ahead, the motorcycle outriders stopped cross traffic so the presidential motorcade could speed through the red light.

"And there was clear evidence in the personal effects of the two soldiers that they had failed to pay substantial gambling debts to organized crime."

The articulate lines she had rehearsed earlier deserted her now, smothered by her anger, disjointed by the surreality of the situation.

"You . . . you really don't get it, do you?" Lara asked rhetorically. "They want you to believe that it was an accident. What about the dead Koreans in Tokyo? How do you explain that away?"

Durant shook his head. "People thought the same thing when Ebola exploded on the scene. We're seeing all sorts of new diseases emerge, even in urban areas thanks to global air travel."

After a long moment of silence, the president spoke. "I think that the"—he searched for a word—"the *troubles* you have experienced recently at your former company have taken their toll and these latest unfortunate events have added to those in a way that has warped your judgment."

"Warped? *Me?*" Lara leaned toward the president. The world's most powerful man shrank away. "You'd rather play with your putter than look at the facts that we have murder and a medical disaster on our hands. Now *that's* warped, sir."

"Lara, please calm down." Durant leaned over and placed his hand on Lara's forearm. She jerked her arm away as from a fire.

"I think the stress has made you reach conclusions that are not warranted," Durant said. "Neither the president nor I wish to see you damage your reputation by appearing to be some sort of conspiracy freak like those people who live by themselves in the desert and see UFOs every night."

Lara leaned back in her seat and answered the question with an exasperated sigh. When she spoke it was quiet and more to herself than to her traveling companions. "I really do not believe you two." She shook her head slowly. "Don't you want to know?" She looked back and forth at the two men's faces.

The president shrugged his shoulders. "There are many things I don't *want* to know," he said. "The older I get, the more things there are that fit into that category."

The sounds of cheers came from outside as the limo slowed in preparation for running another red light. The president leaned forward, toward the untinted section of window, and waved to the crowd. The limo pulled forward. The president craned his head to watch his adoring public until they were out of sight. For just a moment, he admired his own reflection in the tinted glass.

Lara turned her head and looked out at a world darkened by more than glass and weather. Trees rushed by as the limo made a right turn onto Wisconsin Avenue.

"So do something," she said quietly as she turned back to face him.

"Don't you understand? There's nothing to be done," Durant said. "There's not even enough for us to put investigators on. What are we going to do? Send the FBI out to San Diego to nose around a traffic accident? Put the CIA to work looking into some unpaid gambling debts?" He shook his head.

"Then I'll resign," Lara said. "I'll go to the *Post*; blow the whistle. They like me."

The limo turned off Wisconsin Avenue onto an affluent street with manicured lawns.

"Don't kid yourself," the president retorted. "Sure, they'd love to quote you. They'd love to nail me again for something . . . anything. But when they start checking out your story, they'll find a CHP or a sheriff's deputy in Southern California that will swear there's no evidence of foul play. And what's their guy in Tokyo going to find? A closed police report, two more *gaijin* who found out that the *yakuza* don't kid around." He shook his head, then looked out the window. After several winding, tree-lined blocks, he pointed. "That's the house I want. After my second term's over."

Lara opened his mouth to speak, but the president waved his hand. His voice was soft when he finally said, "You truly don't understand. If Kurata was behind all this—please understand that I'm speaking hypothetically here—but if he were behind it, he has resources and influence that assure that his hand will never be seen, only felt. They can make sure that no matter how hard you try to prove this conspiracy, nobody will believe you. You don't have anything but a hunch. They have resources. They can ruin you without actually killing you."

"That may be so," Lara said, suddenly calm and resolute. "But morally, I have no other choice than to try and stop this."

"But, Lara!" Durant said. "Surely you—" The president waved him silent.

"I regret you have reached that conclusion," the president said, his voice now stiff with formality. "Thus I have, regretfully, accepted your resignation."

"But I'm not resigning!"

"You really don't understand, do you?" The president's voice was soft with amazement.

19

THE NOONDAY TOKYO SKY WAS BRIGHT AND FILLED WITH GIANT *KANJI* CHARACTERS.

"Glory to the emperor," the message said as stiff winds aloft began to warp the skywriting and waft the characters toward the city. Even as the first message began to smear across the sky, the flight of ten Australian-built Kingsford Smith KS-3 Cropmaster aircraft were already regrouping over Tokorozawa for another pass, another message.

On the ground, large lunchtime crowds gathered—in parks, on corners, at windows, on the roofs of office buildings—to watch the pilots and their messages in the sky.

"I think they are right," said a blue-suited *sarariman*—office worker—to his coworkers as they sat around their company's rooftop lunch tables in the Tokyo ward of Minato. "It is time we reclaimed our heritage."

"The Americans are too weak anymore to tell us how to worship, what to believe," offered an obese but identically uniformed companion as he lighted his third after-lunch cigarette.

"They have certainly focused all of Tokyo's thoughts on these matters," said a third. "Every week, every Monday, they give us something to think about as we begin the work week." He bummed a cigarette and lighted it. "What dedication. It's almost a year now, and they have never repeated the same proverb twice."

"I've instructed my wife to give preference to their products when she shops for food," said the obese man.

"You must consume half their yearly production of rice," joked the first *sarariman* as he exhaled a deep breath of smoke. The obese man frowned as his companions laughed.

"Don't make light of what these monks have been able to accomplish with their hard work," he countered. "If you think they are right," he challenged the first man, "then you should buy their products too, in order to support their activities."

There were nods, then silence as heads craned up to catch the next message.

"It is very expensive to do this," the fat man persisted. "I understand the beauty and precision of the *kanji* comes not only from the skill of the pilots, but from a special computer system designed by Kurata-*sama's* nephew that gives each pilot his own path to fly."

The third man snorted. "The computer is already in the cockpit," he said. "Those are agricultural airplanes the monks use for their farms. I read an article in *Asahi Shimbun* that all aircraft like that have computer displays with global positioning satellite systems that program a spray pattern and keep track of the plane's position so they don't miss an area of the field or spray one part twice. I agree that the *kanji* are artful. I, too, appreciate their words every week, but it is not so expensive as you say because they already have the computers and equipment."

The fat man sulked. "Those who do not contribute to that which they enjoy are parasites. These are good men, patriots and monks devoted to Buddha. They give up all their profits from their good works."

"Well, I think they are extreme at times, even cultlike." The first man flicked off a half inch of cigarette ash, inhaled, then said, "Besides, I think they have simply found a good marketing angle and are exploiting patriotism to sell rice and soya."

"I thought you said you agreed with them," the obese man said.

"I agree with their sayings," the first man said. "I think they do the Japanese spirit much good. But I think we need to be realistic."

"More like cynical," the fat man said as he stood up. "Belief must be unconditional," he said. "When the tide shifts, those of us who believe will remember the cynics like you."

He waddled angrily away.

The second man lit another cigarette from the butt of his last one, exhaled a round cumulus of smoke. "I think he has bought into more than just the sect's food."

"Yamato lives in your blood," Kenji Yamamoto read the sky message. "Not bad, *neh?*" he said to Akira Sugawara as the two men stood amid the throngs in Shinjuku Imperial Park and watched the sky.

"No. Not bad."

Yamamoto looked down at the palm-sized computer in his right hand and focused on the LCD display and the bar graphs; moments later, the bars began to grow as the built-in air sampling analyzer started to register the marker compounds that had been added to the skywriting chemicals so dispersion could be accurately measured.

"The wave from the first message is arriving now." He pressed a special key, which began to log the data—time of arrival, concentrations of the inert marker virus. Scattered around Tokyo—but with special interest to those prefectures and neighborhoods that harbored Koreans—an additional two dozen identical monitors held by others from the laboratory sampled the atmosphere.

"Come!" Yamamoto said urgently as he tapped at the collector's display. "Come *on!* What is wrong with this?" He looked at the display, tried to generate some enthusiasm despite his misgivings.

"Solar flares," Sugawara said as he took the Palm from Yamamoto. "Very intense for the past several days. Very bad for instruments. It interferes with the electronics. The Web site for the world warning system for solar weather is warning that strong, possibly severe geomagnetic storms are possible."

"How is this possible?" Yamamoto asked. "I was not aware—"

Yamamoto looked up at the tall young man in whom Kurata placed so much trust. Yamamoto struggled to control his feelings. Despite Rycroft's imperious orders to the contrary, Yamamoto still felt the process was not going properly. One word, just a sentence to this young man, might fix the problem.

"Unusual levels of particles and radiation from the sun collide with the earth's own magnetic field; it can cause a geomagnetic storm that affects radio and television transmissions and satellite communications. It can even cause unexplained computer crashes and malfunctions in semiconductor chips. The effects can also distort or interrupt navigation satellites. Remember, our pilots rely upon global positioning satellite signals for both safety and the beauty of the *kanji*. A bad or distorted signal from the satellite could mean disaster."

A loud beep sounded from Sugawara's Palm. Both men looked at it as, moments later, data began to arrive from the other monitors, transmitted by the devices' built-in cellular modems. The data hesitated and surged.

"The wireless link is affected also," Sugawara said as he commented on the irregular pulses of data. "The error-checking software is causing delays as it demands that possibly corrupt data be re-sent."

Yamamoto nodded as he and Sugawara watched a familiar pattern emerge in the data.

Finally, Sugawara said, "It is now precise. Six times in a row, the delivery has been faultless. We are now ready." He struggled to conceal the dark certainty that gathered in his heart that told him that he was playing with evil.

Sugawara looked up from the Palm computer. "Are we sure no one can possibly connect this with Daiwa Ichiban? With Kurata-*sama*?"

Yamamoto sighed. "I have told you this so many times that if you were not so young, I would suspect you of senility. First of all, the authorities will not go all out to investigate the deaths of Koreans. The deaths solve a problem; the bureaus do not want that problem to return."

"But the international community—"

"Have no influence. Look at China where goods are made by slave labor under the cruelest conditions possible. The world continues to buy those goods." He shook his head. "Even if we were to take out advertisements in the biggest newspapers and tell them exactly what happened and who did it, the furor would blow over in weeks. The conscience of the West is blinded by the consumer goods it is addicted to."

Sugawara looked away to keep Yamamoto from seeing the dismay that boiled up from within. What Yamamoto said was true; the world had no conscience. The U.N. and the United States uttered platitudes of outrage, backed up by little or nothing. As much as Sugawara wished it were not so, Kurata seemed to be right when he accused the Americans of being cowardly, gutless, and unwilling to sacrifice for their shallow creeds and flimsy beliefs. Sugawara dragged his concentration back to Yamamoto's words.

"The sect members know nothing." Yamamoto continued. "For a discount price, they have been receiving the canisters of skywriting sprays through an Australian wholesaler owned by a German chemical company, itself a subsidiary of NorAm Pharmco. The blame, if things were discovered, would rest with a string of round-eye companies. It is they who would be charged with racial genocide.

"The sect members know nothing," he reiterated. "Besides, the sky proverbs have been appearing regularly for nearly a year with no adverse effects; people love them, have grown used to them. Further, the incubation period is ten days, which means that those stinking garlic eaters will start to die midday on a Thursday. They're no more likely to associate the sky proverbs with the Korean cleansing than they are to think the Osaka earthquake was the result of the newspaper arriving at the door."

He paused, looked up from the Palm computer, and scanned the sky. "There"—he pointed—"the third proverb: *Un wa yusha o tasuku*. Fate aids the courageous. It is so!"

Yes, Sugawara thought to himself, and *Ja no michi wa hebi*. Snakes follow the way of serpents.

They watched the display silently for nearly half an hour as the messages drifted into nothingness.

Sugawara struggled with his loyalties. How could he be right about the evilness of Operation Tsushima and everyone about him wrong? His head, his duties and obligations, told him that could not be so, but his heart told him yes. Why did he feel this way? He had been raised in a strictly Japanese home. How could he think so differently from his parents? From Uncle Kurata?

The question had hounded his nearly every waking minute. He didn't know why. Sometimes things just were. It seemed to him that there were absolutes in right and wrong, good and bad. No matter how some people liked to live their lives in a miasma of relativistic limbo that justified their own behavior and sanctioned their personal prejudices, his heart told him that there were universal principles that demanded allegiance.

But even if he was correct and everyone including Kurata was wrong, what could he do about it? What resources did he have? What could one person do?

Disclosure was out of the question. Kurata had a cleverly crafted contingency plan in the event anyone suspected human intervention in what was supposed to look like a natural phenomenon. Kurata would disclose that an internal investigation had determined that NorAm Pharmco and a group of American Defense Department Strangeloves had concocted the whole affair without the knowledge of Kurata or anyone beyond the corporate borders of NorAm. To make amends, all of NorAm's assets—valued in billions of U.S. dollars—would be donated to the United Nations and dedicated to providing free or low cost drugs for the Third World.

The firewall had been built, deniability established, amends carefully structured to cause barely a ripple on the surface of Daiwa Ichiban's overall bottom line. Much of it had been done with Sugawara's help, and this blackened his heart.

"Come!" Yamamoto said, closing the small computer. "Let's get back to the lab and give them the good news: the rehearsal is over."

And it's time for me to act, Sugawara thought.

Lara Blackwood clambered down through the main companionway hatch of the *Tagcat Too*, pursued relentlessly by a savage wind that assaulted her with raindrops the size of shooter marbles.

"Damn!" She pulled the hatch shut and stood dripping for a moment over a brass grate in the deck at the foot of the steps that drained to the bilge. The *Tagcat Too* swayed gently against its mooring lines. Finally Lara made her way to her stateroom, dropped a small duffel on the floor next to the door, and stretched at the aches in her back and shoulders. Stress, tension. She'd had too much of it and not enough exercise.

She looked down at the duffel and thought of the bomb it contained: floppy disks and papers, the distilled essence of her case against Kurata and the White House. It was all there: the data pulled off the Web from around the world, the details of her conversations with Jim Condon, Ismail Brahimi, with Kurata in the White House, the president in his limo, and with Peter Durant, and the coup d'état that had finally forced her from her own company.

On top of it all was a copy of the *Post* folded back to the story on her genome conference. The reporter's byline was circled in red highlighter along with the time of their 10:00 A.M. appointment for the next morning.

Lara slumped against the door frame, rubbing at the bands of pain that ratcheted at her forehead. She needed a solid night's sleep to be ready for the *Post*. Bent by the tension of the past two days, she made her way from stern to bow and back, turning out lights, checking that hatches and portholes were closed and secured. Finally, she made her way to the nav station and checked the outside Web cam images. Seeing nothing unusual, Lara set the alarm and went into her stateroom. She turned down her bed and picked up a slim leather clip holster and pulled from it the silver Colt .380 automatic she had loaded with fresh rounds just hours before. She ejected the clip, pushed at the round on top, worked the slide, tried the trigger, and then reassembled everything and placed it next to her bed. Finally, she got in bed, pulled up the covers, and turned out the light.

For several seconds she felt guilty about not brushing her teeth and then she fell deeply asleep.

Hidden eyes pried through the midnight gloom and watched the shadows that played behind the portlite curtains of the *Tagcat Too*.

Across the freeway, behind the eighth-story windows of a nondescript high-rise apartment block, Horst Von Neuman sat patiently on a comfortable folding chair beside a tangle of electronic gear. A tripod-mounted directional microphone pointed directly at Lara's boat; next to it, a dish antenna, aimed at the same target. A compact night-vision scope hung from a lanyard looped about the man's neck. The earpiece from the microphone amplifier filled his left ear; a wire from his two-way radio led to his right ear.

Von Neuman nodded as he looked down at the dish antenna that snared faint radio signals, known as Van Eck radiation, given off by Lara's computer keyboard, printer, and video monitor. From the dish, a cable ran to the TEMPEST surveillance unit, itself a small portable computer, but one which had been specially shielded to prevent its radio waves from leaking out into the hands of strangers. Few personal computer users realized that everything they produced on their systems could be picked up by total strangers using such unsophisticated gear as an ordinary television set and a handful of components from Radio Shack.

Most were also unaware that the tables could be turned on the average PC's delicate chips and circuits. The man looked at the parabolic dish aimed at Lara's laptop. It was receiving data now, but if necessary, he could flip a switch and transmit a powerful surge of radio waves in the microwave band. The circuits in Lara's PC would act like makeshift antennas and pick up the signals, which would then overwhelm Lara's PC, causing it to crash for no apparent reason. At higher power levels, the radio waves could actually cause permanent damage to the circuits.

Von Neuman watched as the LCD screen on the TEMPEST unit scrolled continuously with the same information that was appearing on Lara's laptop. At precisely midnight, he picked up the encrypted wireless and checked in with Sheila Gaillard. He reported that other than a litany of curses, the woman in question had said nothing, had no visitors, had visited the head and flushed the toilet four times, and had been occupied with her personal computer for more than six hours.

"Be ready," Sheila told him, then hung up.

20

Akira Sugawara followed Kenji Yamamoto up the metal stairs to a catwalk that branched away in all directions, making a twisted path among the tops of Laboratory 73's larger fermentation tanks and bio-reactor vessels. Sugawara thought it looked a little like a winery, something like a brew pub, a lot like a miniaturized oil refinery, tanks and pipes and fractionation towers shrunk to fit inside this cavernous metal building behind the main laboratory.

Their footfalls echoed on the metal treadway and punctuated the hum and suck of pumps that like hungry steel hearts kept this biological system alive.

Around them, great gouts of liquid surrated through thick clear Pyrex veins the diameter of sewer pipes that ran willy-nilly but always changed direction in precise ninety-degree elbows heading off for some other tank buried deep in the bowels of the beast. Here—in this tank—the liquid was cloudy and brown, there—coming out of that precipitator—it was clear and bile-colored; over there it had the color and consistency of pineapple juice. Throughout, large carboys of reagents hung like blood-fat ticks from this pipe and that, dripping precise, computer-controlled amounts of their contents into the system like hormones and gastric juices.

At each junction and every choke point lay an electrically actuated valve controlled by a real-time computer that sampled the process from thousands of nervelike sensors wired throughout the apparatus. The computer adjusted the flow, the temperature, the pressure, and the chemical composition as needed. This central nervous system orchestrated the synapses of hundreds of electrical relays that chirped now like a chorus of mechanical crickets.

This was not the bright world of the gleaming glass assemblages of flasks and tubing that cluttered the workbenches of the laboratories. This was not a place of experimentation, but one of work, not a place of questions, but one of production. Here the perfected processes of the labs were sealed up so the business of death could be efficiently conducted.

It made Sugawara shiver. Everywhere Sugawara looked, he saw evidence of his guilt. He had designed the computer control system, had written much of the code. His hand guided death through its paces.

Yamamoto liked to tell visitors that this system lived; it respirated and metabolized and grew and produced waste. Sugawara knew it was true, and it gave him the creeps. This was a Mary Shelley monster with no face that would invisibly creep out of the laboratory and do its work before the global villagers could light their torches and storm the castle.

"As you can see, the yield here is precisely as predicted." Yamamoto had stopped to pull a long continuous sheet of graph paper from a recorder. He held it up for Sugawara to see. "There is absolutely no doubt this batch fills our requirements for potency and for inactivation after the prescribed time period."

He let the paper fall and turned to make his way toward a computer screen.

"As you know, we must be very precise in the manufacture because the genetic differences between any two groups of people are very, very small." Then he lowered his voice. "Although it does not make Kurata-sama and his allies happy to realize it, there is very little genetic difference between ourselves and the Koreans." He stopped, said emphatically, "The differences are not numerous, but they are significant culturally, *neh?*"

Without replying directly, Sugawara followed him, pondering the implications that Operation Tsushima's production chief had left hanging.

Potency, limited life, genetic specificity: these were the three hallmarks of the ethnic bomb they had produced. For the third time that morning, Yamamoto had mentioned the first two and not the third. Sugawara followed the older man toward the computer terminal. Sugawara's heart grew lighter as he thought about being able to use a process flaw to postpone Operation Tsushima. He now regretted his original resistance to taking the tour.

Yamamoto had pressed for this tour every day for nearly two weeks. Sugawara had postponed him day after day. He had seen all of this monster that he cared to see, and he just couldn't summon the psychological energy required to tour the entrails of the beast again. The toll had emptied him, left him exhausted.

Again, he wondered how he had come to think like this. He cursed the events—or the genetic mutation?—that had made him think so differently, so independently, from the way in which he was brought up, the way his family lived, the way he was expected to behave.

Was it his stay in America?

Over the past weeks, he had stared into the darkness while others slept, trying to run the frames of his life backward, looking for the point when he had changed, when he had gone wrong. Perhaps, fixing that time or event in his mind would allow him to change back into a way of thinking he was bound to.

But try as he had, he found no epiphany. He couldn't remember a time when he hadn't been exactly who he was now. It was possible, he had begun to accept, that he had always been flawed, but that he had just been able to get along without too many people noticing. Until now. Perhaps it took something as hideous as Operation Tsushima to focus his thoughts, to force the decision he must make: either he must put his Western, individualistic impulses behind him or he must split with the way of his people, betray his family, default on the *giri* that bound him to them all. He couldn't see even the slightest atoll in the gulf between these two decisions. Failure to make the complete leap would leave him in an agnostic swamp, directionless, uncommitted, unfaithful to either of the poles that clutched at his heart.

He wanted to be alone to struggle with these thoughts, to wrestle with the waking nightmare that had overtaken him. Taking another tour of the facility was the last thing Sugawara needed, but the older man would not be denied.

"You are Kurata-*sama*'s eyes and ears—and strong young legs," Yamamoto had persisted. "You must be able to answer any questions our lord may have for you. It is your duty. You would not want to let him down."

Yes, Sugawara had thought, *I do want to let him down, but I haven't the courage to do so.* Finally, Sugawara realized that the older man's persistence and increasing stridency in pressing for the inspection perhaps meant he had something he wished to communicate, but—as was the way—he could not do so directly.

Sugawara followed Yamamoto down a short flight of steps to a mezzanine platform nestled in the lee of a tall stainless-steel tank.

Sugawara knew if he went to Kurata and told him directly that there was a problem with the process, then it would force the issue into the open, with the result that someone would need to be blamed, to lose face. Such people could be dangerous.

What's more, Sugawara knew he might be wrong about there being a problem with the process. Yamamoto could truthfully reply, "I never said that."

Sugawara knew *he* would then lose face, credibility, his influence within the organization. He would probably be denied access to information he needed to follow the course of the project.

The two men stopped on the small mezzanine platform, which was no larger than a Ping-Pong table. Yamamoto turned on a hanging light and, in the illumination from the naked bulb, pointed at a small glass tube running with a colorless liquid.

"This is the final serum before it's incorporated into the respiratory microsomes," Yamamoto said.

Politely, Sugawara leaned forward, although he knew there was little to see, just a barely visible flow of death as it moved into the patented machinery that would encapsulate bits of the Slatewiper vector into special microscopic dust motes that could be aerosolized without damaging the vector.

First developed by Dr. Ishii and later perfected and patented by NorAm Pharmco as a way to deliver delicate organic drugs via lung inhalers, the microsome was a protective shell no more than a few molecules thick wrapped around the vector. The particle size was carefully manufactured to be the perfect size to be carried deepest into the lungs with every breath, right down to the alveoli, where only a single layer of cells separates the air from the capillaries where oxygen and carbon dioxide were exchanged.

Here, the microsome would dissolve instantly, releasing the Slatewiper vector where it could pass directly into the bloodstream.

The process ran through Sugawara's mind as he watched the liquid flow.

"The quantities are precisely as needed," Yamamoto said. "Please let

Kurata-*sama* know I have faithfully followed Rycroft-*san*'s instructions to the letter."

The older man touched him lightly on the shoulder. When Sugawara turned, he saw Yamamoto looking directly at him. "To the letter, faithfully." Then the older man waited for a moment, then bowed slightly. "To the letter, faithfully." He said it again. Then without another word, he set off toward a set of stairs that led down.

Yamamoto's cryptic repetition caught Sugawara's attention. *"To the letter, faithfully."* He thought very hard about this, then the fog cleared.

"So *that's* it!" Sugawara said quietly to himself. "That's what he wants me to know." There was something wrong with the process and it was Rycroft's fault. But older, traditional Japanese could never bring themselves to criticize others so directly, especially if the people were their supervisors. Open rebellion was out of the question, but Yamamoto wanted Kurata to know that Rycroft's faulty instructions had been followed faithfully, right to the letter.

Silently, Akira cursed the traditional penchant for circumlocutory communication. But Yamamoto was of the very old school and would not, under any circumstances, get into a direct conversation that involved accusing his supervisor.

Sugawara stood there, watching Yamamoto hurry toward the microsome staging area, obviously unwilling to talk further about the matter. To Yamamoto, the message had been sent and received: something was wrong with the process, something that was Rycroft's fault.

Opportunity came to those who watched for it. This was surely what he had been waiting for. This was the wedge he needed to drive between Kurata and Operation Tsushima and to delay it, perhaps giving him time to do something more permanent.

Beautiful, he thought happily. This is beautiful.

Sugawara followed a short distance behind Yamamoto. Sugawara had to figure out how to use the information, how to build a consensus against Rycroft. Sugawara knew he couldn't move directly against the arrogant Britisher; that would offend Kurata. Besides, Rycroft had his own supporters who wanted nothing to derail Operation Tsushima. The project had a life of its own, a momentum that might be impossible, finally, to derail.

For a moment Sugawara considered saying nothing, letting the juggernaut roll on. There would be many more deaths—Japanese as well as Koreans—but he could blow the whistle afterward and bring to the nation's attention what happens when politicians create an atmosphere of racism and elitism, the consequences of ordinary citizens going along with it all.

For an instant, he remembered his history lessons and realized that this political arrogance and a compliant populace was what created the conditions for the attack on Pearl Harbor, the Pacific War, and the humiliation that followed. Japan's leadership and its population had never been forced to acknowledge their culpability for the history of the past half century. In denying their responsibility, they were now on track to repeat it.

It was a tempting idea, Sugawara thought as he entered the clean room airlock with Yamamoto and stopped to change into gowns and slippers. But the lesson for his countrymen would cost the innocent lives of hundreds of thousands of Koreans, people who had already suffered enough under Japanese oppression.

Besides, he thought, slipping on paper booties and a paper hat that looked like a twisted version of a chef's toque, there was no way he could sit on the information. He had no idea how many other people to whom Yamamoto may have given—or would give—the same tour, leading them toward the same conclusions. There was no way to take direct action and no way to avoid indirect collaboration with Yamamoto.

The trick, Sugawara thought as he finished fastening the white disposable paper lab coat, was to exert just the right amount of pressure at the right place so the outcome was neither what Kurata expected nor what Yamamoto wanted.

Sugawara followed the older man into the clean room. Then as the clean-room door closed automatically behind them, Sugawara had the feeling of other doors in his life slamming shut as well.

21

THE TELEPHONE STARTLED LARA BLACKWOOD AWAKE. She reached first for the .380 automatic before realizing there was no threat. She flashed on an absurd vision of putting a couple of slugs through the phone so she could go back to sleep. Instead, she checked the clock: just after 2:00 A.M. The phone rang again, but its trill was nearly covered by a howling gust of wind from outside and the subsequent barrage of rain hammering down on deck. Lara recognized the marina's phone number on the caller ID and picked up the receiver.

"Blackwood."

"Sorry to bother you, Ms. Blackwood." It was Sumter Jones, the night watchman. "I've got a crazy man at the gate says he's got to talk with you. Now."

Instantly Lara felt her fingers tingle. She sat up and swung her legs over the side of the bed. "Crazy man have a name?"

"Yeah. Big name," Jones said. "Peter Durant. I recognize him from television."

What could be so wrong that Durant had to visit in person in the dark of a driving rain?

"Be right there," Lara snapped. She shut the phone, pulled on a sweat-shirt and jeans, and made her way to the foul-weather gear locker just to the left of the main companionway steps. She shrugged into her Gore-

Tex, clipped her cell phone to her belt, then grabbed her keys and a flashlight and started up the steps. She stopped, returned to her stateroom for the .380 automatic. Then with the holster clipped to her belt, headed into the soaking, wind-whipped night.

Durant had *never* visited the boat. She had let him know at the beginning that she considered it off-limits, an intolerable violation of her personal life. Something was badly wrong for him to show up now. Less than a minute later, Lara found Peter Durant and Sumter Jones standing by the chain-link security gate. Jones was dressed in a yellow slicker; Durant wore only jeans, sneakers, and a sweatshirt. He was soaked.

When Durant saw Lara, he threw himself forward and clutched at the gate's wires. "Thank God, you're here!" he yelled hysterically as he grasped at the gate with knuckles so white they almost shone by themselves in the dark.

Pulling out her own keys, Lara nodded to Jones that he could get out of the rain now. Jones hesitated. Lara looked at the man's dark face, could tell by the look in his eyes he was concerned for her.

"It's okay, Sumter," Lara said. "I work with him. It's okay." Lara pulled out her keys and sorted through the wad for the long one that opened the gate.

Jones gave her a final, doubtful look, then turned and walked back to his quarters. Out of the corner of her eye, she saw him looking through the blinds and wondered if he had the rusty museum piece of a revolver he had shown her once.

"It's too horrible for words," Durant babbled almost incoherently. "I've sent Peggy and the kids away to her parents for safety."

Then he started to cry. "I never knew until now! Oh, God!"

Finally unlocking the gate, Lara stepped through and stood helplessly next to her colleague for several moments. "Come on down to the boat," Lara said finally, placing her hand on his shoulder. "It's dry and warm there."

"No time, no time." Durant pulled away and ran-stumbled toward the parking lot. "Not enough time. Come on, come on!" He lurched among the cars and trucks jamming the spaces closest to the gate. Lara watched him make his way to a minivan in a poorly illuminated corner of the lot.

"They're coming!" Durant yelled. "Read while you can." He stood with his hand on the door and waited for Lara to follow.

As Lara walked toward the minivan, Durant slid the side door open and waved impatiently. "Come on, come *on*!"

Climbing in amid the clutter of child seats, toys, crumbs from half-eaten cookies and crackers, the inevitable flotsam and jetsam of childhood, Lara froze when she saw the buff, legal-sized expandable files with the glowing orange fluorescent letters that demanded, "Four-zero security, not to be removed from documents vault." Lara knew the vault in the White House basement. She had been there accompanied, according to the regulations, by an armed guard who was to make sure no documents were removed, altered, or copied.

The files in Durant's minivan were splattered with fresh blood.

"What the hell did you—"

"No," Durant snapped. "Don't talk! No time, no time!" He snatched one of the blood-splattered files from the seat, pulled from it a sheaf of papers, and thrust them at Lara. From the corner of her eye, Lara saw Durant cover his face with both hands, rub as he visibly struggled to pull himself together.

"Go ahead," Durant demanded. "Read it. I'm hysterical, but I'm not fucking crazy."

But now, as Lara read the papers in the dim yellow illumination of the minivan's ceiling light, her insides connected with a deeper blackness than she had ever experienced.

"Dear Christ," Lara said softly as she looked at her old partner. "Tell me this isn't true."

Durant's mouth worked silently, searching for and failing to find words. Silently, he handed her another file.

22

THE RAIN DRUMMED HARDER AGAINST THE MINIVAN'S ROOF AS LARA READ THE SECOND FILE. She never imagined she could feel a deeper, darker, more desperately cold emptiness. Wordlessly, Durant handed her two more files.

"This is too much," Lara said. "It can't be. This just can't be. These kinds of bizarre conspiracies just don't happen like this except in cheap thriller novels. How could the president do this? How could Kurata?"

"Believe it," Durant said. His voice was more even now, more collected. "I put a guard in intensive care to get these."

"How?" Lara struggled for words as she tried to comprehend the horror on the pages. "Why?"

"Your name started coming up a lot in the past twenty-four hours," Durant said. "Plus I couldn't help thinking that maybe you were right and all those deaths weren't coincidences. The more I asked, the harder they stonewalled me. I'm nominally your boss. At least I was, with a right to know *everything*. So I eavesdropped a lot more and paid attention to what was said. And when I heard these files were coming out of the vault for shredding, I arranged a peek after they came out."

"And you—"

"Requisitioned them."

"There's no doubt they're authentic?" Lara asked.

"No doubt."

Lara rested her face in her hands for a long moment, then looked back up at Durant.

"They *used* me," she said bitterly. "The thieving pigfuckers *lied* to me and stole my company so they could kill people."

"Now they're shredding all of your files," Durant said.

Lara Blackwood slumped in the minivan seat and let the enormity of what she had done hammer its way home. It was the sharp sticky dark corner of nightmares that were too horrible to bear; but try as she did, Lara couldn't make herself wake up from this one.

Durant continued. "If you look closely," he said, "you'll see that every one of the files carries the double-nine code for external control."

Lara leaned forward and bent over the folder, face close to the paper trying to make out the words in the dim light.

As she bent over, Lara heard the unmistakable whine of a slug ripping through the air next to her ear. She turned to warn Durant and saw his face turned into a bloody gray pulp. Two more bullets slammed into Peter Durant's chest, blew flesh, blood, and body fluids all over the inside of the van.

Explosive bullets. Lara leaped backward, out of the line of fire. Lying flat by the minivan's rear door, Lara wiped blood and bits of Durant's body from her face. She tried the latch, but it was locked. She barely heard the muted *phut* of a silenced weapon as three more slugs smacked into Durant's now-lifeless body, churning the flesh like a meat grinder. Pieces splattered and clung to the sides and ceiling of the minivan.

Lara dived through the minivan's rear window and hit the pavement in a shower of tempered glass particles. The pounding rain and wind pummeled the glass bits, scattered them wildly.

Another *phut!* More glass hailed down around her as the rear windows of the minivan blew out. Lara rolled until she could scramble between two cars. A rear taillight lens blew out just inches from her face. The warmth of what she recognized as her own blood ran down her cheek, mingling with the cold rain.

With her right hand, she fumbled the .380 automatic from beneath her foul-weather gear. It smelled of Hoppes No. 9 cleaning solvent. Another *phut!* A shower of lead clawed its way across the pavement just inches from her feet. They were trying to skip-shoot under the cars to wound or force her out. To stay at rest meant certain death, especially if she continued to wear the bright yellow foul-weather gear.

Lara pulled her keys from the foul-weather gear's pockets and stuffed them in her jeans. Next, she shrugged out of the rain gear and crept toward the front of the car. She stopped when she got to the broad aisle between rows. Another shot rattled behind her.

Move! Move! Lara urged herself on.

She waited for a strong gust of wind to help obscure her unseen attacker's visibility, then launched herself across the aisle between cars. Far behind her, a slug thudded into a fender.

Without stopping, Lara zigged up the next aisle, zagged behind a delivery van, and dashed into the relative safety of darkness cast by a broken streetlight.

She stood there for a long moment in the shadow of safety, breathing deeply. What she wanted most was to get to her big armored Chevy Suburban, but it was parked at the perimeter of the lot, too far within the gauntlet of gunfire. They had cleverly blocked every exit.

Looking about her, Lara squinted through the curtains of rain and assembled a plan, partly from what she could see, partly from what she could remember. She pushed the doubt from her mind: it could work . . . it *had* to work. If she was quick and fast and gave the athletic performance of her life.

Suddenly movement! She threw herself flat on the pavement as a slug pounded into the Suburban's door. Lara rolled and rolled as the slugs tracked her. She followed the muzzle flash and saw a shadow move against the darkness. She paused for just an instant and quickly fired three rounds at the shadow.

A man's scream split the darkness. She fired at the source of the sound and the scream stopped abruptly. She heard a gun hit the pavement. Lara got to a crouch and saw the shadow mounding on the asphalt, unmoving. There were more killers in the dark waiting for her. The rain thrummed on the vehicle roofs around her and lashed at her head as she ran through her moves in her mind one more time, then in a single fluid motion she sprinted toward the marina.

Slugs followed her, shattering glass all around her as she zigzagged toward the marina gate, keys in hand. Slugs compassed her every step of the way.

At the gate, she took shelter behind a concrete rubbish bin as she fished out the gate key. Slugs tore great chunks of concrete out of the bin. Fear accreted cold and hard in her belly as she began to imagine that her plan would not work, that time would unravel faster than she could act.

"You can only do what you can do," she mumbled to herself. "So do it."

Just then a siren screamed over the shrieks of the rain. Reflexively she searched the darkness, looking toward the sound as its pitch rose and fell. Her assailants' guns had been equipped with suppressors, but not her own. Sumter or someone must have heard her shots and called 911.

23

BLINKING INTO THE STINGING RAIN, HER SKIN SOAKED AND NEARLY NUMB FROM
THE STORM, LARA GRIPPED THE GATE KEY AND LOOKED TOWARD THE ENTRANCE
GATE, THE HARBORMASTER'S OFFICE AND BEYOND IT, THE COLLECTION OF BUILD-
INGS AND AWNINGS UP ON THE SHORE OVERLOOKING THE DOCKS. There was
the Rusty Pelican Deli, next to that a boat brokerage, an outboard motor
repair company, two competing supply stores that sold overpriced brass
and stainless-steel fittings.

She peered through the curtains of rain as they ebbed and flowed,
obscuring her vision completely one instant, offering her a clear view
the next. She waited for the next onslaught, then moved, praying the
key fit into the slot. It slid in the first time. She turned the key and pulled
open the gate.

The rain cleared as she sprinted through the gate. Expecting a sniper's
bullet any second, she kept driving with her feet, propelling her down
the dock ramp deeper into the shadows toward the *Tagcat Too*. Instants
later slugs tore through the fiberglass decks of boats on either side of
her, zeroing in on her. She ducked behind a dock box as a fusillade tore
through the dock where she would have run.

The sirens grew closer. But the bombardment from her assailants continued. She would be dead before they arrived. She thought for an in-

stant of Durant, the files, and the horrible truth that would lay in wait for her should she survive the night.

The wind and the rain drew a blanket over the night again and she sprinted through the impenetrable darkness straight to the *Tagcat Too*. Without hesitation, she unlooped the mooring lines from the boat's cleats. The wind immediately began to push the boat away from the dock. She leaped aboard as slugs began to search the night for her. She disconnected the shore power and the landline phone cord, then leaped through the companionway. Slugs glanced off the steel hatch as she slid it shut.

Belowdecks she started both diesels, and ran them to full throttle. Then, using both the radar and night-vision Web cam images to guide her, she used the belowdecks, foul-weather helm to steer the *Tagcat Too* away from the dock and into the night.

"Oh, God," she said softly as she began to shiver, as much from fear as from her storm-soaked clothing. "Thank you, God."

The *Tagcat Too* slewed and swayed under the vicious wind gusts. It took all her concentration to keep the big ketch in the narrow channel that led to the Potomac. One wrong move and the winged, torpedo-shaped keel filled with ultra-dense depleted uranium would snag on a mudflat or, worse, collide with the concrete pilings that lined the channel. She'd then be at the mercy of the storm that could pound the steel-hulled craft into scrap metal.

She and the naval architects who designed the *Tagcat Too* had made sure that it would be able to withstand the world's worst weather and waves in the Southern Ocean. But that held true only in the open ocean where there was only water and more water to pound against.

The channel was narrow, and the powerful gusting winds could ebb or blow at just the wrong time and send her crashing into concrete pilings that would rip through even the *Tagcat Too's* strong steel hull. Total concentration banished the cold, stilled the shivers, emptied her of thought, of emotions, of fear. She *became* the action; she *was* the doing. There was only action, and it freed her.

In the night-sight video display, set on wide angle, she sensed rather than saw the concrete piling approach, her own personal Pillars of Hercules. Her hands assumed a life of their own, caressing the rudder joystick, manipulating bow thruster power.

Then suddenly the last of the pillars receded into the darkness.

She turned to port and charted a path right down the middle of the

Potomac. Only then did she take a deep breath and turn on the weather radio. What she heard terrified and exhilarated her at the same time.

"The National Weather Service has issued a hurricane warning for the coastal regions of North Carolina, Virginia, Maryland, Delaware, and New Jersey, with wind gusts over one hundred miles per hour and storm surges in low-lying areas of twenty feet or more. Evacuations have begun."

The radio told her that the eye of the hurricane had stalled off Cape Hatteras; the navy was sending its ships to sea to stay ahead of the approaching storm and to keep them from the dangers of shallow water; twelve people had been killed so far, all of them passengers in a church van that had tried to cross a swollen stream in rural South Carolina. The stalled hurricane was spinning off bad weather and tornadoes all along the Atlantic coast.

She thought about the old saying about being between the devil and the deep blue sea and realized that she was—once again—there. She had braved hurricane force winds before. And lost.

She could not shake the cold stone that sat on her heart and told her that this was Cape Horn all over again. Only this time there would be no one to fish her out of the water.

24

THE HOTEL BALLROOM, PANELED ALL THE WAY TO THE TOP OF ITS THIRTY-FOOT CEILING IN RARE TROPICAL HARDWOODS, WAS MASSIVE, DESIGNED TO HOLD HUN-DREDS OF SEATED GUESTS. The elegant crystal chandeliers were dimmed almost to complete darkness. But instead of the International Conference on Derivatives Securities Sales that had used the room less than twenty-four hours before, there was only Edward Rycroft who stood at a solid mahogany podium and faced a curious conference room in which twelve men sat in twelve private, curtained alcoves equipped with a comfortable chair, a small table with refreshments, and room for the heavily armed bodyguards that these men, for very good reasons, went nowhere without.

The men and their security entourages had entered the darkened ballroom by different doors, all at slightly different times prearranged in advance. None wished his face to be seen by the others. They were a notorious collection of civil and military officials from a dozen countries known for ethnic strife. None was particularly happy with being seen by Rycroft and his assistant, but that was the price to be paid for having a new ability to feed their megalomanical obsessions of remaining in power no matter how much their people had to suffer for the privilege.

In the far back of the room, faded into the expensive shadows, stood

Jason Woodruff who watched each of those assembled and tried to deduce which of them would pay the most.

"In summary," Rycroft concluded, "the ultimate value of the gene-specific weapon we are offering you is several-fold. First, it allows pinpoint targeting of precise populations that may be too intermingled with beneficial populations to remove by conventional means. Second, the barrier to entry is much higher than, for instance, with nuclear weapons. The capital investment in research and production facilities and the remarkable depth of scientific"—Rycroft paused—"shall I say, *genius* required makes it unlikely the weapon can be duplicated anytime soon, if ever. Third, because of its design, the weapon cannot be defended against, nor can it—in its final form—even be detected. When our design is combined with an existing disease pathogen, it becomes the ultimate stealth weapon which also insulates its users against war crimes accusations."

Rycroft paused and drank from his water glass. This was a biotechnological tour de force, and it was his show. "Finally," he resumed, "we cannot overlook the essentially attractive feature that our weapon not only leaves untargeted populations unharmed, but it also does not damage or permanently contaminate buildings, infrastructure, homes, production facilities, or other expensive assets. Conventional war is expensive and absorbs financial resources better spent purchasing products from our companies. Conventional wars destroy markets and ultimately depress our bottom lines. Thanks to the Slatewiper, conventional wars are now financially obsolete."

He looked around the room and found only rapt attention.

"So, with that introduction, please allow me to offer you a few more details." He nodded at Woodruff who dimmed the lights and turned on a slide projector.

As soon as the room was dark, Rycroft pressed the cordless remote control and a slide of a chimpanzee appeared.

"Mother Nature is remarkably stingy," Rycroft began. "She believes in reusing available materials rather than creating new ones. That's why our genetic composition varies by less than two percent from this fine simian specimen."

The projector clicked, and up came an image of four microscope photos.

"Here you find yeast cells." Using a laser pointer, he indicated the upper left quadrant. "Counterclockwise, cells from a horned toad, from a mushroom, and from a sea cucumber. While their genetic component differs from ours much more than that of the chimp, they still share many of the same genes and enzymes we do."

The next slide, likewise partitioned into four, showed the faces of people from four racial categories: Caucasian, Asian, African, American Indian.

Rycroft paced along the wall, just beyond the cone of light that connected the screen to the projector. "On average, any two people on earth vary in their genetic makeup by only about zero-point-two percent, one-fifth of one percent. Of that zero-point-two percent, most of the variation—something like eighty-five percent—is local variation among people. This local emphasis is what makes the weapon we are offering you so effective."

Slide of a group of African pygmies.

"There are very large and detectable genetic differences between groups of pygmies living only a couple of miles apart."

Slide of people in Tyrolean hats, cows with bells, snow-covered mountains in the background.

"Likewise, the genetic makeup of people in Swiss Alpine villages are distinctly different from village to village."

Slide of a rawboned family in front of a house trailer.

"This was taken in the American state of West Virginia, where again, there are distinct differences between villages only a few miles apart. Despite the increased mobility of a small minority of the world's population, most people still marry and breed within very narrowly drawn geographic, ethnic, racial, linguistic, and religious groups." Around the table, each of the attendees nodded enthusiastically.

In rapid succession, Rycroft made his way through slides of a man wearing a yarmulke, a woman covered with shawl and chador, a group of children in front of a sign for the Sarajevo airport, a huddle of old women amid the ruins of the Grozny train station.

"While many people think of the Slatewiper as a racial weapon, racial differences account for only six percent of the zero-point-two percent of variation among humans."

The slide of the four races reappeared.

"Indeed, racial genetic differences are not distinct. They are simply more visible manifestations of the other more significant variations I mentioned before."

The screen went blank as an opaque slide chunked into position.

"It is not so important *why* there are genetic differences." Rycroft's voice filled the dark with an eerie resonance. "It is just important that there *are* differences."

He paused as a graph appeared on the screen.

"And even more important to you is the fact that we can quickly find and use those differences."

He used the laser pointer to draw attention to the first graph. "While zero-point-two percent is a relatively small fraction, when it is multiplied against the roughly three *billion* nucleotide bases in our DNA, the result is some two *million* nucleotide differences. This is significant in a system where a single nucleotide in a sensitive position can produce fatal genetic disorders such as Huntington's chorea, cystic fibrosis, and Tay-Sachs."

He walked over to a sideboard and poured a glass of the fresh-squeezed orange juice that was there for his consumption alone. "The trick, as you can imagine," Rycroft said after pausing to swallow, "is in locating those two million or so different nucleotides. We use a powerful new technique called representation difference analysis, a shortcut that compares the genetic makeup of two individuals, subtracts out all the identical segments, and leaves us with how they are different. We use a proprietary semiconductor which performs the entire process on a single biochip."

A slide showed a schematic diagram of the technique.

"Because of the variations among individuals even in the same remote villages, it's then necessary to take many different samples to determine which of the two million nucleotides are present in one group and *totally* lacking in the other. It is this difference that is the margin between life and death."

Another slide appeared, this one a flow diagram of a laboratory process.

"We have perfected the process of locating these significant differences and of creating the Slatewiper—a custom-tailored organic vector that is inactive *unless* it is in the presence of the specific nucleotide sequence that exists *only* in our target population. In other words, our custom bug recognizes a specific gene in the target population and is activated by this gene and only by this gene. It is harmless to all other populations.

"As director of research for GenIntron, I made three key discoveries that have made the Slatewiper possible. First of all, I identified the regions of each human chromosome most likely to contain the unique sequences that we need."

Rycroft took another sip of his orange juice and resumed pacing along the periphery of the projected light. "These unique genes are found among the vast stretches of DNA that do not actively function as genes."

A slide appeared showing the small portion of each gene that actually produced proteins, the larger sections that did not.

"These stretches encompass more than ninety percent of a person's DNA. Until my pioneering work at GenIntron, most of the scientific establishment denigrated these DNA areas as junk DNA."

Actually, he thought, this part of the work had been done by Lara Blackwood and that Islamic wog. But he was dead and she would be soon.

"These areas are known as 'introns,' " Rycroft pressed on. "Formerly skeptical scientists have now been forced to agree with us that many introns play key roles, including the structural shaping and regulation of active, protein-producing genes. They have enabled GenIntron to produce gene therapies for abnormalities linked with specific ethnic groups, and they are half of the key to the Slatewiper."

Rycroft warmed to his presentation, the high priest looking out on the rapt, upturned faces of his acolytes; their faintly illuminated gazes hung wordlessly on his every word. In the scant scattered light thrown off the projector's main beam, their bodies sank out of sight in the dark, giving their faces the appearance of disembodied heads, floating in blackness like white theatrical masks.

"The other half of the key lies also in the human introns." Rycroft's voice shaped itself to the pulpit he now commanded. In many ways, he was, right now, the most powerful man in the world. He intended to stay that way. "The second key discovery I made was a genetic fossil that lives in the genes of every human being." He coughed, cleared his throat. "It's long been known that some of our introns are the remains of ancient retroviruses that infected our predecessors millions of years ago—perhaps five, or more likely ten million years ago—and, as retroviruses can do, inserted themselves into their chromosomes.

"Retroviruses, you may know, are called 'retro' because they have a very crude structure, in the evolutionary sense, in that their genetic code is not DNA, but a single strand of RNA. However, once they are inside a host—such as ourselves—a special enzyme converts the RNA into viral DNA, which is then spliced into our DNA. Once it is spliced into our genes, it forces the cell to produce more and more viruses until the cell finally bursts and dies."

The room grew so quiet now that the projector fan sounded like the winds of a small gale in the enclosed space.

"Fortunately this very potent retrovirus mutated before it could wipe out the entire human species. The mutated retrovirus genome, however, still lives in our every cell, not as 'junk' DNA, but as a fossil message from the very beginning of our species, reaching out to us, spelling out the history of prehistory in eloquent phrases of the four nucleotide bases— guanine, cytosine, thymine, and adenine."

Lowering his voice for dramatic effect, Rycroft looked around, trying to make eye contact with each person as he spoke. "We're lucky that mutations are a daily occurrence in our genes, for my research has revealed the discovery of one particularly lethal retrovirus intron. This intron is the clear, living proof of a retrovirus that nearly wiped out the human species in a cataclysmic epidemic, a global disaster—the extinction of the entire species—stopped only by a chance mutation. This virus was a slatewiper, and in its nonmutated form, it was one hundred percent fatal."

An opaque slide fell into place again, casting the room into eerie darkness. People shifted uneasily in their seats. Rycroft's voice filled the darkness.

"Every human alive today carries the lethal Slatewiper gene in every cell," Rycroft continued. "All of us carry the Slatewiper with the same single-nucleotide-base mutation. We all have this mutation because those without the mutation died."

He paused. The room rustled as those present squirmed uncomfortably with the thought of primitive death lingering in their every cell.

"It is, in every sense of the word, an infection transported across the eons from the very dawn of our species, death carefully preserved by life." Pausing to let his words sink in.

"Once I discovered the mutated Slatewiper gene, the work was just beginning. It was no simple matter for me to develop a method for turning on the original gene so it would produce the original, invariably lethal Slatewiper effects. If it were so simple, the human race would not have survived this long.

"In GenIntron's maximum containment biosafety labs, I determined that the Slatewiper could be activated with a form of synthetic DNA that uses six bases rather than the usual four. Not only that, but I found that when the synthetic pathogen activated the Slatewiper, it became aggressively contagious from one member of the target population to the other, thus assuring maximum impact with minimum up-front resources. This almost undetectable vector carries both the factor that recognizes the target population and the trigger that launches Slatewiper on its deadly trajectory. This is a small, unstable, completely synthetic, mostly protein-based particle that resembles a very small yeast cell. It lives in the environment for a day, two at the most. It is so unstable that every lab technique—save the special one I developed—that could be used to detect the particle destroys it.

"Remember, the Slatewiper vector is not a virus. It is not infectious on its own. It simply triggers the resurrection of an antediluvian gene that does the actual killing.

"As I conclude my talk, I'd like to pay tribute to Dr. Shiro Ishii whose pioneering work on the aerosol dispersal of glanders and other disease vectors makes the physical aspect of our work possible. Dr. Ishii's aerosol dispersion research played a key role in the development of NorAm Pharmco's revolutionary inhaler for the respiratory delivery of medicine.

"We at GenIntron licensed this technology for the delivery of our gene therapies. This work was thoroughly tested and subtly improved upon by the army, and our CIA back in the 1950s and '60s with large-scale tests involving releases of harmless bacteria into—among many areas— the New York subway system and the prevailing northwesterly winds of the San Francisco Bay Area. A small extension of this pioneering work will make it possible for us to deliver the Slatewiper to Japan's Korean population when Operation Tsushima begins less than two weeks from today. Following that theater-level test, we"—looked at Woodruff—"will be in touch with you to discuss your own specific needs."

Rycroft then bowed. "That concludes my talk." He grimaced as the lights came back on. The room erupted with excited questions.

25

INSIDE TOKUTARO KURATA'S KYOTO ESTATE, IN THE ROOM ON THE TOP FLOOR THAT HIS UNCLE HAD ASSIGNED TO HIM, AKIRA SUGAWARA SAT CROSS-LEGGED IN THE DARK ON THE TATAMI MATS AND LISTENED TO THE RAIN POUNDING THE TREES OUTSIDE.

He tried to think of anything but Sheila Gaillard, Horst Von Neuman, and the contract killers they had hired to kill Lara Blackwood. The attack, she had reported, had been a success. Blackwood had fled on her boat, but even such a large personal craft would certainly be destroyed by the approaching hurricane.

He shook his head like a horse shedding flies, as if the motion would somehow banish the sinking feeling he had that her death, indeed all the deaths before her, were very wrong. The effort made him feel even worse. Such thoughts were not honorable; they dishonored his duty to his uncle.

But how had he gotten into this position? It often seemed to him that it had always just been this way, but he knew that things had happened little by little, drawing him subtly into Kurata's web, performing first this job and then that one. Each act seemed innocent in itself, wrapped as they were in duty, family loyalty, cultural imperative. But now, he thought, when taken as a whole, the stream of events had swept him inexorably along, carrying him at some point from innocence to evil.

Step by step, Kurata had pulled him in deeper and deeper, each act blacker than the one before, more incriminating. Threats, *giri*, the material rewards lavished on his parents for his good performance—all bound Sugawara to the path blazed by his uncle. He had tried to steel himself against the meaning of what he was doing. For a while, the usual bureaucratic tricks worked: these weren't people, they were "units" or "parasites" or "lives not worth living," a "disease that needed eradicating."

But when their faces escaped the tyranny of numbers and euphemisms— such as they had the day he tearfully viewed the broadcast of the death throes of entire families on the hospital lawn in Tokyo—pain cut into him and slashed at the commitments that bound him so tightly to Kurata and his cause.

Sugawara thought of the war crimes and the guilt and knew certainly that he was now guilty of many things. Slowly, the sounds of polished wood sliding upon wood raised themselves above the radio chatter and the steady tattoo of heavy rain upon the roof. He knew this sound well; the shoji screen of his room was being opened. His heart jumped. There had been no knock. This must be Kurata.

"Good evening, Kurata-*sama*," Sugawara said as he opened his eyes. Dim illumination from the security lights outside filtered into the room and hazily outlined a man stepping into the room. Sugawara's heart raced, propelled by guilt and fear. It was as if the old man could read his thoughts and had come to prod him back on the right path.

"Good evening to you, Nephew," Kurata replied as he slid the screen shut. He walked toward Sugawara. In the dim light, it was possible to make out a package in his hand.

"Events progress well, I hear," Kurata said as he knelt next to the table and then sat down.

"Yes, Honored Uncle," Sugawara replied. "It will be over soon." He did his best to hide the disappointment in his voice.

For several minutes, the two men listened to the radio's operational chatter without speaking. Assets would soon be converging on the marina.

"You have served me well," Kurata said finally. "You have earned my trust."

"I am only your humble servant, my lord," Sugawara replied.

Kurata nodded in the dark, accepting his due. "Yes. You have done well. But you cannot do better unless you know more, more of our ultimate goal, more of the strategy to reach that goal."

Sugawara wanted to scream, "No! No, do not tell me! Knowing only drags me deeper, gives me another trust to betray! Burdens me further with *giri*."

Instead of speaking his mind, Sugawara did as expected and said, "I am honored by your trust, Kurata-*sama*."

"Yes," Kurata said. "Then listen well." He paused, then asked, "You are familiar with *hakko ichiu?*"

"The eight corners of the world under one roof, the roof of Yamato," Sugawara said immediately.

"Very good," Kurata said. "For that is our goal."

Struggling to still the seething anger, fear, frustration, and sense of impending doom that filled his heart, Sugawara replied, "With a thousand apologies for my impertinence, my lord, but was that not the goal of the national government before the Pacific War?"

"Of course," Kurata said. "An honorable goal, with regrettably bad execution."

Replying as he thought his uncle would expect, Sugawara asked, "Please enlighten me, my lord."

"The generals did not succeed in bringing about *hakko ichiu* because they acted too soon. They also strayed from their roots and fell into the Western trap of open confrontation."

Catching his breath, Sugawara was shocked. Like the rest of Japan, he had never before heard Kurata utter anything but praise for the wartime military and government. It was, after all, the great Kurata-*sama* who had led the national enshrinement of Tojo and the other generals into the shrine at Yasukuni, led the charge against politicians who dared suggest Japan owed the world any apologies for its actions in the Pacific War.

"Yes, I hear your concern," Kurata continued. "These were great men with honorable intentions. But, like many of our great men of that time, they allowed their thinking to be clouded by Western thoughts, confused by Western principles, straitjacketed by Western strategies. They first should have listened to the great Shumei Okawa."

Sugawara nodded his familiarity with Dr. Okawa, a hero to contemporary Japanese conservatives. While holding no formal position, his concepts had guided the neonationalists during the 1930s. He had played a key role in the assassination of two Japanese prime ministers and in the invasion of Manchuria. Indicted by the Allies as a Class-A war criminal along with Tojo, he was not executed but was released in 1948, a free man.

"Okawa urged Tojo and the rest to wait," Kurata continued. "To wait for the perfect time. But they were seduced by their weapons and itched to use them. They forgot the first rule of the samurai that the most skillful sword never leaves its sheath."

"Un wa yusha o tasuku?" Sugawara asked, citing an ancient proverb that "fate aids the courageous."

"Hai," Kurata replied. "Fate aids the courageous, but fate has no patience with the foolhardy. *No aru taka wa tsume o kakusu.* The Western philosophy of open confrontation is not our way. It violates our principle that we should act without appearing to act until victory is *assured*. A clever hawk hides its claws."

Like all Japanese children, Sugawara had been brought up to abhor direct confrontation. Even a straightforward "yes" or "no," second nature to Westerners, was unacceptable. It could put oneself on record too soon, thus causing a loss of face should it be necessary to change the opinion.

Direct confrontations were to be avoided because they made it inevitable from the outset that there would be an obvious and public winner and a loser. Losing meant losing face, and losing face was far worse in the long run than winning or losing the discussion that prompted the confrontation initially.

A humiliated man was a dangerous man who would, eventually, seek revenge. Therefore, if one was prepared to openly confront another and to win the exchange, one needed to be prepared to kill the loser. It was the only way peace could be had in the long run.

"That is why the brave but misguided men of the Pacific War did not achieve *hakko ichiu*. They fought the white man using the white man's rules, and they lost. We are winning, now, because we have returned to the wisdom of our ancestors."

The radio squawked at them from the table.

"And it is that wisdom and strategy I wish you to make part of your very being, my nephew, for it is you who will inherit the fruits of our work."

Closing his eyes, Sugawara bowed deeply. "I am most honored by your trust and awed by the responsibility you are investing in me." *I don't* want *it*, Sugawara thought silently. Tell me no more.

"Good," Kurata said. "Remember that the seeds of our new victory lie in the gutlessness of the Americans and their allies. Even though their technology brought about the end of the conflict, they had no *dokyo*—no stomach, no nerve—for victory. Instead of playing the proper role of victor, the United States government saw an opportunity to—as they would say—cut deals. They have no principles. That allowed us to manipulate them, allowed us to take action against them without seeming to take action.

"They gave all our scientists freedom from prosecution in exchange for a small portion of their research. Their weak war crimes trial indicted *no* members of the ultrapatriotic societies, no chiefs of the Kempeitai secret police, no members of the *zaibatsu*—Mitsubishi, Mitsui, Yasuda, Kawasaki, Sumitomo—despite the fact that they all participated extensively in what the Americans call atrocities."

"Why, Honored Uncle, were these citizens not prosecuted?"

"The Americans were greedy and wanted to use these men for profit. Making money quickly is more important to them than principles," Kurata said. "Instead of conducting themselves properly as victors, they tried to, as they would say, make a quick buck. They wanted money and material things immediately. They did not look into the future to see that business, finance, and technology were the battlegrounds on which future wars would be fought, won, and lost. Americans sell their technology to us, then buy it back in products at ten times the price; they sell it to us once and buy it back a hundred million times. This is why they will always lose."

A sudden bolt of lightning flared into the room and dazzled both men. In that brief instant, Sugawara saw Kurata's face, captured as if by a photographer's flash; the look of near-trancelike fanaticism in his uncle's eyes frightened him. But even more, Kurata's gaze had a hypnotic, paralyzing quality that made Sugawara feel as if he were bound to the older man, pulled even closer by unseen bonds. Thunder clapped in the darkness; Sugawara twitched, tried to erase the flash image of his uncle from his thoughts.

"They are degenerate people," Kurata continued calmly, as if the lightning and thunder had not happened at all. "They are all made that way by a disintegrating racial backbone and because they are controlled by the international Jewish conspiracy, the Elders of Zion.

"We maintain our principles because we have *tan'itsu minzoku shakai*— a monoracial culture, not a polluted, mongrelized race as in America. Prime Minister Nakasone was correct when he told the world that the United States was on the decline because the niggers and Mexicans had polluted the race and lowered the level of intelligence.

"Such people are easily used, bought, and manipulated," Kurata said with an increasingly evangelical fervor. "They will serve us as long as we allow their corporations to make a modest profit, as long as we sell them televisions and cars. Their whore-politicians will allow this as long as they continue to accept our money. As long as we underwrite their debt and foolish spending, they can do nothing about it.

"Understand that the Jew-controlled banks and corporations saw us as the ones to be manipulated," Kurata resumed. "They, in turn, misunderstood us as usual, and considered our silence and cooperation as acquiescence.

"Remember, we do what we do because it is right. It is honorable. It is our destiny. The Americans and the other mongrelized nations do what they do for greed."

Kurata paused for a multiple lightning flash that strobed into the room. Great rolling booms followed.

When the thunder had receded, Kurata picked up his narrative.

"Since the Pacific War, we have acted without seeming to act," Kurata said proudly. "We won without seeming to win. We are now at the top, and the Americans don't seem to realize it."

"Begging your indulgence, Uncle," Sugawara said. "My studies indicate the Americans are not stupid people. How could they fail to notice this?"

In the dim light, Sugawara saw his uncle nod. "The white people are not so dumb," he began, "but they are arrogant and their arrogance blinds them so that they see the world as they wish it to be rather than as it truly is. Just consider: *never* in all the years since the end of the Pacific War has the Japanese government *ever* referred to the United States as an ally."

"*Ah so*," Sugawara said. "I remember now, even from my history books in school. During the war, Nazi Germany was our *domei koku*, but the United States is referred to as *joyaku*, a relationship."

"You have learned your lessons well, my nephew," Kurata said. "As you know, *joyaku* defines an inferior position. Yet, in more than half a century, the Americans have never noticed that not one bulletin, not one treaty, not one communiqué or any other document has ever referred to them as our ally. That is blind. That is stupid."

He stopped as urgent chimes from the radio sounded. "Where the hell is everybody?" demanded a voice that both men recognized as Gaillard's. The "assets" answered one by one. The stories were similar: the storm had flooded streets for one; a second was jammed behind a rain-induced traffic accident; the third was just blocks away, making a detour around a tree that had brought power lines down across Independence Avenue.

Kurata smiled indulgently. "They are such excitable children." He paused and let the sounds of the wind and rain fill their ears.

There was a rustle of cloth as Kurata handed a book to Sugawara.

"This is a book you should take to heart," Kurata said. "Learn it."

"Thank you a million times," Sugawara said, bowing deeply.

"The book is actually a collection," Kurata explained. "The three works inside are Kamakage's work called *The Jewish Plot to Control the World*, Yajima's scholarly piece, *The Expert Way of Reading the Protocols of the Elders of Zion*, and Satio's piece, *The Secret of Jewish Power That Moves the World*."

"*Hai*," Sugawara acknowledged. "I have heard of them all. They have sold millions of copies in the homeland."

"You must use these as your textbooks," Kurata instructed him. "After all, only we—the people of Yamato—stand between the Jews and their domination of the world. Always remember: Yajima summarized the situation best when he wrote that 'to create confusion and then exploit it for their own profit is the standard operating procedure of international Jew capital.'

"The Jews are sneaky," Kurata said. "Just because they are losing to our superiority doesn't mean they have been beaten. Just look at our country's recession and the economic problems of the mid-1990s which resulted from Jew manipulation of the financial markets.

"Most importantly, you must remember to avoid direct, overt confrontation. For as long as the Americans and their allies do not realize that they have been defeated in the current economic war, we will be able to enjoy all of the benefits from a conquered nation without having first to destroy its assets and rebuild it.

"All of this makes Operation Tsushima even more important," Kurata continued. "Sometimes it is necessary to physically remove people. But we do not wish to destroy their assets to do so. That is wasteful and counterproductive. Operation Tsushima will allow us to remove the offending pests from the land without them, or the weak sisters of the world, realizing there has been any deliberate act. Operation Tsushima will give us the final way to act without seeming to act."

Sugawara felt another small piece of himself die.

26

A VICIOUS TAILWIND SHOVED AT THE *TAGCAT TOO* WITH MEAN GUSTS OF RAIN AS THE POTOMAC RIVER GAVE WAY TO THE CHESAPEAKE BAY AND NIGHT YIELDED TO A BATTLESHIP GRAY MORNING WITHOUT DAWN. Lara Blackwood studied the radar and watched the banks of the river recede on both sides. Signal clutter danced about the radar screen like snow. Despite the visual static, she easily spotted the channel buoys equipped with radar reflectors to make them stand out under just these conditions. She saw nothing else. No shipping. No boats.

But then, she knew, she was never home free since the radar could not pick up storm debris floating in the water. Lara stifled a yawn as she turned the helm slowly to the south and engaged the helm's autopilot. She grabbed an insulated plastic mug from its double-gimbaled holder, drained the last sips of cold coffee from it, then stood up.

Using the handrails to steady herself against the boat's heaving and lurching, she made her way to the galley and prepared another pot of coffee. Like the coffee mug holders, the stainless-steel coffeemaker was double-gimbaled, allowing it to remain more or less upright even as the boat pitched and rolled. With the sole exception of the horrific thirty-six hours that preceded the sinking of the *Tagcat* off the Cape of Good Hope she had almost always managed to use gallons of strong black coffee and short, frequent periods of sleep to avoid tapping into the supply of amphetamines she carried for extreme emergencies.

As the new pot of coffee brewed, she went over her plan again in her head. Until she sorted out what was going on, Lara decided that she was safer if the people who wanted to kill her thought she was dead. She made her way forward now, collecting things to help make that seem likely.

At the foot of the companionway stairs, she piled clothes, ice chests, life preservers. She made her way to the forward head and kicked the teak and mahogany door off the hinges. She dragged that back and stacked it on the pile on the floor by the companionway stairs along with the toilet seat and the foam rubber pillows from the forward cabin.

Then she pulled her storm gear from the foul-weather gear locker and stepped into the bib pants, fastening the suspenders securely. She then stepped into her boots and pulled the Velcro fasteners of the pants tight at the ankles. Next she got into the matching Gore-Tex jacket, put on a baseball cap, and drew the jacket's hood over that. She shrugged into the safety harness, fastened the D-rings securely, and coiled the line temporarily around her waist. Finally, Lara pulled on a pair of Gore-Tex gloves with rubber grip-dots on the palms and fingers and opened the hatch.

Rain and wind poured in as she swiftly shoved the pile of items on the floor through the hatch opening and into the storm-tossed cockpit. She started up the steps, then paused as she pulled a large orange plastic cylinder from its bulkhead mounts and carried it out with her into the hurricane. She unwound her lifeline's six-foot-long nylon strap from about her waist and snapped the sturdy stainless-steel shackle on to one of dozens of mounts stationed all over the *Tagcat Too*.

She stood there for a short moment to get her bearings, watching as the wind sheared off the white roiling tops of the waves and hurled them at her head. Then she began throwing everything into the maelstrom: head door, toilet seat, pillows. Everything. All she had to do was lift it high enough and the wind simply took it into the gloom of dawn.

Next, she pulled herself out of the cockpit and on deck, hooking and unhooking the lifeline cable as she made her way to the white cylinder with the rounded ends. Every step was calculated, every handhold double-tested as she wrestled with a malignant wind that wanted to rip her off the deck and toss her into the unforgiving sea. Finally, she reached the life raft canister, quickly unlatched the fasteners, and rolled it off the deck and into the sea.

"They won't believe I'd do such a stupid thing," Lara said to herself as she watched the self-inflating life raft bob away and vanish in the maw of the storm. It was an extreme act, she knew, but one that she knew was required to provide the verisimilitude necessary if she was to have any chance of convincing the hounds that further searching would be futile.

She knew it could also be fatal if anything happened. All she had now was the inflatable dinghy that hung from its stern davits. It was certainly not storm worthy and in heavy weather would be little better than an oversized rubber ducky.

Back in the cockpit, she picked up the bright orange cylinder and extended the antenna. It was an EPIRB—emergency position indicator radio beacon—that would transmit an internationally recognized distress signal that would alert rescue authorities. Not that they could do anything for the time being, she thought as she pressed the waterproof switch to turn it on and tossed it into the ocean.

As she watched the EPIRB disappear into the storm, she felt her heart shift like plates along a fault line. *We measure time in our lives,* she thought, *from the major shifts that set us careening off in new directions: Before Christ, Anno Domini, since the divorce, after mother died, before the wedding, after the birth.* Calendars ran commerce and airline schedules, but for each person, the memories of personal temblors set and reset time.

There had been life before her father had died, then after. There had been life before GenIntron, then the reluctant after. And now this. What would the after be like? Lara shook her head slowly and made her way back to the hatch and successfully down below in search of fresh coffee and of all the marbles she had to have lost in order to be out sailing in a hurricane.

It was hard to tell if the new *onsen*—hot springs baths—at Fuefuki were indoors or out. Sitting on a submerged rock at the rim of a lushly veg- etated tropical pool carved out of black volcanic rocks, Edward Rycroft let the hot waters of the alum-enriched *onsen* hot-massage the knotted muscles at the small of his back as he idly pondered this question. Things were going quite well, he thought as he let the hot water soothe him. That stuck-up bitch Blackwood was most certainly dead. Four days in a hurricane was certainly more than even the super woman herself could handle. And then there was the money that Woodruff's little scheme was about to bring in. An amused smile gave his face an almost kind, harmless look.

Not surprisingly, their first big-money customers came from the Middle East. The Saudi businessman fronting the bill for the drooling, wide-eyed fanatics who thought their twisted brand of Islam was the only way were no surprise. No surprise at all. There had been so many of those bloody wogs knocking at the door.

Rycroft's smile deepened as he recalled the other meeting. The one with the other bearded men in black. The ones from Jerusalem with money from the ultra-Orthodox extremists who wanted to make sure the modern-day Arabs and Palestinians went the same way as their biblical descendants when the conquering tribes of Israel ethnically cleansed the promised land. The irony warmed him, but not nearly as much as the justice for which he had waited a lifetime. Justice delayed was bitter, but would soon be sweet.

He squinted now through the limbs of a camphor tree at clouds flexing across the sky and tried to determine if the ceiling panels were open, or whether the sky and clouds were simply more clever images from the high-resolution Ikeda-Grunwald projection system custom-built for Kurata. Nothing was too good for his employees.

That he couldn't tell the difference bothered him. Annoyance scrabbled about just behind his sternum, crablike and prickly. Rycroft tried to ignore the uneasiness, glancing around, looking for distraction. What he saw made the feeling worse: perfect pools of steaming water set here and there under a canopy of tropical hardwood trees, and all around, perfect rain forest vegetation right down to moss in the rock crevices. Hundreds of millions of yen had been spent re-creating an indoor imitation of a genuine *rotenboro*. Only Kurata's wealth could have produced an imitation of life that was so perfect it was impossible to tell whether it was a real jungle or just an architect's elaborate deception that preyed on the bather's willingness to be deluded into the appreciation of beauty.

Did it really matter anyway? If it fooled the experts, if it smelled and tasted as good, then did anything else really matter? Rycroft mused about this, looking around at the naked Japanese men lounging in the big pool just beyond a brake of palm trees. Some chatted in communal groups—*hadaka no tsukiai*, "companions in nudity"—others lounged in ones and twos. Men ambled along the jungle paths smoothed among the boulders, making their way from the personal hygiene areas to either the large pool or to one of the many smaller, Jacuzzi-sized areas like the one in which Rycroft sat.

The men wore *yufondoshi*—hot water loincloths—as they walked to and fro. Most also carried a *furoshiki*, a small, handkerchieflike piece of cloth in which personal articles are kept. As was the custom among Daiwa Ichiban employees, each of their *furoshiki* were embroidered with their own *hanko*, personal seals, registered with the authorities, which the Japanese used for signing documents and letters instead of a personal signature.

Rycroft looked over at the two *furoshiki* bundles resting on the pool edge near his head. One was a plain *furoshiki*, the other was sewn with his *hanko*. He had brought both. The embroidered one contained his wallet, keys, and watch. The plain one contained a razor-sharp knife and a packet of papers.

Rycroft smiled as he gazed on the *hanko* and thought of the commotion he had caused when he first requested his own. A *gaijin*! Most Japanese bath houses bar entrance to Westerners and their clumsy manners and ignorance of customs and hygiene. Rycroft had proven himself an astute, devout follower of Japanese customs, mastering the speech like a native, and an exception had been made. Kurata made sure that exceptions could be made.

Exuberant noises came from the large pool as a group of young *sararimen* splashed in their corner. Rycroft looked over at them and made a wide, slow inspection sweep of the room, his eyes resting more often on the single bather here and there. The solitaires seemed to be meditating, or perhaps simply praying that the mineral-enriched waters would cure their rheumatism or nettle rashes, as the signs claimed in the outer rooms where bathers vigorously scrubbed every square centimeter of their bodies before entering the communal baths.

What patent nonsense.

Certainly water was relaxing and perhaps the heat could stimulate circulation to an extent. It was possible the relaxation might have some positive psychosomatic effects, but cure? Rycroft looked about and fought successfully to keep a sneer of disgust from distorting his face.

These were apes. Evil, hairless, yellow simians, whose feet were mired in the muck of voodoo, superstition, and irrationality, even as their automatonlike minds continually pushed the outer limits of technology.

He hated them. Damn these yellow pests!

Underwater, Rycroft's fingers made fists, relaxed, then balled up again. They thought he had learned their customs and language because he *liked* them, wanted to be a sort of honorary Japanese.

Fools! Blind arrogance.

Rycroft remembered being four years old when the Japanese troops burst into their home in Singapore, where his father was a minor British banking official. The house on the hillside offered no escape route save down the road up which the Japanese troop truck came.

Jammed into a large wicker trunk used as an end table for a lamp, Rycroft and his sister, older by a year, quivered as the platoon of soldiers first beat their father into semiconsciousness, then took turns gang-raping their mother, sometimes three at a time. Rycroft remembered thinking even then how they jabbered like the monkeys that lived in the forest in the hills above.

Finally, when they had all ejaculated somewhere, one pulled a revolver and shot his mother in the face. He remembered how horrible it was to see her body jerk as the slug slammed into her. But that didn't kill her and neither did the next two shots. Finally, one of them, laughing, pulled off his belt and strangled her with it.

Either he or his sister must have made a noise, because instants later the soldiers were opening the lid of the large wicker trunk.

Rycroft would always remember the way his father, naked, slippery with his own blood, wrenched away from the soldiers and tried to come to the aid of his children. Rycroft would never forget the swift, well-practiced way the Japanese officer in charge pulled a dagger from his waist and, in one clean lunge, cut open his father's belly from breastbone to scrotum. There would never be a horror like seeing the pink and gray avalanche of his father's entrails spilling from the wound onto the floor.

An expression of horror, confusion, apology played over the elder Rycroft's face as his eyes fixed those of his son. Then the head jerked. The eyes went wide, then closed. As hard as he tried, Rycroft could never remember the sound of the rifle shot.

Moved by some primal instinct, the young Rycroft tried to protect his older—and smaller—sister. He would always remember the laughter as they pulled him off his sister and separated them.

As the soldiers carried his sister away, they kept repeating a phrase over and over. He never saw her again.

The Japanese officer took Rycroft as a pet, a slave, a novelty. They taught him to read and speak Japanese so he could function as a servant, "as befitted his status as one of the inferior races."

As he became fluent in Japanese, he learned the meaning of the phrase the soldiers had repeated as they carried his sister away: "Fresh meat for my skewer."

All of this played through Rycroft's head as he sat in the swirling *onsen* and tried to calm himself for the act to follow. Swallowing against the anger, he gradually flushed the memories from his mind. Just in time.

"Rycroft-*san*."

A voice came from behind. Rycroft craned his head and saw his production manager, Kenji Yamamoto, walking toward him, *yufondoshi* about his waist, wooden clogs on his feet, *furoshiki* dangling from one hand. Yamamoto bowed; Rycroft bowed, but slightly less as befitted his station as Yamamoto's boss.

Rycroft sat back down as Yamamoto shed the loincloth and slid into the hot water.

"Ahhh! The instant you enter is always the most intense, is it not?"

"Undoubtedly." Rycroft waited for Yamamoto to settle himself. "I do not like the way you are casting doubts on me and my methods, Kenji."

"*Hai*," Yamamoto said noncommittally.

"I will not allow this to continue."

"It pains me to confront the situation in this manner," Yamamoto said as he cupped pool water in both hands and poured it over his head. "But I believe there is a flaw in the method. Indeed, I have been conducting some additional laboratory analysis, which, even though still incomplete, indicates that this batch of the Slatewiper might be less selective, be activated by more than just the Korean genetic sequences."

"You've disobeyed my orders on this." Rycroft struggled to keep his voice calm and low. "I have told you there is no such problem, and in your own stupidity, you have pressed ahead. These are grounds for your immediate dismissal, you know."

"*Hai*, Rycroft-*san*. This I know. It is the risk I take because I believe the current process endangers both the targeted population as well as the entire Japanese race."

"You're a stupid creature, Kenji," Rycroft snapped. "This was not your decision to make."

"Nor yours any longer, I am afraid," Yamamoto countered. "Respectfully, I think that the decision rests in the honored hands of Kurata-*sama*."

"Perhaps," Rycroft said. He gave Yamamoto a chilling smile, and then turned to grasp the plain *furoshiki* that sat next to his own. He handed the bundle to Yamamoto, who took it reluctantly and gave Rycroft a questioning look.

"Go ahead, you stinking Jap bastard, open it up. Take a good look at your past and future."

Yamamoto's face showed no evidence of having heard the racial slur. He set the bundle on a dry spot at the edge of the pool and deftly untied it. He sucked in a breath through pursed lips as he saw the dagger. His hands, however, went first to the envelope, which he opened.

Rycroft watched Yamamoto's face pale, his usually straight carriage sag, as he read first one document, then the next. His hands began to shake.

Finally, Yamamoto turned to him and said, "What does this mean?"

"It means I have irrefutable proof that your great-grandfather was Korean, Kenji. You have the copies, I have the proof." Rycroft felt the warm intoxication of victory rush from his belly to his head like a hot, visceral wave.

"What it really means is I can ruin you and your family and your wife's family. A few words and your son will be shamed out of Tokyo University and the best husband your daughters will ever get is some slaughterhouse *burakumin* or maybe the guy who gets to dislodge shit clogs in the sewers."

Rycroft paused. In a lower voice he said, "All that can be different if you do the right thing."

Defeated, Yamamoto bent his head; he opened his mouth as if to speak and then closed it. Rycroft pulled himself out of the pool as Yamamoto looked over at the knife.

As Rycroft wrapped his *yufondoshi* around his waist, slipped his feet into his wooden clogs, and picked up his own *furoshiki*, he saw Yamamoto look up at him, then reach over and slip the knife from its scabbard.

Rycroft calmly walked away. As he neared the washing area, he turned and saw the pool water run red as Yamamoto's face slipped beneath the surface.

Out of sight now, Rycroft heard a scream. He smiled. Yamamoto's dossier would be on Kurata's desk in the morning.

27

FEET WIDE AND BRACED AGAINST THE CONSTANT ROLLING, PITCHING, AND YAW-
ING, LARA BLACKWOOD STOOD IN THE COCKPIT BEHIND THE *TAGCAT TOO*'S
WHEEL, FACING AFT. She tinkered with a short loomlike rack of color-coded
lines. Collected here for safety and convenience was every control line
necessary to properly sail the boat without having to leave the relative
safety of the cockpit and without the necessity of using the electrical
controls in the event of power failure.

She carefully surveyed what little sail she had out, just little hand-
kerchiefs for the jib and the mainsail, nothing at all for the mizzen mast
at the stern. But it was sufficient; in wind such as this—gusting to 70
miles per hour here, 150 miles from the eye.

Lara fought the bilious dread in her gut as the *Tagcat Too* slid up the
crests of mammoth waves and down into troughs that reminded her of
the Southern Ocean that had once defeated her. At the crests of the waves,
she could see great white streaks of foam whipped up by the storm and
straggling along in the general direction of the wind. In the troughs, she
looked up and watched as the violent wind decapitated each wave crest
and hurled the resulting foam into the air where it condensed and added
to the falling rain.

She squinted up at the sails, making fine adjustments to the wheel
and the sheets as she did. What little sail was flying needed to be pre-

cisely balanced. The jib was close-hauled, back-winded, and bellied across the foredeck; the main was also close-hauled on a port tack; the wheel was hard to starboard. As she adjusted the sails and wheel, the boat eased its athletic lunging and lurching and settled itself into a less violent rhythm.

The maneuver was known as heaving-to. It provided stability and allowed the boat to move with the waves and weather. With sails and rudder properly set, the craft could drift almost indefinitely without further attention. Of course, it also meant she was making little headway. But more important now, the maneuver allowed a relative respite for some rest.

Rest! Dear God! How she needed rest.

After one last adjustment to the main sheet, Lara made her way forward to the companionway where she unhooked her lifeline, opened the hatch, and climbed down where the warmth seemed tropical in the absence of the driving rain; silence from the howling wind thudded in her ears with every beat of her heart as she secured the watertight companionway hatch in case a wave broke across the cockpit.

Lara stood for a moment at the foot of the companionway steps and closed her eyes against the fatigue. After a moment, she was aware of a welcome aroma. Coffee. Shedding her wet outer gear on the grate that drained into the bilge, she made her way toward the galley and poured a fresh cup to chase the chill the weather had left inside her.

She took the cup and sat down at the navigation station and called up the latest weather maps. The U.S. Eastern coastline edged the left side of the screen, the British Isles and Europe on the right. A broad mass of gray clouds covered most of the Atlantic Ocean in between.

As she had hoped, she had managed to position the *Tagcat Too* along the edge of the hurricane so that it would carry her along without smashing her to bits. The eye, she saw from the map, was still about 150 miles mostly south and a little west of her position. According to the GPS, her latitude and longitude put her better than halfway to England. Or, she thought hopefully, maybe the Netherlands depending on the storm track. At an average of twenty knots—about twenty-two regular miles per hour—for a little over three days, she and the *Tagcat Too* had covered 1,650 miles, not all of it straight or she'd be even closer to Europe.

A weather alert window popped up with a warning from meteorologists that this hurricane could be another astounding one like the Great Gale of 1703 which made it all the way from the Colonies in November of that year and ripped the roof right off the queen's bedroom in London, wiped out the port of Bristol and half the British navy.

Lara shivered to think she was surfing the edge of history in the making, moving along with the weather system as it headed east-northeast and carrying the *Tagcat Too* with it. She also knew that the clouds would give her cover from anyone searching for her, and the storm would prevent any doubters of her faked sinking from launching a search. Ordinary satellites couldn't see her, and the high seas would confuse radar so badly that even the military satellites that could see through the clouds would have a hard time separating her from the wave clutter.

The boat felt stable; the electronics said they were on course. Lara set the radar, depth, and change-of-course alarms that would awaken her in case of danger and then went to the dining salon and lay down on the bench and tried to think of anything she had missed.

The *Tagcat Too* rode the steep waves as well as any hove-to boat ever had. The thought made her happy, satisfied. She had designed the boat, and it was performing now better than she had a right to expect. Leaving the helm in the care of the autopilot was not her first choice. But the point had come where the danger of leaving the helm unattended was far less than the threat of a fatigued helmsman apt to make serious errors or nod off when the electronics were not engaged.

Slowly, she reclined and tried to will her muscles into relaxing; her shoulders were like double-knotted steel cable; her knees throbbed with the stabbing pain that comes from standing on them for days.

As her mind raced toward its first sleep since the current madness began, scenes flashed through her thoughts like bright, full-color slides in a perfectly darkened screening room.

Flash! The phone call from Tokyo; curiosity.

Flash! Peter Durant; confusion.

Flash! Bizarre tabloid images of Denis Yaro and Jim Condon, dead in Tokyo; anger.

Flash! The Blue Room, Kurata; betrayal.

Flash! The president and his ridiculous tam-o'-shanter; disgust.

Flash! Newspaper, Ismail dead; sorrow.

Flash! Durant's head exploding, raw fear.

Flash! Flight; fear, exhilaration.

The last thing that went through her mind before the screen went blank was her amazement that she was still afloat, alive.

Akira Sugawara sat at a pea green Formica table in Laboratory 73's employee lounge and nursed a cup of vending-machine tea. Glancing frequently at his watch, he stared at the CNN news on the television in the corner and tried to hide the desolation that emptied his insides and made him feel like an empty locust husk left on the trunk of a pine tree, the back split where real life had climbed out and flown away.

An attractive Caucasian woman read the news; in the background, a wall of television monitors blinked and changed in no particular synch with her words. An icon appeared over her left shoulder, a drawing of a sailboat in the final moments of sinking beneath stormy waves.

"The search for possible survivors in the hurricane sinking of a pleasure yacht in the Chesapeake Bay is called off. CNN correspondent James Nations reports from the decks of the coast guard cutter *John Brady*."

The picture cut to the rolling decks of a ship. Pewter clouds scudded by low to the water; mist fogged the camera lens. In the background, a helicopter lifted off. The *thwack-twang* of the copter blades drowned out the reporter's initial words. ". . . eye is now some two hundred miles northeast and still packing hurricane-strength winds. It is a very large storm that you can see is still spinning off unsettled weather. Coast Guard officials say they have suspended the search and rescue efforts to locate the yacht *Tagcat Too*. I have with me Captain Mary Evelyn Arnold, who is in command of this coast guard cutter. She says they have located debris that indicates the yacht has, indeed, sunk, that there is no chance of there being survivors."

Sugawara took a sip of the tea, made a face, and watched as the television image panned back to show the reporter and the cutter's captain, both clad in fluorescent orange foul-weather gear. Next to them was a pile of debris.

"What leads you to conclude that further searches would be futile?" the CNN reporter asked.

The captain blinked into the camera lights, clearly more comfortable in the face of a raging hurricane than with the television camera. "Well," she said, bending over to retrieve an orange cylinder the size of a fire extinguisher. "This is the craft's EPIRB—that's Emergency Position Indicator Radio Beacon—which is automatically deployed only in the event the crew is forced to abandon ship or in an emergency when the conventional radio fails."

"What other evidence convinced you further search was fruitless?"

The camera panned, following the captain's gaze, over to a large pile of crumpled fabric and rubber.

"This is the yacht's life raft," she explained. "In addition—" she pointed with her hand—"we have a large collection of other items clearly marked—as is the life raft—with the vessel name *Tagcat Too*—life jackets, an ice chest, clothing."

"What can you tell us about the bodies found at the marina where the boat was home berthed?"

"Nothing," the captain replied tersely. "That's a matter for the police there."

"Aren't they relying upon your judgment in deciding whether to maintain their fugitive hunt?"

"You'll have to ask them that," she replied. "Murder's not my cup of tea."

"Do you believe that this could be a clever ruse?" the reporter persisted. "I understand Lara Blackwood is an accomplished sailor."

Arnold nodded. "She is one of the world's best and my understanding is that with that sort of skill and a lot of luck her boat is capable of surviving the current weather."

Draining the last of the bitter dregs from his cup, Sugawara watched as the television panned to the reporter, zoomed to a close-up. "And for more on that, we take you to CNN's Judy Paige, live at the marina in Washington."

"Thank you, Jerry," said a woman dressed in a yellow slicker with boats in the background. "Police are playing this one very close to their chests and continue to say only that the suspect in this case, biotechnology entrepreneur and White House advisor Lara Blackwood, may have been involved in some scheme to sell information that could be used to manufacture deadly bioweapons. They will not officially say anything else, but privately we understand that law enforcement is receiving satellite imagery from the National Reconnaissance Office and from the military to try and ascertain whether or not the vessel in question has actually sunk. But our sources tell us that the police launches and helicopters and the fixed-wing airplanes are now idle, mostly confined to their bases due to the continuing bad weather. Back to you in Atlanta."

Like a man slogging through knee-deep mud, Sugawara got up from the table. The disinformation campaign to brand Lara Blackwood as a criminal had begun and would result in her death even if she survived the storm. His part in her destruction gnawed at his very soul.

Looking at his watch, he made his way from the employees' lounge. He and his uncle were to teleconference with Gaillard in just minutes. He began to understand what he had to do to rescue his own soul.

"I think she's still alive," Sheila Gaillard said, sitting alone in a hotel room with a view across Lafayette Park to the White House. On the desk in front of her sat a laptop computer equipped with a microphone and small camera. The secure teleconferencing software encrypted her words and image before any data reached the hotel's broadband connection and decrypted the streams of images and words from Japan: from Kurata at his Kyoto estate and Sugawara at the lab. Images jerked and hesitated with the ebb and flow of global Internet usage. Often annoying, Gaillard thought, but always secure.

"The coast guard and other government sources said they thought she was dead," Sugawara said. "Why do you think she's still alive?"

"I know it. I feel it," Gaillard replied. "As you know, Kurata-*sama*'s contacts made arrangements for the U.S. Navy to fly one of its P3 Orion submarine hunters over the area. The aircraft's sophisticated magnetometers would have no trouble detecting the large metallic hull in the shallow waters of the Chesapeake Bay. They found nothing."

"It's a very big bay," Sugawara countered.

"It's a very big boat," Gaillard snapped. "Besides, I've had the opportunity to go over some downward-looking satellite radar scans that had been spirited out of the National Reconnaissance Office, again thanks to Kurata-*sama*'s thoughtful contacts at the White House. An eager-to-please young man gave me an assessment of the photos and while the hurricane has things pretty well obscured, there are some very interesting things he found, including a set of unexplained reflections in the North Atlantic. While their computer analysis indicates a high probability that it's a spurious reflection caused by the waves, or some sort of metallic debris in the waves, I'd be willing to bet it's her."

"Why?" Kurata asked. From the image on the screen, she could see that Kurata was dressed in traditional silk clothing.

"If you draw a line between the mouth of the Chesapeake Bay and the reflections and then extend the line farther to the northeast, it points like an arrow toward Holland. Blackwood's connections to Holland are very well known and I don't believe in coincidence."

No, this was no coincidence. She believed in her hunches. She lived by them. Others died by them. She *knew* that unexplained radar reflection was the *Tagcat Too*.

"And your recommendation would be?"

"To prepare for her in Holland. We have substantial contacts there. They can be on the lookout for her boat, for her. We can also extend the publicity campaign about her crimes to Europe so that police agencies can assist the search."

"I believe it is a good strategy," Kurata said. "You have my fullest support."

"Thank you, Kurata-*sama*," Gaillard said.

"Akira?" Kurata continued.

"Yes, my lord?"

"I want you to go to Amsterdam and provide all the assistance this operation could possibly need, especially your considerable talents in computers and the matters in which you excelled as part of the Imperial Japanese Army."

Sugawara flinched. In private Kurata never referred to the Self-Defense Forces by their proper name.

"*Hai*, Kurata-*sama*."

"And take with you all of the information on *Shinrai*."

"*Hai*."

"You have undoubtedly noticed that *Shinrai's* top leadership are near Amsterdam."

"*Hai*."

"Take this opportunity to see how many of them you can eliminate."

"As you wish, Kurata-*sama*," Sugawara said with an enthusiasm he did not feel.

"Excellent," Kurata said. "You are a vital part of the resurrection of Yamato, my boy."

When Akira Sugawara logged off the teleconference, his mind now knew precisely how it was going to follow the path his heart commanded.

28

THE ANTIQUE POLISHED BRASS CLOCK CHIMED THE TOP OF THE HOUR AND AWAK-
ENED LARA EVEN BEFORE HER WATCH ALARM DID. Reluctantly, she opened
her eyes and squinted through the fatigue, scarcely believing that the
hour had passed so quickly. Her eyes fell on the clock; it made such a
wonderfully archaic contrast with the chips and digital wizardry that
formed the nervous system of the *Tagcat Too.*

Salvaged by her father during one of his Scuba dives, through the
wreck of an American freighter sunk by Nazi U-boats off the coast of
Sardinia in 1944 and lovingly restored by him, the clock had been one
of his favorite things. It always made her think of him fondly.

Her gaze dropped from the clock to the papers and books littering
the table, all piled up against the rails that prevented items from sliding
off in heavy weather or when the boat was under sail and heeled over.
Her research on Kurata and the war criminals he had appointed to the
GenIntron board.

With the *Tagcat Too* still stable, she leaned over and skimmed the
papers, feeling the heat of her anger chase away the last wisps of sleep
from her head. Her eyes fell on a 1994 book she had checked out of the
library: *Prisoners of the Japanese* by Gavan Daws.

As the sea rocked the *Tagcat Too,* Lara picked up the book and revisited pages she had marked earlier with yellow Post-it notes. At page 258 she read, "At Khandok, for the benefit of some Japanese medical students, a POW was tied to a tree, his fingernails were torn out, his body was cut open, his heart cut out. On Guadalcanal, two prisoners were caught trying to escape, and to stop them trying again, the Japanese shot them in their feet. A medical officer dissected them alive, cutting out their livers."

Physically nauseated by the book's irrefutably documented revelations of the lowest, grossest horrors imaginable perpetrated by Japanese officialdom, she wanted to close the covers against the book's brutal, horrible truths, and yet her fingers kept flipping through its pages, each successive yellow sticky another creative abomination that made her wonder how people could be so resourceful in sadistically torturing others to death.

It made her believe in evil. The next highlighted passage concerned Unit 731's operations outside the Chinese city of Harbin. "The *Kempeitai* [secret police] brought them prisoners for guinea pigs: men, women, and children, Asians and Caucasians. They were called *maruta*, meaning logs of wood. Some were infected with disease: cholera, typhoid, anthrax, plague, syphilis, and glanders. Others," the passage continued, "were cut up alive to see what happened in the successive stages of hemorrhagic fever."

"Dear God," Lara cried as she closed her eyes against tears.

A cold deep blackness yawned inside of her as she realized yet again that when she sold GenIntron, she had sold not only her life's work and all the secrets she had discovered to the enemy, but it was an enemy capable of crimes imaginable only to those whose fantasies were driven by pure evil. She had sold these monsters a new and more powerful science capable of wreaking nightmares far more hideous than those practiced and encouraged by the Japanese government in World War II.

"The Western Japan Military Command gave some medical professors at Kyushu Imperial University eight B-29 crewmen," the book continued as Lara opened her eyes and forced herself along to the next Post-it note. "The professors cut them up alive, in a dirty room on tin tables where students dissected corpses. They drained blood and replaced it with seawater. They cut out lungs, livers, and stomachs. They stopped blood flow in an artery near the heart to see how long death took. They dug holes in a skull and stuck a knife into the living brain to see what would happen."

Lara felt the contents of her stomach rising; she swallowed against it and continued to read, finding the next marker, the next highlighted passage.

"At Kendebo," she read, "the *Kempeitai* chopped the head off a fighter pilot, then his body was cut up, fried, divided among 150 Japanese, and eaten, after a speech by a major general. Ob Chichi Jima, a Japanese general, issued orders in the Bonin Islands that captured airmen were to be killed and eaten; he and other senior officers ate the flesh at private parties. An admiral put in a request for the liver of the next airman."

Lara ran to the head and threw up into the toilet.

29

IN THE DIM HALF-NIGHT OF 3:00 A.M., AKIRA SUGAWARA MADE HIS WAY THROUGH THE SLATEWIPER PRODUCTION AREA, UP ONE SET OF STEPS, ALONG A GANGWAY, DOWN MORE STEPS.

Absent the background noise of the day, every gurgle and bubble sounded large, ominous. Relays clicked; valves opened; liquid death rushed through pipes. The organism respired and metabolized and excreted—it lived—all about him, Sugawara thought, as he made his way through its bowels toward the rear of the production facility building.

Most of the overhead lights were turned out, leaving only an occasional bank of fluorescents here and there for safety's sake. In the dimness, the process control computer screens stared at him with wide Cyclops eyes; they filled the passages with ghost light that painted him with the color of the moment, first red, then blue, green, pale gray, red again. He walked down the last flight of steps to the polished concrete floor.

He tried to walk confidently, honestly, to present the video surveillance cameras with the image of a man on a mission.

He felt like a thief as his footsteps echoed off the concrete. He just *knew* he must look like a thief. Somewhere in the security office, there must be an agent watching him on the video saying to himself, "There goes a thief," and reaching for the alarms. With every step, Sugawara expected to hear the Klaxons go off, feared he would soon feel the thuds of footsteps as security converged on him.

But he was Kurata's anointed one. Only Kurata himself could challenge him. And Kurata was asleep. Sugawara prayed he was asleep.

Reaching the airlock at the end of the production facility, Sugawara punched in his security code. There was the slightest of electronic delays; Sugawara's heart hung between beats. His mind knew it took a moment for the computer to recognize the code and release the latch, but his heart knew—just *knew*—they were on to him, that the latch would not open, that he would turn and find Kurata there behind him, accusing him.

He had his story ready. He had packed and—as they had discussed earlier—was on his way to Narita to catch his flight to Amsterdam when he had a premonition, an intuition, that something was not right. He couldn't shake the feeling and decided to look about for himself. It was probably nothing, just nerves raw from the death of Yamamoto and a lack of sleep and the unsatisfactory course of events in Holland.

Deep in his heart, he didn't think Kurata would buy it. He prayed it wouldn't come to that.

The latch released.

Sugawara sighed, stepped into the airlock, and turned on the light. He squinted and blinked against the brightness, stared up at the surveillance camera and quickly donned the disposable white booties, lab coat, and hat. This done, he stepped through the door and turned right. He passed airlocks into the higher biosafety level areas and headed for a room he had visited only once before.

No sirens; no alarms.

His heart raced. *Not yet, not yet, not yet, not yet.*

At the end of the corridor, he glanced up at another surveillance camera, punched his code on another keypad, and waited another heartstopping eternity for the latch to click. It did.

Sugawara checked his watch: 2:17 A.M. The KLM flight to Amsterdam wasn't until five.

He had no friends, no allies, no trustworthy allies in Japan. The police wouldn't stop Kurata; they would not buck a powerful man like him even with irrefutable proof. The consensus for Slatewiper ran too deeply through the government—all the way to the new prime minister—for the government to investigate, much less take action. Further, there was the firewall that protected Kurata, a deniability and damage control sequence Sugawara had helped to construct.

Sugawara needed help but there would be no help in Japan, no help until he had first helped Lara Blackwood.

But to do that, he needed proof.

He had a gigabyte of proof on a small data tape cassette in his pants pocket, an object the size of a Fig Newton that seemed to weigh half a ton, and felt like it glowed white-hot and shouted "Thief! Thief!" with every step.

Somewhere, he knew, the main computer's administrative program had registered his access, had logged the files from which he had copied. He hoped the virus he had injected into the computer would mask the access, make it seem like a routine data backup. But it might not. It might just have triggered silent alarms.

But data was just data. Slatewiper was real: you could see it, touch it, watch it kill. It was the ultimate proof, and he had no doubt that Lara Blackwood could unravel its secrets far more readily than any other person in the world.

If he lived long enough to get it to them.

Looking around the small room, Sugawara saw black-topped laboratory benches, a vapor hood, cabinets, machinery. A huge Dewar fumed in one corner, and a label said it contained liquid nitrogen. He hurried toward the phalanx of huge oil-drum-sized barrels that lined the far end of the room. They were almost chest high, painted with a grayish-beige enamel and trimmed with chrome strips. Each had a thick lid on top like a lady's large pillbox hat. They looked like giant Thermos bottles that, in reality, they were.

There would be questions; answers would come from the surveillance cameras and the computer logs and the missing inventory. He would be implicated, hunted. That much he knew.

The key question was how long it would take for them to realize he had become a traitor. Would they discover his treachery before he had time to contact Blackwood? Would he arrive in Amsterdam only to deliver his proofs to Kurata's goons and his life to a bizarre and painful death only Sheila could conceive . . . and enjoy.

Yamamoto's death could confuse matters, make people forget routine matters. Or would it put people on the alert? Allow them to catch him sooner?

A clack sounded behind him.

Oh, God!

Sugawara whirled.

He saw no one; the sound came from the door closing, the latch re-catching. He took a deep breath and closed his eyes for a moment. He let the breath shudder out and headed for a clipboard hooked on the wall next to the line of barrels.

He checked the clipboard's list and nodded.

Then he bent down, opened one cabinet door after another until he found one with rows of what looked like ordinary, wide-mouth Thermos containers.

Constructed along the same basic lines as an ordinary Thermos, these had much thicker glass walls and a higher vacuum between the walls to keep the contents hotter—or in this case, colder—for longer. In addition, the space between the glass vacuum flask and the plastic outer walls was filled with an aerogel designed to block the transfer of heat in or out.

Sugawara took a Thermos over to the large Dewar vacuum flask. He set the Thermos on the adjoining bench and placed the cap in a shallow metal cup. Then he opened the big Dewar; clouds formed as the liquid nitrogen inside the Dewar condensed vapor in the air. From the wall, he took a pair of safety goggles and slipped them over his eyes, then slipped his hands into a pair of insulated gloves.

Nitrogen, a colorless, odorless, nonpoisonous gas, makes up more than seventy-eight percent of the air people breathed, but in its liquid form, it could cause instant frostbite. Physicians commonly used it to remove skin growths.

From reading the papers Unit 731 had successfully kept from the Americans, Sugawara knew that a number of the researchers had conducted experiments with prisoners to see what effect nitrogen had on them. They plunged the limbs of prisoners into the liquid and discovered that the flesh froze steel hard and glass brittle. For fun, some of the researchers would strike the frozen limbs to see how the flesh would shatter. When it thawed, the flesh looked as if it had been shredded by knives. The victims usually bled to death. Lab protocols called for not treating them in order to follow the progress of the experiment to the end.

Even more gruesome experiments involved pouring liquid nitrogen down the throats of people and splashing it in their eyes. The one caused an excruciating death, the other, blindness. He felt ashamed whenever he thought of the secret experiments.

Sugawara grabbed a contraption that looked like a metal can with a pour spout attached to a long handle. Holding this by the insulated grips, Sugawara plunged the can part through the nimbus of vapor and into the Dewar; he heard the liquid nitrogen sizzle and fizz as the room-temperature warmth of the can caused the cold liquid to boil for just an instant. Then the dipper cooled down to the same frigid temperature and filled.

He pulled the fuming dipper from the Dewar and poured it carefully into the Thermos he had taken from the cabinet. At first, the nitrogen sputtered and boiled into vapor, then as the interior of the special Thermos cooled, the violent agitation calmed and allowed him to fill it to the top. He followed the same procedure with the Thermos's special cap.

As the Thermos and cap cooled to the temperature of liquid nitrogen, Sugawara glanced again at the clipboard and went to the Dewar on the end and opened its pillbox-hat top. Again, cloudbanks of condensation rose from the opening.

Grasping the top of a metal handle, Sugawara pulled upward.

A gleaming wire rack packed with sealed ampoules emerged from the liquid. He stood still for a moment, transfixed by the sight: row upon row of certain death, all in suspended animation, ready to be thawed, ready to kill.

Because each batch of Slatewiper was programmed to self-destruct after approximately three days, each new batch was immediately frozen to prevent the biological clock from ticking until Kurata was ready.

Sugawara reached with his free hand and grabbed first one and then a second ampoule, concentrating on getting a firm grasp despite the insulated gloves. He looked at the two slim vials, each with its own unique bar code and serial number.

He replaced the rack, closed the top, and walked over to the Thermos; both it and the special top had stopped boiling, indicating that they had both cooled down completely.

Working quickly now, Sugawara emptied the liquid nitrogen back into the Dewar, placed the two ampoules into the now-chilled Thermos, fished the top out with a pair of tongs, and secured it tightly into the mouth of the Thermos.

He closed the top of the Dewar, went to the Thermos cabinet and grabbed a special aerogel-packed top, and screwed it on.

Only then did he replace the goggles and gloves on the wall.

Finally, he went to a huge freezer and opened the door. Inside were form-fitting, nylon carrying bags designed for the Thermos. Each had a thick wall of freezer gel similar to that used for athletic injuries, only designed to be frozen to frostbite temperatures.

He unfastened the Velcro top. It sounded like machine-gun fire in the silence. The sound startled Sugawara and loosed a tremor that started at the base of his spine, worked its way up between his shoulder blades, and set his hair on end.

Hands shaking slightly now, expecting to hear alarms any moment, Sugawara slipped the special Thermos into its carrying bag and resealed the Velcro.

Then he turned and headed out, into a future so uncertain he wasn't sure he'd even reach the street alive.

30

LARA PULLED A BOX OF ORANGE JUICE FROM A CUPBOARD IN THE GALLEY, PUSHED IN THE PLASTIC STRAW, AND DREW DEEPLY ON IT. She quickly finished off the rest of the box, grabbed another one, and took it with her into the dining saloon.

Standing there, legs wide for balance, she sipped at the juice and looked down at the table covered with her research. She was stunned at the large number of war criminals—monsters—who had risen to high positions in Japanese society, had been honored, celebrated, venerated, sometimes *because* of the atrocities they had committed rather than *in spite* of them.

She sat down and picked up the list she had extracted from the reluctant data.

One name truly shocked her. She had met the man, a Nobel Prize winner. She had respected him, respected his work, accepted the fact he had deserved his honors and awards. But it was clear now that the man had vaulted to his positions of prominence over the unwilling and suffering bodies of innocent people. His patents had been written in blood. How many more like him were there?

The thought made her shiver.

Distracted, Lara now heard the static fuzzing from the television set and looked over at it, hanging overhead from a sturdy steel bracket. A faint picture bearing the CNN logo faded in and out, nothing that was intelligible. She had left the volume up so she'd catch the news as soon as reception improved. The last newscast she had seen was the one where she had been declared a murderer, a felon on the run.

The unusually poor television reception and the intermittent connection from her normally reliable satellite system was undoubtedly from the solar storms that were making news on their own. Despite the hubris of technological advancement, people were still very much at the mercy of nature, she now concluded.

Lara sipped at the orange juice and marveled at the undeniable story of a forgotten Japanese-sponsored holocaust in which six million innocent civilians had died horribly. A holocaust the American government had willingly covered up in the name of developing more and better Cold War weapons. It was a strategy that was coming back bigger and more horrible than ever.

Behind her, Lara heard fragments of speech from the television struggling to break through the static as she put down the book and picked up *The Other Nuremberg* by Arnold C. Brackman. She was a voracious reader. Why had she never heard of the book? Could it be that the American media was so afraid of offending the Japanese that they simply didn't write about such books? She loosed a sigh, opened the book, and read the highlighted passage aloud.

The last surviving judge at the Tokyo, Japanese War Crimes Trials, B.V.A. Roling of the Netherlands, expressed the view that the United States should be "ashamed because of the fact that they withheld information from the Court with respect to the biological experiments of the Japanese in Manchuria on Chinese and American Prisoners of War . . . '[I]t is a bitter experience for me to be informed now that the centrally ordered Japanese war criminality of the most disgusting kind was kept secret from the Court by the U.S. government.' "

"Unfucking real," she said to herself as she put the book back on the table and headed for the galley. She tossed the orange juice box in the trash, then went forward and started one of the diesels so its alternator could charge the batteries and provide AC voltage to run the coffeemaker.

31

MEN WITH SERIOUS FACES CRUISED THE STREETS OF AMSTERDAM'S RED-LIGHT DISTRICT, CAREFULLY INSPECTING THE MERCHANDISE, CAREFULLY AVOIDING EYE CONTACT, FERVENTLY HOPING NOT TO RECOGNIZE OR BE RECOGNIZED.

Window shopping.

The men walked, strolled, stopped, stared, and loitered on the rolling, brown-red, brick-paved streets and sidewalks that still glistened with the night's downpour. Each of the men tried unsuccessfully to give the impression he was just out for a bit of healthy walking and—oh, my!—had wandered completely by happenstance into the flesh quarter.

Over their heads, clouds had begun to wear thin enough to let the noon sun flash through an instant at a time. Weather forecasters had announced on television that morning the storm from America had stalled in the North Sea and was breaking up. It would produce some spirited showers and thunderstorms with hail so farmers were advised to protect their crops.

The men trolling for sex were hot, bloated sacks of fucklust who walked stiffly as if some great tumor were eating at their groins. Despite their masks of feigned nonchalance that fooled no one—especially the whores who had seen it all too many times before to keep count—this was serious business. This was commerce.

In the midst of them swam every now and then a wide-eyed duo or trio of young men just past adolescence who ogled, snickered, and murmured self-consciously among themselves. Their direct stares and open wonderment nipped annoyingly at the heels of the older men's faux-casualness.

On the Oude Zijds Achterburgwal, a familiar scene played.

"Go away, boys, you're bothering the customers," said one of the working girls good-naturedly.

"We have money," one of the boys said with a pout.

"Then spend it, or keep moving."

She makes them feel like boys again, unsure, maybe a little scared. They look at each other, and an unspoken decision reached earlier—probably over a hamburger and fries at the McDonald's just off the Damrak—plays across their faces.

One of them turns to her. Now that they're actually looking at her, they start to realize she's got the beginnings of a terrific mustache and is maybe thirty pounds overweight, which helps keep her breasts in good selling order but does nothing for the rest of her. In the back of their minds they know she's as old as their mothers.

Still the boy presses forward, opens his mouth. "We were wondering if—"

"No deals, no bargains, no group discounts," she says, knowing what's coming next. "The three of you? No problem. Three times the price."

They walk away.

The entire play was viewed through the world-class optics of a set of Zeiss binoculars that sat on a specially made tripod inside of a third-story room of a cheap, anonymous tourist hotel across the street and less than half a block down from the whore's window.

As the boys straggled away, Sheila Gaillard took a long drag on her tenth cigarette of the morning and watched through the binoculars as a tall, thin man in a khaki raincoat moved away from a group of parked cars, made his way purposefully to the whore's window, negotiated quickly, and went inside. The window curtains closed.

"With your eyes closed, they all look alike," Sheila muttered to herself as she exhaled smoke through her nostrils. Who had told her that?

Sitting back now away from the binoculars, she stretched and sucked again on the cigarette.

Hunching forward to the binoculars again, Sheila moved them just slightly so they panned away from the whore's curtained window and stopped next door on a series of canal houses that had been converted to a gay-oriented hotel and sexual funhouse. It was owned by the former general manager of GenIntron's Dutch subsidiary who had resigned to follow the small head at the end of what Gaillard understood to be a very large erection. From the files she had been able to pull together, the owner was the closest friend in Holland that Lara Blackwood had. Business and tax filings indicated that Blackwood had provided start-up capital for the enterprise in exchange for a modest equity stake.

Gaillard moved the binoculars and focused on the sex shop next door that was conducting a booming business. As she watched, a well-dressed woman walked out, carrying a thick, three-foot-long, anatomically correct, double-ended dildo under her arm like a baguette. As the woman reached the sidewalk, a chauffeur-driven Mercedes pulled up; the driver leaped out and opened the door for her.

She was good-looking, Sheila thought as the Mercedes moved away. Sheila grew moist and allowed herself to linger on a quick fantasy of herself, the woman, and the big dildo.

Her fantasy vanished quickly as Sheila recognized the brisk loping strides of a man down on the street making his way toward her hotel. Horst Von Neuman, one of the thousands of former East German Stasi agents loosed on the world by the collapse of the Wall. While the rest of the world knew them as brutal, cruel men without scruples or any evidence of human decency, she found them dedicated, reliable, talented, resourceful. Best of all, they had few qualms about doing almost anything for the right amount of money. Before the collapse of communism, they'd had experience inflicting every sort of pain, torture, degradation, and death on their countrymen, neighbors, and—not infrequently— members of their own family.

Horst and many of his colleagues had fled the East or gone into hiding before the fall of the Wall, taking with them computer disks, files, photos. These men and women had formed a loose network, like some latter-day ODESSA, and survived by blackmail; by spying, interrogation, and murder for hire; by maintaining contacts with those in the German government who believed the collapse of the Wall had not been a good thing at all.

Horst was one of the better specimens, Sheila thought as she watched him cross the street, approach the hotel, and disappear from sight as he entered the hotel entrance three floors below her.

Von Neuman was tall, certainly more than two meters, a gaunt man with almost-white hair, pale, easily sunburned skin, a nose sharp like a hatchet and high cheekbones that seemed so sharp she was always surprised they didn't slice their way through the skin beneath his eyes. He was intelligent, but not so much so that he failed to follow her orders down to the smallest detail. He also had a piece of meat between his legs that could support a stellar career in skinflicks.

Sheila lit a new cigarette from the butt of her old one and got up from her chair. She was at the door when Horst knocked.

"Taps are done," the tall German said without preamble as he walked in; the tails of his oversized, olive-colored raincoat flowed behind him like a contrail. "Transmitters will feed directly into the recorders." He nodded toward the collection of miniaturized electronics sitting on the chipped, cigarette-scarred particleboard bureau next to Sheila's bed. They were the latest Japanese units made by one of Kurata's companies—a tenth the size and an order of magnitude more sensitive than the best gear the FBI could get its hands on. Kurata had told her that as soon as his company finished the next generation, which was even smaller and more sensitive than these, he'd sell the old generation to the U.S. government.

"They'll 'ooh' and 'ahh' at the technology, like little children at Christmas," Kurata had said, "and compliment us on our prowess, never realizing we've sold them obsolete products for a hundred times our cost."

Sheila closed the door and watched Horst walk over to the window and look down the street at the hotel. He seemed satisfied with something he saw there, because he nodded and then turned around. She walked halfway across the room and sat on the foot of her bed, gazed at the digital miracles that Kurata's people had packed into packages no larger than a portable CD player. Some were as small as a Walkman.

He unbuttoned the oversized raincoat that hung on his Ichabod Crane frame like a tent. Von Neuman shrugged his way out of the raincoat. He wore another coat underneath, only this one was sturdy canvas covered with pockets, loops, and pouches, all bulging with tools, wires, electronic circuit boards, test gauges, and other assorted paraphernalia. He unzipped the front of this second coat and pulled a wad of folded paper from an inner pocket. He walked over to Sheila and handed it to her.

Sheila unfolded the paper as Von Neuman shed this second coat, stepped away, and hung the coat on a bent nail pounded into the cracked plaster wall next to the door. He pulled a hard pack of Marlboros from his shirt pocket and tucked a cigarette in his mouth. He walked back to her, bent over to light the cigarette from hers. The smell of his sweat stirred her groin.

He paused to suck on the cigarette and walked over to the bureau of electronic gear. "I'll also program the cellular scanner to look for the owner's ESN—the electronic serial number—of his cellular. That's no problem." Another long drag on the cigarette.

"Lovely." Sheila nodded and blew smoke.

Her cellular telephone rang. She looked over at it sitting next to the chair by the window. It rang a second time.

Horst retrieved the phone and handed it to her.

Sheila pressed the green button on the keypad.

"Hello," she said.

"Please activate encryption, public key 7666."

She pressed the function key and the four numerals to load the encryption software.

"Sugawara here. Ms. Gaillard?"

"Yes?" Damn! She hated Kurata's snippy nephew, resented the authority the old man delegated to this little snot.

The connection crackled with static. Why was the connection so bad?

"I received a call from our source at the National Reconnaissance Office. The cloud cover's beginning to break, and they think they have a craft that fits the description of the *Tagcat Too*."

"Yes!" Being right was almost as much fun as sex. For just a moment, the euphoria made her head as light as her first cigarette did.

"How is . . . progress in Amsterdam?"

"Progressing well," Sheila answered vaguely. "I think the old farts from *Shinrai* are sniffing around this too. I think we may have to take them completely out this time."

"They have been a source of frustration to Kurata-*sama*, that it true," Sugawara said. "But will their deaths accomplish anything?"

"Yeah, one less thing to worry about," Gaillard snapped. "I'll give Kurata a complete report later."

She hung up abruptly.

"She's coming," Sheila said as she placed the phone back on the table and walked over to the tall German. "All we have to do is wait, and they're ours."

She pressed her breasts into his hard chest, reached down to massage his groin. He came to attention immediately. She pushed him backward onto the bed and unzipped his pants.

32

THE *TAGCAT TOO* SAWED ITS WAY THROUGH CONFUSED SEAS THE COLOR OF SCUM. Swirling fog banks the size of supertankers glided past in the gathering gloom. Under full sail now in the waning winds, the steel-hulled ketch rode easily up and down the ebbing storm swells that came now from the south.

All day, desultory rain had fallen from swift gunmetal clouds that raced across the sky. What was left of the hurricane had unexpectedly snagged a new, southerly branch of the jet stream and dashed itself against a powerful high pressure cell off the Azores. What it left was inclement weather that, after the hurricane, made for smooth sailing.

Lara Blackwood stood with one hand on the wheel, legs apart to steady herself against the constantly moving deck and the extreme heel of the windward tack. She let the fine cool drizzle settle on her face as she zipped up the foul-weather gear jacket and adjusted the baseball cap on her head.

She had encountered more and more shipping traffic since passing through the Straits of Dover on her way north up the coast of Holland: long sleek tankers, boxy loaded container carriers, hulking car transporters and ferries, mammoth tankers of all description, and, salted among them, rusting buckets eking out a dwindling profit from all the money not spent on deferred maintenance.

The fog had made dodging the ships a challenge, and now, dotting the marinescape, there were offshore oil rigs, blinking with more lights than a Vegas casino.

She leaned closer to concentrate on the helm's waterproof display, which mirrored the laptop screen on the nav station below. She frowned as the GPS headings swung wildly under the influence of the solar flares. She picked out a large image on the radar display and decided to tack. Suddenly the deep throbbing of big powerful engines that had been faint background noise just a minute before grew suddenly louder. In the fog, the sound seemed to come from every direction at once.

All at once, a great black towering bow loomed out of the darkness.

"Jeez!" Lara cried as she watched a massive liquid natural gas super-tanker burst out of a break in the fog like a Redball freight and slash its way across the ketch's former course.

"Dear God!" The hull was close enough to see the welds on the plates and make out the Plimsoll lines. Her heart making sledgehammer beats on the back of her sternum, Lara craned her head back, saw the huge breast-shaped LNG domes sitting above the hull.

A fog bank swallowed the tanker, bow first.

"Holy shit!" The tanker had been closer than the radar image had indicated. Were solar flares affecting her radar or the electronics too? She bent over the display and hit the hot-key that pulled up the radar image full screen. She studied a brilliantly colored computer-generated map filled with enough moving, blinking objects to challenge the most skilled videogame aficionado.

The map swarmed with red blinking icons that designated possible collisions. The red blinking icons were outnumbered just slightly by amber ones. The blue area on the display was bounded by the press of land on both sides, England to the west, the Netherlands to the east. She saw the irregular blobs of the southern Dutch coastline—the Westerschelde that led to the Belgian harbor of Antwerp, to the north, the newly reclaimed polders and the shallow, drying waters of the Oosterschelde and Grevlingenmeer. The display showed the *Tagcat Too* was steering a compass course of sixty-five degrees—roughly northeasterly—about thirteen miles northwest of Hoek van Holland, the entrance to the world's busiest port, Rotterdam harbor. As she watched, a green ship icon—too far away to be a collision threat yet—emerged from the canal leading from Rotterdam.

No, she thought. The display looked normal. It had to be fatigue, she thought. Not the electronics. Time for the last of the amphetamine cache.

Lara watched and nodded, took a good look at the chart, then stared intently off the starboard side. She looked again at the chart, placed her finger on the chart. "The light at Scheveningen should be right about there," she said to herself.

Then she pointed toward two flashing lights through a hazy parting of the fog banks. "Yes," she said quietly. The lights were right where she had pointed.

"One, one-thousand; two, two-thousand," she began counting. At "ten, ten-thousand," the lights flashed again.

"Nailed it," Lara said softly. "Two lights flashing every ten seconds." She double-checked the chart. "That's Scheveningen."

Close, she thought. Just a few more hours.

Suddenly, the computer began beeping again; a warning screen appeared showing two converging lines with the icons of a shipwreck at the intersection.

She heard the deep pitch of yet another set of massive ship's engines as she began another tack. Then an urgent beeping alarm sounded from the nav station. Lara looked and saw a flashing red ship's icon bearing down on the *Tagcat Too*.

Where the hell did that one come from?

She took one step toward the companionway steps when the world turned upside down in a maelstrom of shrieking metal against metal; the groans of tortured steel reverberated through the hull.

For a moment, it seemed as if she were hanging weightlessly, upside down as the cabin rolled under her in slow-motion. Then the lights went out.

33

THE *TAGCAT TOO* CLANGED LIKE AN OIL DRUM FILLED WITH METAL SCRAP AND BROKEN GLASS. Everything was black, the darkness exploded with horrendous shrieks of metal scraping against metal, palpable standing waves of sound that resonated inside the hull and made her insides ring with every sound.

Everything lurched and jounced.

For just a moment, the dim illumination of the boat's emergency, battery-powered lighting system unveiled the darkness. In the instant before even those lights went out, Lara surveyed the now-dim and unfamiliar scene: cushions, books, debris scattered all about, nothing where she had ever seen it before. Then she realized she was lying facedown on the padded insulation that covered the overhead surfaces.

The *Tagcat Too* shuddered and wallowed; the noise of the grinding metal penetrated Lara's head like a deep sharp pain that made her think of newspaper stories about a construction worker who had fallen from a scaffold and been impaled through his head with a stub of steel rebar sticking out of a poured concrete form.

The enormity of what was happening seized her like a cold fist around her heart. The thin sleek hull of the *Tagcat Too* was being sledgehammered to bits by the thick steel plates of some oceangoing Goliath. How much time? How much more punishment could the hull take before it split a seam and spilled into the North Sea's cold, unforgiving waters.

A violent rending, a great explosive snap reverberated through the cabin and hammered her facedown. Then as suddenly as it started, the grinding stopped. The belly-deep thrum of a ship's engines and the backwash from its screws filled an otherwise anxious silence that lay heavy with hope and sour with fear.

Lara took a long shuddering breath as the deck started to tilt again. The *Tagcat Too* groaned over, swapping ceiling for floor. Lara—along with the seat cushions, duffels, and the rest of the debris—slid first to the side walls, then to the floor as the boat regained its balance. The hull swayed and yawed like a crazy carnival funhouse with tilty floors.

Then the rush of water filled the air. Lara's insides froze at the sound; she had heard it only once before in her life. Just seconds before the *Tagcat* went down off the Cape of Good Hope.

She rushed to the locker beside the companionway and pulled her Doomsday duffel from it. Recuperating in Cape Town, she had plenty of time to think about the sinking and what she would do differently. One of those items was to have a survival pack that also contained items of convenience she had missed after her rescue: a change of clothing, makeup, money, and more.

With the *Tagcat Too* shifting under her feet, she grabbed her purse, the .380 automatic, and the boxes of new ammunition, stuffed them in the watertight Doomsday duffel, grabbed a flashlight from the bracket by the nav station, and started up the companionway. She stopped abruptly and with desperation on her breath set down the duffel and scrambled into her stateroom. Going to the top drawer of her earring collection where she kept her favorites and the most valuable. She cleaned the shallow drawer out in two scoops of her hand and stuffed them in a cargo pocket of her foul-weather gear.

Zipping up the pocket, she made her way through the ankle-deep water that rose steadily in the passageway. She grabbed the duffel and shot up the companionway steps. On deck, she felt a fine salty tang on her tongue; her nose filled with the unmistakable sweet/pungent sulfurous stench of partially combusted number two bunker oil. She followed her nose and made out the stern of a huge, fully loaded container ship disappearing into the fog. Lara made out the name, *Abraham Lincoln*, on the stern and watched her immense hulk gliding through the night, black on black on gray. The fog was breaking up, at least locally, and she could see the dazzling light displays on the oil and gas platforms to the east. Craning her head, she saw stars and a half-moon through gauzy filaments of fog.

Just then, she heard a Klaxon sound from the decks of the *Abraham Lincoln*. The collision had been noticed; engines would be reversed, a message sent to authorities with the latitude and longitude duly noted; rescue parties would be launched. People would come bearing goodwill and a rescue that would land her in jail.

Squeezed now between death from the sea and disaster from those who would try to save her, Lara climbed up on deck struggling against the sadness that filled her as she prepared to abandon ship. Again. She stood silently for a moment, playing her flashlight about the deck and marveling at the gnarled kinetic web of wounded rigging that laced across the deck like a net of steel snakes, squirming and clutching at them with every move the boat made. Water poured into the cockpit, pressing the boat lower and lower into the water.

In the distance, she heard the engines of the *Abraham Lincoln* reverse, heard the churning of the sea as the screws chop-washed backward. She lowered the inflatable dinghy into the icy water, tossed in the Doomsday bag, then climbed aboard. As water began to wash over the highest parts of the *Tagcat Too*'s deck, Lara started the outboard and let it idle for several seconds before cranking the throttle handle to move her a few yards away.

Dread scudded through her heart as she watched the *Tagcat Too*'s deck awash, then disappear. When the mast slid graciously down, it reminded her of the unhurried dignity of the broadcast tower atop the World Trade Center. Again, the deep, infinitely black loss that had filled her on September 11 returned now, and settled darkly into her heart with an irresistible, innervating weight that pinned her motionless to her seat.

Tears came finally as the instruments and antennae at the top of the mast sank from sight. She gazed at the spot for a long time. Diesel spilled from the *Tagcat Too*'s tanks slicked the water with dark rainbows from the distant lights. When she was sure she would remember the vision the rest of her life, she turned her face toward the lights of Scheveningen harbor, brought the inflatable about, and twisted the outboard's throttle wide open.

34

LANDLUBBERS THINK THE SEA SMELLS LIKE SOMETHING. They visit a harbor or trek down to the seashore and find a characteristic fishy-iodine smell.

"This is what the sea smells like," they tell each other and take a deep breath.

Lara Blackwood knew the sea had no smell at all, that the littoral odors that assaulted the landlubbers' noses came not from the sea but from the frothy decomposition of algae and sea life, all churned and aerosolized by the constant grinding of waves.

You couldn't smell the sea, but you sure could smell the land, she thought, as she leaned against the rough painted walls of the public rest rooms and showers of the Marina Scheveningen.

She pulled in a long pulsing breath through her nose, like an expert sampling wine; in the harbor air she found hints of diesel and gasoline, rotting algae under the piers, wafts of burning bunker oil from the big ships in the outer harbor, the sharpness of disinfectant from the rest rooms, the round sweet smells of bar soap from the showers; from the noisy ventilation fans of the nearby bar and restaurant filled with yachties—both transient and resident—came the fuggy, burning manure smells of tobacco smoke shot through with vapors from the deep fat fryer.

The sounds of people having a good time in six languages on a Friday night drifted across the docks; lighting from the docks spilled into the water and swirled with the gentle waves from a passing dinghy.

No one had paid her any special attention during her ride into the harbor mouth, nor as she made her way through the big Voorhaven into the Eerste Binnenhaven, the first inner harbor where the big ships docked—and through the narrow canal into the Tweede Binnenhaven, where the small craft marina lay. All manner of small craft from inflatables like hers to larger pilot ships and work vessels plied the harbor at all hours. There was no customs or passport demand because people didn't arrive from foreign lands in small rubber boats. Hers had been just one among many tied up at the guest docks next to the marina's bar and restaurant.

Lara let out a deep breath and closed her eyes for just a moment as she struggled against the fatigue that rumbled toward her like a distantly heard avalanche. The immediate threat was gone; the amphetamine hangover was on its way. There remained only to find a safe place to sleep, to rest, to recharge.

She opened her eyes and looked down at the Doomsday duffel: it was all that was left of her former life. Lara felt a sadness then that hurt like the ends of a broken bone grinding in her heart. The *Tagcat Too* rested now on the floor of the North Sea along with the awards, the Olympic medals, and all the photos of her dad. Everything that could remind her of the past had remained aboard the *Tagcat Too* and was now deep under the waves.

She heard a metallic snicking sound and turned just in time to see the door to the women's toilets and shower room open. For an instant, a woman was backlit by the fluorescents inside, then the door closed. Lara picked up her duffel and stepped inside.

She showered, luxuriating in the hot water, washing away the smoke and the sweat, the grime. As she let the water drill into her shoulder muscles, her mind went again to what her next steps had to be. She had to stop Kurata from killing, but how? And how would she survive long enough to answer the question? Ismail was dead. So were Peter Durant and the doctors in Tokyo. Kurata would dog her steps.

At some point they would realize she was alive and come hunting for her. It was vital, she knew, to alter her appearance before anyone saw her.

Somewhere she had once read that most attempts at disguise—stage mustaches, wigs, radical makeup—fooled no one because they looked fake. She remembered from that somewhere that the goal had to be *al-*

teration, not disguise, that it had to be done with clothes and products that people used and lived in every day.

She struggled to recall the many physical descriptions of her that had appeared in newspapers, magazines, and television. As she went over them in her mind, she realized that they all defined her in terms of her strength, height, eyes, and breasts.

Stepping from the shower, she combed her fingers through her wet hair as she looked at herself in the mirror. At least in Holland, her height would not stand out and strength was not something anyone could see if she kept her clothes on. And no earrings. Reporters had written stories on her collection. Kurata certainly knew about it as well and so would the people looking for her.

Lara looked more closely in the mirror, then set to work.

By the time Lara stepped out of the rest room, there was no sign of her breasts; she had taken an elastic bandage from the first-aid kit to bind them flat. She had trimmed her hair short and tucked it completely inside a Nike baseball cap; even in a well-lighted place, she could keep the bill pulled low to hide her incredible eyes in shadow. She wore a plain navy blue sweatshirt over faded Levi's. She wore her deck boots.

Outside, she stuffed her foul-weather gear in a trash bin. They were both marked with her name and the *Tagcat Too*. They'd be discovered soon enough, but better not to advertise by wearing them. Next, she threw the duffel into the scorched inflatable and motored away from the well-lit guest dock to the deep shadows where she disconnected the fuel tank and placed it on the concrete riprap. It was now mostly empty and a perfect flotation device.

Next, she took the Swiss army knife from her pocket and slashed at the inflatable's four air compartments and watched the sturdy little craft sink along with the most reliable outboard she had ever had.

Finally, she picked up the anonymous red fuel can and duffel and picked her way across the riprap to a sidewalk where she left the can. It had been years since she had last visited the harbor, but she remembered there was a trolley line just outside the marina that would take her into Den Haag—the Hague—and to the central train station. From there, she could catch the train to Amsterdam.

35

Amsterdam Central Station smelled of wet concrete and ozone when Lara Blackwood stepped onto the platform just after midnight, Saturday morning. She stood there for a moment as a swirling clot of teenagers filtered past her, chatting loudly in round, back-of-the-throat Dutch sounds. Two tracks away, a train bound for Paris and Rome pulled slowly away in a shower of sparks as its three engines raised their pantograph arms and made contact with the electrical wires overhead.

Lara coughed, looked around as a moist gust of wind carrying motes of drizzle whirled through the open ends of the huge semicylindrical dome and slaked the dust on the platform. The smell of coffee wafted from the restaurant; a man walked out of the public rest room, still zipping up his pants.

Lara tried to shrug off a shiver, but it still made ice tracks up her spine as she shouldered her duffel and made her way past a line of porter's carriages with metal-spoked wheels and down a short flight of steps to the passenger tunnel that led under and gave access to all of the tracks.

The crowds grew thicker as she walked up the slight incline leading to the main terminal area. She had been through Amsterdam's Central Station many times and walked as confidently as a native, blending in with the crowd.

The crush grew thinner as they entered the main room of the station; ahead, the lights of the Damrak gleamed through the front doors. As she passed the newsstand by the front entrance her eye caught sight of something very familiar—her own face.

"Oh!" she said softly to herself and stopped.

Something like cold footsteps marched behind her breastbone as she looked at an old publicity photograph of herself on the front page of *Het Parool*.

Below that was a photo of the *Tagcat Too*. Reading Dutch had never been her strong suit, but she could make out enough to tell it was about her presumed death and, equally troubling, about being a suspect in a plot to sell bioweapons secrets to terrorist countries. The deal had gone sour, according to the article, and she had killed Peter Durant. It was unbelievable to her, but in the aftermath of so much thievery and lying among the icons of corporate America and the twisted, fiendish plots of terrorists and other lunatics, she supposed that the public was now willing to accept even the most preposterous situations as truth simply because the incredible had happened once too many times.

The cold steps in her heart moved lower now, stamping out a dark empty dread in her belly. Lara glanced toward the cashier's booth where a young dark-skinned woman—Indonesian maybe—was concentrating on a small-screen television playing a music video. Her lips moved silently with the words. Without attracting the vendor's attention, Lara made calmly for the station's main doors. Outside, a fine mist swirled about her in the peachy orange streetlights as she made her way across the Stationsplein, crossed the wide bridge over the haven canal, and made for the traffic lights at the Prins Hendrikkade.

The light changed, and she headed down the east side of the Damrak, past a tourist information stand shuttered for the night, standing watch over a phalanx of glass-topped tourist boats bobbing gently in the early morning darkness. To her right, a yellow tram rattled past, its power bar sparking along the overhead wires. At the Old Stock Exchange, she turned left, away from the brightly lit street that a sign on the side of a tall brick building identified as the Damrak. Ahead, she saw a dark warren of narrow alleys dimly lit by the flashing lights from porno shops.

Lara made her way along the Oude Brugsteeg, past stores with multicolored flashing lights and display windows filled with huge plastic penises, an inflatable sheep's ass, and lurid photos graphically displaying more full-color gynecologically and urologically correct photos than the Kama Sutra.

She came to the Warmoesstraat where the Oude Brugsteeg jogged to the left and became the Lange Niezel. Her footsteps clopped loudly in the narrow alley bounded by rough brick walls. She crossed the Oude Zijds Voorburgwal and finally arrived at the Oude Zijds Acherburgwal where she turned right, passing the marquee of a small gay cinema currently showing *Teddy's Rough Riders* and *The Crisco Kid.* In less than half a block, she came to a tall windowless brick wall painted white and delineated from the walls to either side. A plain door painted black was set in the middle of the white-painted wall, flanked by two gaslights in old-fashioned carriage-style glass and frames. A brass-captured lens of a peephole stared out at Lara's eye level; light could be seen behind it. To the right of the door, a discreet polished brass plate the size of a business card sat on the door frame just above a lighted doorbell. The brass plate pronounced this the entrance to "Casa Blanca." Lara looked up and squinted to see the vague outlines of something that might be a trompe d'oeil painting of a large house.

She pressed the doorbell. Moments later, the peephole went dark, electric lights winked on over the door for just a moment, and instants later the rattle of a bolt was followed by the *snick-click-thunk* of a well-oiled deadbolt.

The door swung open to reveal a very tall, lean, dark-skinned man with heavy eyebrows, a Zapata mustache, and the Mexican facial structure that came from the combination of Indian and European genes. The man had dark black eyes and was dressed all in black: silk shirt, baggy trousers, espadrilles. The shirt was open to his navel, revealing a hairless chest (*electrolysis*, Lara thought) covered with gold chains that draped down to his flat muscular belly. He was easily a hand taller than Lara. Santiago Rodriguez. Her old GM.

"May I help you?" the man said formally. The look on his face clearly said he didn't like what he saw on his doorstep: a rumpled, wrinkled woman, her face in the shadows of the baseball cap.

"I came to check on my investment."

The tall man frowned at her words like someone trying to catch an errant thought. Lara watched the big man's face run the gamut from confusion to shock to recognition and joy.

"*Amiga!*" The man spread his arms wide and took a step forward. He embraced Lara and lifted her off her feet. "I thought you were *dead*; I thought you were dead." He hugged her for a moment, then stepped back. "Well don't stand out there, come in. Come in!" He took her duffel.

Lara followed the tall man into an elegant sitting room with slate blue carpeting and a collection of antiques ranging from Bergere and cabriolet chairs to an unusual love seat. Oil paintings in ornately carved gilt frames covered the walls; statuary lined the room, including a marble she recognized—Michelangelo's Rebel Slave. Rodriguez saw her jaw drop.

"It's a *very* good copy," Rodriguez said. "I've done a little redecorating since you were here last." He watched as Lara made her way to a small desk unobtrusively tucked into the far corner of the room, and behind it a rack of keys and mail slots.

"And some expanding, I see."

"Twenty-three guest rooms, all furnished with antiques or reproductions so faithful they could be sold as such to the most discriminating and knowledgeable buyers."

Rodriguez smiled. "Come on over here." He walked toward a leather wing-backed chair seam-lined with round brass tack heads. "I was just having a glass of a very good tawny port before turning in."

Lara saw a small pie crust table with a cut-crystal decanter beside a single sherry glass. Rodriguez set her duffel next to the wall behind an identical wing-backed chair, then went to a mahogany Queen Anne, opened the glass doors, and pulled another sherry glass from it.

Lara made her way to the chair and sagged into it.

"That's better." Rodriguez filled their glasses from the decanter.

They sat, raised their glasses.

"Your health," Rodriguez said. The glasses tinked.

"And yours," Lara said.

They drank.

After a moment, Rodriguez spoke, his voice full of concern.

"So. How are you?"

"Tired. Glad to be alive, I suppose."

Rodriguez nodded. "I read the paper. I was wondering how long it would take you to get here."

"I'm fortunate to be here."

He nodded slowly. "There have been people knocking on my door, looking for you." He paused.

Lara felt her heart quicken.

"Some were policemen," Rodriguez continued. "But they acted secretively, as if they were not visiting on official business."

"How could you tell?"

He smiled. "You well know that in my business I meet a lot of policemen . . . and women, both as customers and as officials."

"I don't suppose my investment here . . . or our friendship is any secret."

"True, true," he said. After another sip, he said, "I expected the police. But then there were others. First, a tall German man with a sharp face and cold eyes. Then very late last night the most curious of all, an old man." Pause. "I actually got the impression that he was concerned about you. When he left, he said something truly odd."

"Which was?"

"The old man said to me: 'If you do see her, please tell her that there are others who also seek the truth.' "

"The truth. That's all he said?"

Rodriguez nodded. "And he left an E-mail address. One of those anonymous ones." He fished around in his shirt pocket and pulled from it a large Post-it Note and gave it to her. "He said that if you wanted to contact him, to send an E-mail with a way to contact you."

Lara shivered. "This is too spooky."

"Uh-huh. And I think there was something vaguely familiar about him. I can't put my finger on it."

Lara shook her head slowly and placed her drink on the table. "This is so bizarre." She paused. "I am so tired, I have no idea what could be happening here."

"Did you kill the man in Washington the paper said you killed?"

"What? Of course not!"

"Of course not. And have you been selling bioweapons secrets to terrorist cells?"

"No! You know me better than that!"

Rodriguez smiled. "Yes, I certainly do, but it looks as if people in very high places want the world to think differently. Differently enough so that they can use law enforcement to hunt you down."

He paused to let the silence punctuate his wisdom. Then, "What is it that you know that they don't want you to tell the world?"

Wearily, Lara leaned back. The words spilled out beginning with her abrupt eviction from GenIntron. It felt so very good, the weight in her chest seemed to melt away as she described the phone call from Tokyo, the bizarre conversations with Kurata, the president, Ismail Brahimi, and Peter Durant. Then she told him of the violence, the deaths, the discoveries of what she believed Daiwa Ichiban was up to, and then the nerve-shattering voyage that ended in the loss of yet another boat.

Then a look of horror widened her face. "Oh, my God!" She leaned forward. "I am so stupid coming here like this! This is such an obvious place to look for me. I've put you in danger."

He shook his head.

"There is a reason why there are no windows on the ground floor of my hotel and why the only two entrances are fine wood veneer over steel."

Lara raised her eyebrows.

"Even in a country such as Holland, there are people who would harm gay people doing what they do in the rooms I charge them for. We have had fire bombings, pipe bombs, deranged individuals with knives and pieces of pipe." He set down his glass and got up.

"Come," he said as he walked to the desk with the keys and stepped behind it.

Lara followed him.

"See." He pointed to a panel of six small displays, each displaying an image from a closed circuit television camera outside. "I have very good surveillance, solid doors and walls, and"—he pointed to a red button next to the camera displays—"a panic button that summons the police at the Warmoesstraat, just a couple of blocks away."

Lara shook her head slowly.

"Never in my wildest dreams did I ever think I'd get tangled up in something like this."

Lara placed her hand over her mouth, trying not to yawn. Without success. Lara felt embarrassed as her gaze met that of Rodriguez.

"I'm really a poor host," he said. "I *must* know everything else, but only after you've had enough sleep to remember it all."

"Thanks," Lara said and yawned deeply.

Rodriguez grabbed a shiny brass fob from the rack.

"Follow me." He went to her bag, picked it up, and headed for a set of steep, narrow stairs. Lara followed him closely.

"I have one room left," he said, calling behind him. "You may find the decoration a bit jarring, but as you well know, there are many among my clientele who find it . . . stimulating." He disappeared around a corner; Lara hurried to catch up.

On the fourth floor, Rodriguez stopped on the landing and held the door to the hallway open for her.

"Number 410," he said, handing the key to her. Lara stepped through the door.

When she turned on the lights, the room fairly leaped at her: pale gray walls and black marble floors sucked the illumination from the Italian-design halogen lights that hung from the ceiling. The rest of the room was decorated entirely in chrome and black leather. There were Bauhaus chairs and tables that looked like dentist chairs, or maybe gynecologist examining seats, chrome miniblinds, black suede draperies.

Scattered about the spacious room were gleaming chrome frames that bore a distant family resemblance to Nautilus exercise machines. There were padded black leather straps with buckles, just right for a wrist or ankle—attached to black nylon ropes that fed through pulleys and blocks. Lara saw that the pulleys were attached to shackles that allowed them to be moved about the room from one attachment point to another.

In the middle of the room, the bed sat like a stage, four-poster in inspiration, only made of shiny chrome pipes generously festooned with D-rings. It was all very much like a sailboat, except the lines and blocks here were designed for hoisting people rather than sails.

"Wow," Lara said quietly as she bent back and caught sight of herself in the mirror that covered the entire ceiling. She watched as Rodriguez looked up at her with a broad white smile on his face.

With no further words, they walked in and closed the door. Lara stuck her head in the bathroom, which was by the entry door, and was relieved to see that—other than a large Jacuzzi-style tub—the gray, black, and chrome room was functional, prosaic, and not designed for anything other than normal functions.

Then she made her way to an arrangement of a dozen delicate black leather roses with brilliant chrome stems, leaves, thorns. They rested in a large cut-crystal vase that threw off rainbows from the halogens. The crystal vase was filled with what appeared to be mercury covered with a thin layer of mineral oil; the rose stems made dimples in the surface of the mercury; a single chrome leaf floated on the surface of the mercury.

Rodriguez caught her questioning examination of the roses.

"It's by a very famous artist from Germany who regularly reserves this room," Rodriguez said. "I'm told it's worth a fortune, and yes, it's real mercury, but the mineral oil keeps any harmful vapors from escaping."

"Fascinating," Lara said. She turned; her jaw dropped as she caught sight of an odd collection of what appeared to be statuettes at the far end of the room. Pyramidally phallic things, most of them about two feet high, like the traffic barriers she had seen lining the sidewalks to keep cars from parking there she supposed. They lined an entire wall from a louvered closet door all the way to a set of French double doors on the opposite wall.

"These are new too," Rodriguez said proudly. "What you see is the most complete collection of 'Amsterdamjes'—little Amsterdammers, both the real and the kitsch, the functional and the imitative, the historical and the contemporary." He set her duffel down on a luggage stand.

Lara walked over to the Amsterdamjes and saw that some looked very old, some new; most were round at the top, but some of them—abstract designs someone would try to call art, she decided—were dunce-cap pointed and looked sharp enough to cut. She gingerly tested the top of one with her index finger. All of the designs were marked with three "X"s arranged vertically.

"Museums regularly make me offers to buy the collection."

"I must say this is the most striking room I have every been in," Lara said. "I wonder, though, how anyone manages to sleep here."

Laughing loudly, Rodriguez grabbed one of the leather wristlets on the bedpost and pulled black rope a couple of feet through its block. "They don't buy this room to sleep, not this one."

Lara felt her cheeks flush. "No," she said slowly as her eyes followed the chrome lines of the bed. "I don't suppose they do."

She turned and moved to a set of French doors framed by more black suede. She saw the doors gave out onto a small balcony that overlooked the steep roof of the adjacent building.

Lara turned. "I suppose there's always a first time." She smiled as she saw Rodriguez giving her a questioning look.

"First time?" Rodriguez asked.

"To sleep," Lara said. "First time to sleep here."

Rodriguez laughed.

36

THE SOUND OF GUNFIRE INTERRUPTED LARA'S CONVERSATION WITH HER FATHER AS THEY SAT IN THE *TAGCAT TOO*. The feeling of being profoundly at peace was palpable as she showed him the cabinets that held her collection of earrings. He gave her a deep, warming smile when she told him that of everything in her collection, the star sapphires from Kashmir were her favorites and would always be.

He disappeared with the first crack of gunfire and took the *Tagcat Too* with him. Then there was darkness filled with more shots, shouts, explosions, expletives, barked orders, and screams. One of the voices was Rodriguez's. There were Dutch voices, German, and English.

Lara woke up and got instantly to her feet. The red LED clock on the bedside table told her it was just shy of 4:00 A.M. She pulled the .380 Colt from her Doomsday duffel, pulled the slide to chamber a round, and swiftly made her way to the door and made sure it was locked. Breathing deep shuddering breaths, she put her ear to the door for a moment. The violent noise seemed distant, below her. Muscling a heavy armchair in front of the door, she next pulled on her Levi's and the clothes she had left strewn on the floor in her weary lunge for sleep.

The sounds of violence grew louder, closer. Lara deliberately compassed the room for any avenue of escape. There was only the window opening out onto the steep roof of the adjoining building. She looked warily at the slick wet tiles, then went quickly into the bathroom. Not even a window.

"Terrific," she muttered as she zipped up the Doomsday duffel and tucked her head and right shoulder inside the strap, letting it rest snugly on her left hip.

Loud voices barked on the other side of the door. Something hammered on the frame, resounding like a cannon. Then again. The door began to splinter. Lara clicked the safety off the Colt, raised her arm, and fired a single shot at the door, just above the back of the chair.

A man screamed in pain. The hammering stopped. From beyond the door, footsteps clattered urgently. Lara allowed herself a faint smile as she listened to the muffled curses and urgent orders. The dominant commands were coming from a woman in both English and German.

Odd, Lara thought as she unlatched the window and slid the double-hung pane up. Suddenly the door erupted in a hailstorm of automatic weapons fire. Lara lunged through the window to escape the deadly reach of their guns only to find herself sliding face first down steep tiles well lubricated by the previous day's rain. Desperately she reached for any handhold; the Colt clattered off ahead of her. In the faint glow of refracted streetlights, Lara watched the gutter racing toward her and realized she'd just rip it off if she couldn't check her speed.

There! A pipe venting plumbing below stuck up a foot from the roof. But it was too far away. As the pipe grew nearer, Lara tried to get to her knees, to position herself to grab the pipe. But it was too slippery. Vaguely, she heard angry, excited voices behind her, above her. Desperately, she rolled over on her back and stretched out her legs to make contact with the pipe.

She could see the window now and with a calm, almost out-of-body detachment watched as a clot of people leaned on the sill. Lara watched as a woman raised a weapon and aimed it at her.

In the next instance, the crook of Lara's outstretched knee caught the vent pipe and swung her around in a violent circle. Then Lara heard the report of a gun above; then felt a storm of terra-cotta shrapnel as the slug gouged the tile where Lara had been about to pass. Another gunshot and another.

Lara reached for the pipe, but her momentum down the steep roof and the moisture broke her grip. But it also broke her speed and turned her around so that she slid slowly, on her back and feetfirst toward the gutter. Gunshots followed her, getting ever closer. When Lara's feet touched the gutter, she gingerly inched her way under an eave that blocked her from the sight of her attackers.

Breathing deeply, Lara rested for several seconds, and then tested the strength of the gutter. It collapsed under her immediately, spilling her off the roof and another ten feet onto the top landing of a metal fire escape. Stunned by the fall, Lara struggled to take a breath where none would come. Finally, the first breath came and the next. She pushed herself up to her elbows, amazed to find the worst pain in her thigh where she had struck a potted plant.

Lights went on behind the window that looked out over the fire escape. Excited voices grew louder. Lara scrambled to her feet and swiftly made her way to the ground, landing in a pile of old boxes and trash in the alley at the bottom. At just that instant, a blue van bounded down the alley and skidded to a halt. The doors exploded open like a grenade blast.

Four very large balaclava-masked men dressed in black leaped at her.

"Come with us," one said urgently as he lunged for her. "We're your friends."

"No! Stop! Let me go!" She threw an elbow at the man's face and the wet crunching sounds of breaking bone crackled through the dim alleyway. The man's legs buckled; he collapsed into the men behind him. Lara sprinted away, but seconds later a flying tackle took her down to the damp, irregular pavement.

The next handful of racing heartbeats and shattered seconds were filled with men, hands, weight bearing down on her, a glove over her mouth, a needle prick in the back of her thigh, and then the dark warm comfortable melting feeling that came from powerful sedatives taking effect. Lara felt metal. Handcuffs? And then the hands that grabbed, handled, lifted, carried. Finally she fell gratefully into the dark churning maw of darkness.

37

VOICES IN A VOID. Words without meaning. Sounds without context. Blackness.

Then, by tiny degrees, Lara Blackwood felt herself becoming herself again. Consciousness returned slowly, bringing with it fear and memories: of men and uniforms and needles bearing narcotic dreams.

She felt smooth fabric under the side of her face, smelled the musty, stale tarry odors of a house lived in too long, the dusty motes of old books and wood.

With each beat of her heart, the words she heard made more sense, grew in content, and created context until, finally, she could make out two distinct voices speaking Dutch. They didn't realize she could understand them.

The voices seemed friendly; they had removed her restraints. Even more assuring was the absence of the sounds made by every bustling bureaucracy—be it hospital or police station. She heard none of the constant chaotic background noises of phones ringing, feet stepping, papers rattling, voices murmuring, chairs scraping, drawers rattling, doors closing, throats clearing, file drawers rumbling.

Instead, she felt a gentle breeze from an open window and heard, distantly, the voices of children playing.

Then a knock at the door, a muffled Dutch voice on the other side asked if it was all right to enter. From near her, another Dutch voice gave assent. A knob rattled; hinges squeaked; a concerned voice spoke English. "How is she?"

"She's," said an old man with a Dutch voice.

"*. . . an old man . . . I actually got the impression that he was concerned about you.*"

Behind the dimness of her closed lids, she remembered Rod's description.

"*When he left, he said something truly odd . . . the old man said to me: 'If you do see her, please tell her that there are others who also seek the truth.' *"

Lara's heart quickened, but she damped her first impulse to open her eyes, get to her feet. She remained as still as a sleeper, hiding behind gray-pink eyelids and trying to learn as much as possible before deciding how to act. She was lying on her right side, facing the conversation.

Finally Lara opened her eyes and spoke: "Are you the man who also seeks the truth?" Her speech was slurred, her tongue dry and swollen.

"Ah! The sleeping beauty awakens."

"Oh, my!" Lara exclaimed when her eyes focused on a remotely familiar face of an elderly but vigorous man. "You—aren't you Jan De-Groot?"

"The same." He gave her an Old World bow.

"Professor . . . professor emeritus at Leiden University," she said vaguely. "You were formerly head of research at Eurodrug."

"I am guilty of all you charge." He smiled. "And this"—he indicated the other Dutchman, a mature but much younger man than DeGroot— "is Richard Falk, the second in command of the Dutch Armed Forces and the founder, along with me and several others, of *Shinrai.*"

"*Shinrai?*"

"It's the Japanese word for truth," Falk said. "We are a network of people around the world, including many Japanese, who would like to see a just conclusion to the situation which has swept you up."

"The situation?"

DeGroot took over. "For fifty years, politicians and novelists have concentrated on the horrors of Nazi Germany, telling tales of the ODESSA and plots to create a Fourth Reich—straw dogs!" He sniffed loudly. "Perhaps their efforts, and certainly the German admission of guilt, the Jewish cries of 'Never Again,' and the continuing pressure against the rise of neofascism there all serve to keep that Aryan evil at bay.

"But all the while, this concentration on Germany has distracted people from the Japanese holocaust and medical atrocities, their virulent racism, the very Wagnerian sense of superiority and destiny that still burns in Japan today."

Lara heard him take another deep breath. The Dutchman's speech impediment seemed to get worse as the subject matter grew more emotional.

"You see," DeGroot continued, his voice calmer now, "except for our Japanese allies, most members of *Shinrai* all suffered at the hands of the Japanese in World War II. The Japanese killed millions of innocent people and those—like us—whom they did not kill, they maimed physically and emotionally. There is nothing more indelibly imprinted upon memory than seeing loved ones, comrades at arms, tortured, dismembered, disemboweled, defenestrated, exsanguinated, vivisected, alive and right before your eyes.

"It would probably be correct to call us fanatics," continued DeGroot. "While most of us have lived outwardly normal lives and many of us have achieved substantial recognition in our careers, there is nothing else in our lives that matters even one percent as much as the justice the Japanese have denied us and the world.

"We've labored for half a century to bring the arrogant Japanese to the same point of contrition that Germany accepted more than half a century ago." He paused and in a lower voice said, "The old saw about those who forget history being doomed to repeat it—it's very true and poignant here: the Japanese have never been punished, never been forced to face their hideous acts, never accepted responsibility. Unless they do, they will do this all over again, and the world will be a worse place for it."

"You are just the latest victim," Falk said. "And perhaps you can help us prevent any more."

The lobby of the Casa Blanca smelled of stale cigarettes, rancid coffee, and fresh fear.

Sitting at attention on the edge of a gold brocade sofa, Constable Joost Van Dyke squinted against the tears that washed down his face from the woman's constant cigarette smoking. He had been unfortunate enough to be the first policeman to respond to the emergency call of gunshots on the Oude Zijds Acherburgwal. He found the front door to the trendy gay hotel and funhouse demolished by what appeared to be professionally crafted explosives and inside a charnal house. The owner was dead, as well as two guests who had unwisely opened their doors to see what the clatter was about. Three others were wounded. On the top floor, he found the body of an often convicted and too-often paroled Northern Irish thug who appeared to have hired out his gun one too many times.

The darkness had been filled with detectives, ambulances, morgue wagons, and a steady stream of police officials from headquarters, steadily increasing in rank, all asking him the same questions as the dawn turned into morning and morning approached noon.

Then came the woman who reminded him of a cobra he had once seen at the zoo. She was a formidable woman: tall, blond, a face that carried the lethal beauty of a cobra and a voice that cut through to the bone. She arrived at the hotel accompanied by his watch commander who had brought him to the café.

The woman stood over the sofa on which Van Dyke sat alone.

"All right," she said, puffing smoke out with each syllable. "Let's go over things one more time."

Van Dyke threw a pleading glance at his watch commander to please do something, *anything* about this snake woman, to please let him go. Van Dyke's commander shook her head imperceptibly. She stood like part of a small but silent Greek chorus next to the chief of all Amsterdam's police, the diplomatic liaison from the mayor's office, and the number two man from the U.S. embassy. A personal request from the U.S. president to afford the snake woman every possible courtesy had been passed quickly through diplomatic channels and had dropped like a ton of cobbles on Van Dyke's head. The continuation or denouement of his promising career rested on the quality of his answers.

Van Dyke nodded at his commander, tried to take a deep breath, and found himself choking again on the tobacco smoke. The woman rolled her eyes as he took another sip from a foam cup of water.

"Sorry." Van Dyke cleared his throat and looked again at his notes. "As I said, I observed five people come out of this place of business from the time I called headquarters until backup arrived."

Sheila looked at him silently.

"All naked or partly clothed men."

She nodded. Still silent, still waiting. To strike? he wondered.

Behind him and up the stairs he could hear the rustlings of the detectives and forensic lab techs as they scoured the hotel for evidence.

Again he explained what had been found: besides the bodies, the teams had, so far, found a .380 automatic on the ground behind an adjoining canal house, and a single .380 casing on the floor of room 410. Also, head hairs from the pillow in room 410 and in the alleyway, a single earring with one of the most stunning star sapphires anyone had ever seen including old Wilem at the station who was once stationed in India and knew sapphires. Also fresh footprints and tire treads in the alley. A number of fingerprints had been lifted from room 410 and its key. They expected to receive a data file momentarily from the American FBI to see if any of the prints matched the American fugitive, Lara Blackwood.

"Yes, yes, I've heard that before." She waved her smoldering cigarette about, spreading the stink like a farmer's honey wagon. "I want to know what *you* saw. People, vehicles—anything out of place for that time of the morning."

Helplessly, the constable looked at his notes and found nothing written there. He shook his head and wondered if he should begin the mourning for his career. Then something he had not previously remembered!

"A van," he said brightly.

"Can you remember the color?"

Van Dyke shook his head. "Dark," he said apologetically.

Closing his eyes, he tried to visualize the vehicle.

"It was driven by an old man," Van Dyke said finally. "Someone vaguely familiar." He looked up at her. "But after a certain age most old men start to look alike."

"Thank you, Constable, for that last perceptive observation," Sheila said acerbically. "You may go now."

Uncertainly, Van Dyke looked over at his commander. She nodded her assent. Hurrying, Van Dyke made his way to the outside, where he greedily sucked in great lungfuls of air uncontaminated by the toxic stew of burning tobacco that polluted the café.

As the constable stood by the door, two of the forensic technicians who had previously searched the café and its rest rooms exited the mobile crime scene van and made their way into the hotel.

Sheila Gaillard stretched, acutely aware of the effects her hard round breasts had on the men around her, all of whom tried, unsuccessfully, to look away. Her gaze locked with the Amsterdam mayor's; she gave him a small, willing smile. He might prove to be useful, she thought.

At that moment, two white-uniformed men approached the booth.

"Pardon me," one of the uniforms said, "but you said to contact you the moment we had preliminary results."

Sheila turned. "Yes?"

"The suspect's fingerprints match fresh latents found in the room, on the key, on the windowsill, the fire escape, and the .380 Colt pistol found in the alley."

Murmuring filled the room. Finally, the mayor asked Sheila, "I can understand why Daiwa Ichiban would send you, one of its security personnel, to help us track down someone from the company who has committed these heinous crimes, after all, you have access to the people who knew her best. But I'd like to ask you if you have any idea . . . any idea at all, what could cause someone so talented and brilliant as Lara Blackwood to suddenly snap and become a criminal? After all, I remember her well in the years before her Olympic competition . . . she raced in many regattas here and I personally awarded prizes to her." His voice was sad, reluctant to believe.

Gaillard shook her head and concealed her joy that they had bought into the spin story she had created. "Perhaps there is a medical reason," Sheila said generously. "Perhaps a brain lesion?" She shook her head slowly in mock sadness. "We may never know."

The mayor nodded.

Sheila turned to the Amsterdam police chief and said, "In light of this recent incident, would it be possible for you to broadcast a composite sketch and lookout report?"

The police chief nodded, then stood up. "Just to law enforcement, or to the media as well?"

"To the world," Sheila said. "Then she will have no place to hide."

38

LARA SAT AT A GLASS AND CHROME TABLE THAT FILLED ONE END OF A SPOTLESS, WHITE TILE AND PLASTIC KITCHEN. The room and its furnishings were so clean they hurt the eyes. At her side sat Falk, across the table, two more people: Beatrix VanDeventer, a Dutch woman who sat on the World Court in the Hague, and next to her, Henry Noord, the Netherlands' liaison with Interpol and former chief of the Rotterdam Police Department. By the door, two young men with military haircuts and side arms stood at informal parade rest, not eating. Four more like them were deployed throughout the house and on the street. One had a bandage over his nose that Lara had excruciatingly broken.

At the head of the table, DeGroot spoke reluctantly about his World War II experiences at the hands of the Japanese. Myriad scars and discolorations did more than hint at the ordeal he had survived. He had told them that he was the only survivor of a virus that had killed every other human guinea pig. Normally, the mortality rate on experiments was one hundred percent because they killed the survivors to dissect them and find out why they had not died.

"But I was the miracle man and they kept me around as a sort of pet—poking, prodding, drawing blood, clipping out tissue samples here and there—all without the benefit of anesthesia, of course." In addition, his careful observation of the Japanese medical experimenters and the access that his "pet" status provided allowed him to absorb experimental techniques and lab processes that led to many of his pharmaceutical patents.

Like Noord, Falk, and VanDeventer, DeGroot was in his late seventies or eighties, vigorous, energetic living proof that age and a certain amount of brutal torture did not inevitably bring disability.

"After the war, at university, they thought I was this boy wonder," DeGroot had said. "I developed three vaccine patents before even graduating. But remember, Japan had a functional bacteriological warfare operation they used to kill countless Chinese with anthrax, plague, cholera, glanders. They also needed to develop and test vaccines to protect themselves against their own weapons. What my professors and classmates thought were brilliant insights into the biological process were simply the result of my observations and indelible memories of hideous experiments done on innocent, unwilling human beings."

He had been married and divorced twice. "It's difficult to live with a man who screams at nightmares even in the day when he is awake," he had said matter-of-factly.

His patents had brought him millions, yet he took only a small portion for himself. The rest went to the support of *Shinrai*, or for the care of survivors victimized by the Japanese. "Since neither the Japanese, nor the Americans, nor any other country will lift a bloodstained finger to help these poor wretches," Falk spat.

DeGroot picked up his fork and took a bite of the vegetable curry that had been brought in by Falk and VanDeventer.

"Amazing," Lara said as she sipped at her wine. "The network—this *Shinrai*—is truly amazing."

Shrugging, DeGroot swallowed, took a sip of wine. "We help each other because we must." He took another sip of wine, then continued. "You see, we are like Kurata's assets, only just the opposite. Kurata's people are salted through many governments and corporations and are bent by money. We are not so many as they. We are bent the other way, and by conviction rather than money."

"We are the polar opposites of Kurata's people," said VanDeventer. "Like magnetic poles, neither of us would exist without the other."

"We are *very* analogous to Kurata's organization," Falk added. "We are at the same levels of responsibility and power. We are in places to observe the flow of pertinent information, in positions to direct certain assets and take action under the guise of officially sanctioned activities."

"Indeed," DeGroot said. "Our people are in just the positions that

Kurata likes to subvert. As a consequence, many of our congregation have been approached and, after consultation, have allowed themselves to be recruited so we might monitor their activities more closely."

In the ensuing silence, a songbird chirped an evening song; breezes made stirring sounds in the trees; the toasty smells of burning leaves drifted in like faint shadows on overcast days.

"Unbelievable," Lara muttered. "Whole secret worlds, battling spheres of influence—wars actually—all happening in the dark." She shook her head.

"It is a long tradition, going back centuries and centuries." VanDeventer wiped her mouth with her napkin. "Modern Westerners have deluded themselves into thinking that just because governments and people are *supposed* to behave in a certain way they *will* behave in that manner." She shook her head. "I was a very young law clerk to Roling, a great man and the Dutch judge at the Tokyo War Crimes Trial. I learned then that civilization is a thin veneer that inadequately buffers the animals at our cores."

"Especially the Japanese."

"Why especially?" asked Lara as she scooped the last bite of curry onto her fork.

"Because they like to regale us with their pious assertions about how civilized they are," VanDeventer said. "Yet they took medical atrocities beyond even the Nazis; they ate human flesh! This is not civilization; it is hypocrisy."

"We know now," Falk said, "that the Japanese had a very advanced atomic bomb program. They had accomplished more than the Germans and had plans to incinerate Los Angeles. Yet, they play entire symphonies on the bleeding heartstrings of the world—'Hiroshima! Nagasaki! Oh, poor us!' and they don't tell anyone that they certainly would have used their A-bomb first had they been able. There is no doubt that without dropping the atomic bombs, troops invading Japan would have been met by a massive biological warfare counterattack."

"Ishii's production man—Karasawa—had his systems going twenty-four hours per day," said DeGroot, "turning out plague, anthrax, typhoid, and cholera among others. Archives at your Fort Detrick estimate the Japanese had made enough to infect half of the planet."

"Further," Falk continued, "records of the Japanese High Command show there was no moral compunction about using the new weapons—no hand wringing such as took place here in the United States. In their racist world, everybody but the Japanese themselves were inferior, animals to be slaughtered when necessary for the glory of the emperor."

"I'm not sure I mentioned it," DeGroot said, "but the Unit 731 weapons nearly stopped dead the American advances in the Pacific."

Lara shook her head. "No, you didn't mention that."

DeGroot nodded. "You may remember that the tide of the entire war against Japan turned with the fierce battle over Saipan in 1944."

Lara shrugged and shook her head vaguely. "School history classes seem to start with Pearl Harbor and skip right right to Hiroshima without touching much in between."

DeGroot frowned, then continued. "Well, it was. It was a bloody battle with fourteen thousand Americans and twenty-four thousand Japanese killed in the fighting. Additional thousands of Koreans died as well. They were basically slaves brought to the island as common labor. But when the battle started, the Japanese slaughtered them all—men, women, children—because it was feared they would stage an uprising and side with the Americans."

"Dear God," Lara said quietly.

"Well, Ishii's Unit 731 had prepared a surprise for the invaders. He equipped a huge assault team with bubonic plague weapons. The assault team's ship was sunk by an American submarine before it could reach Saipan. Otherwise, the war might have been very different."

"The point to all this," VanDeventer said calmly, "is that—Japanese protestations aside—civilization is unreliable, and nations rarely do anything for moral reasons. Peace is still maintained through superior firepower."

"Even though that firepower may actually be economic or some other force that can destroy without destroying," Noord added.

"Private wars," Lara said.

"It's the future," DeGroot said. "The best attacks are those the target cannot detect; the best battles are those the combatants don't know they are fighting, and the best victories are the ones that the defeated don't recognize."

"These are the wars of the future," Falk said. "The opening skirmishes are being fought today. We have had already a dozen Pearl Harbors, and the public is unaware of most of them, seeing only the collateral damage—air traffic control failures, power blackouts, new viruses and antibiotic-resistant bacteria, aircraft crashes, ship sinkings, millions of dollars hacked from banking systems, major telephone switching failures, satellite malfunctions. The public has no clue, no clue at all."

"The public *thinks* it knows what is going on," VanDeventer interjected, "what with the information overload that exists today they feel they somehow *know* everything that is going on."

"Naive," Noord commented. "So much goes on—probably the most important things that shape people's lives—that is unseen, off the record, off the books."

"The public has no clue," VanDeventer said.

"I disagree," said DeGroot, who had been silent as he worked through the curry that had grown cold. "There is a hint; unfortunately the first hint is often death."

The landing lights of the Valkenburg airport grew closer.

Sitting directly behind the copilot in the Daiwa Ichiban corporate helicopter, Sheila Gaillard stared through the darkness and watched as the small airport east of Leiden came into view.

Next to her sat the chief of the Amsterdam police force. Two plainclothes officers sat in the seat behind.

Quietly she fumed as she lit another cigarette, adding to the smog that packed the cabin like sedimentary rock layers. Fucking cookie pusher diplomats. She *knew* that Blackwood's trail led to DeGroot's house—or it would. She could not prove it but she *knew* it in her guts. Following the meeting at the Casa Blanca, she had tracked down the timid constable Van Dyke and had pulled up an Internet photo of Jan DeGroot.

"Yes," the constable said reluctantly. "That *could* be the man I saw. But it was very dark and, and they all tend to look alike."

But the higher-ups in the police department refused to give such thin evidence the respect Sheila believed it deserved.

"No, we will positively *not* authorize any intrusion on a Dutch citizen's home on the basis of the information you have." They had been adamant.

"Blackwood is a dangerous woman," she had argued. "Mr. DeGroot's life could be in danger."

They did not budge.

"You will not set foot on the property," she was told brusquely. "We will have one of our own people talk to him, ascertain if there is any substance . . . any danger."

Sheila attacked the cigarette, drawing down half an inch of ash in a single suck; she flicked the ash on the helicopter floor with her dead butts and cursed the Dutch and, for lack of a better target, Kurata's smarmy nephew, Akira Sugawara.

She had contacted Sugawara and asked him to have Kurata intercede with the Dutch. Kurata's reply was that she would have to appear to cooperate with the Dutch.

The ground rushed up to meet them as the helicopter pilot used a police emergency to gain a priority slot to land.

As they approached their designated landing spot, Sheila saw a Leiden police car and another unmarked one beside it.

A fucking parade, she thought. *All we need is a big fucking parade with sirens and maybe a Macy's float of Goofy or something.* At least it would distract attention from her own surveillance team who should already be discreetly in place. But the police visit would tip off DeGroot—one more opportunity thwarted.

Shit, she thought as she ground her cigarette butt out on the helicopter's carpeting. Just fucking shit.

"The point," DeGroot said as he led the way from the kitchen to the overstuffed living room and settled into a wing-backed chair, "is how we stop this terrible thing and how we can keep it from happening again."

"*Shinrai* has supporters, people all around the world, in Japan as well," Falk explained. "Mobilizing them, however, takes time."

The telephone rang.

DeGroot picked up the receiver. "Yes?"

He frowned for several moments and replaced the receiver.

"It seems," he spoke calmly, "that we have a friend and an emergency."

Faces turned expectantly toward him.

"The caller identified himself as *maruta* and said he was a member of Kurata's organization."

A faint collective gasp filled his brief pause.

"He said that a small contingent of police are on their way here at this very moment."

"Do you believe him?" asked Lara.

"There is no profit in failing to believe him, at least for the moment."

"What are we going to do?" Lara asked.

"*We*—that is me and my friends—will do nothing," DeGroot said. "To do otherwise would endanger our new friend, if indeed he is a friend."

"But—" Lara started to speak.

"You will wait in the Jew closet."

"The what?"

"You remember the *Diary of Anne Frank?*"

She nodded.

"The title in Dutch was *Het Achterhuis*. In Dutch *achterhuis* means, literally, 'behind the house' and refers to the hidden caches that many Dutch people prepared to hide their Jewish friends from the Nazis."

He got to his feet. "Come, I will show you."

Lara followed him into a rear bedroom and watched as he parted the clothes hangers and inserted the point of a small screwdriver into a depression that looked as if it belonged to a finishing nail. One of the rear wallboards of the closet clicked loose.

"Does *maruta* mean anything?" Lara asked.

"Literally, it is Japanese for log," DeGroot said as removed the loose board and reached into a space behind it. "But it actually means even more. A lot more."

A mechanical click sounded, and a portion of the rear wall swung inward, revealing a dark, cramped space.

"Anyone the Japanese wanted to use as a medical guinea pig was referred to as a *maruta*—a log."

He motioned her inside the hidden space.

"Ishii and his men would requisition *maruta* along with toilet paper and typing paper," DeGroot said. "When there was an oversupply, they'd slaughter them so as not to waste food and space," DeGroot continued as Lara climbed into the hidden space.

"There are many things which—try as I might—I will never forget," DeGroot said. "One of them . . . one is a film of Unit 731 technicians interviewed by intelligence officials in Tokyo."

Lara scrunched to one side of the double-coffin-sized space to allow the door to swing back toward the closed position.

"When the interviewer asked him how he could conduct experiments on human beings, he told them, and I remember his reply word for word. 'Sometimes there were no anesthetics. They screamed and screamed. We didn't regard the *maruta* as human beings. They were just lumps of meat on a chopping block.' "

Lara shivered.

"Dehumanizing others is the first necessary step to cruelty and war crimes," DeGroot said as he closed the door. Blackness closed in on Lara as she heard him refasten the door of the Jew Closet.

Sugawara stood by the pay phone as he tried to steady his knees. His heart was light with the rightness of what he had just done. His belly boiled with heavy black dread over what would follow. The reports from

Gaillard were confidential, restricted to him and Kurata. His actions could be traced. This much he knew. But he knew he had to follow the new path he had chosen, for there was no returning. He had burned every possible bridge to the past and there was nothing more to do.

Finally, he turned and headed for the KLM departure gates.

39

RENEGADE TIME CAREENED PAST LIKE OFF-SPROCKET, FAST-FORWARD FILM—NOW OFF TO AN ANGLE, NOW STUTTERY STRAIGHT, NOW RUNNING RAGGEDLY AT ANOTHER ANGLE, PIE-SHAPED PROJECTOR LIGHT BURNING INTO THE SCREEN.

Lara tried to organize the shattered fragments into coherent thought.

There had been the Jew Closet, then muffled voices as VanDeventer and Noord said their good-byes.

Hurried footsteps, rattles at the door to the Jew Closet, bright lights and DeGroot, motioning frantically not to say a word. He shoved a child's erasable tablet at her—the type with a clear plastic sheet that you wrote on with a stylus and erased by pulling up the plastic sheet.

Written on both tablets was, "Say nothing. Follow me quickly. Use this for all communication until we tell you otherwise. HURRY!"

She followed DeGroot along a hallway. At the end, Falk and his bodyguards waited at an open door.

"It is always such a pleasure to see old friends, eh, General?" DeGroot said conversationally.

"Ah, yes," Falk replied lightly, "but there seem to be fewer each year." Despite his light tone, Falk's face was a taut web of lines and gristle, his eyes sharp and alert. He looked away, through the door, then motioned them to move quickly.

"Afraid that's a consequence of living so long," DeGroot said lightly.

For eavesdroppers, Lara thought. DeGroot said earlier that the house was expertly swept for bugs on a regular basis, indeed had been just hours ago in anticipation of her arrival. Maybe they figured someone might have directional microphones or those lasers you aimed at windows.

They went through the door now.

Lara made her way down two steps into a spacious, American-style enclosed garage large enough to house a luxurious workshop that looked like a hardware store tool display; an old, battered Citroën, rust showing through gray paint; and a gleaming new, black Chevrolet Suburban with tinted windows, resting like a main battle tank, so large and dark it seemed to suck the light away from the rest of the room.

Falk's bodyguards stood around the hulking Suburban. Lara headed toward the Suburban's open rear door. DeGroot grabbed her arm; with his head, he motioned her toward the Citroën. She hesitated, frowned as DeGroot's grip tightened. Reluctantly, she allowed herself to be led toward the Citroën, a large sedan model shaped like a giant streamlined beetle.

DeGroot opened the rear door; Lara got in. One of Falk's armed men was at the wheel. DeGroot paused for a moment, cleared his pad, and began writing a message, his face frowning, obviously annoyed at the delay.

He turned the pad and showed it to Lara.

"On the floor. Lie down. Stay down until I tell you. Very important. Life or death."

Lara nodded as she climbed in, surprised by the spaciousness of the interior. There were jump seats attached to the back of the front seat, as if the Citroën had once been a taxi or a limo. She noticed then the tinted windows in the rear and decided it had once been a limo, maybe two decades past.

A large remnant of new household carpeting covered the floor. Lara lay down.

DeGroot covered her with a black muslinlike cloth.

Almost as soon as the rear door closed, the engines of both vehicles roared into life; Lara heard the grumble-grinding of garage doors opening.

Then they were moving. Then stopping, turning, moving again. Bouncing. The Citroën vibrated evenly with the deep rumbles of a powerful engine, obviously new and well maintained. It accelerated quickly and effortlessly; it took bumps and turns like a race car.

A radio in the front clicked, no words, just a series of clicks as if someone distant were simply hitting the transmit key but saying nothing.

More turns, more clicks. A stop, and then the engine accelerated; regular thumps like expansion joints and higher engine revs hinted to Lara they were on a freeway.

"You can sit up now." DeGroot's voice seemed biblically loud as he broke the silence.

Lara rolled onto her back and sat up. Pulling herself onto the seat, she looked forward through the windshield and saw they were, indeed, on a freeway. Lara saw a marker, E10, flash by.

"What's happening?"

"The telephone call—*Maruta*—said the police were on the way, that they had been told that perhaps you were holding me hostage." He gave a short laugh that sounded almost like a cough. Lara recognized the sound now as DeGroot's way of trying to deal with his speech impediment.

"Obviously an excuse for someone to look for you."

Three quick clicks came over the radio speaker; DeGroot leaned over, picked up the microphone, and pressed the transmit button twice.

"Falk's behind us; someone's behind Falk," DeGroot said. "Someone who's not the police."

"Not the police?" Lara asked.

A nod from DeGroot. "Thanks to our Mr. Maruta, we staged a nice little scene for the police just as they arrived. After we hid you in the Jew Closet, Falk and I walked out with Noord and VanDeventer, talking about what a lovely evening we had had and how we would be joining them for coffee.

"It was a lovely little tableau, and certainly illustrated that we were in no danger. They offered to post a guard in case you showed up; I pointed out that Falk and his bodyguards would be visiting with me for several days and that there was no need."

More clicks on the radio: two slow ones followed by four in quick succession.

An exit approached; the driver quickly turned off the E10 onto Plesmanlaan.

DeGroot looked into the darkness and said, "My laboratory is near here. This area is known as Leeuwenhoek. The Dutchman who invented the microscope is from here." Pause. "I love the feeling of history, of continuity I get from working here."

The Citroën rumbled on, more slowly now. Three quick clicks sounded on the speaker.

"They're still with us," DeGroot said. "There's no doubt we're being followed."

They rode in silence for several minutes as each thought about the car—cars?—in pursuit. The Citroën made its way around a traffic circle. They passed by the train station, then they turned onto a street with another tongue-twisting name: Wilem DeZwijerlaan.

Three more rapid clicks on the speaker. The Citroën slowed and turned left on a narrow road. "Leidseweg" said the sign. Moments later, three more quick clicks, a pause, then two more.

"They're still there," DeGroot said. "Two of them."

Lara looked through the tinted rear glass and saw the headlights of three vehicles.

"But not for long," DeGroot said, his voice carrying with it . . . what? Satisfaction. Anticipation.

"Noord and VanDeventer will be in position by now," he said cryptically. "We have practiced this for quite some time, never convinced it would really be used."

Lara gave him a quizzical look.

"Just wait," DeGroot said. "Very soon, you'll see how the mouse fights the tiger."

40

NIGHT FOG GATHERED ON THE BOTERHUIS POLDER EAST OF LEIDEN, ROLLING OFF THE WATERS OF THE JOPPE, SNUGGLING INTO THE DIKE-ENCLOSED FIELDS LIKE QUILT BATTING.

Tatters of the fog, lifted by a gentle breeze, detached themselves like diaphanous ghost shadows and made their languorous way across the narrow Leidseweg. These were the timeless, the original, poltergeists, from the German word meaning "ghosts from the polder." The Dutch called them "*poldergeests.*"

Hunched in the rear seat of a rented 900 series Mercedes, its headlights out, Sheila Gaillard squinted through the night, concentrating on the taillights ahead, giving no thought to the fact she was witnessing an ancient cycle that had insinuated itself into the mythology of nations around the world. The Mercedes was empty save her and the driver, a Flemish Belgian borrowed from NATO.

A rented BMW raced through the fog half a mile ahead of them, and beyond that, by another half mile, the taillights of the massive, dark Chevy Suburban. Beyond that, barely visible now, the dented Citroën.

"Fuck all," she muttered as the taillights disappeared again into a fog bank. The driver slowed.

"Faster," Sheila barked.

"But it is dark; I have no lights," complained the driver. "We could die."

"We *might* die," Sheila growled. "You're very right about that." She paused and caught his eye for just a moment in the rearview mirror. "But if you lose them, you *will* die."

She smiled.

"Slowly."

The Mercedes surged forward and burst out of the poltergeist.

Gaillard took no satisfaction in winning her tiny point from the driver. Instead, she burned with the humiliation of seeing DeGroot walk from his house, of having him laugh at the suggestion he might be in danger, of having the Dutch police laugh with him . . . at her.

Not willing to endure the humiliation any longer, Sheila had them drop her at the train station, where she taxied back to the surveillance teams watching the DeGroot house. Two surveillance teams, hastily cobbled together with assets of uneven abilities who had never worked together before. Ill-equipped and understaffed.

"Fuck all," Sheila muttered. The driver cast her a worried glance that almost made her smile. "Fuck, fuck, fuck."

With Kurata's wealth and influence behind her, she had rarely lacked for resources and cooperation, but things had happened too fast to prepare in a country where the people were as close to incorruptible as possible. Fucking proud Dutchmen and their fucking prickly sense of duty. They weren't perfect, but—she thought ruefully—there was good reason Kurata's organization had fewer assets here than in any other place in the world.

"Fucking Dutch," she muttered aloud, ignoring the driver's anxious look. He sped up, thinking this was what she wanted

And damn Kurata. "Appear to cooperate," she muttered. "Fuck you, Tokutaro." Double whammy: no resources and no commotion. He'd blame *her* if they lost the Blackwood bitch.

She shifted on the backseat now, tried to stretch the cramped muscles in her calves and thighs. Too much sitting, too much inactivity.

"What's that?" she asked as, up ahead, brake lights brightened: first the Suburban, then the BMW. "Slow down."

Instants later, the radio on the seat next to Sheila crackled, first with the encryption tone, and then a voice.

"The Suburban's stopped," a voice from the Beemer reported.

"You stop too." Sheila thought quickly. "If they don't move within a couple of seconds, turn around and wait somewhere near in Leiden. I don't want them to get a make on you."

"Acknowledged."

Sheila told her driver to stop and back up into a small turnout by a pump house. With the Mercedes concealed by the small structure, Sheila climbed out and watched the scene play out in front of her. As the taillights of the Citroën disappeared in the distance, Sheila watched the BMW turn around, head toward and then pass them.

Moments later, the Suburban's brake lights went dim. Sheila raced for the Mercedes.

"Fast now," she ordered, slamming the door after she leaped in. "As fast as you can."

Battering their way through the fog banks, the Mercedes jounced on the narrow rough road; the Suburban's taillights moving quickly. They came into a small hamlet: Warmond.

"Don't get too close now," Sheila ordered as she scanned the roadway for signs of the Citroën. Blackwood had to be in there, she and the *Shinrai* assholes.

"They will be too smart, won't they—the men in the Chevy—to lead us to the other car now that it is out of sight?" The driver ventured the thought Sheila had been avoiding.

She ignored the driver.

Fuck all, she thought as the Suburban wandered through a small village and out the other side, moving cautiously, seemingly oblivious to surveillance. There were signs for a *jachthaven*—a yacht harbor—two of them. The dread in her belly told her that even at that moment Blackwood could be boarding a boat and there was no way to follow it.

"Keep following them," Sheila said. "We've got nothing to lose."

The driver shrugged.

When the village ended, the road made a sharp turn and they lost sight of the Suburban for a moment. Then, as the Mercedes came around the curve, Sheila saw the Suburban pass over a small drawbridge, which immediately began to open.

"Motherfuck."

The Suburban quickly disappeared from sight on the other side of the bridge.

"Fuckers."

As the Mercedes drew to a stop at the bridge, Sheila got out. "Molensloot" said the sign, referring, Sheila assumed, to the narrow canal that looked almost narrow enough to jump over.

As she stood there, a cabin cruiserlike boat made its painfully slow, deliberate way toward the bridge. Of course it would move slowly,

Sheila thought. Staying in the bridge shadows, she made her way down to the water level as the motorboat approached.

In the moonlight, she noted the boat's registration number. Then, for the first time that night, she smiled.

41

DAWN TAGGED THE KLM 747 FORTY THOUSAND FEET OVER THE SIBERIAN STEPPES, NORTHWEST OF LAKE BAIKAL. Inside, on the first deck, almost to the very front of the first class cabin, the soft peeping of Akira Sugawara's digital watch pulled him out of a nightmare: Kurata was testing new blades on him, cutting off fingers, toes, cleanly chopping at arms and legs an inch at a time. Each excruciating blow brought great gouts of blood and screams from Sugawara for Kurata to just end his suffering and kill him cleanly. With every plea came Kurata's mocking laughter; with every new sword to be tested, Sugawara's flesh healed whole, ready to be painfully mutilated once again.

Sugawara startled awake, his mind carrying the acid residue of fear, his limbs still throbbing with dream-pain. Looking around him through sleep-glazed eyes, Sugawara saw the empty seat next to him. The rest of the no-smoking section was mostly empty; the clean air he breathed ended abruptly four rows to the rear where great roils of cigarette smoke collected about the mostly Japanese passengers.

Taking a deep breath, Sugawara swallowed against the lump of fear in his throat, sat up, and checked his watch: 8:51 A.M., Tokyo time. He rubbed his face, pushed the button that levered his seat into its upright position, and pressed the call button for the flight attendant.

Only then did he lean over and touch the special Thermos in its special holder. Destiny passed easily through airport X-ray machines and fitted handily in the space beneath an aircraft seat: carry-on death.

He sat up, ramrod straight, and reached for the expensive phone on the back of the seat in front of him. Were they on to him yet? Was the alarm out for his hostile welcome in Amsterdam? Akira dialed in the Tokyo number and moments later entered his user name and passcode to access the voice mail system where Gaillard left her status reports for him and Kurata. He frowned as he listened to the evil woman's obvious progress. Her success would only push him closer to failure.

"Hai?" the flight attendant said. "What may I do for you?"

Sugawara looked up at the very tall, blond man in the KLM uniform. He spoke perfect Japanese. They always surprised him, these Dutch, with their facility for languages, for accommodating foreign cultures. "It is very good for business," a Philips executive had told him one day at an electronics conference in Tokyo. "It does not make good sense to try and do business with a people if you cannot speak their language, understand their culture, no?"

Sugawara nodded politely at the man, listened for any last hints that Gaillard or Kurata were on to him, and then disconnected the call.

"I believe I slept through breakfast," Sugawara told the flight attendant as he replaced the phone in the seatback fixture. "May I have some coffee?"

"Of course," the flight attendant replied. "Would you also like the full breakfast? We saved that for you."

"Yes, I would like breakfast very much." Sugawara glanced at his watch again: 8:53 A.M. Television coverage of the dedication in Tokyo would have started, but Kurata would not be on until 9:00 A.M. Akira tugged at the small personal television screen attached to the center armrest, manipulated it into position, and turned it on.

The first images displayed the 747's speed, position, local time, and temperature of the air outside the aircraft. Next came a map with a little icon the shape of the 747, displaying their position over Siberia.

Flipping through the channels, Sugawara quickly found the live satellite feed from Tokyo by using the new phased array television antenna designed for the in-flight reception of live signals. The picture was fuzzy and faded but tolerable; the screen carried an apology that informed viewers that solar activity was degrading broadcast quality.

On the screen, he saw long lines of limousines parked near the side entrance to the Yasukuni shrine. In the background, a small group of protesters yelled, "No pardon for war criminals! Cabinet ministers stay away." The picture shifted to a parade of somberly dressed men gathering in an empty area just next to the Kudan Kaikan Hotel.

Sugawara slipped on his headphones as the television commentator was telling viewers that more than 400 of the 751 members of the Diet—including most cabinet members—had just attended prayer services at the Yasukuni shrine to honor Japan's war dead. They were now making their way across to the groundbreaking ceremonies for the new War-Dead Memorial Peace Prayer Hall. According to the commentator, there would first be a Shinto consecration of the site followed by remarks by Tokutaro Kurata, chairman of the Daiwa Ichiban Corporation, which had donated one hundred twenty-five million dollars of the new prayer hall's one-hundred-fifty-million-dollar cost.

The television commentator's voice had pronounced notes of admiration when he said, "Kurata is well known by all Japanese as the defender of Yamato." The screen cut to a picture of Kurata walking alongside the prime minister, surrounded by a platoon of cabinet members.

The commentator went on at length about Kurata's climb from torpedo kamikaze to the wealthiest man in Japan and the number one defender of "our nation's unique culture."

The camera lost sight of Kurata and immediately cut to a shot showing the front of the Yasukuni shrine.

"These are the people for whom Kurata has waged his battles," said the commentator. The picture showed masses of ordinary worshipers. In their midst, groups of World War II veterans dressed in their uniforms marched up the steps in tight formation, tossed coins in the offertory boxes, and clapped their hands to summon the spirits of their fallen comrades. As the men walked away, they were surrounded by people in civilian dress.

"Bystanders ask each of the veterans many adoring questions," said the commentator. "The curious—mostly too young to remember the Great Pacific War—ask the grizzled old veterans how they received their medals, which battles they fought in, how many Americans they killed?

"Their interest in a war they cannot remember," said the commentator in a more somber voice, "is a testament to the efforts of Kurata and the War-Bereaved Families Association, and the new Peace Prayer Hall will be a huge and lasting monument to all."

A monument to atrocity, Sugawara thought angrily. It made him feel guilty for being Japanese, genetically evil for being a blood relative of Kurata's.

Damn you! Sugawara thought silently as the cameras once again caught sight of Kurata as he made his way through a fawning crowd and walked up to the podium.

There was no such thing as genetic guilt, no gene to inherit the bad karma of previous generations. Just because Kurata was evil, just because those in the bloodline had acted evilly, didn't mean that he, too, was evil.

Instead, he thought, as the crowd quieted for Kurata's address, it seemed as if societies had their own cultural genomes—traits and habits, prejudices, norms and beliefs—that were passed along almost like genes. And perhaps among the cultural genome were societal genes for guilt and evil. The group-think, consensual manner of Japanese society made it easier for evil to flourish because it denounced the moral man who might stand up and yell, "Stop!"

Blood rushed through his ears like wind through autumn leaves. Sugawara knew the only way to cure himself of the cultural evil that infected him was to exercise his own personal decisions and faith; he had to stop listening to the group and start accepting individual responsibility for his actions. It really meant that the life that had nourished him had to die. He bit his lip as Kurata began a talk filled with familiar sentiments.

"Japan is at war again," Kurata said, speaking without notes. The television camera showed shocked audience reaction.

"More than fifty years after our honorable war to liberate Asia from the white man's rule, we are at war against forces that would rip our country apart, which would stain the honor of our loved ones who died fighting that just war, revisionists who would tell lies about the role of our great nation.

"We may have lost the physical aspects of the Greater East Asia War," Kurata continued, "but just look at what we accomplished: there is no more *Dutch* Indonesia, no more *American* Philippines, no more *French* Indochina, no more *British* Malaysia, Burma, Singapore."

Applause rippled through the audience. Kurata bowed slightly to acknowledge the applause.

"This was a great accomplishment," Kurata continued. "We accomplished our goal to form the Greater East Asia Co-Prosperity Sphere at great cost and sacrifice to our nation. But enemies both within our society and outside it would deny the truth, denigrate our accomplishments."

The flight attendant brought Sugawara's breakfast and set it on the tray. The man's impassive eyes glanced at the television screen, at Sugawara's face, then away. Sugawara felt ashamed.

It's not what you think, Sugawara thought. He wanted to say, *I'm not one of them.*

"Can I get you anything else?"

Sugawara shook his head.

"These enemies, roused by foreigners and other impure people, have raised a host of ridiculous lies to support their cause: 'What of the rape of Nanking, the Bataan Death March, the killing of millions of Chinese and other Asians, forced prostitution and so-called medical atrocities?' " The crowd fell silent, mouths gaped at the open mention of these hurtful things.

"These are lies," Kurata said quietly. "They are the victor's history, written to justify the means and the will of the white men who have tried—and rightfully failed—to destroy our culture. Lies . . . *lies* . . . *LIES!*"

The crowd cheered; cries of *"Banzai!"* rose above the general noise level. Sugawara felt nauseous; he sipped at his orange juice, ignored the food.

The crowd took more than a minute this time before it quieted.

"That is why we are here today," Kurata said. "Our new War-Dead Memorial Peace Prayer Hall will tell the truth, our truth, the real history. It will rise two hundred feet above this honored ground, next to the moat of the Imperial Palace and just across the narrow canal from the Budokan where our beloved emperor conducts his solemn ceremony each August 15 commemorating the end of the Greater East Asia War. It will rise tall for all to see the truth, to expose the lies, to exult our well-deserved glory, to honor the fallen war dead to whom we owe more than we can repay in ten thousand lifetimes."

The crowd cheered.

"With your support, we made sure the Diet did not issue a humiliating apology that would have disgraced the war dead," Kurata continued. "Apology! Hah! Those self-righteous Caucasian racists should apologize to *us* for putting us in a position in which we were forced to defend ourselves and all other Asians."

Again, cries of *"Banzai!"*

In the distance behind Kurata, skywriting filled the cloudless sky. "Glory to the emperor" said the writing. "Hail to the defender of Yamato."

The knot in Sugawara's gut ratcheted down as he watched the skywriting drift across the sky; harmless now, lethal just days from now.

It was then that a giant yawning ache of emptiness opened around him like a sickness, swallowing him in a throbbing maw of loneliness. He had never felt so alone in his life, so far from the supporting hands of friends and family, so divorced from the supporting fabric of society. If he fell now, there would be nothing, no one to break his fall.

As cheers resounded from the crowd in Tokyo, as Kurata yielded the podium to the priest who would dedicate the ground, Sugawara thought of his childhood, of his parents, of simpler times when decisions were made by others and theirs by society.

He felt guilty for the shame he would bring on his family and of the disgrace that would shadow them. He thought of the retribution if he was caught by Kurata. From experience, he knew nothing in his worst nightmares could compare with the real-world punishments Kurata could create.

He was afraid. He had been taught that a samurai was fearless and that courage was born through the banishment of fear.

As the KLM 747 hurtled over Siberia somewhere above the Lower Tunguska River, Sugawara wondered if it could truly be called courage if one's seemingly brave actions sprang merely from the act of putting oneself in a position from which there was no retreat. He certainly had no retreat; that much was clear to him even if it had not dawned yet on Kurata.

He thought of this, of Holland, of frozen death riding under his seat, of Kurata, Blackwood, Sheila Gaillard. He thought of all of this and knew he had taken the big leap.

Only one question remained: was he going over the chasm, or into it?

42

Thick fog began in darkness—the midnight sky—and ended in darkness—tame waters only God knew where. In between was some kind of muddled grayness, not totally dark, not easily navigable. Lara Blackwood imagined that life was a lot like this to most people.

She sat in the stern of a small fiberglass powerboat, perhaps twenty feet long, with twin, very quietly muffled outboards at the stern linked by cables to a steering wheel and controls amidships. DeGroot was at the wheel, Falk by his side. They were just barely visible through the murk.

For nearly four hours, DeGroot had piloted the boat through a steady succession of locks and canals, sloughs and sluices, ponds, lakes, and ditches, only occasionally looking down to refer to his chart and the handheld global positioning satellite receiver.

The boat passed under what seemed like a hundred bridges and for a long time paralleled a heavily trafficked road that carried the surf-like chords of constant freeway traffic just yards away but unseen in the fog.

The narrow canal widened as it came to a dead end; DeGroot turned the boat around and put the motors into neutral as the boat glided toward a low pier and then bumped gently against old car tires affixed along its edge. Lara remained silent.

In the next moments, Falk and Lara tied the boat up to the dock; the smells of wood smoke filled the air.

They all followed DeGroot along a wooden walkway across a narrow strip of marsh. A white, two-story house gradually emerged from the fog. As they stepped up to a covered porch lit by a low-wattage bulb, the door opened, spilling bright light from the interior.

"Good evening," said a silhouette backlit against the light. "Come in and get warm."

Lara followed the group in and found herself introduced to Bernard Claes, tulip farmer and government employee.

"This is a working tulip farm—tulips and other bulbs—it makes a profit and more than pays for itself," Falk said. "It just happens to belong to the Dutch government.

"A safe house," Falk said. "For conferences, confidential meetings, that sort of thing."

As they entered the farmhouse's living room, blue light flickered off one wall, the flickers syncopated with the low voice of a television newsreader. Interlaced with the newsreader's voice was a droning, artificial sound with a computer lilt. The wood fire hissed and popped.

As she watched the television, the picture cut from the newsreader to a wide shot of a narrow, cobbled street. The video looked jerky, grainy, amateur. Despite the poor quality, Lara immediately recognized the facade of the Casa Blanca hotel in Amsterdam. Dread shafted through her like a grinding armature of supercooled steel.

The bottom fell out of her stomach as the video closed in. The voice-over explained that the video had been obtained from a tourist on an early morning walk who had discovered Santiago Rodriguez impaled on a two-foot-high Amsterdamje.

Lara felt the room spin, shift; the light assumed a weird glowing brightness as she heard Rodriguez described as a successful hotelier, a respected Amsterdammer, leader of the European gay community.

Nausea rushed into the void in her belly as the newsreader calmly described how Rodriguez had been found alive, the phallus-shaped parking barrier rammed full length through his rectum, its top pressing against the bottom of his heart.

Rodriguez, the television said, died following seven hours of surgery. The victim had been a very strong man. Police said they had found blood and tissue samples from at least four assailants under the victim's fingernails.

"Dear God," Lara said aloud. She had killed Rodriguez. She had led the killers to Casa Blanca, and they were sending her a message about what would happen to others who helped her.

43

THE ENORMITY OF EVENTS STRUCK AKIRA SUGAWARA LIKE A FIST, SLAMMING INTO HIS BELLY AND WORKING ITS WAY UPWARD, TAKING HIS BREATH AWAY.

Locked in the toilet stall at Schiphol Airport, Sugawara knelt in front of the toilet and bent over as the next wave of nausea squeezed his entrails, ridding itself of the final bits of the fine meals KLM had served him.

He retched, gagged. The wave passed.

Pulling off a wad of toilet paper, he wiped at his lips and swallowed at the sourness in his mouth as he glanced over at the special Thermos.

The impossibility of his position pulsated in his belly. What could he have been thinking of? How could he have stolen this from Kurata? They would hunt him down and kill him. The snake woman, Gaillard, would make him suffer for hours . . . days.

Had they already discovered his treachery? Had the alert gone out? Would he enter Daiwa Ichiban's Schiphol offices and find that death had gotten there ahead of him?

He bent over and gave the toilet a gut-twisting dry heave, then sat back on his heels.

How could he have been so stupid?

One voice in his head told him his only hope was to contact Kurata, confess, return the stolen Slatewiper vials, throw himself upon Kurata's mercy.

But Kurata was not known for mercy.

The best that could happen now, Sugawara knew, would be quiet, inevitable death and disgrace.

Shakily, Sugawara got to his feet and flushed the toilet. He shook his head. He was too far along the path to return. He had taken a running leap at the chasm, jumped. Life was ballistic now, its arcing path leading somewhere unknown. He was in flight, and he had to ride the parabola.

Stumbling out of the stall, he carried his bags over to the sinks and washed his face, rinsed his mouth, careful to avoid soiling his suit.

He combed his hair and checked his watch. The interpreter and driver he had ordered would be at the curb soon. The service had been told he was a scientist carrying samples of bull semen. They had located for him a breeding and sperm storage operation half an hour from the airport that would be happy to replenish the liquid nitrogen for his special Thermos.

Then, only then, would he be ready to check in with the Daiwa Ichiban office.

Taking a deep breath, Sugawara took one last look at himself in the mirror, then left the rest room to find out where the trajectory of his life would carry him.

"Words deceive us, Matsue-*san*."

Tokutaro Kurata broke the meditation of the long silence. He sat on a rough stone bench next to the bent figure of Toru Matsue, the ancient family retainer charged with teaching *Nihonjinron* to Akira Sugawara following the young man's return from college in America. The two men had come to Kyoto for the brilliant fall colors of the leaves and for the clear perspectives that meditation could bring far from the bustle of Daiwa Ichiban's roiling hives of activity.

"Sometimes, I think we substitute words for true thought," Kurata continued as a wan breeze, chilled by the late afternoon, ruffled the leaves of a single bamboo plant in the stone garden. "Furious activity cannot replace purpose."

He fell silent and gazed out at the dry landscape garden of Daisen-in. Created in 1529 by the poet, painter, and tea master Soami, the dark craggy rocks and coarse brown and buff sand raked to resemble river currents represented mountains and streams and, in them, an illusion of the earth that pointed to the ultimate illusion of life itself. A stone boat made its way through sand currents.

"Master Sugawara is a troubled young man," Matsue said finally. "I fear his contact with the Americans has made his adjustment difficult."

Kurata nodded silently.

"He is a good man," Matsue continued. "He wants to please you, to do right."

"But he is troubled because he doubts sometimes that pleasing me and doing the right thing are the same?" Kurata listed his head and looked at the old man beside him.

"*Hai*, Kurata-*sama*," Matsue said. "As always, you are perceptive."

Again, Kurata nodded as if it was his due. "The truth is always close. To find it, we have to abandon words, logic, metaphysics, and seek enlightenment. Otherwise we become like the great masses who stand in water and cry for a drink."

Matsue remained silent. The afternoon faded into evening, the chill wind seeming to blow daylight away like smoke. He shivered, but not just from the cold; something dark other than night was approaching.

Kurata turned toward the garden gate and made a series of motions with his hands; moments later one of his bodyguards brought a small blanket and placed it around Matsue's shoulders.

"Many thanks, Kurata-*sama*. The years have taken a toll on my body."

Kurata dipped his head to acknowledge the thanks. "In the worlds of words and logic, Akira performs well despite his conflicts. What we can see and describe goes well." He turned his head again toward the garden, searched it, as if for answers. Again the breeze blew, keener, cooler.

They sat there silently for more than half an hour as the remains of daylight drained from the sky. When Kurata spoke again, his voice was firm, decisive.

"I sense trouble, old friend," Kurata said finally. "Something that runs deeply beneath my ability to express in words. I fear that, perhaps, I have placed too much trust in him too soon." He paused.

"I have failed to instruct him properly," Matsue said.

Kurata shook his head. "The best gardener cannot grow flowers from stone. No, the events of the most recent few days have given me pause to reflect. I can only say we should look very closely at our young Sugawara. Retrace his steps; look at his actions over the past days, weeks; determine if there is any good reason for the unease I cannot begin to define in words."

Standing, Kurata extended a hand to Matsue. The old man took it gratefully and levered himself upward. The blanket slipped from his shoulders to the ground. Kurata picked it up and placed it back around the bent, old shoulders.

"Only time will tell if young Sugawara can measure up to the destiny that can be his," Kurata said. "He has the greatness of *Yamato minzoku* to fulfill, the responsibility of his birth to accept. We are the *shido minzoku*, and we, our family, are the guiding lights of this very unique and pure race." He turned toward the garden gate, walking slowly as Matsue shuffled alongside.

"*Yamato minzoku* remains strong because we are pure," Kurata said. "We are pure because we remain strong against pollution. Sugawara will ascend as is his right, or he must die. There is no other choice in the way of purity."

"*Hai*, Kurata-*sama*."

44

THE IMPACT WAS AN EXPLOSION, THAT BEGAN WITH THE *SWOOFT!* OF THE ALU-
MINUM BASEBALL BAT WINGING THROUGH THE AIR, THE *SMACK!* OF THE BAT AND
THE LONG TEARFUL KEENING OF AN OLD WOMAN LIVING IN A HELL BEYOND PAIN.
Beatrix VanDeventer twisted in agony on the cold, gritty concrete base-
ment floor of her house and begged for mercy.

Sheila Gaillard laughed and prodded her with the tip of the bat.
VanDeventer groaned again.

"We can keep you alive for days," Gaillard said. "Horst is medically
trained in these things." She looked over at Horst Von Neuman, standing
in the shadows near the staircase. From upstairs, she heard the footsteps
of her other assets as they dissected the house above for clues.

"You'll get mercy when you tell me the names of the rest of your
pathetic little group."

VanDeventer groaned again.

Sheila shook her head as she wound up with the bat. "It's your call."

Sheila Gaillard's cell phone rang, giving the unique tone that alerted
her to an encrypted incoming signal. The phone rang again, its delicate
tones almost lost in the cavernous basement.

Sheila set down the twenty-five-pound barbell weight she was using
on Beatrix VanDeventer's shins and reached for the telephone.

"Leave me for a moment," she ordered Horst Von Neuman. "Go up and see how they're doing. I want to confirm this bitch's information, make sure she didn't deliberately give me wrong information."

The phone rang again; VanDeventer's keening pleas for death were faint now. Von Neuman nodded and set off for the stairs, casting long shadows in the cavernous basement.

Gaillard rubbed the perspiration off her hands, went to her purse, and—after glancing at the map marking the location of the Blackwood bitch—pulled out the telephone, pressed the receive button, and said, "Yes?"

After a pause, she said, "Kurata-*sama*, how good to hear from you."

She stood there, looking down at VanDeventer and enjoying her low groans of agony in one ear, and the welcomed news from the phone in the other.

Sheila smiled.

Sugawara drove slowly along the well-kept, tree-lined street, slowing as he approached the massive three-story brick house. He pulled the rented Volvo to the curb and took another look at the map and sheet of handwritten directions he had been given by Sheila's people at the conference room they had commandeered at Daiwa Ichiban's Schiphol offices. Her people had been deferential, respectful. There had been no orders issued to detain him or ship him back to Tokyo, or worse, to turn him over to the snake woman.

Still, the hot cramps of fear never left him. Sugawara looked over at the seat next to him, at the small blue airline carry-on bag with the KLM logo that he had bought at the airport. The Slatewiper Thermos sat at the bottom, tucked in among papers, a sweatshirt, toiletry items. Sheila Gaillard was fast, unpredictable, and he was prepared to move quickly with her.

The dark brick house was set back from the street by a broad, tree-studded lawn set with elegantly landscaped flower beds placed with a professional designer's flair. A very tall wrought-iron fence with medieval lance pickets lined the sidewalk. World Court judges lived well, he thought.

The driveway gate was open, leading to a brick-paved lane lined with shrubs. Sugawara eased the Volvo up the long curving drive and parked it behind a Mercedes and a BMW.

He got out, slung the carry-on bag over his shoulder, and walked up the broad steps; the door opened before he could ring the bell. A tall, thin man he had never seen before—one of Kurata's "assets" obviously—

opened the door and nodded. Sugawara stepped inside.

"Follow me, please," the man said politely with a German accent.

"Of course."

They walked down a side hall. The floors were covered with worn Persian carpets, the walls hung with oil portraits he assumed were VanDeventer's ancestors.

At the end of the hall, the thin man opened a door outward that led onto a set of stairs leading down. Nothing in his life could ever have prepared him for the scene of pure horror and suffering that greeted Sugawara when he reached the bottom of the stairs.

The smell hit him first—the coppery notes of fear laced among the low sulfur and ammonia smells of human offal. As his eyes adjusted to the harsh light, he saw Beatrix VanDeventer's tortured and swollen body sprawled on the concrete floor in a wide smear of her own fluids. Her eyes were glazed, wide with pain, her swollen lips whispering, for what he couldn't hear.

He stopped suddenly and closed his eyes, praying this was a horrible nightmare and he'd wake up soon.

"Welcome, Akira," Sheila said.

Akira! She had never been this familiar with him before. He opened his eyes and tried to keep from looking at the charnel on the floor; her gaze held different but equally shriveling horrors of their own.

She was dressed in a tight-fitting jumpsuit made of stretch synthetic material that form-fit her enormous surgically augmented breasts; she held an aluminum baseball bat in one hand.

"Kurata-*sama* called to say you were on your way," Sheila said. Then to Von Neuman, who had followed Sugawara down the stairs, she said, "Take his bag."

Fear exploded in Sugawara's belly like gasoline on an open flame. He started to turn, started to flee, grabbed for his bag. But the tall, thin man was very quick and very strong and the grisly scene had stunned Sugawara motionless. He felt the helpless, half-sentient immobility that roots a dreamer's feet to the ground as roaring trains bear down screaming and snorting fire and steam.

Fighting to piece a whole out of the shattered scene, Sugawara found himself relinquishing the bag and stumbling backward as the tall man spun him into a straight-backed chair.

Breathing quick panic gasps, Sugawara stared at Sheila.

"Your uncle's worried about you," Sheila said. "He wants me to keep an eye on you."

Flaming fear damped itself into a black-hot dread that settled into Sugawara's belly, into the deepest parts of his soul.

"I want you to cooperate with me," Sheila said as she walked up to him and stood over him, so close that his face almost touched her mons. She knelt in front of him, grabbed his face, and pointed it toward the broken judge.

"I want you to see what happens to people who do not cooperate." She leaned over and prodded the broken old woman with the bat; a low moaning sound like a dark wind soughing through derelict old buildings filled the basement.

"This is the sort of thing that makes me happy, Akira."

Sugawara felt nauseous; he heaved once, then again, but kept from vomiting.

"Excellent," Sheila said as she stood up and walked over to Sugawara's carry-on bag. Unzipping it, she rummaged around and quickly pulled out the Thermos container, as if she had known it would be there all along.

She pulled open the Velcro closure to the gel bag and slipped out the Thermos. "Well, well," she murmured, "what could this be?"

45

AKIRA SUGAWARA SAW THE BALANCE OF HIS LIFE BEGIN TO TIP AWAY.

For a freeze-framed moment, he saw Sheila Gaillard holding the Thermos container in its special gel carrier; her smiling gaze was a mask of pure evil, her eyes glistening with insanity. From the corner of his eye, he saw the thin German leaning toward him, on the floor, the disfigured, discolored remains of World Court Judge Beatrix VanDeventer.

Sounds came to him acutely in this frozen moment on which his life would turn: footsteps and thumps from the floors above, the distant susurrations of traffic, the subtle hissing of the hot-water heater located off in some corner of this crowded basement filled with boxes, fiberboard wardrobes, old furniture, and the other accumulations of a lifetime.

He had seen Gaillard at work, heard her talk of the many more numerous times when she had acted out of his sight. He knew she counted on compliance for immediate control; after that, after she consolidated her dominance, there was no escape.

As the thin man leaned forward, as Sheila pulled at the Velcro on the Thermos carrier, Sugawara knew he had one chance—slim to hopeless—and it would pass in the next half second. Better, he thought, to die trying to escape than to pray for mercy that would never come and to end up beaten into fragments, dismembered, disemboweled, or defenestrated alive like the victims of Ishii's Unit 731.

Focus, he thought as he fell back on the extensive Zen-based martial arts training he had practiced since early childhood. Find the center, visualize the motion.

Then, with a purpose so deep it surpassed conscious thought, Sugawara launched himself from the chair, snatching the Thermos from Sheila's hands.

"Hey!" she cried as she raised the bat.

Cradling the Thermos like a football, Sugawara lunged over a sofa and heard the *swooft!* of the bat parting the air behind him.

Strike one.

He scrambled to his feet and made his way toward the darkest part of the basement. But there was to be no hide and seek with Sheila, who sprang, catlike, right behind him.

"Stay by the stairs," Sheila barked at the thin German as she closed quickly on Sugawara.

Sugawara veered off behind a wardrobe just as Sheila swung the bat at him again. The splintering sounds of smashed wood filled the air just behind Sugawara's head.

Strike two.

He ran, scrambled, dodged, then realized she was herding him back toward the stairs. He stopped suddenly and faced Sheila. The movement froze her for an instant; he caught a glimpse of a raptor's face, smiling, enjoying the pursuit. She licked her lips and gave him a smile that was completely sexual.

"Come on, sweetheart." Her voice was low, husky. "You know me well enough to know you can't avoid the inevitable." Her eyes were captivating, compelling. He knew she could freeze her prey like a cobra.

He tore his eyes away from her gaze. Then, hearing the tall German's shoes grit on the concrete to his right, Sugawara hurled himself to the left and slipped effortlessly into the inky black darkness between two packing crates. The first two steps went fine. Then something ropelike tangled one ankle, and he went down hard, striking the side of his head against one of the crates.

Like an unseen fist, the concrete floor rushed up at him in the darkness, slamming into his side, knocking the breath from him.

The gloom spun around him like half-drunken sleep for an instant.

He didn't hear her approach. He sensed rather than saw her looming over him. He lay perfectly still on his side in the narrow aisle and tried to control his breathing—through his mouth, in slowly, out slowly—ignoring the need, the mortal compulsion to take in great greedy lungfuls of air.

Even without the bat, he knew she was far more skilled at the martial arts than he; she could effortlessly disable or kill with just her bare hands.

He was no match. Any second a blow would arc out of the darkness, and the game would be over. He needed a weapon, an equalizer. His mind raced and a slim thread emerged. But for it to work, he needed time.

He thought frantically. Was she right-handed or left? He tried to visualize her drinking, using a fork. Then he saw her in the basement, prodding the poor woman with the bat . . . held in her right hand.

Putting his life in this one vision, he rolled against the crate that would be on Sheila's right; it would blunt her swing or force her to use her left hand. As he rolled, he fumbled with the closure on the Thermos.

At the same instant, he heard a dark *swoofting* and then the white-hot lightning that flashed behind his eyes as the bat connected with his left hand. His arm went numb for an instant as he rolled over onto his back and kicked at the darkness.

Another blow thudded into the sole of his left shoe, sending a shuddering vibration straight to his hip. He did a half roll, half backward somersault, as the metal bat smashed into the concrete where his head had been, making a tiny spark that flashed in the dark.

Struggling to his feet, Sugawara willed his left arm to work, pinning the Thermos to his side as he pulled the lid off with his right hand. Then he made his way round the corner of the crate, again moving to his right, her weak spot for swinging the bat.

There was dim light here; Sugawara crouched as close to the floor as he could and prayed for luck.

A split second later, the bat came whistling around the corner and slammed into the packing crate a foot above his head.

Strike three.

Standing up, he saw the dim outline of Sheila's face as she wound up for another swing. Sugawara then did the unexpected; he stepped toward her, inside the swing arc. He watched her smile as he drew close. She dropped the bat. But before she could bring her deadly hands into play, he swung the Thermos and sloshed the liquid nitrogen into her face. He visualized flesh frozen solid, instant frostbite; he replayed the stream of liquid splashing against her open eyes.

The banshee scream that pierced the blackness seemed to make Sugawara's spine resonate with the pain he had inflicted.

"Sheila?" the tall, thin man yelled. Sugawara heard his footsteps hurry toward them.

With no time to spare, Sugawara set the Thermos on the ground and picked up the aluminum bat. As he bent over, he saw the faint glint of one of the Slatewiper vials on the floor; it looked intact. He wondered for just an instant if they had both sloshed out, if one had broken.

Then Sugawara stood up and saw the beam of a flashlight bouncing in the darkness. Sugawara hauled back on the bat just as the thin man came lurching around the corner of the crate, gun in hand.

The wet crunching smack the bat made as it slammed into the tall German's face made a percussive counterpoint to Gaillard's moans of pain. The German folded up and dropped to the floor like a shot bird.

Without consciously thinking, Sugawara pocketed the German's gun— it felt like some sort of automatic in the dark—then used the flashlight to survey the scene. Sheila Gaillard was on her knees in a cloud of condensation from the liquid nitrogen. She cradled her face and moaned as she rocked back and forth.

There was no change in the rhythms from the upstairs noises. The men there had, no doubt long ago, become inured to tortured screams coming from the basement.

Pulling out the German's pistol, Sugawara saw it was a Beretta. He quickly found there was a round already chambered. He clicked off the safety. Then keeping Sheila in the gun's sights—he knew she could be lethal even wounded—Sugawara picked up the one intact Slatewiper vial he could find and put it back in the Thermos.

His left arm tingled and the shoulder throbbed. But his arm worked. As Sheila continued to moan, Sugawara reclosed the Thermos, slung the carrier strap over his shoulder, and ran for the stairs.

A moan from the tortured woman stopped him. She was whispering something. He walked over to her and knelt down. Her eyes opened and through the blizzard of pain reflected there, she fixed him with a poignant gaze and whispered, "Kill me. Please. Kill me now."

Shocked, Sugawara stood up. He looked at the gun in his hand. He even pointed it at the gray-haired woman's face. He closed his eyes.

But he couldn't do it.

Embarrassed, he opened his eyes and glanced away from her. It was then that he saw the map and the legal pad covered in handwritten notes he recognized as Sheila Gaillard's.

He grabbed the map, ripped the notes off the pad, folded them roughly and stuffed them into his flight bag along with the Thermos. He took the steps upward three by three.

As he opened the front door, a cry of alarm sounded.

"Stop," he heard someone cry as he bolted out the front door and sprinted for the rented Volvo, fumbling in his pocket for the keys. Instants later, a man appeared at the door. He raised a gun. Sugawara dived behind the rear quarter panel of the BMW as a shot slammed into the car's rear tire.

There were more voices.

Sugawara leaned around the trunk of the BMW and loosed a wild shot that failed to hit its target, but nevertheless sent the gunman diving for cover.

Sugawara lunged for the Volvo, opened the door, threw in the flight bag, and climbed in after it. More men appeared as he inserted the key in the ignition and turned it.

Pointing the Beretta at the men, Sugawara fired through the rolled-up passenger side window. The window disappeared in a hail of tempered glass granules. One of the men returned fire, then ducked behind a pillar.

The Volvo's starter ground, then caught immediately. Sugawara ducked down, slammed the gear into drive, and floored the accelerator.

The Volvo weaved forward, lurched around the BMW, ran off the driveway, narrowly missing a large elm tree. The erratic movement threw off the gunmen. But they knew he'd have to leave via the open gate.

As the Volvo approached the street, the gunfire grew more accurate, slamming into the body, exploding the windshield, the rear windows. Sugawara had reached the street when he felt a slug hammer into his side.

46

THE EARLY AFTERNOON SUN CAST LENGTHENING SHADOWS AS THE INCREASINGLY ABBREVIATED DAYS SLOUCHED OFF TOWARD ANOTHER HIGH-LATITUDE WINTER. Warmed by the day, Lara Blackwood strolled pensively atop a small levee that bordered the tulip farm. "Tulip farm" was a misnomer they had learned, because the operation actually grew all sorts of bulbs as well as hothouse roses for the international market. It had started with tulips two hundred years ago and the name had stuck.

She looked away, at a distant field where some odd contraption of a machine was being pulled by a tractor through a field of plants she could not identify. Dust spummed up behind the machinery, roiled briefly, and began to settle in the windless day. Lara wiped at the perspiration on her forehead.

Reaching the end of an earthen dike, she looked to the west and wondered how she could have done things differently. So many people dead. So many more to die. Nothing she could think of alleviated the heavy dark stone that weighed inside her.

Finally, she turned and made her way to the unpaved levee-top lane that led from the main road to the tulip house. A rank of greenhouses obscured the old farmhouse from here. From the direction of the main road, she could see a dust plume signaling the arrival of a car.

The sounds of the approaching car grew louder as she approached the first of the greenhouses.

Suddenly a horn sounded—urgent, long, loud. Lara turned to see a battered Volvo weaving toward her. As it grew near, she could see bullet holes in the windshield. She watched horrified as the car suddenly veered off the road and bulldozed through the glass walls of the nearest greenhouse.

Glass erupted in a shower of fragments that reminded Lara of an alpine avalanche. She ran toward the gaping hole. The horn was still blaring as she climbed over the tangles of mangled rosebushes and approached the Volvo, which had come to a stop against a steel pillar that supported the roof trusses. Bullet holes pocked the rear fenders and trunk.

The smell of gasoline permeated the air; Lara stopped in horror as she saw gasoline trickling from the rear of the car. In less time than her mind could register the danger, Lara saw the first small flames licking at the fuel; she froze for a moment. Then she forced something to shift in the pit of her stomach and rushed to the Volvo, stepping through the gasoline.

Slumped over the steering wheel, Lara found a young Japanese man. She tried the door, but it was jammed. Several bullet holes pocked the door, one right through the latch.

"Oh, wonderful. Just too freaking wonderful," she mumbled to herself.

As the smell of gasoline grew stronger, Lara made her way through the tangle of rosebushes, thorns grabbing at her legs, to the passenger side door, which opened easily.

The young man regained consciousness as Lara leaned in to grab him. Blood soaked Lara's hands as she wrapped her arms around the driver and pulled him toward safety. She had just gotten the young Japanese man out of the car when suddenly, the man twisted away with surprising strength, flung himself into the Volvo. Lara pursued him.

When she pulled the driver out for the second time, the man clutched a cylindrical object covered in fabric. Lara started to take the object from him. The young man gripped it like life itself.

"No! Don't! Keep your hands away!" he cried in unaccented English. Lara pulled the young man away from the Volvo.

"Do not . . . do not open," the young man mumbled. "Death in there. Death in there. Don't open."

Just then, the gasoline ignited with a whump.

47

A POMEGRANATE AND PEACH SUNSET SPILLED THROUGH THE WINDOWS OF THE TULIP HOUSE'S BEDROOM, CASTING A GLOW ON THE PEOPLE GATHERED AROUND SUGAWARA'S BED.

No one had yet turned on an electric light, so engrossed were they all at the story Sugawara had unraveled for them. Absent modern lighting, the tableau was painted with the warm colors and natural modeling of light and shadow that gave the whole scene the feel of something painted by Vermeer: Sugawara in bed, propped up with pillows and covered with a quilt bearing the tiny, even stitches of a woman who had no idea that her work would play a role in a pivotal scene of history; in chairs to one side of Sugawara's bed were Falk, Noord, and the physician they had flown in by helicopter from Rotterdam. Their long Dutch faces, plucked directly from an earlier century, lent verisimilitude. Only a thick plastic bag of blood hanging from the stainless-steel intravenous fluid rack and the tube to Sugawara's arm anchored the scene to the present day.

The physician had determined that the bullet that wounded Sugawara had entered just below his left shoulder blade and came cleanly out under his arm. It missed all the major arteries by fractions of a millimeter. "He is young and healthy and in good shape," said the physician. "Lots of fluids, and he will be fine."

By the window, Lara sat in a straight-backed chair, her face painted with the sunset—warm and roundly shadowed in contrast to the brightness of her eyes; the black shininess of her hair flowed with the gold of dusk.

And in a dark corner by the door where sunset had already ceded to night sat an intense, silent Chinese man who had arrived just minutes after Sugawara's accident. Lara struggled to remember the Chinese man's name; introductions had been hurried, the scene chaotic as they sought medical care for Sugawara and struggled to put out the fire without calling the authorities.

As hard as she tried to recall, all Lara could come up with was "Al-Bitar's Man." He was well financed by an Asian semiconductor firm and the head of the Asian operations for *Shinrai*. He had originally come to arrange for their passage to Singapore. That was probably about to change with what Sugawara had to say. Xue, Lara remembered finally, pronounced something like *"Schwerh."* Victor Xue. That was the man's name.

Only DeGroot was absent. The same helicopter that had brought the physician had carried DeGroot and Sugawara's Slatewiper sample to the renowned drug researcher's lab at Leiden University.

In the hours since DeGroot's departure, Sugawara had stunned them with his detailed revelations of Kurata's organization and Operation Tsushima.

"Well, I believe we must assume the worst," Falk said with a nod to Lara. With DeGroot absent, the aging army officer had assumed command of the group. "That means we must be prepared to stop this thing."

Heads nodded, agreements were murmured. Noord turned on the bedside lamp as the last embers of the day faded to black.

"When did you say this was supposed to take place?" Noord asked.

"I didn't yet," Sugawara replied as he reached for the glass of milk on the bedside table and took a long thirsty gulp. "But it will be"—he closed his eyes for a moment—"in precisely five days."

A collective gasp filled the bedroom.

"Five?" Noord's mouth was open, his jaw worked, but no further words came out.

Sugawara nodded, then finished the milk.

"I'll get you more," Lara said, reaching for the empty glass as she scanned his face. What she saw were strong, angular lines and deep compelling dark eyes that radiated a deep solid intelligence despite the painkillers the doctor had given him.

She had been struck at his strength when she pulled him dazed and bleeding from the flaming wreck and the tenacity with which he gripped the Slatewiper samples right up to the point where the loss of blood dropped him into the dark void of unconsciousness.

"And just how is the Slatewiper to be delivered?" Falk asked.

Sugawara describe the skywriting and the religious cult's agricultural commune.

"They are quite secretive, paranoid actually," Sugawara said. "And very capable. They are located in a remote valley west of Tokyo."

Falk made a low frustrated whistle.

"Five days," Falk said. "Remote, well guarded, paranoid." He took a deep breath and loosed it audibly.

Then, to Sugawara, Falk said, "You're absolutely certain anyone in an official position to stop this Operation Tsushima has already been co-opted by Kurata's organization?"

With a nod, Sugawara said, "I am quite certain. I, myself, have had a hand in this matter." His face flushed; he hung his head in shame. "Remember, he is a very powerful man who controls members of the Diet, and exerts enormous power over the bureaus, even the justice ministry and law enforcement. While I believe there are some people in less senior positions—younger people—who would be willing to help, but they have no power so long as they remain in positions of minor importance. They certainly will be no help in the short run . . . and that is what counts."

Noord shook his head and looked at Falk.

Falk, too, shook his head. "No time for a physical assault. Too far away; besides, we need to wipe out the actual bug and the facility that produced it. And both sites are heavily guarded. We'd need something bordering an invasion to accomplish this, and there's no way to keep things quiet."

Grim nods all around.

"Not to mention," Lara said, "the fact that a physical assault would risk releasing the Slatewiper into the environment." She thought for a moment. "But all we need is a little time. And thanks to Mr. Sugawara, we've got the irrefutable proof of Kurata's involvement. All we need to do is delay all this to give us time to let the world know."

"No time." Sugawara shook his head. "Kurata and Daiwa Ichiban are too rooted, too powerful for such revelations to have an immediate effect. In the long run, perhaps. But five days is not enough time for people to believe us."

Lara nodded slowly as she and Akira held each other's gaze long enough for felt, unspoken connections to link, a communication too deep for conscious thought to articulate.

"All we need," Noord said. "All we need is magic," he said darkly. "Or an act of God to stop this Operation Tsushima and disable the facility that produced it."

The room hung with a funereal gloom for a very long time.

Finally, Lara spoke. "Not magic," she said. "And not an act of God." Heads turned expectantly toward her.

"We've got to fight science with science," she said.

For Sugawara, the room faded in and out like a bad television signal, not quite gone, not quite there, an unsteady image unclear beneath the static of pain that throbbed in his side.

It had helped to talk, to confess. The pain of the words, the deep bites from the new reality he had created for himself, distracted him from the throbs of the bullet wound. As time went on and he described Kurata's operation in details never before heard by outsiders, the enormity of it all had begun to press against his heart like a great stone.

Day by day, he had lived the life decreed by his uncle. Like most people, he had worked day after day, a task here, an accomplishment there. He realized he was like those people who live in beautiful mountain resorts and drive to work each day, eyes on the road and looking at mundane life as it stretched a few hours out, never noticing the scenery.

Only, it was a vast web of evil that he had missed.

But now as Sugawara undertook to tell these strangers everything he knew, as he ordered the information to make it most understandable, the pieces assembled themselves into a frightening whole that made him even more ashamed of his participation. If only he had started looking at the whole thing sooner rather than just focusing on each of the pieces that had passed through his hands. Realization sat like a bottomless blackness in his belly and made him want to die.

". . . science with science," Sugawara tried to ignore his pain as the beautiful woman who had saved his life spoke. Her voice sounded to him like music. Like a symphony.

"One of the West's famous scientists, Louis Pasteur, remarked once that 'Chance favors the prepared mind.' I think I have made a chance connection that may show us a path to our goal here." She paused. Around her, heads cocked, jutted forward; eyebrows arched; people leaned forward in the chairs. "First I have to tell you a story," Lara continued and then related to them the problems she had experienced with the *Tagcat Too*'s electronics including the loss of her boat off the Dutch coast.

"Yes!" Sugawara said. "I know the same phenomenon. It disrupted the skywriting and even the measurement instrumentation in Tokyo."

"This is all very interesting, in an intellectual sort of way," Noord said. "But what does it have to do with stopping Slatewiper?"

"I think it has everything to do with it," Falk said. "If I can leap ahead, I think Ms. Blackwood is suggesting that we undertake to use an electromagnetic weapon against our adversaries."

"If I remember correctly, we used something like that in Iraq and again in Yugoslavia, didn't we?" Lara asked.

Falk smiled, then nodded enthusiastically.

"An electromagnetic weapon?" Noord asked.

"Electrical circuits—especially microprocessors and computers—are extremely vulnerable to various types of electromagnetic radiation particularly at certain high frequencies just short of the visible spectrum," Sugawara said. "I have studied this in school and received training regarding it as part of my service in the Self-Defense Forces. Light, radio waves, television, microwaves—these are all electromagnetic radiation."

Falk nodded slowly and then spoke. "You are right, Ms. Blackwood, about American use of these. You may recall during the Persian Gulf War there was much made of how the Americans blanked out the Iraqi air defense system before sending in its aircraft." Heads nodded. "Not much was released about just how this was done, except for some mentions of smart bombs and the like."

The military man paused, as if deciding whether to continue and how much he should say. Sugawara reached for the glass of milk and drank deeply from it.

"Well, these were electromagnetic pulse weapons—EMP for short."

"EMP?" Noord asked.

"Back in 1962," Falk said, "the Americans detonated a nuclear weapon in the atmosphere over the Johnston Atoll in the Pacific some eight hundred miles south of Hawaii. Operation Starfish, it was called, and it was a scientific and military turning point." He leaned forward, elbows on his knees. "You see, when they pulled the trigger on Starfish, the streetlights in Honolulu went black; burglar alarms went off. People with a newfangled type of radio with transistors found they no longer worked—the electromagnetic pulse from the nuke had fried the silicon in the transistors.

"Well, today's semiconductors are a million—maybe a billion—times more delicate, so all it took was half a dozen EMP weapons to fry all the chips in Saddam's air defense system."

"The Americans nuked Iraq?" Noord interjected.

Falk smiled and shook his head. "We've learned to produce the EMP without the nuke. Scientists at Los Alamos and Lawrence Livermore Labs along with a California company called Maxwell Laboratories have developed the technology. In fact, the technology for one particular type of EMP bomb—known as a flux compression generator—is so simple and well known that the Chechen rebels built one and used it in 1996 to blank out a sophisticated Russian security system in order to enter a highly controlled area."

"Fascinating," Noord said.

"How does it work?" Lara asked. "I'm a biologist but I know a lot about physics."

"And I am neither," Noord said. "So please use smaller words for me."

"In simple terms," Falk said, "EMP is a very short—from a few billionths of a second to a few millionths—but very, very high intensity field strength of up to fifty thousand volts per square meter. Indeed, a cylinder the diameter of two golf bags and no taller than me can produce a pulse more powerful than a lightning bolt.

"When this pulse finds a handy antennalike object—telephone or power lines, an aircraft fuselage, metal fences, home wiring, metal circuits inside an appliance or computer, the metal contact prongs on a semiconductor chip—it can induce electrical currents measured in the thousands of amperes," Falk continued. "By contrast, arc welding needs only a hundred amps, sometimes less. It's a very short zap that welds things to hell."

"You need to realize that every modern appliance, airplane, automobile, industrial controller—almost every modern device—contains microchips," Xue said. "Fry the chips with EMP and cars stop, airplanes fall out of the sky, factories halt, processes stop. You can't microwave a meal, watch TV, or play a video game.

"At Dr. Al-Bitar's main corporation, Singapore Electrochip, which so generously supports *Shinrai*, we spend a great deal of time trying to minimize effects from electromagnetic radiation. We have a number of defense contracts from around the world to produce so-called hardened chips and circuits to be used in devices and vehicles designed to survive an EMP from nuclear war."

"I remember," Lara said vaguely. "During the Cold War, a Soviet pilot flew his Mig—a Mig-25 I think—to Japan. When they opened it up, the electronics were filled with vacuum tubes—not chips."

"And the West laughed at the antiquated components," Falk said grimly. "Just long enough for them to realize the Soviets weren't using yesterday's technology, but tomorrow's, designed to survive the EMP of nuclear war."

"I recall as part of my job at Electrochip coming across data on this very topic," Xue said, "which described a fairly small device which was cheap and within the capabilities of a garage technologist. There has been some discussion—but not nearly enough—about how a few such crude garage EMP devices could be used to fry corporate and financial data centers, Internet hosting operations, and telecommunications switching locations. In a technology-dependent country such as the United States, that could be a far bigger disaster than even the World Trade Center disaster. They could even be used to destroy law enforcement and emergency response radio communications over a large area in advance of a terrorist attack."

Xue got up suddenly and left the room.

"Precisely," Lara said enthusiastically. "Which is why EMP is the solution to our particular challenge. It can fry the avionics in the skywriting aircraft. They will sit on the runway or in the hangars while the Slate-wiper deteriorates. It can fry the process control computers in the Slate-wiper production facility. This buys us time to marshal our legal, political, and public offensive to stop Kurata once and for all."

Xue returned with a computer case. From it, he pulled out a slim laptop with a titanium case and set it on Sugawara's bedside table. Xue opened it and turned it on.

Falk let out an audible exhale. "Matra BAe Dynamics has developed e-bombs for the British which are designed to be delivered by a 155-millimeter cannon or rocket." He paused. "But of course, those weapons are guarded almost as closely as nukes. That means I can't possibly acquire one or more of them for our use."

"Well, if the Chechens can build one, then so can we," said Lara.

Falk's expression was incredulous. "In five days? You're going to build the—That's impossible! It took years to develop."

"Then that will just have to be enough," Lara replied.

"There might be another way," Xue said as he bent over and tapped at the laptop's keyboard. "There." He picked up the laptop and turned it for all to see.

"This is the Russian's MC-1 flux compression generator." Falk, Noord, and Lara crowded around to see. Xue made sure Sugawara had a good view.

"I remember seeing this on the Los Alamos Lab's Web site some time ago," Xue said, "and I am quite surprised to see that they still have all this information available in light of the New York attacks."

"So?" Noord asked.

"The MC-1 was developed under the direction of nuclear bomb scientist Andrei Sakarhov at the Soviet Union's most secret laboratory, Arzamas-16. Since the fall of the Soviet Union, the Russians have sold a number of these to Sweden, Australia, and, for all we know, to anyone with about one hundred thousand dollars in ready cash."

"I'll pay for it if you can get it," Lara offered without hesitation. She looked at Xue and then to Falk: "I don't suppose you have any contacts that might be useful?"

Falk shook his head doubtfully. "I will think very hard, but in five days?" He shrugged. "I do not think this would have a high degree of probability for operational success."

Xue set the laptop back on the table and tapped at it again. "Damn," he said quietly. "Signal is weak here and the wireless modem keeps dropping the connection." Moments later he smiled.

"I think we can easily build what we need in the time period allotted." Again, he turned the laptop around for all to see.

"This is the blueprint for a very efficient flux compression generator," Xue said. "As you can see, it is remarkably simple, something I could build in a weekend from things I already have in my garage . . . with the exception, that is, of the C-4 explosive and the RP501 detonator specified."

Falk whistled in amazement. "You could use Semtex as well. And the detonator is as common as they come. You could get them anywhere."

"It's astonishing to think that any terrorist with a modem and the ability to type in 'Google' can have this same data in seconds," Lara said.

Xue nodded. "Some twelve-gauge wire, epoxy, aluminum tubing, and a few odds and ends of aluminum stock and Plexiglas."

In the ensuing stunned silence, Xue stood up. "I will leave now to make our other arrangements. I will be at Electrochip's Amstelveen offices if you need me. With Dr. Al-Bitar's permission, I believe I can arrange discreet transportation for us all as well as technical support."

As he left the room, the telephone rang; Noord picked up the extension on the bedside table and listened. He nodded, then his face went visibly white, like someone had powdered it with talc.

"It's DeGroot," Noord said as he let the hand holding the phone receiver fall into his lap. "He says the analysis of the Slatewiper sample shows that something is seriously, profoundly wrong. DeGroot says that it looks to him like Rycroft was trying to make Slatewiper kill Japanese instead of Koreans, but in the process produced a bug that is totally non-ethnic-specific."

"Dear God," Lara whispered. "That reactivates the Slatewiper intron in all our genes. Prehistoric death, gentlemen, flowing in all our veins. It nearly wiped out our species millions of years ago, it would have if not for a mutation." She shook her head. "Millions of years in the bottle and now this arrogant madman is about to let it out again."

Hours later, the obsession clawed at her every thought. As she lay in the dark, physically disabled by fatigue, Lara's insomnia fed on the anger and mortal fear she had carried from Sugawara's bedroom. She tossed in bed twisting her sweatshirt and warm-up pants that had served as nightclothes since fleeing Washington. Washington? It seemed like a lifetime ago. She had gone from CNN appearances to fugitive overnight. Shaking her head, Lara leaned over and grabbed her watch off the bedside table: 1:16 A.M.

Five days. Countdown to doomsday. She thought about her role in the impending holocaust. She had uncovered the Slatewiper gene to begin with, in giving Rycroft the resources to take things where they never should have gone. She had sold the company to Kurata.

This ache of guilt gave over to the fear of what could—would certainly—happen if this mutated, antediluvian virus were to be reactivated in the bodies of billions of people. It would make Ebola look like a head cold. Slatewiper was not some rare virus whose main reservoir was confined to a dark forest or remote plain. It lived in every cell of every human being. How would it spread? she wondered. Once Kurata's vector reactivated a person's Slatewiper gene, once that person sickened and died, would the virus spread from person to person, self-replicating and no longer in need of the initial boost Kurata had given it? She thought it would become self-sustaining, by aerosol—sneezes, coughs, perhaps even a lover's sigh.

Each time she followed the scientific reasoning deeply enough, she started to fall asleep. But the reasoning always led directly to death, and sleep would slip away until, finally, the relief of darkness covered her eyes.

48

AN URGENT ALARM, A SHRILL HIGH BEEPING PIERCED THE CALM, COMFORTABLE DARKNESS OF SLEEP. Lara startled awake, her eyes taking in the darkness, the unfamiliar room. Her sleep-drugged mind struggled, but memory flooded into her mind, placed her in time, and space.

Shaking her head, she sat up.

From beyond the windows came a rattle of pops and cracks; small-arms fire.

A white flash spilled from the window. An instant later the glass rattled as a dull *whump!* hit the outer wall like mud thrown against a cardboard box.

"They found us," Lara said to herself as an alarm clanged in the dark and the sounds of anxious voices, barked orders, and sharp acknowledgments filled the house. She jumped from the bed and pulled on her warm-ups and shoes.

From outside, the small-arms fire intensified; more explosions rocked the house. The firefight outside sounded as if it was growing louder. She opened the door and heard voices. She followed them to the kitchen where she found DeGroot, Falk, and Noord huddled in what appeared at first glance to be a huge walk-in pantry. As Lara drew near, she could see the "pantry" was, in reality, a combination armory and electronic command center. The three men were clad in soft body armor that stretched from wide collars that reached almost to their ears all the way down their torsos to their groins.

Falk turned from a computer screen, saw Lara. The soldier got up and selected a set of body armor from a wall rack.

"Here," he said, tossing her the garment. "We've got some hostile visitors."

With practice remembered from the executive protection training she had received when the armored Suburban had been delivered, she slipped on the body armor, heartened to find the Kevlar reinforced with ballistic ceramic plates for protection against heavier calibers or special body-armor-piercing rounds. It made the gear heavier, but safer.

The outer cover of the body armor was like a windbreaker covered with zippered pockets. Most of them, Lara noted, were filled: a two-way radio with earplug, flashlight, basic first aid supplies, a syringe of morphine, a folding knife-tool, flares, tricolor greasepaint for camouflage. Everything was thoughtfully designed to make the body armor into a basic combat and survival kit for surprise emergencies such as this one. Someone had given this a great deal of consideration; Lara thought perhaps that someone had been Falk.

As she fiddled with the pockets, Lara glanced at the computer screen as a dozen or so red dots advanced. The green dots numbered only five or six; four were dead, the rest falling back toward the center of the display, the tulip house, she surmised.

"Infrared," Falk explained, nodding at the screen. "That and a combination of ground radar." The military man's face was grim and covered with sweat. "We've got a tiny IFF transmitter on each of our men displaying the green."

"Looks like the uglies are winning," Lara said.

Falk nodded grimly.

"Tried calling for help?" Lara asked.

Falk nodded. "Telephone's been cut; radio and cellular are jammed."

"How can they jam it all?" Lara asked.

"Computers," Falk said. "Spectrum analyzers . . . directional, focused here. As soon as a signal is detected, the spectrum analyzer adjusts the frequency of the jammers and . . . ka-bam!"

On the screen, another green light had remained still for too long. Lara prayed the man had just taken cover.

"Somebody's got to be monitoring those frequencies, especially the ones reserved for the military," Lara suggested.

Wearily, Falk nodded. "But not so much as during the Cold War," he said. "I fear any investigation of the radio emissions will be in time only to find bodies."

The explosion of a grenade whumped outside, and the still green light Lara had prayed for disappeared from the screen. Falk saw the same light flicker out and crossed himself.

In the ensuing silence, they heard Akira Sugawara walk slowly through the door, the color mostly returned to his face, his carriage straight and strong, bare from the waist up except for the bandage on his shoulder. She thought briefly about the resilience of youth and then the sight of his lean, muscular physique captivated her, enhanced by his victory over the pain of his injury. Her eyes followed the way the well-defined muscles flowed so beautifully from the pillars of his neck down the pyramid of his shoulders to the elongated muscle mass of his arms that looked like those of a basketball player. Beneath his shoulders, his chest was muscular and broad with well-defined pectorals that led into a flat, washboard abdomen.

He met her gaze, open and directly. Lara saw his eyes widen. Surprise? Confusion? For just a moment, their mysterious darkness wavered with indecision. She held his gaze with her own for another split second, then looked away suddenly.

Sugawara cleared his throat. "What's happening?"

"Your former associates seem to have located us sooner than we had expected," Falk said as he handed him body armor. Trying not to watch but unable not to, Lara watched Sugawara as he pulled on the body armor with an easy familiarity. Despite his wound, he showed no pain and moved without any hesitation or limitation.

"Ms. Blackwood?"

Lara turned to see Falk handing out M-16s with extra clips snugged into an elastic pocket arrangement fitted to the stock. Each of the automatic weapons had a fat tubular starlight scope attached at the top. Lara accepted the weapon and looked it over, satisfied that its mechanical functions were identical to those she had fired at the range near Washington.

"The device at the muzzle is a laser sight," Falk said. "But it doesn't use visible or infrared light that our assailants are likely to detect. It shines, instead, in a special part of the far ultraviolet the night sights only on these weapons have been modified to detect."

Lara nodded.

"Good," Falk said, then turned back to an urgent voice from the radio.

Just then, a massive explosion rocked the entire house. Lara fought to stay on her feet. Sugawara cried out as his wounded side slammed into a chair. The main lights flickered out, replaced by a dimmer glow as emergency power took over. The acrid stench of high explosive drifted into the kitchen, wafted by fresh air from outside.

Without warning, a series of flashes outside were followed by a thunderous battering that tore through the house.

"RPGs," Falk said calmly. Rocket propelled grenades.

An instant later, the unmistakable smell of fire came from the direction of the living room, followed by a hungry crackling and a wavering, growing light from the flames.

Amid the din, Lara heard Falk and the despair in his voice. "It's no good," the soldier said darkly as he looked at the computer screen. "They're lost . . . lost. Every last one of them."

As Lara looked at the still green dots on the computer screen, she knew the soldier was talking about his men, the soldiers guarding the tulip safe house who had been borrowed from their units for a "training exercise."

"Come!" They heard Noord's voice somewhere beyond the maelstrom. "Regroup!" She heard affirmative replies from the handful of soldiers who had been stationed inside the house with them. Then instants later running footsteps and more shots.

Explosions volleyed into the house from every direction, a constant barrage that seemed to make the floor lift beneath their feet. Smoke filled the room, the heat from the flames palpable around them.

A near-hit detonated just beyond the kitchen window, fractured the special armored glazing, hurling shrapnel into the kitchen.

The concussion knocked everyone standing to the floor. Shrapnel whistled audibly through the kitchen and augured harmlessly into the walls and ceiling. The living-room flames flared brighter; Lara felt her flesh crawl as the fire growled louder—like a living thing—fed on the cross ventilation opened up by the new hole in the kitchen wall.

"Into the cellar," Falk commanded as he grabbed the remaining three M-16s in the armory, then rushed to open an ordinary door next to the "pantry." Flames grew brighter as they headed through the door and down the stairs just as an RPG round slammed into the wall of the kitchen, pulverizing the outer wall of the "pantry." Just then, a ragged hammering of automatic weapons fire tore through the jagged hole in the wall and pocked a shaky line of craters across the kitchen wall. Plaster showered down.

Falk's body danced with a burst of automatic weapons fire, hammered and battered but still alive until the slugs climbed above the body armor and punched his head into a great red misting geyser of death.

Sugawara pulled Lara to the floor as slugs filled the space around them, probing for more life to end. The crackling of flames grew louder, the air hotter. They choked and coughed at the smoke. Somewhere, out of sight, a bullet-riddled, fire-weakened wall crashed; the fire grew brighter, stoked by the falling wall; up in the night sky, a vigorous stream of embers climbed into the darkness. Gutted walls towering with flames surrounded them. Lara smelled the stench of singed hair. It was like being in a skillet. "Come on." Sugawara tapped at her shoulder. "Let's get out of here. Stay low." Crawling through the debris, she followed him through the flame-lit darkness to a gaping hole that had been blown in the kitchen wall. Then suddenly they were in the dark, cool night air with the heat to their backs in the lee of the kitchen Dumpster. Behind them, and above, an exterior wall burned fiercely; a gentle wind blew the smoke and flames toward them. Lara looked back as, on the far side of the house, a wall collapsed slowly inward, urged along by the breeze. She unslung the M-16 and looked around, trying to fix in her mind the direction of the shooting, attempting to separate the sounds of friendly gunfire from that of the attackers, hoping to assess the size of the enemy force left. She saw that Sugawara seemed to have that figured out and was scanning a patch of darkness with the starlight scope on his M-16.

"We probably should move clear of the house before it collapses on us," Lara said as she looked up at the tottering wall beside them. But before Sugawara could reply, sharp white flashes chipped at the night, followed instants later by the sounds of an automatic rifle.

"Down!" Sugawara said as he shoved them into the cover of the Dumpster. Slugs gonged into the Dumpster metal, worked their way down. Lara scrambled back, pressing herself next to Sugawara as the bullets reached for them. Dirt flew up just inches from her face.

They stayed like that as an exchange of gunfire erupted. Lara could hear the M-16s of Noord and his small contingent, and the answers from a host of other weapons. The exchange continued furiously, punctuated by curses and screams of pain. Then a lull.

And in the ensuing lull, the sucking, roaring sounds of hungry fire that leaped into the night sky and animated the shadows around them. Certainly that could be seen across the flat polders for miles and miles, Lara thought. Someone would see it. Someone would investigate. But when they finally did, would there be anyone left alive?

In the fire-fed shadows that danced about them, something caught the unconscious attention beneath the floor of her thoughts. A shadow out of step. It moved all wrong, stayed too long. She got to one knee and whirled around just in time to see a man near the corner of the house. Swiftly she raised her M-16 and pulled the trigger. Slugs chiseled away the wooden siding, then stitched across the man's face as she adjusted her aim.

It was silent again, but for just a moment. Then a sharp, cold woman's voice filled the lull.

"Very nice shot, dear."

Lara whirled and found she was looking straight into the muzzle of a stubby, bulbous weapon, the Heckler & Koch MP5A, being held by a tall, striking blond woman with a smile like pure evil.

A large armed man clad all in body armor and ammunition pouches and hung like a Christmas tree with grenades flew past her. Lara turned her head in time to see Sugawara's attempt to bring the muzzle of the M-16 to bear on the big man. But the man's quick hands grabbed the M-16's muzzle and kicked Sugawara in the side of his head, wresting the rifle away from him and sprawling him face first into the ground.

49

IN THE NEAR DISTANCE, SMALL-ARMS FIRE RATTLED AND CRACKED AND POPPED IN A LONG BARRAGE THAT POUNDED EVERY SHRED OF SILENCE FROM THE NIGHT AND CARRIED THE BRUTISH NOISES OF DEATH FOR MILES ACROSS THE FLAT STILL POLDERS.

Lara froze in place as the fearful cannonade of her own heart battled inside her with a white-hot rush of anger that sizzled like molten steel.

"You two have caused me quite a bit of trouble," Sheila Gaillard said.

Sugawara got to his knees and hands and looked over at Gaillard. The big man with the body armor kicked him solidly in the ribs. The blow sent Sugawara rolling over on his back. The big man moved in for another blow.

"No," Sheila said firmly. The man stopped as immediately as a well-trained setter. Moments later Sugawara propped himself up on his elbows and shook his head unsteadily.

Gaillard was well lit in the firelight, her usually spectacular breasts sheathed in body armor, a bandage on her face, a patch covering her left eye. Flames flickered in her face as she turned and took a step toward Lara; she leaned over and placed the muzzle of the H&K on Lara's forehead, and pushed hard enough to slam her back on her heels into the dirt.

"Bang!" Sheila said softly. Her face glowed with pleasure. "All I have to do is pull the trigger and blow your fucking Nobel Prize right out of that pretty little head of yours . . . just another splatter of bloody gray ooze dripping all over the ground." She smiled broadly. "Just a handful of dripping jelly. The be-all, the end-all of humanity." She looked at Lara. "The seat of intellect, the fabric of a billion trillion electrical impulses we call consciousness . . . the soul."

She paused again. Then: "Do you think you have a soul, Ms. Black-wood? One that will go on and on after I pull the trigger?" Lara mar-veled at her own odd inner calm as she watched Sheila's index finger curl around the gun's trigger. There was no doubt in Lara's mind the safety was off. She could twitch and set off the round herself. Sheila's henchman stood nearby, his own MP5A pointed at Sugawara, his finger eagerly wrapped around the machine gun's trigger.

Lara saw Sheila's smile vanish then as the finger on the trigger tight-ened. Lara decided she might as well die trying. Just as she started to roll away, a tortured, shattering sound filled the night as a groaning surrender came from the towering wall of flames above them. The angle of the firelight abruptly changed.

Sheila whirled and looked toward the source of the frightening sound. The exterior wall just above them swayed like a drunk for a moment. The thug next to Sugawara turned too as the wall began to lean ever so slightly in their direction.

It was all the time Lara needed.

In one swift, smooth movement, Lara batted Sheila's machine gun away and performed the sit-up of her life. Hearing Lara's grunt of ex-ertion, Sheila whirled, leveled the machine gun, and squeezed off a long stuttering blast at full automatic.

The wall started to topple still slowly, still reluctantly. Pieces from the top spilled flaming debris that announced the imminent collapse of the wall.

The slugs from Sheila's H&K flew wildly and blew large wet holes in her henchman's belly. Sugawara rolled away. Lara sprang to her feet as Sheila regained her composure and aimed for a second shot. As she watched Sheila bringing the muzzle to bear, Lara lunged forward and landed a vicious kick that sent the blond woman staggering backward toward the foundation of the house. But Sheila Gaillard rebounded, whirled, and again brought her weapon to bear.

From Sugawara's direction, Lara heard a burst of automatic weapons fire. Gaillard went to her knees, still holding the H&K, still trying to get off a final shot. Then from the flaming wall that loomed above them came the final groans of burned and tortured wood screaming.

"Come on!" Sugawara shouted. Lara ran with him into the darkness.

Dawn burst upon Tokyo with a crispness that seemed to have painted every leaf gold or red or yellow overnight.

Deep inside the Slatewiper production laboratory, Tokutaro Kurata followed Edward Rycroft along a catwalk. With every step, Kurata tried to visualize the leaves and recall the sense of inner peace they had given him during the drive from his office that morning. He searched for the center he knew the leaves would give him if only they would replay again in his mind.

Kurata frowned as the image abandoned him to the production facility's jungle of pipes and retorts and bioreactors and computers and the gurgling, susurrating death that flowed all around them.

They stopped on a landing. Rycroft pointed at a clot of white-garbed workers at the far end of the facility.

"That is the last of the lot we need," Rycroft said as he watched the workers. Kurata followed his gaze. "Another forty-eight hours, and that batch of precursors will come out the other end. We'll have more than enough of the Slatewiper vector to do the job, a good three days ahead of schedule."

Rycroft looked at Kurata for approval.

After a long moment Kurata nodded. "You have done very well," Kurata said, angry at himself for allowing his fatigue to show in his voice. The night had been sleepless, the hours filled with anger and bitterness since the departure—the defection, the *betrayal*—of his nephew. Kurata struggled to center himself now and succeeded in capturing an image of the leaves, but only a veiled one, as if viewed through sheer curtains.

"But things have not gone well of late," Kurata continued in a steadier voice. "Yamamoto's death still troubles me; my nephew has brought shame on his family and me; there is no word from Sheila Gaillard. At the least she has failed me again; I fear she may be dead."

Yes, but look on the bright side: DeGroot's dead, Rycroft wanted to say, but he kept the thoughts to himself. DeGroot had always been a rival, a brilliant molecular geneticist Rycroft saw, along with Lara Blackwood, as competition for the Nobel. With them out of the way, Rycroft felt the coveted medal—and the long-overdue recognition of his brilliance that the prize would bring—was naturally his. Overdue but deserved like the riches that would come from his own entrepreneurial sale of the Slatewiper to the first customers that Woodruff had brought to them. The thought made him smile. The first batch went to a camouflage-clad band of militant Palestinian terrorists who wanted a Slatewiper to wipe out Jews. The second batch went to a bearded, black-hatted gang of ultra-orthodox Zionists who wanted a repeat of the genocide that had cleared Canaan the first time. But the joke was on them. The two sides were so genetically similar, he was able to cut corners and give them both the same Slatewiper batch. A pox on both your irrational houses, he thought as Kurata's words brought him back to the present.

"While we are free of DeGroot and his immediate band of meddlers," Kurata said, "Blackwood and Sugawara are still loose. My sources tell me an inspection has failed to find any evidence of them at the site."

"Yes, but they are only a handful," Rycroft said. "What can they do?"

"What can they *not* do?" Kurata said, more strongly than he intended, as he watched Rycroft stiffen. Continuing in a calmer voice, Kurata said, "They have defied the American and Dutch police, a hurricane, and everything I have been able to throw at them." He fell silent as a computer beeped an alarm; below them, a white coat moved quickly to study the computer screen, reset the alarm, then rushed purposefully off.

"It is almost as if they lead charmed lives," Kurata said vaguely. "As if they are the visible manifestations of some inevitability that cannot be stopped, an idea whose time has come."

"You don't truly feel they are threats to Operation Tsushima?" Rycroft asked.

"Of course they are," Kurata replied. "To think otherwise is arrogant, perhaps stupid, and certainly unwise." Kurata saw the look on the white man's face and remembered how easily the man could be offended. It disgusted Kurata how easily the man could be provoked into showing his emotions.

"We must be prudent and assume they may be able to repeat their remarkable successes one more time."

"How can I help you?" Rycroft said.

"I would like to move the timing of Operation Tsushima up as soon as possible."

Rycroft nodded. "As I said, we will be done in forty-eight hours, but I heard there is some problem with the aircraft, something to do with navigation."

Kurata nodded. "We are experiencing a series of very strong geomagnetic storms caused by solar flares," he said. "I have anticipated the need to alter our plans without raising alarms and have increased the number of skywriting flights. Unfortunately, the intricate aerial choreography relies upon precise electronic navigation including satellite navigation signals. We have had to cancel flights because of this."

"In the middle of the show, yesterday, I heard," Rycroft said.

Kurata nodded. "I want you to divide the Slatewiper vector in half," Kurata said. "I want the first half to be loaded into the aircraft today."

Nodding, Rycroft said, "You remember that the vector will begin to self-destruct in three days?"

Kurata nodded. "If the planes do not fly in three days, I want the second part ready to replace it." He fixed Rycroft with a long, serious look. "I have been personally looking at the reports of the space weather and geomagnetic storm activity. There are windows when things are fine. Sometimes the windows are only a few hours wide, but they are there.

"When the heavens are right, I will have death in the air."

50

THE INTERIOR OF THE HALF-EMPTY 747 JET FREIGHTER WAS COLD, DARK, LOUD, AND CROWDED. Strapped into Spartan jump seats amid towering pallets and sealed containers destined for Singapore Electrochip sat Victor Xue, Lara Blackwood, and Akira Sugawara. They were dressed identically and warmly in grayish-green quilted nylon parkas and pants to ward off the chill of the unheated cargo hold. The faint transitory fog from their breathing animated the immediate hold area.

Xue had paid the crew a lavish, all-cash bonus to divert the fully loaded jet so that its three undocumented stowaways could make a dark, unseen passage to Osaka, Japan. As arranged, the pilot would claim an equipment malfunction shortly after entering Japanese air space and make an un- scheduled stop in Osaka for "repairs." Afterward, he would continue to his scheduled destination in Taiwan.

Lara shifted, trying to get her long legs into a comfortable position in the cramped temporary seat bolted to the bare floor. As she moved, her shoulder and arm seemed to burn where they brushed against Akira. He gave her a smile, dim in the faint cargo bay illumination, but bright enough for her to tell that he shared the same strange, unspoken connec- tion that had linked them.

It was an odd feeling, she thought. Part of it felt like the giddy exhil- aration of high school infatuation, and the rest? She struggled to define feelings that defied examination. Perhaps they were sharing the emotional bonds of combat survivors who know that neither would have survived without the other? Certainly that, she thought. But there was more. There was a sexual element, an urge she could not deny. Sex and danger seemed like unlikely companions, yet it was logical, she thought, for evolution to make those in the shadow of death want to create new life. It was an undeniable imperative like that which drove Lot's daughters to trick him into having sex with them so they could make sure the human race continued. Was she simply gripped by the feverish evolutionary lust that had developed over the eons to assure the survival of selfish genes, or was there more to it?

Just maybe, she thought as she found his hand and gave it a gentle squeeze, maybe it was love. The thought embarrassed her because she knew too well from research and study that what most people called love was a biochemical phenomenon whose molecules and pathways were well understood. And did it really matter? Lara wondered about this as the jet's engines backed off and the aircraft began to level off at its cruising altitude. Victor Xue unbuckled his seat belt then and made his way to his carry-on bag. He unhooked the bungee cord around the handle that kept it secure and took it over to a waist-high pallet of boxes.

"Come on over," he said as he took off his right glove, used it to manipulate the latches on his carry-on and pull from it a sheaf of papers. He spread the papers in neat stacks on top of the palletized boxes. Finally, Xue reached up and turned on the bright cargo loading lights. An intense glare suddenly flooded the cabin with harsh light.

Lara and Sugawara unbuckled their seat belts and gathered around the makeshift conference table.

"This is an enlargement of the blueprint off the Web," Xue said. "We have copies of this and several others in a warehouse near the Osaka Airport. I have a team assembling all of the necessary supplies and a small number of people gathering there to build the devices."

"You really don't waste any time, do you?" Lara asked.

"We really don't have any to waste," Xue said. "I know that we think we have five days, but there's no good reason that might not be moved up, especially if there is a break in all of the solar activity."

Akira and Lara nodded.

"So here's what we've got to work with," Xue said as he leaned over the drawings. "The main feature is the pipe-within-a-pipe construction." Lara and Akira bent forward to follow Xue's gesturing hand. "The inner pipe is filled with explosive and is held in exactly the center of the big pipe using an insulator. A Plexiglas disc should work." He pointed out each end.

"Then we coil number twelve copper wire around the outer jacket. To keep the whole thing from disintegrating too soon, the whole thing is encased in some sort of insulating material. Concrete can be used although I think the military probably uses some sort of very strong composite material to save weight. Basically, we can find everything we need for this at a well-equipped hardware store."

"Except for the explosives," Sugawara said.

Xue shrugged. "Maybe even that, if your local Ace Hardware's in Somalia or Teheran."

His attempt at humor won short grim laughter.

"But seriously," Lara persisted.

"Almost anything will work," Xue said. "C-4, Semtex—you name it—will all do the job. Everything I have found indicates that machined blocks of PBX-9501 are ideally suited because it produces a detonation wave burn perfectly matched to the compression of the magnetic field. But because C-4 is so reliable and available, I've arranged for a shipment which should arrive in Osaka about the same time we do. It may not be ideal, but it's safe, shapes easily, and will save us some time."

He stopped as the jet hit a patch of turbulence that tossed them about and drew a chorus of groans and creaks from the strapped-down freight containers.

"I hate that," Lara said, grabbing the pallet for balance. "It completely freaks me."

"You can sail across the Atlantic in a hurricane, but a little turbulence freaks you?" Akira asked.

Lara shrugged. "We all have our weaknesses." *What are yours?* She wanted to ask him.

"So how does it produce the EMP?" she asked Xue.

"Well, the whole device is a way to transfer the energy of the explosion into a very powerful electromagnetic field," he started. "The whole event starts when we discharge a bank of megajoule capacitors like those made by Maxwell Labs into the helical coil of number twelve wire which is called the stator. Capacitors can be trickle-charged with electrical power much like a small stream feeding a vast reservoir that is contained by a dam. The capacitors can be discharged much like blowing up the dam—only after discharge the capacitor is not destroyed but can be recharged. This is the same principle that allows the small, low-voltage battery on a common camera strobe to produce a jolt of fifty thousand volts or more through the flash tube."

Xue paused as he looked for signs of understanding. Lara and Akira nodded knowingly. "Pretty basic stuff," Sugawara said.

"How big are the capacitors?" Lara asked. "I assume they're a lot bigger than the rice- and pea-sized ones on a computer circuit board."

"The ones I envision are the size of oil drums," Xue said. "Fortunately, there are suitable versions that are used by companies who do metal forming using nonexplosive flux compression techniques. That makes them fairly easy to obtain if you know where to look."

"Like doing a Google search for flux compression metal forming," Sugawara said.

Xue nodded.

"How do we get from the intense magnetic field to something that fries chips?" Lara asked.

"Well," Xue continued, "when the start current peaks in the stator coil, the explosive is detonated. Remember, the explosive is contained in a metal cylinder known as the armature. The explosion expands the armature cylinder and forces the metal pieces into the highly charged coil which is at maximum current. This short-circuits the stator's electromagnetic field coils which actually traps the intense current within the device. As the explosive burns from one end of the device to another, it compresses the magnetic field farther and farther until it produces a single, incredibly intense electromagnetic field which is released just microseconds before the entire device disintegrates."

"Wow," Lara said softly. "So simple."

"Well, yes and no," Xue said. "Almost any garage terrorist can slap one of these together in a matter of hours and take out the local phone exchange, Internet hosting facility, or law enforcement communications center. But for maximum range and impact, we'll need to run tests on the stator coil to see how long it takes for them to reach maximum current. Then we need to know how long it takes to set off the explosives and get the detonation wave to the coils. If we do this, we can use a simple circuit to trigger the detonator just before the current peaks in the stator coil. We also need the proper shaped charge for the explosive, but in this case, that'd be pretty easy to deduce. If you do it right, the current of the EMP pulse that comes out can be sixty times larger than the start current . . . and possibly more."

"All from converting the explosive energy into electrical energy," Sugawara said. "Amazing."

They were all silent for a long moment. The steady drone of the 747's jet engines filled the pause.

"Could you . . ." Lara searched for a complete thought. "Could you use one EMP device to . . . uh, pump another one so that you'd have a multi-stage device that would be even bigger?"

Xue nodded. "Oh, yes. That's what you find in the military versions. Since a deliverable EMP bomb can't be encased in concrete and attached to a bunch of oil-drum-sized capacitors, they start with smaller capacitors and use multiple stages."

"So," Lara said slowly as the magnitude dawned on her, "instead of having two e-bombs that each multiply the current sixty times, if you combine them so one pumps the other, then you get sixty times sixty—"

"Holy shit! 3,600 times the original current," Sugawara blurted.

"And if you could manage a three-stage device it would be more than 200,000 times bigger than the input current."

"But the timing would be critical . . . millisecond . . . microseconds," Sugawara said. "You would have to make sure you didn't blow up the second and third stages too soon . . . or too late."

Suddenly the 747 pitched aggressively. The yawing lurch threw Xue and Sugawara to the deck. Papers flew like confetti from the pallet they were using as a table. With one hand, Lara grabbed the pallet and spread her legs, bent at the knee, as if she were back at the helm of the *Tagcat Too* in a storm. The familiar movement and the resulting muscle memories triggered a deep black sense of loss that had been bound by unrelenting fatigue, terror, and activity until just this moment. Her free hand went to the single star sapphire earring, the only physical thing she had to remind her of a life that she now doubted she would ever see again.

Moments later, the cargo deck regained its equilibrium. Xue climbed to his feet using the cargo straps for handholds. Still sitting on the deck, Akira grimaced and rubbed at his wounded shoulder.

"Are you all right?" Lara asked, her voice deep with concern.

Sugawara nodded as he struggled to his knees. "I'm okay." He got to his feet. "Everything works just fine, but the stitches took a direct shot and it hurts like fire."

"I hope you didn't pull them." Lara said.

"Nope. I've done that before and I know what it feels like." He rubbed at the shoulder through the slick parka fabric. "It'll be fine."

"That was a good one," Xue said as he bent over to gather the scattered papers. Lara and Akira helped chase down the errant documents.

Akira did move well, Lara thought as she watched him bend over to pick up the papers, effortlessly using both hands, not favoring one side or the other.

Finally, when they had placed all of the scattered papers back on the pallet, Sugawara spoke.

"All of this"—he indicated the EMP bomb documents with an arc of his hand—"are a very good idea." He paused. "But I believe we should have some last-ditch plan for physically destroying the aircraft on the ground, something in case the EMP bomb doesn't work. Even if the Slatewiper escapes in the process, it's better that it contaminate a small area rather than being sprayed over all of Tokyo."

"Yes, but getting close enough to do that, given the weapons at our disposal, probably means this would be a suicide mission. There is every likelihood we would be contaminated in the process," Xue said. "Remember, the Slatewiper that DeGroot tested was pretty nonspecific."

"What in the world could have gone wrong with that," Lara asked rhetorically.

"I think that Rycroft was tinkering with the process," Sugawara said. "The plant manager tried to tell me something about that. He thought the process had been improperly changed in order to speed things up. I suppose it could have been that."

"Regardless of why it happened, what you're proposing would be a suicide mission," Lara said. The concern was clear in her voice.

Sugawara looked around him. "I'm willing to go it alone," he said.

Lara shook her head and moved closer to him. She put her hand on his forearm and said, "I helped create this monster. I would rather die stopping this thing than to live knowing I helped set it loose."

The two of them stood eye to eye for a long moment, exchanging communications that ran deeper than words.

Xue waited patiently, a wise, knowing smile on his face. Finally, he broke the silence. "Dr. Al-Bitar can obtain certain weapons that could increase the odds of such a mission succeeding," Xue said.

Akira and Lara looked at him and nodded their agreement.

"Good. Now, I'd suggest we get some sleep," Xue said. "We've got a busy period that will begin as soon as we arrive."

Wordlessly, Lara led them single file through the shadow-steeped alleyways of strapped pallets and containers, back toward the cargo door where the aircraft's loadmaster had left sleeping bags, water, and a crate of granola bars that she found far too sweet. Xue picked up his sleeping bag and quickly disappeared among the freight.

Akira bent over stiffly to pick up his bedroll.

"How is your shoulder?" Lara asked.

Akira stood up slowly. "Stiff." He rubbed it gingerly. "But I've hurt worse before."

"That's good," Lara said genuinely as she picked up the bundled sleeping bag.

The two stood silently like that, looking at each other for a long moment in the dim netherlight as the deck hummed beneath their feet.

"Well," Lara said. She chewed self-consciously on her lower lip.

"Well." Akira nodded and shifted uncertainly from foot to foot.

Lara's heart was taken with the rare formula of strength and vulnerability she saw in the faint bas-relief of his face. She remembered his bravery in the battle at the Tulip house that now seemed so distant, and recalled his calm grace in the midst of chaos. But beyond that, she marveled at, admired the deep emotional strength it took for him to navigate the mine-laden depths of family and culture, to see beyond them to the irrevocable moral choices he had to make.

Lara thought of that as her eyes mapped his face and compassed every part of it. His eyes seemed exotic, almond-shaped, deep and dark. They excited her. She felt her usual assurance and self-confidence desert her, leaving her uncertain and bereft of any notion of what she should say, should do. She wanted to hold him. Her body told her it wanted more. Her mind told her that it was all absurd, some version of post-traumatic stress disorder.

"I, uh . . . I guess we should get some sleep now," he said.

Lara nodded. She wanted to tell him that sharing body heat would be really good for them. But instead, she simply nodded. "Uh-huh," and watched his back disappear into a corridor of the night.

"Good move," Lara muttered to herself as she wandered among the pallets. "Smooth. Got what you wanted there." She shook her head as she found an alcove, rolled out the sleeping bag, and lay down in it.

Moments later her heart hit double beats when she heard footsteps and Sugawara appeared.

"I found this." He held out a shapeless form in the darkness. "It's a tarp, but it'll help keep you warmer than just the sleeping bag."

And so would you, she almost said. "That's very kind of you." She took the tarp. "Thank you."

Silence drew them together again, the time and the space filled by mutual need, uncertainty, attraction, fear of rejection. Finally, Lara said, "Would you like to share the tarp?" For an awful moment, she was shot through with adolescent insecurity; gone was the woman who sailed the seas alone and built biotech companies. Instead, her world narrowed to the emotional, biological pinhole focus of billions of women before her: would this man reject her or not?

"Uh, uhm . . . sure." He hesitated. *Surprised?* Lara wondered. "Sure. Yes. That would be very . . . nice. I'll just go get my sleeping bag."

He left Lara awash in her own emotions and returned just a little too quickly. This excited her too. He had obviously hoped for this, had brought his sleeping bag and stashed it close by.

Lara moved over to make room for him in the space she had selected. He spread out the sleeping bag, climbed into it, and then spread the tarp over both of them.

They lay still like that for several minutes. Then tentatively he offered his arm and shoulder to her. Lara accepted his offer and snuggled as closely to him as the bags and winter clothing would allow. She kissed him modestly good night and then they fell quickly asleep as the giant aircraft rushed on toward destiny.

The rising sun climbed above a landscape hung with hazy curtains of smog and distance that draped from ridgeline to ridgeline, growing denser and turning Tokyo's skyscrapers into vague silhouettes that towered above the harbor.

Tokutaro Kurata stood on the roof of Laboratory 73, gazing at the morning sunlight until the noise of an automobile sounded on the ground below. He looked down as a plain Mitsubishi sedan pulled away from the loading dock and made its way to the first of the security gates. Edward Rycroft stood next to him, hands jammed in the pockets of his white lab coat; he was watching a hawk in the distance hover, whirl, and dive out of sight behind a grove of camphor trees.

"They will tell no difference?" Kurata asked.

Rycroft shook his head.

"The pellets look the same as the ones we've been giving them for months now." His voice was sharp, irritated. "They think it's a surfactant— something that dissolves in the skywriting chemical to make the chemicals vaporize more uniformly, keep the nozzles from clogging."

He turned to face Kurata. "Relax. By this time tomorrow, the whole thing could be done."

Kurata looked over at him. "Forgive me for not being myself. The dishonor of my nephew has troubled me greatly."

"Of course," Rycroft said more evenly.

"What do you hear from the solar forecasters?"

Rycroft smiled. "Decreasing intensity. The geomagnetic disturbances seem to be migrating farther north. It's not unreasonable to expect we will have a window for noon tomorrow."

Kurata smiled broadly.

51

DEEP IN THE RUGGED JAPANESE LANDSCAPE, A LANDSLIDE TRIGGERED BY SOME LONG-FORGOTTEN EARTHQUAKE HAD FASHIONED A MASSIVE DAMLIKE BARRIER ACROSS THE MOUTH OF THE VALLEY, TRAPPING A SMALL LAKE AND ISOLATING THE VALLEY FROM THE WORLD BELOW. The valley was an almost perfect bowl; steep mountains sloped down to flat fields graded level by the silt of eons. Paddies filled with the commune's famous rice clung to the sides of the mountains, hanging from the slopes like water-filled half bowls stepping their green syncopated way halfway up to the peaks. Paddies filled in the high end of the valley as well, so the very flat land in the middle was surrounded by a "U" of rice paddies that began and ended at the berm and lake at the lower end.

The flat land was planted in the commune's prized vegetables. Beef cattle grazed alongside a packed gravel landing strip used by the commune's agricultural aircraft. All of the commune's food was grown organically, but their pilots were valued for their ability to precisely deposit chemicals on other farmers' fields. A metal hangar sat near the edge of the lake, a huddle of smaller buildings crowded close.

If an observer had been standing along the edge of the ridge road that made its way up the spine of one of the valley walls, the observer would have seen guards patrolling the double lines of tall chain-link fence that drew the exact shape of the commune's property.

Some of the commune's detractors had told editors at the *Asahi Shimbun* that the fences were prison walls to keep unwilling cult members from returning to the world outside. Commune elders scoffed and pointed out the repeated attempts that had been made to steal its pure and valuable food. Not to mention the commune's detractors who were a very real threat to the farm and the physical well-being of its inhabitants. A cursory government inspection invited by the commune and reported in the *Asahi Shimbun* seemed to allay fears it might be another armed cult like the one that had planted nerve gas in Tokyo subways.

On this day, the observer on the hill would also have seen a plain Mitsubishi sedan making its slow way up the single winding dirt road to the compound's gate. The Mitsubishi was waved through, its papers checked a second time as the first gate closed. At last, the sedan made its way to the hangar, where it was met by more scrutiny. Finally, the hangar doors opened, and the Mitsubishi disappeared from sight.

52

IN THE DYING MOMENTS OF THE OSAKA SUNSET, A BIG SIKORSKY HELICOPTER SETTLED GRACEFULLY IN FRONT OF SINGAPORE ELECTROCHIP'S FREIGHT HANDLING TERMINAL. It was one of the largest buildings among scores of similar metal-sided buildings that crowded the cargo sectors, far from passenger terminals and prying eyes. This was a routine event and failed to draw a second glance from any of the jump-suit-clad workers who loaded and unloaded boxes and pallets from aircraft at the neighboring terminals.

Lara Blackwood and Akira Sugawara held hands, crouching in the rear of the craft, carefully hidden by strategically placed boxes and pallets. The helicopter had "coincidentally" been sent for minor repairs at the same maintenance hangar as the 747 that had transported them from Amsterdam. The mysterious Dr. Al-Bitar's money had, once again, purchased discretion, silence, blindness, and cooperation.

Lara leaned against Akira and felt him move toward her in the dim confined space. The contact filled her heart with warmth and security and chased away the cold darkness that had been her constant companion since fleeing death in Washington.

The pitch of the helicopter's main rotor ran down the scales, and moments later there was little more than the free-rotating *swoofting* of the rotors. Unseen voices came from beyond the fortress of cargo. Among the voices was Victor Xue's, issuing requests and other voices responding crisply and respectfully. From beyond the fuselage came the sounds of forklifts and quieter vehicles. The rumble of the helicopter's huge cargo door made the entire craft vibrate.

Moments later thumps came from beneath their feet. Lara and Akira scrambled to their feet and opened a small access hatch in the deck.

"Please check carefully about your seat for all personal items before deplaning." Victor Xue's head bobbed up in the opening. "And thank you for choosing Fly By Night Airlines." He gave them a smile and then held up his hand. "Hold on a moment."

His head disappeared for a moment. Then, "Okay, quickly. Everybody's busy with the freight." They slipped quickly out of the hatch and climbed around a collection of cardboard boxes that nearly filled the back of the full-sized cargo van. Xue whisked them away from the helicopter, around to the rear of the freight terminal, and through an open vehicle door. Xue pressed a remote control to close the door.

"Okay, you can get up now."

When Akira and Lara sat up, they saw a cavernous room with white metal walls and high ceilings two or three stories high. Very bright lights hung from exposed girders, backlit by skylights that covered half the roof. They were surrounded by a ten-foot wall of shipping containers, pallets, and boxes: exactly what one might expect in a freight terminal.

Akira and Lara watched as Xue steered the van left and around the distant perimeter of the boxes, doglegged back right and brought them to a halt at the edge of a broad open space filled with pallets, workbenches, a lathe, a drill press, and other shop equipment along with tables occupied by computers, electronic test equipment, papers, and blueprints. Piles and stacks of pipe, coils of wire, and plastic and metal stock sat haphazardly where forklifts had deposited their pallets. A motorized cement mixer sat idle next to pallets stacked high with sacks of concrete.

In one corner a man in olive-drab fatigues tended to a metal oil drum suspended over a large portable bottled gas burner; what looked like water vapor hung over the mouth of the barrel.

In the far opposite corner, blue lightning stuttered and crackled as a man in brown coveralls lit up the area with an arc welder. The man stopped, tilted the shield over his head, then set to work on the object with a portable grinder, setting off a meteor shower of spray of sparks as he worked. Lara guessed he was grinding off rough spot welds. A collection of dome-shaped tents clustered in a far corner of the building surrounded by enough folding tables, stools, and cooking gear to look like a floor display in a large sporting goods store.

Closer to them, a man in a white lab coat bent over a computer monitor. He stood up and looked toward the van, then began walking briskly toward them, the tails of his lab coat trailing behind him.

"Amazing," Lara said. "How did you get all this so fast?"

"*Shinrai* has many resources," Xue said. "But most importantly, when Dr. Al-Bitar tells someone to get moving, they move heaven and earth."

"Apparently," Lara said, clearly impressed by the extent of the organization. She watched as the man in the lab coat grew closer. He was a lean man of average height with dark skin, a full salt-and-pepper beard, a dark blue turban, and a smile that radiated both confidence and genuine welcome.

"Good evening, Victor!" the man said as he drew near, and extended his hand. "I hope you had a good trip."

Victor shook the man's hand. "Under the circumstances, very good although sleeping on the floor of an unheated cargo jet is not something I'd recommend for anyone older than twenty-five." Then he turned to Lara and Akira. "Lara Blackwood, Akira Sugawara: this is Dr. John LaPorta, head of research for Singapore Electrochip. He's a brilliant physicist who came to us when we acquired a very successful semiconductor company he founded. In fact, his patents and discoveries have paved the way for high-temperature quantum computing."

"Don't believe a word of what he says," LaPorta replied. "I'm just grateful to make a contribution here and there." He extended his hand to Lara. "What a pleasure to meet you, Ms. Blackwood. And to know you are safe."

Lara took his hand and returned the pleasantry.

"And you." LaPorta turned to Akira. "I am also glad to meet someone of your courage."

Akira shrugged as he shook LaPorta's hand. "Thank you, but I am only doing what seems like the right thing."

LaPorta nodded. "And sometimes that is the hardest thing."

He paused. Xue looked to LaPorta expectantly. Then, "We have made some very good progress in a very short time." He looked around the room. "Fortunately, the basic device is very simple and its design easy to come by. We are very nearly done with one very uncomplicated device and have begun to work on a couple of others I have designed that may be far more effective. Come this way, I will show you."

They followed him toward the computer he had been working on.

Xue pointed at the computer screen. "What do you have here?"

"It's a simulation of our e-bomb." He stepped to the keyboard, entered a string of commands, and stood back as the screen began its animation. "The trick is to correlate the shape of the explosive's detonation burn wave form with the magnetic field and the precise initial shape of the stator and armature for maximum output. Since I am not an explosives expert, it's fortunate that detonation burn characteristics of most explosives are readily available in a form which I can use with my own electromagnetic model."

Lara and Akira watched as the graphic simulation proceeded to a conclusion.

"This simulation offers us all we need to shape the initial charge. It also helps me design a charging and detonation circuit that will produce maximum EMP." He paused. "But to be honest, the design is so simple that none of these design tweaks is vital. My sons could build one of these in the garage in a weekend."

"Wow," Lara said. "It's amazing that terrorists haven't been setting these off all around the world. A half dozen of these placed at the right places could take out air traffic control, phone switching centers, Internet hosting companies—it could bring the U.S. to its knees . . ."

Xue shook his head. "But it's not splashy; it doesn't kill people and doesn't make for horrific images on television," he said. "There's no blood, no body parts, no flying pieces of dead babies, no lingering threat of bodily harm. Terrorists live to see gore and suffering. They like to murder and destroy. They wrap their sickness up in politics or religion, but none of that really matters to them. It just gives them cover for their psychosis. They're just butchers and mass murderers and they'll always turn away from the merely effective. Why attack soldiers when you can blast some little girl's party?"

"Charming," Lara grumbled.

"Let me introduce you to the others who will be working with us," LaPorta said as he began walking toward the man with the arc welder. "We haven't much time, so we'll all need to get right to things tonight."

The man saw them coming and set down the grinder and wiped his hands on a carnelian shop towel. When they approached, Lara saw that the man had been welding half-inch-thick steel plate into what looked to her like a cradle or some sort of mounting base.

"This is Satoshi Kakudate," LaPorta began as he introduced Lara and Akira. The man bowed; Akira returned the honorific. "He's one of our most active members. In real life, he's a machinist for the Japanese subsidiary of General Motors. He'll make sure that what we put together will not come apart until we throw the switch."

"I will do my best," Kakudate said in flawless English.

"What are you working on now?" Lara asked.

"It is a frame on which we can put all the other components," he explained. "I am told we may be using heavy materials such as concrete, so I have made it sturdy."

A voice with a subtle Southern accent came from behind them: "So sturdy that the frame will probably be the only thing that survives the blast!"

They all turned toward the source of the voice and found themselves looking at a tall, obviously fit man in his fifties. "Hell, in case of nuclear attack, I'd hide under just about anything Satoshi builds." He extended his hand and before LaPorta could introduce him said: "I'm Charles Brooks."

Xue introduced Lara and Akira, then said, "Charles is a banker—"

"That's pretty cruel, Victor," Brooks said. "Can't you introduce me as some other kind of criminal?" He smiled. "Besides, I'm retired now."

"Yes," Xue recommenced. "Charles has retired from banking and is now working to atone for the sins of his career."

They all laughed.

"That doesn't look like an annuity," Lara said, nodding toward the steaming oil drum. "More like something from *Macbeth*."

"Well, it is more like something the witches would brew up," he said. "I'm here because of a modest background in the military—"

"Charles was a Green Beret," Xue interjected. "Hardly a modest background given that he was so valuable, they've managed to keep him in the reserves long past his prime."

"Thank you for that vote of confidence," Brooks said with mock sarcasm. "Truth is, Ms. Blackwood, that cauldron is a heap of toil and trouble. I'm using it as a big double boiler to melt the C-4 so that we have a uniform cylinder of explosives. Otherwise, if we just wadded it down into the copper armature pipe, there would be wrinkles and voids and other irregularities that would disrupt a smooth burn for the detonation wave. The device would still work, but it would probably not give us as much bang for our effort."

He paused to let the information sink in. Then he looked at Lara and Akira. "I could use some help for one of those pours right now."

"Sure," they said almost simultaneously.

"Do you need both of them?" Xue asked. "I need help unloading the van."

Brooks shook his head.

"Charles and Akira are our two military types," Xue said. "Why not let them get to know each other better?"

"Sure," Lara agreed reluctantly. She wanted to see the explosives casting process herself, but yielded to Xue's logic. If there was to be some sort of last-ditch physical assault, the two soldiers would need to be on the same wavelength.

LaPorta accompanied them back toward the van. They all stopped when they reached his computer. "I am almost finished with the coil and timing circuit design. Satoshi and I will need some assistance winding the coils on the lathe and soldering the electronics." He looked at Lara.

"My pleasure," she said.

"Excellent," Xue said. "I'll need to go take possession of the capacitors and direct the container of weapons that Dr. Al-Bitar has arranged for us."

When Lara and Victor reached the van, he opened the side door, stepped in, and began handing boxes to Lara.

In minutes, they had finished.

"Take that one over to Satoshi, would you?" Xue indicated a tall, thin box with the DuPont logo on it. Lara looked at the label closely as she bent over it.

"Ballistic Kevlar fabric," she read. "Wouldn't that be the stuff used in body armor?"

"Precisely."

"And we need it for what?" she asked as she picked up the box and hefted it easily to her shoulder.

"I'm sure you're aware that ounce for ounce, it's stronger than steel?"

"Right."

"And you're also aware that concrete by itself is brittle, which is why strong construction uses steel reinforcing bars?"

Lara nodded.

"Well, we can't use rebar in the concrete structural jacket around our device because the whole thing needs to be an insulator."

"Ah!" said Lara. "But Kevlar is a synthetic fabric which melts, so my guess is that we put a thin concrete jacket around the device and then wrap it with the Kevlar. The blast pulverizes the concrete which keeps the heat away from the Kevlar long enough for it to contain the blast so it can get the maximum EMP from the detonation?"

"I think you have a future in weapons design," Xue said as he made his way to the now-empty van and got into the driver's seat.

"I think I'll pass on that." She smiled.

"Wise move," Xue said as he started the engine. "I shouldn't be long."

Lara nodded, then turned and carried the box of Kevlar fabric to Brooks and Sugawara. When Lara approached, she saw they were concentrating on pouring the melted C-4 into a long shiny copper pipe about six inches in diameter. Silently, she leaned the box against a workbench where she was sure they would see it, then went over to where Satoshi Kakudate and John LaPorta wrestled a giant spool of wire toward a lathe.

"May I help?" she asked when she approached the men. She saw now that the spool, the size of a small end table, was twelve-gauge AWG copper wire with an enameled coating. A one-inch steel bar ran through the center of the spool that the men were trying to lift into a cradle that would allow it to spin.

"Gladly," Kakudate replied quickly.

Lara was taller than both men by at least a head and certainly twenty years younger. She took one end of the steel bar and the two older men the other. Together they easily lifted the spool into the cradle. Satoshi walked toward the lathe that already had a four-foot-long Plexiglas cylinder fastened in its chuck.

"Thank you," LaPorta said softly.

"Thank you!" Lara replied. "For being here."

"It's the right thing," LaPorta replied. He bent over the spool and found the free end of the wire and handed it to her. "Would you take this over to Satoshi? This will form the stator windings. If you will help Satoshi feed the wire so the windings are very even, I will keep the spool turning and the wire free of snags."

"Of course."

The work went swiftly, interrupted only by the arrival in the outer area of the warehouse of an air freight container. Brooks and Sugawara cast the C-4 into four copper armature cores; Kakudate, Lara, and LaPorta wound four stator coils, splitting each of them into three separate coils to maximize the output. Using Lexan insulator blocks that Kakudate had machined, they assembled the explosive-filled armature so it ran coaxially inside the Plexiglas tubing, precisely down the midpoint of the stator windings. The explosive-filled armature was longer than the Plexiglas stator windings and stuck out a lot at the end where the detonation would start and only a little at the other end.

"That's so we can have the properly shaped blast wave," Brooks explained. "I'll shape the C-4 properly and insert the detonator after the concrete hardens."

Xue returned shortly after 9:00 P.M. with a large truck of capacitors just as they prepared to make the stator structural jackets.

"I can see my timing was off," he said as they pressed him into the dirty task of mixing concrete. "I should have taken more time!"

The assembled e-bombs were covered top and bottom to keep concrete out and then lowered into a plastic chemical drum. LaPorta and Kakudate drilled holes in the sides and threaded half-inch-diameter insulated copper cables through them and attached each one to the free end of a stator winding. The cables were properly labeled, the holes were sealed with plain window putty, and by midnight the last of the concrete had been poured. All seven people were covered with a fine gray patina of cement dust streaked with sweat. They gathered around a stack of bottled water cases. Nearby were cases of vending machine food: granola bars, beef jerky, candy bars, chips, and cheese-food crackers.

"Victor, this is not the breakfast of champions where I come from," Lara joked as she downed her fourth granola bar and washed it down with the water.

"I'll relay your criticism to the chef," he replied.

The assembled group laughed wearily as they tore into the snacks.

Sugawara stood quietly next to her; she felt his body heat, but found it hard to care about it. After sleeping badly in the 747 from Holland and all the work that had just ended, she found that fatigue ruled her mind, body, and emotions. Just as well, she thought, with all the people watching.

"There's a shower over there." Xue pointed to the cluster of tents in the far corner of the warehouse. "I don't know how hot the water will be, but I'd advise everyone to rinse off the cement dust. It can be a nasty irritant." He paused. "There's a pile of towels and other toiletries in the shopping bags by the door." Then he turned toward Lara and Akira. "Since you couldn't pack a bag like everyone else, I bought an assortment of sweatshirts, T-shirts, warm-up pants, and other items. I hope they fit. They're in the cab." He pointed toward the truck still filled with gigantic capacitors. Each had two electrodes sticking out the top, supported by white, crenellated ceramic insulators that looked like ears on some weird cartoon creature.

Akira and Lara walked toward the truck as the others drifted off slowly, toward the tents and shower. They walked silently side by side, separated from each other by fatigue and modesty.

"I am totally hammered," Lara said as she wiped at the dust on her face.

"Yeah." Sugawara nodded. "Sleep would be good. I'm so tired everything looks too bright."

Suddenly the overhead lights flicked off one by one with only a single bank of fluorescents still shining in the corner farthest from the tents.

"Well, they did look too bright there for a while!" His easy laughter brought a quick smile to Lara's face.

She reached over and squeezed his hand. He responded with a warm comfortable grip that felt more comfortable to Lara than any other, ever. Self-consciously, she looked quickly over her shoulder and felt relieved to see that everyone was either in their tent or the shower. All except John LaPorta who had pulled off the plastic sheeting that had protected his computer from the concrete dust and sat there now, engrossed in whatever played across the monitor.

"How's your shoulder?"

"Kind of a dull ache that's always in the background like a headache that just won't go away." He shrugged. "It's annoying, but not a lot more."

"Hmmm. Good."

When they reached the truck, Sugawara climbed up and brought down the shopping bags. He handed Lara the one with her name on it and turned back toward the tents.

"Want to share a tent?" Sugawara asked tentatively.

"Uh-huh, but not tonight. I don't know about you, but I don't want to have to deal with all the winks and stares that would surely get thrown our way."

Sugawara nodded. "Yeah. You're right." He paused as they got near the tents. "But I thought I'd ask."

"That's sweet. But let's concentrate on our mission. If we succeed, then we can see what happens."

"But we will!" Sugawara's voice was incredulous. He stopped. "Of course we will. We have to."

Lara continued walking, and found that pieces of paper with names on them had been taped to each tent. She scanned each tent and located her own.

"I wish I had the same faith you do," she said as she reached her tent. "I often see things differently after a little sleep."

She looked at him standing there. The brave, handsome man who moved with such effortless grace despite his wound looked like a bewildered little boy. It moved her heart.

"Good night," she said and blew him a kiss.

53

MORNING DAWNED ELECTRIC.

The first thing that reached through the darkness of sleep and chased Lara's dreams like sun after the fog was the sound of high-voltage snapping and crackling. In the spaces between the electrical discharges came the hum of a small motor. She rolled over and looked at her watch. It was 6:17 A.M.

She rummaged through the clothes that Victor had bought and found a plain red T-shirt and pulled it on followed by a set of men's large nylon warm-ups. The jacket fit well, but she had to pull the drawstring in severely on the pants to keep them from falling down.

When she unzipped the tent and climbed out, she saw John LaPorta and Satoshi Kakudate tinkering with a bank of the huge pulse discharge capacitors. A Honda generator stood next to them. They were obviously testing the charging circuits for the capacitors.

Where was Akira?

"Oh, man, this just isn't going to work!"

Lara followed the complaint and found Charles Brooks and Victor Xue standing in a far corner staring down at a makeshift table that consisted of a sheet of plywood resting on four oil drums.

Where was Akira?

She pulled on her old sneakers and walked over to Brooks and Xue and saw they were staring down at a topographical map and aerial photos.

"Morning, Ms. Blackwood," Brooks said gruffly. Then he turned toward a line of four identical white delivery trucks at the far side of the warehouse and yelled: "Akira!"

Where had the trucks come from? she wondered. More of Victor Xue's resourcefulness, no doubt. She noted the double rear wheels on the trucks that told her these were designed to carry the heavy loads. They looked, she thought, a lot like smaller versions of UPS vans, only white.

"Yo! Sugawara!" Brooks yelled again.

Akira emerged briefly from the rear of one of the trucks. Lara's heart brightened.

"Come here!"

"Can't now!" he shouted. "Be there in a minute."

Brooks shrugged. "Look at this." Brooks pointed to one of the aerial photos. Lara and Xue leaned forward. "We've got a big problem delivering our gadgets." He tapped his index finger on the topo map. "Lookit—there's a huge horseshoe of rice paddies surrounding the compound. And here . . ." He ran his fingers in a "U" shape on the topographical map. "The contour lines almost merge all along here; this is a sheer cliff we'd need technical rock-climbing gear to scale, and once we did, we'd be up to our hips in rice paddy mud and water."

They all leaned over and studied the map, then the photos.

"Okay, look here," Brooks said, moving his finger along one of the aerial photos. "You can see the dirt strip running along the valley floor here—" He tapped. "Now the fencing comes right to the edge of the valley mouth and this humongous drop-off that looks to be a couple of hundred feet.

"Now here on the topo map." Brooks outlined an arc that took in the horseshoe of rice paddies and the sheer cliff that followed the upper level of the fields. "As you can see, we'd have to slog everything right down to the middle of the rice paddies in order to get within a mile of the runway. That means hauling things by rope down those cliffs and into the mud."

"Things look even grimmer for Plan B—stopping things with an assault if the e-bombs fail." They followed him over to the freight container in the outer part of the warehouse. He walked over to the container, pulled the door open, and went inside. Brooks exited a moment later with a large tube in one hand and a weird tripod-mounted weapon in the other.

"Okay," he said, putting the tripod down. "Here we've got a 30-mm AGS-17 Plamya grenade launcher. Nifty weapon, fires fifty to one hundred grenades a minute. Effective range, half a mile max." He stood the tube on one end, opened it up. "And here, an SA-7 Grail surface-to-air missile, old model without cooled IR sensors. Iffy on jet exhaust heat but no way in hell it could get a target fix on a prop plane."

Brooks looked at Xue for a long moment. "I'm not trying to lay blame or discredit what you arranged on such short notice. It was short notice. But the best thing you've got in there"—he thumbed at the container—"is an 82-mm mortar. Range is a couple of miles, plenty if we set up on top of this ridge." He tapped his index finger on a winding road that paralleled the valley. "Trouble is, there's only a dozen rounds of mortar ammunition, and those are all smoke—no HE."

Xue loosed a deep breath and looked at the ceiling as if expecting divine inspiration or intervention.

Brooks continued. "For physical intervention that leaves us with: (a) secretly infiltrating the compound and sabotaging the aircraft, (b) standing at the base of that big embankment at the end of the runway and trying to plink at the planes as they take off, (c) chartering a fast helicopter—something like a Bell Jet Ranger or a Huey—and flying in fast and low, using the M-16s to strafe the aircraft."

He raised his eyebrows and looked at Lara and Xue. Then he held up his finger. "The first is suicide, given the commune's reputation for paranoia; the second is an existential jerk-off and likely to puncture a tank that could then drip Slatewiper vector from there to Tokyo and back."

"And there's this town here." Lara pointed at the map. "A hit could cause an airplane to crash there and spread the vector. But any of the physical intervention is simply too dangerous. Unless we can destroy the aircraft *before* the Slatewiper vector is loaded, we'll spread it all over the countryside."

"Better to spread it over sparsely populated terrain than over Tokyo," Sugawara suggested.

"Maybe," Lara replied. "On the other hand, their termination sequence could be faulty and this stuff could be so durable that any release could spread worldwide eventually."

The resulting pause was filled with knowing looks.

"Then we must make the EMP generator work; it is the only hope," Xue said.

Sugawara jumped down from the truck and came over at a fast jog, his expression excited.

"What's up?" Brooks asked.

"You want the good news first, or the bad?" Sugawara said.

Lara raised her eyebrows.

"How about the worst first," Brooks said.

"Okay. Sure," Sugawara replied quickly, then took a deep breath to try and calm himself. "Okay. Right." He took another deep breath. "I've been on the Net doing some digging in Daiwa Ichiban's files . . . On and off. I've been watching a Web cast of NHK television which is now reporting that Kurata has arranged a special skywriting tribute to Yamamoto, the guy who killed himself at the company baths."

"And?" Lara asked.

"They hope to do it at noon tomorrow," Sugawara said. "The reporter said the solar wind—geostorms—are easing."

"What's the good news?" Lara asked.

"It comes in two parts." Sugawara ventured a small smile. "First is that Yamamoto is a cousin of Kurata's. I knew that; most of the family did. My uncle liked to hire family. He thought it would make them more trustworthy." He was silent for a moment. "Didn't work in every case." He smiled. "Like mine."

"Right," Brooks snapped impatiently. "Kurata put his cousin in charge of producing Slatewiper. Cut to the chase."

"Well, the chase is this," Sugawara responded. "I hacked into Rycroft's files this morning. Something's been fishy about him and the way Yamamoto told me about how Rycroft made him change the production process. Then Yamamoto killed himself and now we find out that the Slatewiper is somehow not ethnically targeted at all."

"Right, right," Brooks urged him forward. "What's the payoff here?"

Sugawara smiled. "I learned from Rycroft's files that Yamamoto's great-grandmother was really Korean."

Sugawara looked from one face to another as the significance slowly dawned in one pair of eyes after another. "Not only that, but from what I can figure out from the files, Rycroft used this knowledge to force Yamamoto into committing seppuku."

Their stunned silence allowed the vigorous activity from the opposite end of the warehouse to wash over them. Beyond the metal walls of the warehouse came the horns of ship traffic and the throbbing of giant engines.

"Oh, wow," Lara said softly. "If that gets out, your uncle Kurata will be finished with his racial purity buddies."

Sugawara smiled broadly and nodded. "That's why I downloaded all Rycroft's files, converted them to a fax format, and anonymously faxed them to the newsroom at *Asahi Shimbun*."

"It could be over by tonight," Lara said.

Xue shook his head. "They'll think it's manufactured, think it is a political attempt to destroy Kurata. It'll take several days for them to check it out."

Sugawara nodded. "I'll send it to a lot more newspapers and to the American, Chinese, and Korean news bureaus but it'll take time to have an effect."

"But *what* an effect it will have," Lara said.

"Okay. That's cool, but we've got work to do," Brooks said. "Let's get all the devices wrapped in Kevlar and placed in their cradles so we can forklift them into the trucks."

Propwash combed through the grass at the perimeter of the aircraft staging area and stirred a faint fog of dust as the single-engined airplane taxied into position behind its sister ships, following the hand signals of a man in bright yellow overalls. Overalls crossed his arms, and the pilot cut the engine. He climbed out of his cockpit and joined the rest of the pilots who had gathered at the edge of the staging area.

"The special surfactant has been added to your skywriting materials," began the wing leader. "It should keep the materials inside the tank usable, even though things may sit for a day or so.

"The aircraft will remain here, at the ready," said the wing leader. "We will be ready to fly at a moment's notice, starting at dawn tomorrow. If we have a break in the geomagnetic disturbances, we will perform this memorial ceremony early."

He paused, then shouted, "For Kurata!"

In a single voice, the pilots responded, "For Kurata!"

"The defender of Yamato!" the wing leader cried.

"The defender of Yamato!" the pilots responded.

54

"You should understand that I, like the people of Japan, have many enemies." Kurata stood at the broad plate-glass window of his office that gave onto crisp fall views of the city. In the distance, he could see the roof of the Yasukuni shrine and the new monument site just . . . there.

"I have the greatest respect for the *Asahi Shimbun*," Kurata replied. "It would be a great disservice to your reputation and for the great trust that your readers place in you if you were to print such a blatantly political attack."

He paused to take a deep breath as the editor on the other end of the connection spoke. Kurata fought the tarry tide of dread that rose in his chest.

"It is true that my great-grandmother was born in Korea," Kurata said. "But you must realize she was born of pure Japanese parents. My great-great-grandfather—her father—was a textiles and ceramics trader who established businesses there. I hardly think there could have been any sort of genetic rearrangement." He laughed, making himself feel hollow. He listened a bit longer.

"Of course," Kurata said heartily. "My family heritage is a source of great pride; I would be happy to open our genealogical archives for your inspection."

Pause.

"That information is maintained by Toru Matsue of my personal staff," Kurata said. "He and his family are experts at genealogy. He will be able to provide proof your allegations are false."

Another pause.

"You're quite welcome."

Kurata slammed down the receiver. The handset ricocheted off the top of the base and skidded across Kurata's desk, rearranging papers and upsetting an antique vase carefully arranged with tulips. The vase, recovered from an archaeological dig in northeast China and smuggled to Kurata at great cost, spilled its tulips and made a half turn on its side before rolling off the desk and dashing itself to shards on the floor.

Rycroft walked toward his car, a broad, satisfied smirk slashing across his face, the last warm rays of the day on his back.

You're one dead Jap, Kurata, he thought. *You and the rest of your pricks.* He checked his watch. His meeting with Woodruff and the meeting with the first of his Middle Eastern bootleg Slatewiper customers was less than an hour away. He had to hurry.

Humming a flat tune, Rycroft followed his shadow away from the buff brick of Laboratory 73. He carried two briefcases, one a shiny aluminum Halliburton case with the vials to deliver to those bloody wogs and stinking Jews and the other briefcase so overstuffed with papers and floppy disks and computer backup tapes he had had to use strapping tape to keep the contents from spilling out. He'd never set foot in Lab 73 again.

But with the data he had now, he'd get credit for quickly identifying the horrible disease that would devastate Japan and the Middle East. The Nobel would quickly follow. He'd be rich. Most importantly, there would be tens of millions of dead Japs.

Arriving at his Mitsubishi, Rycroft set the briefcases down by the trunk and fumbled for his keys. He rubbed at the Band-Aid on his right index finger. He had cut it opening one of the vials of Slatewiper vector that morning as the "surfactant" pellets were prepared. There had been a local reaction, a patch of small blisters. No problem, he decided as he located his trunk key and shoved it in the lock. Just a small allergic reaction. It couldn't hurt him. Slatewiper was for Japs.

55

THE NIGHT PRESSED CLOSE.

No moon. High clouds that had scudded in just after sunset blocked even the moonlight.

Lara steered the white truck along the two-lane highway following the three other trucks in their convoy. At the front of the procession, Victor Xue drove the lead truck. Sugawara sat next to Lara, dozing. It was amazing, Lara thought, how a relatively minor gunshot wound and a strong healthy body combined for quick recovery. But despite it all, he tired more quickly than usual and had handed off the wheel to her about two hours out of Osaka.

Up ahead, the procession slowed. Right-turn indicators blinked as Xue led them off the main highway onto the winding road that would lead up along the ridge overlooking the commune's property. Akira yawned now. Helpless to stop, Lara yawned as well. Her scratchy eyes welcomed the resulting tears.

She sniffed and drove on as dawn began its struggle with the night.

The landscape sketched itself brighter with the new day's growing light, and grew color where shades of gray had ruled. Lara had an eerie feeling of playing a well-known bit part in an ancient drama, filled with hatred, lacking catharsis. It was a play that would continue regardless of what they accomplished today.

They passed a farmer pulling an empty wagon. Seeing him made her feel a sadness for him, for the others like him who lived here, learned to walk, studied, gave birth, worked, grew old, and died. She pitied the narrow horizons that embraced only the familiar (and anointed it as superior) and rejected the different (and found it inferior). These were people like her, different in no significant physical way, yet they had divorced themselves from the richness of the world, from a richness of experience. She mourned their lost opportunity, their unfulfilled potential.

All for what?

All so that power-hungry people could be left alone by their own people to subjugate and destroy others they arbitrarily defined as inferior. Serbs and Bosnians, Jews and Arabs, Irish and English—the list stretched beyond the mind's ability to comprehend.

What was clear to Lara, as she drove through the dawn of a rising sun, was that people were good and cultures were evil; people were the same but cultures were different and divisive. But there were no people without culture. The good and the evil needed one another to survive.

The science was clear: there was no racial or cultural superiority, but only artificial differences created so that the greedy could be left alone— even encouraged—to loot those defined as different and contemptible. Theft and death in the name of superiority.

Divisions among people were not about race or about right and wrong, but about power and the allocation of wealth and resources. An ancient play that might run for as long as the species survived.

Sugawara broke her train of thought.

"Just up there," Sugawara said. "See that clump of trees? Turn there."

As planned, the other vans continued along toward positions selected from the aerial photos and top maps.

As the other three vans disappeared in the hazy predawn light, Lara turned right onto the narrow, steep road Sugawara pointed out.

She looked over at Akira, and a big part of her wanted to turn the car around and leave, disappear. They couldn't stop the hatred and its violence.

But what about all that they could change? This morning? This time?

All she wanted was to be left alone with him in peace. It was odd, she thought, that throughout history, peace was seldom created by pacifists. Well meaning but ignorant of human nature, they appeased and invited aggression. Their peace was the involuntary servitude imposed by the victor, the Balkans under Soviet hegemony, or the subjugated peoples under Roman rule.

No, enjoying peace with any level of human dignity came through superior force; it was only possible through the willingness to use violence. Any peace she and Akira might enjoy must come after fighting for this right thing.

She breathed in Akira's scent and remembered his touch, how it felt like the future brushing against her. Fear rose in her then: fear of losing him. Oddly, the fear of dying paled beside the fear of not having the life together she knew they could. He gave her a feeling of belonging, a sense of not being alone anymore. No matter, she knew it was an illusion death would shatter sooner or later.

Later, she prayed.

"Stop there," Sugawara said, "by that grove of trees."

Lara slowed and turned off the road. Sugawara would take an M-16 and one of the secure, encrypted cellular phones and walk the rest of the way up the embankment to keep an eye on the air strip. She was to park the truck with the rear doors open and aimed toward the strip.

They rolled down the windows. When Lara turned off the ignition, the sound they heard chilled them as only one sound could: the sound of aircraft engines coming from the top of the embankment.

56

THE BLACKNESS OF THE KYOTO NIGHT EMPTIED FROM THE TEAHOUSE AT KUR-
ATA'S ANCESTRAL HOMESTEAD. Kurata sat silently on the teahouse porch,
gazing into the rising sun. Next to him, Toru Matsue sat so silently Kurata had to glance occasionally to make sure the old family retainer had
not left. A wise man, Kurata thought, but sometimes odd, like his curi-
ously urgent insistence they travel to the estate in Kyoto during Operation Tsushima.

Kurata's heart continued to pound: deep, angry, fast. He found no
center in himself. There were no crickets to listen to in the crisp cold;
instead, the steady ringing of the telephone in the distant main house.
He had never been able to hear it before.

He knew who was calling, and that made him even angrier. First there
had been the *Asahi Shimbun*. Then the television reporters and more
newspaper reporters. Then the foreign press, all asking about the same
set of damning papers they had received anonymously.

The telephone rang again. Why tonight? Why now, when he needed
meditation to quell the unwelcome agitation inside? Why had his hearing suddenly grown so acute as to pull the faint ringing out of the night?

Kyoto had always centered him, helped him to conquer anger, fear,
and frustration. As he tried to visualize the rock garden in the dark, as
he tried to see in his mind the big rock hidden in the night—the rock

that was his ship that always carried him to calmer waters—as he tried to do all this, he knew Kyoto had failed him for the first time in his life.

This failure was a momentous thing. That much he knew. It was pregnant with significance.

Kurata sighed, and from the corner of his eye saw Matsue turn his head. He tried to visualize then the horrible, disease-mutilated bodies of the Koreans; it was then that his center returned like oil, smoothing out the surf of his anxiety.

Fine. It would all be fine. His most enduring legacy, the work of a lifetime would be finished before night came again. Nothing else mattered. The defender of Yamato would strike his greatest blow for the purity and protection of his race.

Edward Rycroft had been forced to accept that something had gone hideously wrong with the Slatewiper vector when the blood-filled blisters began to cover his face. When the ends of his fingers turned blue and then gray and then began to putrefy from the lack of blood, he knew for sure he was going to die.

The Slatewiper's predictable series of small cerebral hemorrhages left his thoughts a jumble of reality and vague childhood recollections. Through the haze, he felt himself fall, grasping for the sink, fingers too damaged to grip the slick porcelain edge. As he collapsed on the bathroom floor and vomited bright red arterial blood, he knew he must die soon.

He saw Singapore, then, and his parents and the Japanese. Instead of his own gags and moans, he heard his parents' mortal screams; instead of the Slatewiper's excruciating pain as it scraped his insides clean, he felt the fear of a small child about to be discovered by his parents' murderers.

Then a warm, dark peace filled him as he realized the dirty fucking Japs would all be dead soon too. A final rictus of death shaped his bloody lips into a smile.

57

LARA GRABBED HER WIRELESS PHONE AND SPEED-DIALED XUE'S NUMBER. Her heart pounded like flak; the ends of her fingers tingled in resonance with the sound of airplane propellers.

Xue answered on the second ring.

"Are you high enough up yet to see the aircraft on the runway?" Lara said without preamble. "Right." She listened then. "Can't you zap the fuckers now?" Lara was silent again for a moment. "Shit. Right. We'll do our best."

Her face was grim when she folded the phone and slipped it into her jacket pocket. Sugawara looked at her expectantly.

"They heard it too," Lara said. "They're trying to get into position, but two of the other three trucks are in valleys that don't have a clear shot at the runway."

"Okay, we've got the best shot of taking them out," Sugawara said. "Drive as fast as you can up the hill. To the compound."

She started the engine and floored the accelerator. The truck groaned up the steep slope. Lara drove intensely; the rear end of the Nissan broke free and slid around the tightest of the hairpins. The engine raced. Tortured rubber screeched.

"Oh, shit!" Lara cried. Sugawara looked toward her as she hauled on the steering wheel, swerving to avoid a large goat that had wandered into the roadway. The truck went sideways for a moment before straightening out. Then just as it looked as if the collision had been averted, the frightened animal darted back into their path. The sickening crunch was followed by a truncated bleating; instants later, the goat's body flew up over the hood and slammed into the windshield in a dirty white whir of hooves and blood.

"Oh, shit!" Lara said as the body blocked her vision; she slammed on the brakes; the antilock mechanism pumped them to a quick halt that sent the goat careening off the hood.

The whole thing took less than ten seconds. Lara cursed under her breath and jammed the accelerator to the floor. She steered around the body, squinting through the cracks in the windshield.

"Once you get to the top," Sugawara yelled. "Don't let up on the speed. Take us right through the gate. If we're in time, we'll block the runway, open the doors, and run like hell before we set off the explosives."

Hanging on to the door handle as Lara threw the truck into the next hairpin, Sugawara closed his eyes for a moment and prayed. He prayed first for success and then that he wouldn't have to shoot anyone. The pilots were not evil people; they were completely unaware they would be carrying a lethal cargo.

They were innocent that way, but guilty in another. They were guilty of lending their talents to the creation of an atmosphere of racial hatred. But did they deserve to die for that? Akira thought not, but he would kill if it meant containing the Slatewiper. Better to shut off a platoon of unlucky seamen in a watertight compartment and let them die than to have the whole ship sink.

He prayed, too, for Lara and for himself. He looked over and watched the intense concentration in her face, the skillful way she threw herself into the last-ditch battle against mass death.

The truck almost left the ground completely as it broached the top of the hill. Lara wrestled with the wheel and kept the accelerator to the floor.

The sentry at the gate whirled toward them, his eyes wide. Then he ran.

Sugawara felt his testicles crawl up the side of his groin as he took in the sight that lay before them. In the distance, one of the aircraft was at the end of the runway and had started its takeoff roll.

Sugawara flipped the M-16 to full automatic and leaned out the window. As they grew closer to the fence at the end of the runway, the airplane grew larger and larger as it gathered speed and began to lift off.

Then from the hills came a thunderous explosion. Then another.

Suddenly the truck's engine quit.

"Oh, hell," Lara cursed. "Now what?"

Sugawara barely noted the silence of the engine over the M-16's cannonade. With an indescribable elation, he watched the airplane waver for a moment; then descend, its tires trailing dust.

The M-16's clip emptied. In the ensuing silence, the loudest sound came from their truck's tires crunching over gravel as Lara struggled to maintain control over power steering gone dead. Akira rammed a new clip into the M-16 and prepared to leap out as the truck slowed to a halt.

Lara brought the truck to a stop. In the distance, the aircraft that had started its takeoff rolled slowly into the chain-link fence at the end of the runway. There was a screech as the metal fencing expanded to stop the aircraft, a creaking as it rebounded.

They smiled at each other then as they absorbed the sweet powerful sounds of silence. The sound of success. Of life.

The sweet feeling of victory evaporated suddenly as the sounds of gunfire and angry, frightened men filled the air.

"Let's get out of here," Lara said as she saw a crowd of people heading for the truck.

"Right." Sugawara fired the M-16 and sent the men diving for cover as he and Lara ran for the hole they had made in the fence. They ran down a small embankment. The sounds of their pursuers grew louder.

"Hold it a second," Lara said as she stopped and pulled the radio-controlled detonator from inside her jacket. She opened the safety cover and pressed the red button.

Another thunderous explosion sounded, this one from the truck that they had just abandoned.

Without waiting, they ran on into the brightening day.

58

Osaka International Airport throbbed with activity.

People lugged bags, swung briefcases, carried duty-free parcels, and cradled carefully wrapped gifts and children through the stale manufactured air that hung foul with jet fuel, anxiety, cigarette smoke, frustration, flatulence, anticipation, rest-room disinfectant, fear, coffee, joy, fried food, and sorrow: the stale, smelly Esperanto of world travel.

At the general aviation terminal, swinging doors spun into the concourse. Lara Blackwood was the first through.

"I tell you, he'll find a loophole to wriggle through if he remains alive," Akira Sugawara said as he followed Lara through. "I must kill him; he's my obligation. I must do this alone."

"Oh, wait . . . wait! Hold on just a bleeping minute!" Charles Brooks stopped suddenly, half a dozen steps inside the doors. Bringing up the rear, Victor Xue failed to anticipate Brooks's sudden halt and ran into him. Sugawara stopped at the sound of Brooks's voice. Lara stopped next to him.

They stood like that for a moment—Sugawara, Lara, Brooks, Xue—strung out in a twenty-foot line; then they gathered next to Sugawara.

"Look, we went over and over this already today," Brooks said. "I thought you agreed that you'd accept our help. There's no way you stand a chance alone."

Sugawara took a deep breath. "Kurata's my *obligation*," he said softly. "He's family; I'm the one who must close the circle on this thing. I do not want any of you to get hurt because of my obligation." He looked around at each of them in turn. His eyes lingered on Lara.

Lara shook her head. "We can be there to back you up," she said. "We want to be there." She fixed his eyes with her own, then said softly, "I want to be there."

Shaking his head, Sugawara said, "It's my fight . . ." He paused as the public address system fuzzed out the announcement of an arriving flight. A gaggle of starched nuns bustled past, all black, white, and holy.

Lara took a deep breath. "We all have an obligation in making sure that Kurata and his companies can't do this again. If you fail, then we all have to try again."

Sugawara shook his head again. "I have to do it myself, or it won't be right. It's my family that did this, my genes, my culture. It won't be right if you go." He made another movement to resume walking; everyone followed him down the escalator to the transportation and baggage area.

"You need to stop all this Bushido bullshit," Brooks said harshly. "Get hold of reality, son. If you fail at your little kamikaze stunt—and I have no doubt that Kurata will eat you alive—then the rest of us have to try and finish him off . . . only without having your considerable talent and knowledge and contribution."

"We don't really have any choice in all this," Lara told him. "You know as well as I do that if we don't eliminate Kurata, he will find a way to keep Slatewiper alive . . . his empire will do that. Without your help, then we'll probably fail. Without ours, so will you. Together, I think we can succeed . . . alive."

"Dr. Al-Bitar will not be stingy with his resources."

Sugawara frowned and stared at the floor. He remained silent.

Finally, Sugawara looked up at these new friends.

"Why do this?" he asked. "Risk your life? You don't have to."

"Because it's right," Lara said.

Sugawara shook his head. "People don't do that anymore."

"Enough do," Lara responded. "You did." She paused. "Otherwise I wouldn't be alive."

Sugawara turned away and stared at the luggage carousels. He took a deep breath and sighed as he turned back to face Lara, Brooks, and

Xue. "Right." He shook his head and finally smiled. "Well, I can't very well fight all of you *and* Kurata."

Lara kissed him; Brooks slapped him on his back; Xue shook his hand. Then they made their way toward the rental car counters.

59

A GRITTY INDUSTRIAL DIMNESS SIFTED THROUGH THE TWILIGHT IN A SOUTHWEST
KYOTO PRECINCT SELDOM VISITED BY TOURISTS: RAIL LINES, SWITCHING YARDS,
WAREHOUSES, FAR FROM THE RENOWNED TEMPLES AND SCENERY OF THE ANCIENT
TOWN AND ITS HILLS TO THE NORTH AND EAST.

Just inside the half-rolled up loading dock door of a freight consoli-
dation warehouse, a muffled *thunk!* sounded dully in the gathering night.

"Awright!" An excited voice. "That's it!"

Inside the freight bay, Charles Brooks squatted next to a gallon can
of oil-based paint, washed clean of its original contents and half filled
with gasoline. Two dozen identical paint cans, sides streaked with paint,
were lined up along the partially open freight door. All had lids tightly
tamped except for the one Brooks now examined; he checked his watch
against the time written in black marker on the side of the can. Gasoline
and linseed fumes clotted the air and made his eyes water.

"Exactly one hour," Brooks said as he stood up and looked into the
can. At the bottom lay the practice hand grenade, the arming lever, and
the remains of two partially dissolved rubber bands. The *thunk* had been
made by the spring-loaded arming lever as it clicked loose from the
grenade body.

At the far side of the freight bay, Lara and Xue looked up from the maps they had spread out over a makeshift table of packing crates. Stacked around them were the boxes of munitions and arms that Al-Bitar's people had trucked in from Osaka, less than an hour's drive southwest of Kyoto.

Brooks placed a lid over the paint can, then stood up. He bent over backward to stretch his back muscles and walked toward them. "One of the medium-sized rubber bands and two of the thin ones," he said as he walked toward them. "As accurate a timer as we're likely to get on this short notice." He snuffed against the tears from his watering eyes as he stopped next to Lara and put his arm around her shoulders; she smiled up at him.

Spread out before them on the makeshift table were maps of the Rakuhoku, the steep mountainous region north of Kyoto. Since ancient times, the mountains here were thought to be inhabited by devils and evil spirits. In more modern times, it was known as the home of Tokutaro Kurata.

Scattered about the maps were photos of Kurata's estate, most of it surrounded on three sides by a mountain lake set amid dense trees and rugged hills.

Brooks pointed at a hand-drawn map Sugawara had constructed for them. "Kurata's estate is laid out in Shinden style, along three sides of a big 'U' with his huge main hall at the bottom of the 'U,' down by the lake. The other two sides are long narrow buildings and walls that stretch from the lake almost to the entrance up at the public road. The interior space is filled with streams, ponds, statues, and gardens. And while it outwardly resembles the Golden Temple, it is easily six or eight times larger.

"Akira thinks his uncle will probably try to confine him here." Brooks pointed to the third-floor drawing that resembled a large cupola.

Lara leaned over and pointed at the drawing. "If I remember correctly, Akira said we'll find motion detectors, pressure sensors on the top of the exterior wall and key steps and walkways, infrared light beams, some thermal imaging, and a colony of Komodo dragons that are allowed to roam most of the outer grounds."

"Don't let their lumbering size fool you," Brooks said. "They're the size of an alligator and can take you down in a split second."

Lara winced. "That's not a pretty picture. Hopefully they'll be lethargic with the night-time temperatures."

"Yeah, well I wouldn't count on it."

Lara leaned over for a closer look at an aerial photo. "Okay, just so I've got it straight: deliveries come up this way?" She traced the route up from Kyoto to Kurata's estate.

"The human food, yes," Xue replied. "The animals to feed the Komodos come from the opposite direction, remember?" Brooks tapped at the map with his index finger. "From a farm that Kurata owns just to feed his dragons."

Lara nodded.

Xue's cell phone rang just then. He flipped it open.

"*Hai.*" Brooks paused to listen and then, in an indeterminate Japanese accent, replied, "Yes, those are the arrangements; thank you. Good-bye."

"Our lookout." Xue smiled as he closed his cell phone. "Kurata's provisioner has started his usual evening rounds."

Food at Kurata's mansion was always fresh, Sugawara had explained. Delivered fresh just prior to each meal's preparation. A fishmonger whose family had served Kurata's for more than 120 years procured the freshest of seafood and then, after making the rounds of other food shops in Kyoto, delivered the ingredients for the entire meal to Kurata's lakeside palace. Including the trips to the fishing villages, it was a task that took more than three hours for every meal. The owner—like his father, grandfather, and great-grandfather—handled Kurata's needs personally when the great man was in residence.

"Okay now, if Akira's right—"

"He better be." Lara smiled.

"Yeah," Brooks agreed. "For his sake as well as ours." He paused. "Anyway, assuming Akira's right, we've got about an hour and a half before the guy gets to Kurata's gate," Brooks said, walking over to the roll-up door. There, he hefted a dark green knapsack from the floor and slung it over one shoulder. He reached for the door switch and pressed a black button; the door clanked upward. Immediately the freshness of a light rain pressed into the freight bay. From beyond came the sizzling susurrations of tires and wet pavement.

"Raincoats inside the truck," Brooks said, turning to Lara.

"You've got the recording?" she asked him.

Brooks pulled the microcassette recorder from a Ziploc bag and pressed the play button. Sugawara's voice came from the speakers, panicked. In Japanese he identified himself, screamed of intruders, assassins, fire, Kurata the target, help, hurry!

"Timing will be critical," Brooks said. "I won't phone the police with that until you let me know you're ready to come out—"

"Or if you don't hear from me by the time the grenades blow," Lara interrupted.

Brooks nodded. "There has to be maximum chaos for this to work." He paused to key in a number into his cell phone.

"Victor?" Brooks paused. "Smoke grenades already in the chopper? Yeah? Good."

Brooks listened for another moment, then: "Okay, then, it's show-time!"

Akira Sugawara stood at the barred window of his room and stared down at the limousines parked on the gravel in the front courtyard. As he watched, a black limousine crept through the twilight, its tires crunching lowly on the gravel. Moments later the limo parked alongside the others. Three men in dark suits climbed out of the limo's rear doors; Sugawara's stomach soured—he recognized the men as government string-pullers, men with influence. People who would help Kurata survive.

Then Akira heard a subtle scraping from behind; he turned. As he did he took in the room, a large, unoccupied, twenty-one-tatami room as wide as three mats were long and seven widths deep. The side walls were lined with alcoves—*tokonoma*—containing Kurata's ancestral collection, including the priceless sword and dagger sets passed down from generation to generation.

As Sugawara turned, Kurata's guard slowly slid open a shoji screen, revealing Toru Matsue who stood in the open doorway. Moments later Tokutaro Kurata joined the old man.

Silence amplified the wind in the trees beyond; birdsongs sounded too loud, gaudy. Sugawara felt perspiration form on his upper lip, trickle down his ribs.

After a lifetime, Kurata broke the silence. "So, Nephew," he said without honorifics or a bow.

"Kurata-*san*," Sugawara said and bowed politely. His use of -*san* rather than the more respectful -*sama* hung palpably between them. His uncle was no longer his lord.

Kurata took one step forward, another and another, until he had crossed the room and stood face-to-face with Sugawara; Matsue followed a respectful distance behind.

Kurata looked his nephew up and down very carefully, like a man trying to decide if he was going to buy a suit being modeled for him. Suddenly Kurata slammed a great, cracking, open-handed blow against

the left side of Sugawara's face, staggering him. Sugawara took half a
step to the side to regain his balance.

"What sticks to the ground when a dog drags his anus on the grass
is more honored in my house than you." Kurata spoke so quietly Sugawara had to strain to hear the insult over the ringing in his ears.

Struggling for control—Sugawara knew that anger only defocused a
man and made him a fool—he acknowledged Kurata's insult with a
polite bow.

"As you wish, Uncle."

He saw Kurata's face soften ever so slightly.

"I had not realized how disgracefully stupid you are," Kurata said.
"You have thrown away your entire future in order to delay the inevitable for only a few hours."

"Hours?" Sugawara asked without thinking.

Kurata smiled victoriously. "The other half of the Slatewiper vector
has been loaded into substitute aircraft. They will fly when I give the
word in the morning."

"But, Uncle," Sugawara blurted, "the vector is flawed! It will kill
everyone! You must not—"

Kurata slapped Sugawara again.

"Lies," Kurata said. He waved his hands in the air, dismissing the
notion like a man scattering flies. "A diversion, another of your devious
delaying tactics."

Again, Kurata slapped his nephew, this time with the back of his
hand. Then he walked over to the window and looked down. "There are
men who understand the future," Kurata said. "Men who know that the
ruthless shall inherit this earth." He shook his head and turned to face
Sugawara. "You have delayed the demonstration they came to see. I will
not allow that to happen again."

"But, Uncle, you will kill everyone, not just Koreans!"

"You had the future in your hands," Kurata said, ignoring his
nephew. "You are my only male heir; all the documents were prepared,
sealed; my empire was yours. This will all be changed in the morning."

Sugawara acknowledged this with a polite bow.

Kurata shook his head. "You have shirked your duty, ignored your
obligations, turned your back on the future."

"Respectfully, Uncle," Sugawara said, "I have turned my back on the
past so that I might better face the future."

"Future!" Kurata snapped. "There is no future without the past, and
you—you miserable lump of offal—have no future."

"Begging your indulgence for my temerity, Uncle, but I believe I have acted with responsibility and faith to my duties."

"Responsibility?" Kurata raised his hand as if to strike his nephew again, then slowly lowered it to his side. "Who gave you the right to define your own responsibility?" Kurata said finally. "You have no right to make such decisions. I define your responsibilities; the emperor defines your responsibilities; ten thousand years of honorable ancestors define your responsibilities. You have a duty to be true to your heritage, to your ancestors."

"Begging your forgiveness, Uncle, but might my honorable ancestors have been men of their times who would recognize I must be a man of my own?"

"Man of *your time*," Kurata muttered, then without warning slapped the left side of Sugawara's face yet again. "You are a man of your blood! Every cell in your body, your very genes are your heritage. You and I and every man before us is born as a vessel for the genes; we are impermanent on this earth but our genes continue for generation after generation. Your sacred duty and responsibility is to honor and be true to the physical presence in your blood of ten thousand years of racial purity."

"Uncle, I am not a machine rented by my genes; I am not a passive urn made to carry the ashes of the past into the future. I control my destiny; I refuse to have my life dictated by dead men."

"Then you are a dead man standing before me."

"And you are a Korean," Sugawara replied. "You must realize that very soon everyone will know this."

Rage seized Kurata. "Lies! All lies!" With the open palms of both hands he threw a series of punishing blows at Sugawara's face and head.

Sugawara took the blows without resistance, and when Kurata had tired, said, "You may beat me all you wish, but this does not change the truth. You may ask Matsue-*san* if this is true."

Kurata's eyes grew large as he turned to his faithful family retainer. "Tell this unworthy dog the truth."

Matsue looked between Kurata and Sugawara for a long moment and then said to Kurata, "As you know, my family has served your honorable clan for more than six generations."

A nod from Kurata.

"And so it came to be that my great-great-grandfather accompanied your great-great-grandfather on his travels in Korea."

Another nod, this one impatient.

"And so it also came to pass that your great-great-grandmother was a barren woman and with her concurrence, your father lay with a Korean woman who gave birth to a son, your great-grandfather."

In that instant, something seemed to crumple inside Kurata. Sugawara thought of a glass of milk suddenly turning to powder. The container was still there, but the contents had shrunk.

"This cannot be true." Kurata's powerful voice was now an old man's. "After all these years, after the work I have done for the purity of the Japanese race. Please tell me it's—"

"It is true," Matsue said. "That is why I insisted so strongly that you come here during Operation Tsushima. I was afraid you might be affected."

"But how could you let me . . ."

"You are still the Defender of Yamato," Matsue said. "It is the protection of things Japanese that is important; they lie in the heart and mind, not in the genes. You are aiming at a higher truth, helping the Japanese people to find their spirit. This higher truth transcends the genetic inconvenience and irrelevancy at issue here."

Kurata shook for a moment, his legs obviously unsteady. Matsue moved quickly to his side, but Kurata waved off his support. Then he walked to a small shrine in the corner of the room and knelt before it. Finally, Kurata stood and faced the room.

"The great Buddha taught us that flesh and stone are but illusions and that true reality is created by the spirit," Kurata said. "Matsue-*san* is, of course, correct that reality lies in the heart and mind, not in the physical presence in the genes. The physical is merely a means to protecting the spirit. Facts must be interpreted by the wise in order to reach the higher truths we seek." He nodded. "This is the truth. Our culture is of the spirit and not of the body and it is that culture which must be protected." His voice had grown strong again.

Sugawara spoke: "But the reality is—"

"Your reality is what I say it is," Kurata interrupted as he strode to a display case and pulled from it a dagger. He returned to Sugawara and held it out. "Your reality is whether you will die quickly by your own hand or slowly"—he looked out the window at the darkness of the park-like grounds beyond—"slowly being torn apart by the Komodos."

Sugawara looked at the dagger but did not move to take it.

"Reality means the last choice you have left is to take the dagger or not," Kurata said.

At that moment, a terrified painful bleating filled the night. Sugawara knew that, on occasion, animals escaped from the feeding pens and were hunted down by the Komodos. The bleating crescendoed again and again. Death and pain filled the darkness. Then as suddenly as it began, the noise fell silent.

Sugawara took the ancient dagger.

60

GLOOM FILLED THE LANE. Mist filled the gloom. Night sucked the details from the world and turned it into a silhouette box of featureless gray and black.

A dark panel truck with its lights out coasted to a stop at the edge of the road, engine off, tires crunching subtly on the shoulder gravel. A moist chill breeze blew through the truck's open cargo doors.

Lara peered through the truck's windshield. Maples that had glowed a luminous autumn scarlet during their daylight reconnaissance drive were now just so many more black on blacker shadows. Low clouds crawled across the sky, barely distinct from the trees. Little of Kyoto's city light reflected here. It was, she thought, like being locked in a closet. Even she was nearly invisible dressed as she was in all black with dark camouflage paint coating all her exposed skin.

"Okay, this is the last one," Brooks said quietly as he set the truck's manual gears, pulled the emergency brake, and climbed into the back of the delivery van, almost empty now save for a cardboard box containing twenty-four fragmentation grenades and, beside the box, a gallon paint can with drips down the side. Paint splotches scrawled Jackson Pollock scenes on the dismantled cardboard boxes covering the floor.

As he had with the other twenty-three cans, Brooks leaped from the rear of the truck and ran to the base of the stone wall that surrounded

Kurata's estate. With practiced fingers, Brooks took a screwdriver and pried up the can's lid and—like the other twenty-three—replaced it loosely on top. Then he ran back to the truck, climbed in, and closed the doors. In the windowless rear space, he pulled out a pencil flashlight and turned it on; the beam shone red from the plastic he had taped over it to protect their night vision. Finally, Brooks settled himself down cross-legged next to the box of grenades.

Lara made her way beside him.

He handed her a grenade. "Put the rubber bands on like so"—he slipped the bands over the grenade—"right here at the lower part where the lever curves out . . . make sure the bands are hooked through the lower pineapple section on the grenade body."

"Got it."

A light breeze swept droplets from the tree leaves and made a small rain shower that drummed on the truck's roof. No other sounds came from the isolated mountain road. From within Kurata's stone palisade came the sounds of livestock. Komodo cuisine for tomorrow, Brooks thought. From Sugawara's descriptions, he knew the Komodos were fed in the afternoon in this most remote quarter of the estate where the screams of the animals wouldn't disturb guests with delicate sensitivities. Sugawara said Kurata liked to visit the pens during feeding time and watch his dragons feed.

"Now," Brooks said, placing the rubber bands around the last grenade. "Let's get these all in the cans." He looked at his watch. "Kurata's provisioner should be arriving at the service gate in half an hour." He clicked off the light and opened the truck's rear doors. Lara dragged the box of grenades as they got out.

She placed the grenades on the passenger seat and fished the binocular night-vision scope Xue had given her from her rucksack, turned it on, and fitted it over her head. She took a moment to adjust the straps and lenses. Gloom vanished in the green glow of electronic image intensification. Then she took a grenade and ran to the paint can they had just planted by the stone wall. There she lifted the lid and pulled the pin from the grenade. She made sure the rubber bands would hold the firing lever and then dropped the grenade in the can and replaced the lid. Lara pressed the stopwatch button on her watch as she ran back to the truck.

She stood on the truck's running board, wedged into the lee of the half-closed door, right arm gripping the window frame, left hanging on to the roof rack.

"Okay, time's slipping away."

Brooks started the truck's engine and pulled slowly away, still driving without light in the gloom. About half a kilometer down the road, Lara tapped on the roof; he braked the truck to a stop. She grabbed a grenade and ran into the night. She wore camouflage pants held up by suspenders; pockets covered each leg and the objects inside slapped and banged against her legs as she ran. Seconds later, she was back, up on the running board, arm draped over the door, two taps on the roof, the truck lurched forward against the clock.

In less than twelve minutes, they had worked their way past the main gate, all the way back to the first can that had been planted next to the wall near the gate used by servants, by employees, and for deliveries.

"Good time," Lara said breathlessly, sliding into the passenger seat as Brooks pressed the accelerator and steered the truck down the hill. "Okay, let's check things: you've got the recorder and Sugawara's tape?"

"Got it," Brooks said, his voice a mixture of annoyance and bemusement.

Lara glanced over at him. "Sorry." He slowed for a curve. "I guess it—maybe I'm a little nervous."

"Me too," Brooks said. "A lot nervous."

They drove in silence for several moments; then Brooks slowed, looking for the spot where the truck would "stall."

"Look," Lara said, "down the mountain." Below them on the serpentine switchback road that gnarled its way up the mountain, a single pair of headlights stabbed at the darkness.

Brooks looked at his watch. "Gotta be him," he said. "Akira said the man was as punctual as a clock."

"Our spot's close," Brooks said as he slowed the van toward the location they had chosen on the drive up. After a long moment, he pulled the truck to a stop.

"This looks good." Brooks nodded to himself. He put the truck in park and set the emergency brake. They could hear the engine of the approaching car as it downshifted for yet another switchback.

Engine sounds—deep diesel thuddings—were now accompanied by tire hums.

"Good luck," Brooks said and gave her a fatherly kiss on her cheek.

As headlights began to paint the tops of the trees around them, Lara grabbed her rucksack and sprinted across the road, concealing herself in the undergrowth there. Brooks got quickly out and opened the truck's hood. Using the penlight flashlight—now stripped of its red plastic—he leaned in and loosened two spark plugs. Finally, he unfolded the emergency reflectors and fastened them into blunt-corner triangles that he erected in the roadway in front and back of the panel van.

Then he stood by the front of the truck, waiting to flag down the approaching truck.

Akira Sugawara paced the room, ignoring the display cases filled with mementos of his family's glorious history. He held the dagger that Kurata had given him in his right hand and the scabbarded tip in his left. With every step, he turned the dagger—step, turn, step, turn—his thoughts kept pace.

Walking now toward the shoji screen entrance, Sugawara saw the guard's shadow cast on the screen's rice-paper covering.

There, Sugawara thought as he slid the dagger out and held it out toward the screen, *right through the rice paper. Wedge the point right through the back of the guard's neck just right and he'd be instantly paralyzed, fall to the floor without alerting the others.*

Just then, he heard a familiar voice—Matsue—and heard the guard respond, *"Hai"* as he bowed deeply.

Sugawara resheathed the dagger and stepped back in the middle of the room as the shoji slid open.

"Matsue-*san*," Sugawara said as he bowed to the old man. The old man made a shallow bow in return. Sugawara looked at him and searched the old man's face for a sign, but there was none hidden in all those decades of wrinkles and a lifetime of mastering the craft of inscrutability. Sugawara saw Matsue's eyes linger on the dagger and then make their way to his face.

"Kurata-*sama* wishes me to inform you that you will be taken to the Komodos before he and his guests sit down to dinner," Matsue said. "He wishes to dine comfortably knowing that this unfortunate situation has been resolved." Matsue paused. Then: "It will be seen as an unfortunate accident by the police that you do not visit your generous uncle frequently enough to be thoroughly aware of the precautions needed." He paused, his liquid brown eyes betraying nothing.

"Kurata-*sama* has already issued orders; they will come for you shortly. You may wish to make sure you are unconscious by that time," Matsue said and then turned on his heel and left the room. The shoji closed with the finality of a guillotine.

Kurata's provisioner had a big truck, not a semi but a large double-rear-wheeled refrigerated van that was about as large a vehicle as the remote mountain road could comfortably accommodate.

Across the road from his truck, the driver obligingly spoke with Brooks. Lara couldn't hear their words over the hum of the refrigeration compressor and the rattle of the truck's idling diesel. The truck's headlights illuminated the van and its emergency reflectors. Deep in the bushes, Lara tightened the straps of her rucksack one more time to make sure it would not flail and flop when she ran. For what seemed like the hundredth time, she touched the objects in her pants pockets and hanging from her belt: reassuringly, she patted the Colt .45 automatic and attached silencer that ran almost the length of her thigh, the wickedly curved linoleum knife honed to a razor likeness for close-in work, the length of high-C piano wire and broom-handle lengths for garroting, and a second length of wire that was woven into the pants' waistband. There was the magnesium dust and the CS canister and the roofer's hatchet on a belt scabbard to take out inconveniently locked doors. She touched each one in its turn, each one in its place. Some, like the Colt, were familiar. Others were strangers to which Brooks had only recently introduced her. He had drilled her over and over. She hoped that she'd remember his instructions when the time came to use them. She prayed even more she wouldn't have to use them. Especially the garrote. She was not sure she could kill someone so intimately.

Moments later, she watched as the provisions truck driver took Brooks's flashlight and leaned into the engine compartment. Lara lunged from her hiding place in the tangled roadside undergrowth and raced for the rear of the provisioner's truck.

Her heart froze at what she saw there: the broad metal undersurface of a hydraulic lift platform was folded up against the rear of the truck, blocking access to the door latches! There was no way in! Not without the noisy and time-consuming task of lowering the lift to give access to the door latches.

Frantically, Lara surveyed the truck. She raced to the front and peered into the cab. No place there to hide. From behind her came the sounds of the panel van's engine starting and the clunk of the hood closing. The driver had found the problem quickly.

Too quickly!

Footsteps approached. Lara ducked into the shadow of the truck's massive rear tires so the driver wouldn't see her.

As the driver climbed up to the cab and slammed the door, Lara pulled her flashlight from her pants pocket and played it about the truck's undercarriage. Sweat rolled into her eyes. She wiped at the perspiration as she surveyed the maze of brake lines, electrical wiring, wire cables, drive shaft, hydraulic lines, and pumps for the lift and the crisscrossing of the truck's support frames.

The driver gunned the engine and put the truck in gear.

Desperately, Lara stashed the flashlight, and as the truck began to creep forward, she crawled under the truck and grabbed the edge of a steel frame member that ran side to side. It was almost like an I-beam but without the generous lower horizontal that she would have preferred. Her fingers began to ache almost immediately.

The truck moved forward, dragging Lara by the heels. Frantically, she lifted one foot and searched for a toehold. After an eternity, she found another side-to-side frame member. Cautiously, she jammed first one foot and then the other, lifting herself off the ground. Lara gripped the underside of the truck with all her strength, willing her mind away from the pain that burned like red-hot nails up each finger and flared in the muscles of her arms, shoulders, back. She knew the pain of hanging on was infinitely better than the pain of letting go.

The truck gathered speed and then almost immediately began to slow. Lara tried to crane her head to see how far down her pack extended. Would it drag and make noise? Would they see it? The truck stopped, then turned left. She would know soon enough.

The truck's tires set up a loud crunching as the road's pavement gave way to gravel. Then a very bright light suddenly enveloped the truck. This was obviously the gate and inspection area by the service entrance. The truck stopped again. This time there were loud voices, familiar greetings, the easy friendly banter of servants connected by their liege. The driver got out and distributed what Lara quickly deduced was the provisioner's usual evening assortment of delicacies for the guards to enjoy.

Instants later the lights went out and the truck lurched forward; Lara's heart raced as the movement tore the three fingers on her left hand away from their handhold. Desperately, her hand flailed for the lost support. She clutched for the support beam as the truck gathered speed. There! The fingers found purchase.

She struggled to consolidate her grip as the truck plunged on into the darkness. Then, a minute—perhaps two—later, the truck hit a pothole; water from the rains covered her, lubricated her hand and feet; the three fingers on her left hand lost their grip again. In an instant, Lara knew she could drop from the truck in a controlled fashion and risk being seen by the guards or try to hang on and eventually slip and fall, running the risk of being crushed by the truck's massive wheels.

This was not a choice.

She let first one foot and then the other drag in the gravel. Then, when she was as sure as she would ever be that her feet were pointed between the rear wheels, she let go.

The skid went well for half a second, which was almost enough.

Lara dropped and began to slow immediately; the rucksack absorbed the brunt of the initial impact and then bore into the gravel with more concentrated force than the rest of her body. The inevitable mechanics of the rucksack's concentrated friction then flipped her into a rear somersault as the rear of the truck passed over her.

As the back of Lara's head struck the ground, a galaxy of stars slam-zoomed before her eyes; instants later pain hammered into her middle back and stole her breath.

Then the dark, dark night turned totally black.

61

THE STENCH OF ROTTING FLESH CUT THROUGH THE DARKNESS AND FILLED LARA'S NOSE. Then she felt a nudge. And a stronger smell of dead, decaying meat. A grunt.

Lara opened her eyes and stared straight into hell: deep, reddish eyes barely luminous in the light from the departing truck. One of Kurata's Komodos slouched over her now, huge jaws closed with a reptilian grin, deciding if she was a meal or not.

Thoughts racing, Lara tried to remember what Sugawara had said about the animals. They liked live prey; did this mean the big lizard would go away or not? Would a sudden movement startle it away or galvanize it into action?

Before she could decide, the big reptile opened its jaws; its putrid breath turned her stomach. As the Komodo lunged, Lara rolled; the pain in her head and back made her light-headed. Suddenly she was jerked back abruptly as the Komodo seized the rucksack and shook it with its powerful jaws.

Just as swiftly, Lara released the strap across her chest that connected the two arm straps; she slid out of the straps and rolled away as the Komodo flung out the dry lifeless mouthful and sprang toward her. As she backpedaled through the night, Lara fumbled with the snap that secured the long pocket containing the .45; at the very least she could shoot the eyes out of the beast. The giant lizard, visible now only as a lampblack form slithering through carbon darkness, gathered speed as it closed in on Lara. Still moving backward, she withdrew the .45 and the thick clumsy makeshift silencer Charles Brooks had fashioned for it.

Then something caught the backs of her thighs, cold, hard, immovable. As the rotting smells of the Komodo grew stronger again, Lara twisted, stretched out her left hand to break the fall. Her fingers touched the cold, rain-slick stones of a low wall as she fell over the edge landing hard on her shoulder; her head and back throbbed in sympathy with the new bruise. As Lara fell, her gun hand slammed against the rocks, knocking the .45 into the darkness.

Lara sat up as the Komodo's blunt dragon head appeared tentatively over the edge of the wall. Frantically, she looked for the .45, could not see it in the gloom. The feculent smell of the Komodo's breath filled the darkness; a frozen armature of terror turned in Lara's guts as she watched the creature's head tilt down, the malignant eyes acquiring their prey.

In one swift movement, Lara got to her feet and pulled the roofer's hatchet from its holster and—just as the Komodo began to open its jaws—brought the blade down hard and swift. With a wet, *shunching* butcher-shop sound, the hatchet blade buried itself deeply in the Komodo's head, just behind the eyes.

There was no bellow, no geyser of blood, just a shudder from the giant creature as it slid back to the other site of the wall, the hatchet ripped from Lara's hand, so firmly was it embedded in the Komodo's skull.

Was it stunned? Lara wondered. Dead? Regrouping? Would others be attracted? Repelled? She took a deep breath and decided not to wait for those answers.

Ignoring the pain in her head and the throbbing in her back, Lara stood in the darkness and let her eyes follow the stone wall up to the complex of buildings. From her earlier study of the book on Kurata's palace, Lara knew this service road made its way to a cluster of utility buildings adjacent to the main building. As she looked into the distance, Lara's peripheral vision caught the dim outlines of her Colt .45 on the ground. She picked it up and ran along the fence in a half crouch, praying for no more encounters with Kurata's Komodos.

Akira Sugawara crouched, wedged into the corner of the room facing the three men Kurata had sent for him. The man in charge was a tall, broad former sumo wrestler. The three men were dressed in track suits and carried long wooden poles.

"Don't condemn yourself," Sugawara said as he waved the dagger at the men. "This is not your fight."

"If Kurata-*sama* tells me this is my fight, then it is my fight," said the former sumo as he brought his staff down. Sugawara leaped to one side as the staff crashed against the spot where he had been standing. At the same instant, the second man brought his staff around; Sugawara ducked under the pole.

Right into the well-practiced path of the third man's staff that caught Sugawara on the side of his head.

Darkness fell.

The rain had faded to a foggy light drizzle as Lara stood in the lee of a six-foot timber stockade wall and peered through the cracks at the back of the single-story, pitched-roof kitchen building. Dumpsters lined the back wall facing her. To the left, a tile-covered open walkway connected the kitchen to Kurata's main palace. Servants in white dinner jackets wheeled chrome-domed carts from the kitchen.

Kitchen staff chattered busily as the provisioner prepared to leave. A man in a tall toque—obviously the chef—and his staff drifted out with the man who had "repaired" the van.

There were more thank-yous now from Kurata's people for whatever the treat of the evening had been. Then, two of the kitchen help went to open the gate; they were accompanied by an armed guard, obviously there to make sure none of the Komodos slipped from where Lara now stood into the protected human compound.

Sugawara had explained that manned security was actually light inside the compound, that the gates, electronically secured perimeter fence, and the Komodos were expected to neutralize most threats. As a result, Kurata relied on very few traditional guards and sentries, relying instead on early notification and very swift quick-reaction squads.

As Lara had watched, there were two guards walking the 360-degree porches that ran around the perimeters of each floor. She timed their rounds with her watch. The guards were amazingly regular, predictable— sloppy sentry work she thought—but good for her because there was a forty-five-second interval when they were both out of sight of the kitchen and connecting walkway.

The provisioner's truck engine started, filling the night with the rattle of diesel rods. Then there was a clashing of gears followed by tires crunching on gravel. Through the crack in the wall, Lara saw all eyes on the provisioner's truck. Even the guard who normally patrolled this area turned his back to the kitchen, rifle at the ready in case some lizard from a bad nightmare decided to explore the open gate.

Now! Lara grabbed the top of the fence and leaped upward, easily clearing the top. She landed, crouched in a shadow that painted the base of the fence.

All eyes still rested on the provisioner's truck. Lara waited in the shadow until the truck came between her and the group of men by the gate. Then she sprinted for the Dumpsters. This was a one-take movie, she thought as she ran. There was no time to hide and wait. The guard would return to his post, the kitchen personnel would be a constant threat of disclosure. So it had to be now: Dumpster to the roof of the kitchen, top of the covered walk to the main building. Then up to the top. One take, no rest.

Lara reached the Dumpsters when she smelled the cigarette smoke; she froze in the shadows and let her nose point her in the direction of the smoker. In the distance, she saw a clot of men in dark suits who looked like professional chauffeurs, standing about smoking. But the stink of the smoke was too strong to have come from that distance. She waited, fighting the urgency that squirmed in her belly.

But not too long. The moment will pass. The guard will return; the kitchen will spring to life.

Then, from just beyond the corner of the kitchen building, the glow of a cigarette and in the brief splash of illumination, the face of a guard, one of Kurata's soldiers. The soldier moved toward her!

Quickly Lara slipped into the darkness between two Dumpsters and realized she had only one right weapon that would kill quickly and silently enough to avoid disclosing her presence to the others. Reluctantly, she pulled from a pants-leg pocket the two lengths of broom handle. Each round piece of wood was about four inches long and had a shallow groove around the circumference at the midpoint. A stiff thin piece of piano wire was wrapped around the groove and twisted tight. She hesitated as she looked at the unfamiliar weapon. She focused on the training Brooks had given her just hours before.

As the guard shuffled closer, kicking gravel with his boots, Lara held one of the broomsticks and let the rest dangle to unkink the wire. Next, she grabbed the free handle and arranged the handles so that the wire made a complete loop, crossing at the handles.

The guard walked past the Dumpsters. Lara hurtled from her hiding niche, slipped the loop of wire over the guard's head, and yanked on the handles with all her strength, closing the wire loop like a drawstring. She felt it tug, stretch, and then cut through the tendons and flesh. She thought it felt a little like those wire cheese cutters.

Then the wire made a single high-C twang. The guard's head separated soundlessly from his head. It made a low hollow melon sound as it hit the loose gravel. Lara ducked out of the way as blood geysered from the collapsing body.

It was all over in seconds. Lara wiped the garrote off on the man's shirt, then stuffed it back in her pants pocket. Next she dumped the guard's head and body into one of the Dumpsters. With the sounds of the provisioner's truck growing fainter, Lara waited by the eaves of the kitchen and studied Kurata's main palace as first one guard and then the other vanished around their respective corners. She hit the stopwatch button on her watch—forty-five seconds.

With time rapidly running out, she scaled the wall to the kitchen roof, clambered her way across the covered walkway to the second story of the main building, and scaled the railing.

The next move terrified her. Even though she had studied the photographs and practiced the moves a thousand times in her mind, preparation paled in the face of execution. As with many Japanese buildings of the era, the tiled roofs of Kurata's palace gently curved downward, then cantilevered their lower surfaces far out from the main body of the building. They formed, essentially, a six- or eight-foot eave that covered the balcony below. But unlike Western construction where there would have been a supporting post running from the floor of the balcony to the edge of the roof, here there was none.

As she had planned in her mind, Lara went quickly to the corner of the balcony and climbed up the railing until she crouched on top, facing out, with one foot on each of the intersecting railing tops. Below her, she watched the kitchen staff walking back to their jobs. The lone guard closed the gate and fiddled with the lock.

Don't look up.

Lara prayed for this, for balance, for success, and then cautiously let go of the railing with her fingers and stood up. The rail was slippery with moisture; she felt her shoes slide just a fraction, then stop. She looked down at the kitchen, using it as a reference point for balance. Finally she was standing. Below her, a white-coated waiter stepped into the rear eaves of the kitchen and lit a cigarette. Without taking her eyes off the kitchen, Lara raised her hands above her head, reaching for the complicated lattice of beams and joists that formed the underside of the eave.

The fingers of one hand, then the next, found the centuries-old wood; the mere touch cemented her equilibrium. She looked up now, searching for a handhold. And as she looked and reached, a cold deadly realization settled in her chest like black ice: she had misjudged things; she was not quite tall enough. The middle joints of her fingers reached only to the bottoms of the beams.

Lara shifted so that only her toes stood on the slippery railing, then stood on tiptoe: almost. Not quite.

Sweat rolled into her eyes. Where were the guards? How far had she cut into her forty-five seconds? Cautiously, she used one hand to clear the tears. She was just inches shy of a firm grip on the beams; Lara knew she had only one option. So she slowly bent at her knees into a half squat, eyes riveted on the beam her hands must find.

thistimeonlychanceonlytimepleaseGodplease

or she would die, from the fall or from the guards.

Then she leaped. One foot slipped at the takeoff; steel butterflies etched fear in her belly. She pushed even harder with the other leg. She rose. Lara watched her hands, willing them higher, willing the beams to connect.

And they did. First the right hand and then her left.

That was when the shout came from below. Lara looked down and saw the white-coated waiter screaming, pointing at her.

Lara ignored him and began to swing, back and forth like a woman on a trapeze. Back and forth. Back took her toward the building, forth into the night. Again. Again. More shouts from below. Then, propelled more by events than her own conscious decision, Lara guided her legs up and then back in a tuck roll. The toes of her boots thudded against the roof tiles above and tried to gain purchase on the wet tiles.

On the ground below, the guard who had closed the gate appeared by the side of the waiter and looked up at her. Lara pushed with all the strength in her arms, shoved her body as far over the lip as possible. She worked her hands out, beam by beam pushing herself backward and upward until, finally, most of her body lay on the roof, feet toward the sky.

That was when the guard took his first shot.

The slug buried itself in the wooden eaves just inches from her right hand. Lara fought gravity and the rain-lubricated tiles as she scrambled desperately backward on her stomach. An instant later the tiles she had just instants before covered with her body exploded in a torrent of automatic weapons fire. She lay there for just a second, gasping for air and breathless from more than the exertion. She pulled the silenced Colt from her pants pocket, checked the magazine, and chambered a round.

A siren slit the darkness as she crawled on all fours up toward the room that Sugawara was sure Kurata would confine him in. As Lara's head drew level with the floor of the balcony that encircled the room at the top, a door opened; a man in a track suit stepped out; he carried a handgun. Lara froze in place as she brought the Colt to bear. The man in the track suit looked down.

Lara aimed, pulled the trigger. The first silenced slug from the Colt caught the man just below his nose and jerked his head back. The second round ripped out the front of his throat. He was dead before his body settled on the balcony floor.

Lara leaped over the balcony railing and as she landed, saw three men in the room beyond the open door. Then she spotted Sugawara on his back, lying in a corner, hands bound with tape, kicking at a massive fat man in a track suit.

"No wounds," cried a smaller man, also in a track suit. "Remember the autopsy." Lara stepped through the door. The big man turned as if he sensed rather than heard Lara enter.

It took four bullets before the big man who looked like a sumo stopped moving. But the small man was quick; he drew his side arm and brought it to bear on Lara. Sugawara scrambled to his feet and, with his hands still bound in front of him, grabbed a dagger from the floor and shoved it into the small man's back. The round from his side arm went wildly through the roof as the tip of the dagger tugged its way through the fabric of the track suit and emerged red and wet just below the small man's breastbone. Bleeding extravagantly, the man dropped his weapon, staggered backward, then collapsed.

"Lara!" Sugawara cried with a smile. An angry red swelling decorated the side of his head.

"Yep," Lara replied. "Last time I checked, anyway." She pulled out the almost empty .45-caliber clip from the Colt and inserted a fresh one before tucking it back in her thigh pocket. Then she went to Sugawara and stripped the tape off his hands and wrists. Underneath was an elastic bandage.

"Things didn't go as well as they might," Sugawara said as he rubbed his wrists. "Kurata laughed off the Korean heritage thing. No leverage there. Gave me the choice of seppuku or dragon fodder." He looked about the room until his gaze stopped on a long dagger lying on the tatami near one corner. He walked toward it.

"Been there," Lara said as she bent to pick up the small man's pistol. "Almost done that." She handed the gun to Sugawara, checked her watch, then pulled out her cell phone. "I'll get the chopper on the way."

"Not yet," Sugawara said as he bent over to pick up the dagger. A scabbard lay just feet away; Sugawara picked that up too and slid the dagger into it.

"What do you mean, 'not yet'?" Lara asked incredulously. "You're so fond of the service here, you want to stick around for more?" She stabbed at the phone's keypad and hit the send button.

Outside, excited voices rumbled a basso continuo to the siren's ragged operatic.

"You don't understand, Kurata's going to ride this one out, blame it on enemies trying to destroy him. He's got a room full of military brass from around the world at a dinner downstairs right now and if I remember things correctly, he's pitching them on buying Slatewiper for their own arsenals—just the thing to wipe out regional and ethnic insurgencies without having to use guns and look like the bad guys."

Lara listened to the telephone line being picked up. "Yep." She paused. "It's time to rock and roll. Tell Victor we'll try to get to the animal pens as we planned." She closed the flip phone and turned to Sugawara.

"Look, all his visitors don't change things," Lara said. "We knew selling to various militaries was the plan."

"Yes, but I'll wager that they've got all the paperwork—proof that could blow this whole thing wide open. Take down a lot more people who lack Kurata's resources for covering it up," Sugawara insisted. Footsteps sounded on the stairs. He slipped the dagger into the waistband of his pants.

"That won't stop the Slatewiper project," Lara said. "Kurata will just keep pressing on."

Sugawara took a deep breath. "Not if he doesn't live long enough to change his will."

Lara raised his eyebrows.

"He told me tonight that I am the sole heir to all his empire," Sugawara said. "Until tomorrow, after I am dead and he can change it without raising eyebrows."

Lara loosed a low whistle.

"You see, I can make it stop."

"You could kill your uncle?"

"After what he's done? Of course."

"He's your own flesh and blood."

"Genetics is not destiny," Sugawara said. "Sometimes you have to do things you don't want to."

The door from the stairway flew open and spilled men dressed in track suits.

62

THE POINT MAN THROUGH THE DOOR CAUGHT LARA'S .45 SLUG IN HIS LEFT EYE; THE
MAN DROPPED THE MACHINE GUN HE WAS CARRYING AND FELL TO HIS KNEES.
The three men behind him tripped over their fallen comrade. Lara shot
the two men who fell on top of the point man; Sugawara shot at the third
man, missed the first time, then connected with two shots in the man's
left breast.

More steps sounded on the stairs. Lara slipped the .45 into her pants
pocket and bent over to retrieve the guards' machine guns.

"H&K," Lara said as she handed one of the three to Sugawara. "Only
the best."

Steps on the stairs grew louder; no voices: these were disciplined men,
Lara thought.

"Here," Sugawara said. "This way." He headed toward the corner of
the room, a blank corner with no cover to defend, solid walls, no windows, no escape route. Lara gave him a questioning look.

"*Chodai-gamáe*," Sugawara said as he bent over and felt around the
edge of the wall panels. With a muffled click, one panel opened. "*Chodai-
gamáe* means 'secret chamber,'" Sugawara explained. "Every nobleman's
house of this era has them, many of them. For hiding guards to ambush
their enemies, to hide from enemy ambush. And sometimes to escape."

"Fuck a duck," Lara said, her voice full of amazement and approval. "Come on!"

Lara took one step toward the *chodai-gamáe*, then stopped. Holding two of the H&K machine pistols in one hand by the trigger guards, she reached into a pocket by her right calf and pulled from it the tear-gas canister designed to work as a spray can for personal protection. Then, as steps grew louder on the stairs, she stepped out on the stairwell landing and set the canister at the edge of the top stair.

Suddenly, in the distance, an explosion followed by a flare of light. Lara checked her watch: one hour, three minutes. Not bad for a rubber band timer. The steps froze on the landing, obviously reacting to the blast.

"You snooze, you lose," Lara said under her breath as she stepped back into Sugawara's room, took one of the machine pistols in her right hand, and then carefully aimed at the canister. The first slug took the top off the canister and sent it tumbling down the stairwell spewing clouds of chemical irritant behind it. Excited shouts erupted from the stairwell followed by the sounds of retreating feet.

Only then did Lara join Sugawara in the *chodai-gamáe*.

It was a cramped little tunnel space. Sugawara replaced the *chodai-gamáe* panel, then beckoned her forward. They cradled their machine pistols in one hand, and made a three-point crawl until the passageway opened up at a vertical shaft with a ladder.

From beyond the walls came the muffled rumble of the second grenade. Lara couldn't help smiling.

"Frying pan into fire," Sugawara whispered tersely as he looked down into the shaft. "This leads to an exit at the bottom of the house, drops right into the water."

Lara nodded.

"But first, we deal with Kurata, agreed?" Sugawara said.

Again, Lara nodded.

"Okay then. On the way down, there's one more exit before we get to the exit at the bottom. It leads to a panel inside the room where Kurata is having his meeting. He likes to set up his podium just in front of the panel."

Lara felt her heart grow hot with anger at these men who had gathered to learn how to kill millions, to commit sanitary genocide. These were the Pol Pots and Hitlers and Milosevics of tomorrow. She would feel no regrets to remove them from the land of the living. If any of them left the room, they would kill and kill and kill again—innocent victims whose only crime was a different skin color, religion, political affiliation.

Without further conversation, Lara followed Sugawara down the shaft.

At the landing that led to Kurata's second-floor gathering hall, the buzz of excited conversation filtered through the *chodai-gamáe* panel.

First Kurata's voice, murmuring like a man talking on a telephone. Then there was a rattle of a phone receiver being replaced. "I have just been informed that we have some sort of disturbance on the grounds. The authorities have been notified and should be here momentarily to supplement my security people and yours."

Another explosion. The conversation buzz grew louder.

"I understand that we all have those who wish us harm," Kurata continued. "I assure you that we are quite safe here. As you know, this room is an inner keep with foot-thick timber walls. And as you know the doors are bolted from inside." Pause. "The irony should not be lost on us that the medieval precautions that were taken centuries ago are so very appropriate for the savage world we live in today."

The conversation grew quieter.

"I suggest that we finish our business while the appropriate security people deal with this disturbance."

"Now?" Sugawara asked.

"Now."

Lara launched herself through the *chodai-gamáe* panel, hammering into Kurata's back, sending the two of them sprawling in a hail of splintered wood and fabric.

"Don't move," Sugawara shouted.

Angry, frightened voices filled the room. Lara rolled quickly to her feet and disentangled herself from Kurata who remained still on the floor beneath the ruins of the *chodai-gamáe* panel. As she got to her feet, Lara saw more than a dozen men, sitting Western-style in chairs set behind tables. Carafes of water and drinking glasses sat before each man. Papers covered almost every horizontal surface.

Anger sharpened itself as Lara recognized many of the men in the room. There were officers from the American military. And nearby sat men who would be classified as war criminals in the worst way if only the U.S. government hadn't sanctioned their inhuman slaughter with foreign aid and the rationale that they were essential for stability in whatever regions they lorded over.

A man in khaki military dress leaped to his feet, toppling his chair to the floor as he lunged for the door. Lara recognized him as the corrupt head of Mexico's intelligence agency, a man known for protecting drug lords and slaughtering the native population who wanted running water and electricity.

The burst from Lara's H&K caught the Mexican intelligence head in the small of the back and moved up; the rear of the man's head seemed to explode, scattering pink and gray and red all over the men surrounding him.

Pandemonium!

Like the dead Mexican, every man in the room flew from his seat and headed for the only door out of the room. Lara and Sugawara cut them down one by one. Until there was no sound left in the room save the pounding on the door as guards outside struggled to enter the room.

In the distance, another explosion sounded; the pounding on the door decreased for a moment and then continued.

Finally, Lara stood up straight in the middle of the carnage and looked around. Now, through the silence came a low grunt of exertion. Akira and Lara turned toward the sound. Their eyes found Kurata painfully limping toward the door, his hand extended toward the bolts that kept the men outside at bay.

Sugawara and Lara both leaped for the door, hurdling tables, bodies, and overturned chairs. Kurata was no match. He scowled defiantly as Lara spun him half around and pinned his shoulders to the wall.

"You may kill me," Kurata said, "but you will not live to see another rising sun."

Lara shrugged. "Maybe." Then she turned to Sugawara: "Yours." Lara released her grip on Kurata and stepped aside, pulling the silenced .45 from her thigh pocket. Lara concentrated on unscrewing the makeshift silencer. There was no reason to sacrifice velocity and accuracy now for the sake of stealth that no longer existed.

Kurata stood ramrod stiff as he glared at his nephew. Sugawara raised the muzzle of the H&K.

"So, you had no courage to take your own life and you want mine instead?" Kurata's eyes locked with his nephew's. Sugawara hesitated for just an instant, snagged on the power of his uncle's gaze. Kurata laughed.

"So, Nephew, not even the courage to kill your enemy in battle?" Kurata goaded him.

The insult galvanized Sugawara who aimed the machine pistol and began to squeeze the trigger. For just an instant, Kurata's hard stare flickered, showing the fear behind.

Sugawara took a deep breath.

And then lowered the muzzle.

From beyond the house another explosion rumbled. The room shook with the frenzy of men breaching the room's security.

Lara stepped forward with the .45. "Let's get this over and get out." But Sugawara held out his arm. Lara stopped as Sugawara took the dagger from his belt and handed it to Kurata.

"What're you fucking crazy?" Lara said as she backpedaled away from the now-armed Kurata.

Kurata gave the dagger a look of recognition and then gazed back at his nephew who stood within slashing distance, gun muzzle pointing at the floor.

"I could kill you now," Kurata said. "Finish the job myself."

"And be cut down by my friend," Sugawara said. "The great defender of Yamato slain by the *gaijin*." He paused. "Better that the *wakizashi* and your hand deliver you from that humiliation." He looked at the dagger, a small sword really.

Kurata seemed to shrink then, to deflate into a tired old man as reality clutched him firmly in its claws.

"*Hai*." Kurata nodded sadly. "You have won this game." Then, Kurata stripped to the waist and sat down on the floor, cross-legged.

He hesitated, then looked up at Sugawara and said: "Be *kaishaku*," Kurata commanded.

Lara looked at Sugawara.

"It's part of the ritual of seppuku," Sugawara explained. "A *kaishaku* is a second, a man who finishes off the samurai after the ritual cuts are made if the cuts do not do so immediately. In the old days, it was done by beheading with the long sword; after defeat in World War II, it was done with a bullet."

Sugawara went to his uncle and bowed deeply.

"*Hai*."

It happened so quickly then. Kurata plunged in the blade on the left side of his abdomen and slashed open a gaping wound that ran sideways, all the way across his belly. Blood oozed from the huge wound; entrails crowded through the opening. Sugawara and Lara stood transfixed.

As Kurata pulled out the dagger—his *wakizashi*—his eyes were fixed in a far distance unseen by Lara and Sugawara. The *wakizashi's* blade dripped blood. Then Kurata calmly looked down and seemed to nod to himself. With steady deliberate hands, Kurata shifted the *wakizashi's* handle now so the cutting edge ran up and down. Gripping the hilt with both hands, Kurata raised the *wakizashi's* point and aimed it at the sideways slash he had already made.

Kurata's hands trembled for just an instant before he plunged the *wakizshi's* blade in to the hilt, straining as he slashed upward. At that instant, Kurata sounded a surprised, "Ah!" and then went silent as great gouts of blood geysered from the wound. The blade had obviously severed the aorta. Death would be swift now. Kurata slumped forward, his face striking the floor.

Leaning over his uncle now, Sugawara spoke privately to himself and then raised the H&K to Kurata's temple and pulled the trigger.

Outside yet another explosion sounded. And just audibly, the thwacking of helicopter blades.

And from just outside the room came the sounds of a chain saw as it bit into the stout door to the meeting room.

Lara went to Sugawara and touched his back.

"Time to go," Lara said.

Sugawara nodded.

Lara followed Sugawara down the shaft, through the trapdoor at the bottom and into the lake. The water was shallow and muddy. They waded along the edge to a huddle of artfully arranged boulders that shielded them from the glare of floodlights that brought daylight to the area around the house. The grounds crawled with armed men.

With a flare of exploding gasoline, another of Charles Brooks's grenade bombs went off across the grounds. As it did, armed men hit the ground, lunged for cover. Lara smiled.

"C'mon," she urged as she hurtled from the cover of the rocks toward the pebble road that led to the Komodo feed animal holding pens. Sugawara followed her.

Rocks exploded all around them.

"Damn! I'm hit!"

Lara turned and through the dense curtains of darkness saw Sugawara crumple and fall to his hands and knees. She reversed her course and reached his side as he struggled to push himself into a sitting position. Beneath the ragged staccato of gunfire, Lara could hear slugs pounding the earth around them.

"Come on." She reached down to help him up, but his knees collapsed and would not hold. She grabbed him in a bear hug and rolled the two of them away from a devastating swarm of slugs.

In the momentary silence, Lara heard the frothy sucking sounds Sugawara made with each breath and smelled the harsh metallic scent of his blood. Bullets searched the darkness for them.

"Go," Sugawara said.

"Forget about it."

The blood made Sugawara slippery, but Lara quickly got him up in a fireman's carry and began to run.

She cut from side to side, zigging as the bullets zagged. Lara half turned and spotted a gunman firing at them from the roof of the mansion.

"This way," she said to herself as she made her way toward the stone wall that paralleled the road.

"Komodos that way," Sugawara grunted through clenched teeth.

"Big lizards don't have guns," Lara said as she hurled both of them over the wall into the shadows. Sugawara clenched his teeth against the pain and uttered only the faintest protest.

Instants later stone fragments flew out of the top of the wall and zinged like shrapnel into the ground around them. Then the shots stopped.

"Reload time," Lara said, springing into a crouch. She got Sugawara into position again and ran as fast as she could along the cover of the wall. Then it began to rain again in earnest. Great slanting sheets of rain drew themselves like curtains between them and the mansion.

"Thank you, God," Lara said softly.

Ahead of her, she heard the frightened bleats and cries of penned animals and, from farther away, the excited shouts of a hunter urging his comrades in for the kill. Instants later the shots resumed, from one machine gun, then two, then too many to count. The shots were wild, fired blindly into the rain.

Lara and Sugawara reached the graying far reaches of the mansion's floodlights and then into shadows. As they approached the animal pen where the Komodos' live meals were raised, Lara's lungs burned with the exertion as she freed one hand and pulled out her cell phone. She slowed to a walk for just a minute to make sure she hit the correct speed dial.

"Nearly . . ." Thud went Lara's feet, deep breath, thud. "There." She said into the phone, "Animal" Thud, deep breath, thud. "Pen." Thud, deep breath, thud. "Now."

Almost magically, the dark dragonfly silhouette of a helicopter with its lights extinguished parted the relentless rain and pitch. With Sugawara seeming lighter than ever, Lara slogged among the animals, through the barnyard muck and mud until she came to the low tin-roofed building.

"Sugawara's wounded," she said into her phone as she stood in the barnyard. "Can't make the roof as planned. Need rope."

The chopper's backwash was driving the rain down even harder and drowned out Lara's words even to her own ears. She prayed they understood her.

Then, for the very first time that night, she was sure she was going to die as the first tentative feelers of gunfire began searching for the chopper's engine noise.

The helicopter edged downward. Lara watched the rescue loop dangling lower and lower. Slugs churned the darkness around her; she heard them begin to strike the helicopter's metal.

"That's good," she said as the rope reached her. She tucked the cell phone in her jacket pocket, tied a bowline in the end of the rope, then straddled the loop.

"Okay, go! You've got us both," she said. She tried desperately to keep the rope across one buttock as the helicopter lifted, slowly at first. Then she heard the helicopter's turbine scream as the pilot tilted his craft nose forward and accelerated up and away with a force that left her hanging on with all her considerable strength for dear life: hers and Akira's.

EPILOGUE

SPRING HAD BEGUN TO ERASE THE WINTER DRABNESS FROM TOKYO'S PARKS. A bright green haze hung among the branches of the trees and stained the dead brown grass.

The brisk wind still carried a sharpness that jabbed at the crowds mobbing the sidewalk in front of the old Daiwa Ichiban Corporation's headquarters. The crush spilled people off the curb and blocked the street like a logjam. Television remote vans lined the opposite side of the broad avenue, satellite dishes craned expectantly upward. Camera crews sidled and wedged their ways among the crowd, conducting impromptu interviews as they fought toward the chest-high temporary dais constructed in front of the building's main entrance.

"We seem to have a partial cross section of Tokyo present this morning," said one television reporter doing a stand-up in preparation for an interview. "As might be expected, we have many here from the Korean community and no one from the Diet, the national government, the city, or the prefecture. This event is seen as political death for public officials." The camera pulled back to show a college-age Japanese woman beside the reporter.

"What is surprising is the very large number of ordinary Japanese citizens who have rejected their political leaders' calls for a boycott and have come out in numbers that have overwhelmed the police's ability to cope. Even more surprising is what is on the minds of those—especially the young—who have gathered here this morning for the dedication of the DeGroot Foundation for International Reconciliation."

Atop the dais, Lara Blackwood and Dr. Hassan Al-Bitar milled about with reporters from around the world. In a far corner, Henry Noord chatted with a collection of corporate and nonprofit foundation executives who had come to lend their support to the dedication. White uniformed attendants served coffee and tea.

Private security guards ringed the dais. In the distance, a protest of right-wing neonationalists staged an aggressively loud, but so far nonviolent, protest against the upcoming dedication. Television pictures had shown large numbers of Diet and cabinet members mingling with the protesters.

Lara Blackwood half listened to the B'nai B'rith executive as she watched one of the many television monitors installed on the dais.

"This is very interesting," she said, then she and they both watched the Japanese newsman interviewing a young Japanese woman.

". . . must repudiate the racist policies that got us into the Pacific War and have brought upon us the scorn of the rest of the world," the woman said.

"Do your parents feel the same way?" the interviewer asked.

The young woman shook her head. "They are somewhere out there." She looked toward the neonationalist protesters. "But they also don't know how to use a computer and they still smoke cigarettes to kill themselves. They're the past; their eyes are shut to the future, their minds closed to new ideas."

The newsman bowed and turned to the camera as the picture zoomed into a medium shot of his head and shoulders.

"There's hope," Lara said to the man from B'nai B'rith.

"One can hope so." He was silent as the newsman began his stand-up.

"Today's events are scheduled to begin in just over ten minutes," the newsman said. He shifted position so the camera could show a wide shot with the dais in the background.

"Less than six months after the most extraordinary series of events to shake the Japanese people since World War II, the fate of the mighty Daiwa Ichiban is still in doubt. The last of the family-controlled *zaibatsus*, Daiwa Ichiban was ruled with an iron hand by the self-proclaimed defender of Yamato, Tokutaro Kurata, who died by his own hand along with his loyal family retainer Toru Matsue. Kurata's sole heir, his nephew Akira Sugawara, was shot to death, apparently by one of Kurata's security guards who is being held along with a score of his co-workers and charged with murder. Sugawara reportedly composed a hasty, handwritten will leaving his inheritance to an American, Lara Blackwood, who is the founder of one of Daiwa Ichiban's subsidiaries, GenIntron. The will is being contested."

Lara watched as the television picture cut to a close shot of the dais taken by a shoulder cam. The newsman's voice continued over the new shot.

"The lack of a clear-cut path of succession has resulted in a tangle of legal challenges that have left the ultimate control uncertain. Members of the Diet have suggested that the company's industrial and economic significance to the Japanese economy is too important to be left in the hands of a foreigner. As a result, they have introduced legislation to nationalize the company and somehow compensate Blackwood. The matter remains one of great confusion and controversy. Meanwhile, the Daiwa Ichiban board of directors has partly validated Sugawara's holographic will by appointing Blackwood as CEO of the entire company.

"If she ultimately prevails, Blackwood said she would regain control of GenIntron and sell the rest of Daiwa Ichiban Corporation's business units to Singapore Electrochip. Dr. Hassan Al-Bitar, Electrochip's chairman, has said that if the sale is consummated, he would take all the former Daiwa Ichiban Corporation assets and place them in a special trust with the stock to be owned by a new foundation which will be dedicated today. The new foundation, currently funded by Blackwood and Al-Bitar, will be devoted to activities that promote social and religious justice and which encourage respect and understanding among traditionally hostile groups.

"The new foundation was created amid bizarre circumstances," the newsman continued. "Blackwood, at one point, was the subject of an intense international manhunt, wanted for a number of murders, until the U.S. government agencies involved revealed there had been a case of mistaken identity. Even stranger were rumors of a grotesque plot by a religious sect linked to Daiwa Ichiban Corporation to exterminate Koreans."

The roar of aircraft filled the morning sky. Lara looked up as the new aircraft they had purchased for the commune appeared in tight formation. The crowd hushed as heads craned toward the skywriting.

"No human race is superior," read the first line of the skywriting.

The newsman continued in a hushed tone. "Rumors of ultra-secret dossiers detailing war crimes and more recent indiscretions on the part of prominent Japanese and Americans citizens have also surfaced along with hearsay that those in the new foundation have used these dossiers to prompt mass resignations in the national governments of both countries and to effect changes in the management of a number of global corporations."

"No religious faith is inferior," read the skywriting's second line.

"While grist for the tabloid mills," the television newsman continued, "none of the rumors or allegations have been proven."

The B'nai B'rith man looked at Lara and gave her a questioning glance. She smiled and shook her head. "Fanciful," she said.

"I think," said the B'nai B'rith man, "that if I had in my possession the sorts of documentation the rumors have alleged, I would publish them, make it all public. Expose the evil for what it is."

"All collective judgments are wrong," read the third line of skywriting.

Lara shrugged. "I've read about the rumors as well," she said. "Now, *if* they were true—which they aren't—I'm not sure I'd do that."

"Why?"

"Well, it would seem to me that even if you get rid of one level of such reprehensible people, there would be no shortage of equally awful folks ready to step up and take their places. Playing all the cards at once would just rearrange the chairs. Threat is more potent than apocalypse," Lara continued. "Once you've pushed the button, you've got nothing left to fight with. Better to use the threat to control than the reality to destroy."

The B'nai B'rith man murmured his understanding without agreeing with her.

"Only racists make them," read the fourth line of the skywriting, and then the name of their author, Elie Wiesel.

"People are fatigued by visions of war atrocities," Lara continued as the master of ceremonies made his rounds, urging the participants into their seats so the dedication could start. "One more set isn't going to help. People are disillusioned with government and business; publication and exposure would only confirm what they already feel without changing things. Isn't it better to quietly use the information to work for change and make things better rather than just destroying things?"

"You sound like you've done a lot of thinking about this." His voice implied he believed the rumors.

"Of course," Lara said. "The rumors involve—partly—me. It's a huge ethical problem, one that deserves great thought." She paused as the B'nai B'rith man pulled out her seat for her. "I'm glad I wasn't actually faced with a real decision on this," she said unconvincingly.

Before she sat down, the B'nai B'rith man asked her: "If—just *if*—this were true"—his eyes searched her face—"and a group like the Foundation used this information to, in reality, *extort* admirable behavior from disgusting people—if this were true—then by what ethical rights would this self-appointed group exercise their immense power, their mammoth influence on human society?"

"*If* that were true," Lara began as she returned his gaze, "it would be a real dilemma, philosophically, given that in a democracy power is supposed to be derived from the people."

The B'nai B'rith man nodded. "But then, the exercise of power has gone on in secret for as long as there have been people, yes?"

"Yes, but I think that—"

Suddenly commotion swept the platoons of television news crews. A gasp swept over the assembled crowd.

Lara frowned as she turned and, along with the crowd, gazed at the large-screen monitors set up behind the dais. A bold BREAKING NEWS banner filled the screen, replaced seconds later by the grave face of a reporter. The scrolling words at the bottom of the screen told the story.

"Initial reports from the Middle East indicate that an unknown but devastating new disease has begun to strike both Jews and Palestinians. The horrible new syndrome, which began in Jerusalem, has so far killed every person who has contracted it. With a live report we turn now to . . ."

AUTHOR'S NOTE

WE ARE NIBBLING AWAY—ONCE AGAIN—AT THE TREE OF THE KNOWLEDGE OF GOOD AND EVIL.

Knowledge has blinded humankind before, and the results have been the stuff of nightmares. The world's top experts in biomedical ethics can cite substantial evidence that the conditions that produced the medical atrocities of Nazi Germany and Imperial Japan still exist today, stalking laboratory aisles and high-tech containment rooms of the world's human genetic research institutions.

This book is based on actual events. Dr. Shiro Ishii, the "Japanese Mengele," was a lieutenant general in the Japanese army. Dr. Ishii headed an official government program that authorized medical atrocities on Allied POWs and Chinese civilians, atrocities equal to the Nazis' worst medical evils. Yet few people know about Dr. Ishii.

Why have we forgotten?

We remember that the Nazis murdered more than ten million Jews, gypsies, homosexuals, retarded and handicapped people, political dissidents, and others judged undesirable by the Third Reich. Yet few people know that the Japanese slaughtered more than six million innocent civilians during World War II. This, too, puts them on a par with the Nazis.

Why have we forgotten?

In the Balkan civil war of the 1990s, the Serbs were internationally condemned for making rape an instrument of war, but we've forgotten that the Japanese institutionalized rape as part of their military policy more than half a century ago. They forced hundreds of thousands of women into organized army-run brothels so that Japanese troops could come each day and take comfort from raping them again and again. These women who were forced to service the basest needs of the Imperial Japanese Army were mothers, wives, sweethearts, daughters, and sisters.

Why have we forgotten them?

Why did the Nuremberg War Crimes Trials so firmly etch the horrors of Nazi Germany into our consciousness while few people are aware, even today, of the Tokyo War Crimes Trials that saw war criminals equally evil?

What does all this have to do with the Human Genome Project?

In the years since the first edition of this book was published as an e-book on the World Wide Web in 1996, I've wrestled with those questions and still don't have any good answers. Unfortunately, much of what I wrote then has come true, or nearly so. The first edition appeared four years before the human genome had been sequenced, and five years before the horrific terrorism and murders of September 11, 2001.

In 1996, many thought a plot about bioweapons using new forms of genetically engineered life was unrealistic. Others thought it preposterous that a single, driven, ambitious wealthy individual could alter the face of global politics by capitalizing on the frustration, hatred, and extremism of a few thousand fanatics.

Of course, that was before Osama bin Laden demonstrated that Islam can be perverted by political evil in the same satanic ways that have warped Christianity and Judaism in the past. I wrote this before Al Qaeda became synonymous with irrational fanaticism and the Taliban a watchword for oppressive, misogynistic, drug-dealing dictators who were willing to take the name of their God in vain and blaspheme all that millions of true Muslims hold dear and holy.

I didn't know then that much of what I wrote would be proved prophetic in 2001. But I pray in the name of God, most gracious, most merciful, the cherisher and sustainer of the worlds, the master of the Day of Judgment, that no more of what I have written here will come true. I would pray that this book can serve not as more prophecy, but as a lesson that ambition, greed, lust for power, racial hatred, and evil will destroy us unless we recognize that we are all brothers and sisters under our skins and that the God we worship is the same, regardless of name.

Lewis Perdue
Sonoma, California
November 25, 2002